THE
WORKSHOP

VOLKER G. FREMUTH

MINDSTIR MEDIA

Published by Mindstir Media
1931 Woodbury Ave. #182 I Portsmouth, NH 03801 I USA
1.800.767.0531 I www.mindstirmedia.com

Printed in the United States of America

ISBN-13: 978-0-9914884-4-5

Library of Congress Control Number: 2014939482

Visit Volker Fremuth on the World Wide Web:
www.volkerfremuth.com
www.thewarehousebook.com

To all my family and friends who offered their honest assessments and support, and to my wife who above all others had to endure month after month of relentless solicitation for critique, advice, and editing as the pages of my story took shape.
Thank you for your patience.

CONTENTS

FOREWARD

A Word From the Author

Being that my "day job" has had me in a leadership position for a segment of a multi-billion dollar conglomerate, both in marketing and more recently as a leader in the transition and consolidation of the company's recent acquisitions, I have had some interesting exposure to the function, dysfunction, and potential corruption of both the private and public sectors. This in combination with a love of history, an interest in world politics, a healthy distrust of politicians, their private sector counterparts, and a long-term fascination with the premise behind my novel has led me to a fertile landscape in which to grow my storyline.

When I first started writing this book, the concept had been winding through the passages in my mind for some time. It was spawned from a fanciful "what if" question, a playful ruse, which I relentlessly attempted to make realistic and plausible. To this end, I drew on my own experience, knowledge, and research. It should be noted that all of the technological, social, economic, and political activities and history are based in fact and manipulated only to help drive the narrative. Indeed, after having finished the first draft, the concepts covered in the book, which were predictive several years ago when I first started putting my thoughts to paper, seemed to be coming more and more fact than fiction. This was both unnerving and reassuring as it suggested a strong relevance of the material and also a driving urgency to get the book published as elements of the plot entered our everyday lives.

The concept that drives the storyline, which will be clear to the reader within the first paragraph of Chapter One, was to consider lore as history and what would the world look like had it been so. The fanciful and pleasing nature of the legend takes on a new and potentially sinister twist when forced to fit the mold of cold hard reality. What seems fun, exciting, precious, and endearing may not be so when you replace fantasy with fact, magic with practicality, omnipotence with resources, and knowledge with the technology of espionage. Then, with this adjustment made, consider how the world might react to the new reality. Keeping the story in this new

1

context palpable led me into an environment which exploited the conundrum that comes when faced with power and knowledge, its practical application, the morality of doing so, and how to protect the populace from those who would seek to abuse it if they could.

Enter reality. If I may now consider the socioeconomic and political environment in which we all live, remember that I had laid the first draft of this book down before the activities of the National Security Agency and the name Edward Snowden became part of our own personal realities.

THE WORKSHOP

1

THE EXECUTIVE

The older gentleman took a last sip of his coffee, tucked an envelope in his breast pocket and readied himself to leave the coffee shop. A man of significant means by the looks of him, his attire belied his well-known image, as he was normally not seen by the public in gray pinstripe. Like his father before him, Xavier Kringle played the part of CEO and spokesperson for the company well. His round, gold-rimmed spectacles, well-groomed white beard, and long white flowing hair which were part of his persona seemed oddly out of place in this context. His normal public appearances were scheduled only for a few months in the year. He was recognized almost more for his attire than himself; the deep burgundy-colored suit with gold thread accents, light-colored fur trim cap and boots, which remained true to the original Victorian costume, were all part of a well-orchestrated, choreographed, and scripted media event. Generous, exuberant and approachable, this was how the public knew Xavier, the head of his organization, yes, but rarely did the public see him as the CEO of a multi-billion dollar company, though most were subconsciously aware of this fact.

Xavier got up and made his way outside of the coffee shop to a small grouping of aides and security personnel clad in dark suits, sunglasses and communications devices. They seemed particularly anxious to address him as he and a partial contingent made their way into a large black SUV-based limousine. Xavier tapped his chest to check for the envelope and got in. The others scurried like cockroaches after a light has been turned on in a dark room to their respective and similarly appointed vehicles, which were parked one in front and one behind Xavier's SUV. The caravan sprung to life almost in complete unison, pulled into traffic and down the city street like an oversized, black, mechanical snake. The long line of vehicles drove down the road with headlights ablaze even though the day was bright.

A reasonably public figure, Xavier Kringle's activities and life remained very closely guarded. Almost completely out of the public eye, most of the year he managed the affairs of the company founded by his kin several generations back, running the complex operations that umbrella a significant purchasing, manufacturing, supply chain, logistics and transportation company that not only was best in class worldwide, but also one of the largest companies to grace the planet. Still, like its sole proprietor, the company was rarely featured in publications or exposés and remained shrouded in an almost diversionary blanket of lore.

Sometimes referred to as "The Workshop," Kringle Works's operations were part of an enormous compound located on a remote island off the coast of Greenland and the northeastern coast of Canada. Nearly central to Baffin Bay, its location had contributed to the incorrect but rarely disputed perception that the business was located on the northern pole of the globe. Largely autonomous, the company retained its independence by maintaining an open-ended and self-renewing contract and treaty between Kringle Works, Canada, and Denmark. The island, the second largest asset of the company, was almost entirely built up to support the company's operations and housing, which would fall purposefully outside almost all global governmental scrutiny, acting and governing itself more like a country than a business. The vast majority of the employees lived on the island and had every convenience one expected from a large city and its suburbs. Shopping, recreational facilities, and other services were all supplied, staffed, and operated as part of the business, making it a significant and globally influential economy in its own right. Yet Kringle Works remained far enough removed that it would fall generally outside of the world's consciousness.

Like so many, Jason Pelham had grown up at Kringle Works. With his father and mother working for the company, Jason was destined to take a job at Kringle Works if he was to stay on the island with his family. This is how it worked at the company; like its executive staff, the workforce was largely dynastic. Jason started modestly after college, taking a job at Kringle Works in the manufacturing division, which though established well before the mid-twentieth century, would resemble a modern laborers' union.

The manufacturing arm of Kringle Works, known as the Employee's League of Fabricators or ELF, which gave rise to a rather fantastical vision of who manufactured the goods at Kringle Works, had a reasonably generous education program to add incentive to its employees. ELF offered collegiate scholarships to both employees and their families if they would contractually agree to work for their organization for a minimum of five years after completing their study. It was a good deal, and allowed one to study abroad rather than accepting the no-cost education supplied by the island's educational facilities. This was Jason's plan. While his father contently remained a part of the assembly line, Jason wanted more, and after an Ivy League business degree gathered in Boston, Massachusetts, USA, Jason's aspirations would allow him to move rapidly through the ranks at ELF leading to a position of line supervisor, then foreman, and eventually to running many of the fabrication operations as director of toy manufacturing. For its size and diversity the toy-manufacturing department was the most sought after.

It was about fifteen years ago when Jason Pelham first met Xavier Kringle. Xavier liked to thank his middle managers personally when they had made a significant difference, and Jason had dramatically increased production to meet an un-forecasted and unprecedented increase in demand, even when faced with tremendous workforce shortages. It had seemed that this was becoming the perfect storm of supply shortages, an unforeseen pandemic of worker illnesses, a dramatic increase in demand, and a year of particularly bad weather across the globe, which would increase delivery times.

That year had been shaping up to become a disaster of desperate proportions within the company's history. Seeing the pending catastrophe, Jason had taken the lead and worked with a number of other middle managers and drafted a recovery strategy to make up for the shortfalls and increase production. The key ended up in a retooling of the operations' raw material lines to decrease waste and streamline the manufacturing lines. The specifics were unorthodox and innovative, but they allowed Jason to increase toy production with only fifty percent of his workforce. He was then able to lend a number of his team to other manufacturing lines, such as the electronics and jewelry divisions, which seemed particularly hard-hit in worker absences. Though some of the other manufacturing directors disagreed and resisted the strategy, successes in Jason's line forced them to comply and in less than forty-five days the plan was fully implemented company-wide. ELF's production was up over fifteen percent by November of that year.

Jason's plan had managed both to overcome the immediate disaster and to have tremendous cost and efficiency implications going forward, which earned Jason a tremendous amount of notoriety throughout the company.

Xavier Kringle reveled in the success of Jason's efforts; the prospect of having averted a near collapse in deliveries for that year, only to emerge more productive and inevitably more profitable, made Xavier almost publicly giddy. He never missed an opportunity to praise Jason's success in the company, and it would lead Jason to move up even more quickly both at ELF and Kringle Works as a whole, largely because of his well-earned reputation, but also because of the open endorsement of Xavier Kringle. Xavier began to value and to rely on Jason's insight and uncommon business acumen more and more consistently. Xavier and Jason spent a great deal of time together and as a result became quite amicable, though their dealings remained largely hierarchical. Even with Jason's rapid ascension and his ever-growing friendship with Xavier, Jason remained extremely respected and popular. Still, some at ELF grumbled and bristled at his success; they almost seemed to genuinely fear it.

It was a balmy thirty-seven degrees Fahrenheit, modestly sunny and prematurely warm for a May morning; pleasant for those who had grown up on the island. The warmer days carried a smell in the air of wet wood, leather, and smoke. Most continued to heat their homes year-round but not Jason. He embraced the climate on the island and allowed the fresh air into his house once the temperature consistently broke the freezing point. This morning was a treat. It was almost like a summer morning, and by now Jason was well into a stride at work. Gearing up since last December for the year's manufacturing at ELF, production would be well on its way by now, and though busy, it was all about keeping the pace up and running.

"As long as nothing runs out, runs short, runs amuck or breaks down, we are on the way to meeting all of The Workshop's supply demands and timelines," Jason chuckled. "What could possibly go wrong?" Jason amused himself while sitting down at a characteristically open window and listening to the drip, drip, drip as some two-meter-long icicles slowly released their grip as the dominant feature outside of Jason's house.

Leaning back, Jason unwrapped the island's own published newsletter, The Work's Weekly, which acted much like a local newspaper with the predominant reporting being mostly about the company. Included would be articles about top employees, production efforts, employee gatherings, general island activities, and classifieds. World news would be gathered by the importation of papers from various parts of the world. The reprinting of some particularly important or relevant material in The Work's Weekly would usually be followed up with some editorializing from prominent company personnel discussing the impact on activities of the company and the island. It was a practice that Jason Pelham had also participated in. This morning the weekly newsletter was a little different. Jason took a sip of tea from a small, white, porcelain cup adorned with a print of holly berries and leaves. He then untied the gold and red twisted ribbon from around the rolled newsletter and pulled a parchment-colored paper from around it. The text, "Directly from the desk of Xavier Kringle," and the company logo adorned the top.

Seeing Jason Pelham's name on a company announcement was not really all that unusual but this one surprised even him. By this point Jason had moved up in the company's structure to become a divisional vice president at ELF, managing most of the manufacturing for gift exports and holding a strong dotted line responsibility for the raw materials procurement, which included some local mining and harvesting as well as importation of materials. In fact, the only ELF activities that did not have a significant thumbprint of Jason's on it was the electronics and entertainment division responsible for the procurement and manufacturing of consumer electronics such as televisions, radios, home theaters, computers, and video games, and the vehicle manufacturing arm of the company which built various forms of transportation equipment from railroads to snowmobiles to cars and trucks which were predominantly used on the island and not generally for export. Jason liked working with the manufacturing lines and was both effective and popular, so it was a surprise to all when Jason was named senior vice president of the Nocturnal Transportation Authority, also known as the NTA. The announcement came directly from Xavier Kringle and was not discussed in advance with anyone that Jason was aware of.

"I think the old man has finally lost his mind," Jason thought.

> *"Directly from the Desk of Xavier Kringle, CEO & Owner, Kringle Works:*
>
> *It is with extreme pleasure and excitement that I, Xavier Kringle, may announce the promotion and transfer of Jason Pelham to the Nocturnal Transportation Authority (NTA), in the newly created position of Senior Vice President, NTA.*
>
> *In this new position, Jason will find himself charged with the operations of all the Nocturnal Transportation Authority's activities including, but not limited to, all of the worldwide deliveries of ELF*

goods for both the specialty deliveries year round, and also the tremendously complex planning, staging, and execution of the annual November and December Christmas Holiday delivery rushes.

Those of you who know and have worked with Jason can appreciate the extensive skill set and level of professional success he brings with him to this new position. I am hoping that in his new role Jason will help to usher in a new era of efficiency and innovation for the Kringle Works in this, an ever-changing world.

Jason Pelham will be reporting to Andre Leopold, Executive Vice President, NTA, with a dotted line directly to me. All of the divisional vice presidents and directors who formerly reported to Andre will now report to Jason.

I know that you will join me in congratulating Jason Pelham and his new team in this most important charter.

On another note, Marcus Millerov, formerly Divisional Vice President of Electronics Procurement & Manufacturing at ELF will now assume Jason's former responsibilities and personnel in addition to his own. Marcus's new title will be Senior Vice President, ELF, and will continue to report to the Executive Vice President, ELF, with the addition of a dotted line directly to me. Please also extend your congratulations to Marcus Millerov in his newfound role.

Note that these moves have been discussed and endorsed by all Senior Executive stakeholders and have been ratified by all actively participating members of the Kringle family.

With respectful regards,
Xavier Kringle"

Jason pondered the note and decided to skip breakfast and close down the house. Even though it was early in the morning, by this time of the year, and with the extremely high latitude of the island, the morning sun was already bright and high in the sky as Jason stepped outside and locked his front door. Wanting time to clear his head, Jason chose to walk to work and take the time to think things out before getting to the office.

"Why would Xavier make this move? Why move me to the NTA when my entire career was at ELF? Why not discuss this with me first? This is not like Xavier," Jason contemplated, and though he was honored and excited by the possibilities, this was still shaping up to be one of the most awkward days he could imagine.

"Maybe I'll just hide in my office for the day," Jason figured, but then thought better of it and decided that he would likely do exactly what Xavier Kringle probably expected and indeed may have planned on all along; Jason would go to see Xavier first thing that morning.

The Workshop's compound was huge. Representing nearly one-quarter of the landmass of the island, it could take as much as one full hour to cross from one side of the compound to the other by snowmobile and longer if by caribou-drawn sleigh.

Entering the compound, Jason Pelham approached the first building, a half-timbered barn with an office in the front. He noted a familiar face. A pretty, fair-skinned woman about eight years his junior. She had an unremarkable beauty, the kind that is comforting more than arresting. Still, clad in fur cap and wool jacket, her rose-colored cheeks reminded him of the cool air; her green eyes and her smile seemed to warm at the mere sight of him; Jason found himself captivated.

"Hey there, stranger, you're up early," the young woman's voice broke the silence.

Sheepishly Jason replied, "Eh … yeah … hi, Krystal …" looking at his feet.

She interrupted,

"So what will it be, gasoline or grain?" Krystal continued, "I know, I know, you're sorry. Come on, follow me to the back, I have someone who wants to see you."

They walked down the center of the large building; both sides were lined with stalls. Each had three to four snowmobiles. Further down, the stalls were gated and each contained a caribou or reindeer. They approached one of the stalls and just beyond the gate was a reindeer. The reindeer watched the duo as they approached, and immediately looked to Krystal for attention, nudging her hand with her nose. Krystal smiled and petted her. Jason reached over to pet the animal and as he did, the reindeer swung her head over to Jason to get more attention. Jason responded by petting her on the nose and neck.

"She missed you …" Krystal suggested. "I missed you. I thought we were going for a ride last night?" Krystal continued, "I guess I understand why, now. Things are changing fast, aren't they?"

Jason did not answer the question.

"Jason, you can have her for the day; tomorrow Xavier is taking all the reindeer for a series of photos …PR stuff … you know? Just bring her back to this entrance." Krystal paused and asked, "So, why didn't you tell me?"

Jason hesitated, "I didn't know; to the best of my knowledge, no one did!" He responded.

Krystal glowered at him, "Oh, well then, you are NOT forgiven!" She handed him some tack. "Take sleigh 362, hitch her up yourself, mister senior VP!" she commanded curtly.

Krystal turned away to hide an involuntary smile that crept across her face, content that she had properly communicated her annoyance, and with her back to Jason, she noted,

"Millerov was looking for you."

"Marcus? Great! What the hell is he doing here? He's an hour and a half early!" Jason whined.

His frustration was punctuated by a groan. This amused Krystal and she broke into a quiet chuckle as Jason walked away.

The trip to the ELF manufacturing building was fifteen minutes from the compound entrance. Jason planned to leave his briefcase in his office and make his way to the executive offices. However, Jason's singular focus for the morning was broken by someone sitting at his desk.

"My office, my manufacturing operation, my supply chain! Mine!" A malicious voice rang out as Jason entered his office. "You know what else is mine now? Your father! He belongs to me now, too!"

The two men snarled at each other.

"Get over yourself, Marcus, I'm not staying … so, make yourself at home," Jason snapped back.

Unwilling to leave his belongings there and compromised, Jason held on to his briefcase and as he turned to leave, he looked over his shoulder at his former desk and said, "The old man is in, then?"

Marcus nodded, "Yeah, he's in … talked this morning."

Jason flicked his head forward. "Uh huh, thanks! Hey, Marcus! Congratulations pal, break your legs or something!" Jason walked out.

Marcus smirked; his eyes followed Jason out the door.

"You too!" Marcus yelled after him, paused and then continued quietly, "Pal!"

Jason, who was normally fond of the occasional treks around the Kringle Works compound, found this particular trip irritatingly long. The sleigh ran a steady course along the ELF manufacturing buildings, passing by rows of windows in which one could see a constant flurry of activity punctuated by the various smells of manufacture; from the extrusion of plastics to the forging of metals, they belched from the line of smokestacks that dotted the buildings' entire length. The familiar route allowed Jason's mind to wander, unfettered by a need to pay attention. He attempted to make sense of this morning's circumstances. Marcus was a good man; he certainly had knowledge to run the majority of the ELF operations, Jason thought.

"He's a jerk, but generally a good man for the job," he said to himself.

Still, Jason could not make sense of such radical changes, not without discussing it with those involved. Or was everyone else informed and just incredibly good at keeping it secret? And if this were indeed the case, why would he be the one who was not informed? Again, the newly appointed senior vice president of the Nocturnal Transportation Authority considered his new challenges. They were exciting, but to be thrust into the position without the time to prepare or learn the operations was perplexing.

"Sir, Mr. Pelham, sir?" a voice jarred Jason from his thoughts. "Mr. Pelham, would you like me to tie up your reindeer for you, sir?"

Jason looked up to see Peter Sharp, head of security, a broad, six feet five inch tall man in a dark green uniform.

"Sir? Mr. Pelham, sir, you should wear your badge where we can see it before you go in here, sir. Would you like me to take the reindeer for you now, sir?"

The hyper respectful and almost submissive tone always caught Jason by surprise coming from such an imposing figure.

"Yes, Peter, thank you," Jason finally answered.

"You should make sure that everyone can see your badge, sir," the burly man reiterated. "Mr. Kringle hired a bunch of new guys for some of the security stations, though I'm sure they know who *you* are sir; just the same, you should have your badge where everyone can see it, you know, just to be sure," he finished.

"I thought you did all the hiring of security personnel at the executive offices, Peter?" Jason asked.

"Yes sir, well … that is, unless Mr. Kringle thinks that he needs to make a few changes personally, I have always done the hiring and the background checks, but I trust he has his reasons … and, after all, it's him that security is trying to protect," Peter answered in an almost rehearsed manner and a mild tone of irritation, which he notably attempted to hide.

"It's okay, Peter, there is a little of that going around; Mr. Kringle knows how well you do your job!" Jason suggested.

Upon entering the building, Jason noticed the faces seemed to have changed at the front desk. Not important, Jason thought, and he proceeded to the desk.

"I'm here to see Xavier--" "Yes, sir, Mr. Kringle has been waiting for you, Mr. Pelham," the unfamiliar guard interrupted and made some notations in a book.

The guard then buzzed Jason through a turnstile gate.

Xavier Kringle's office was nearly fifteen hundred square feet, high-ceilinged, hand-carved wood trim, with highly ornamented and imposing dark wood furniture. The back wall was lined with bookcases and wooden file cabinets. The room was embellished with antiques, and along the side the wall were paintings of each of the dynastic CEOs starting with the founder, Christopher Kringle, who started the company in North America back in the mid-nineteenth century. In front of the back wall was a figure sitting at an overly grand and very ornate desk. A rather large and imposing man, Xavier seemed dwarfed by these surroundings.

As Jason entered the office he spotted Xavier, dressed in a golden-toned robe, his long white hair and beard cascading down. Xavier looked up over his round spectacles. His eyes squinted as a smile crept across his face; he rose, set down a gold pen and some paperwork, then started to walk around the desk to greet Jason. Laughing characteristically, Xavier smirked and leaned on an antique globe that stood at the front of his desk.

"Jason my boy, I was wondering when you were coming to see me," Xavier said. "I was afraid you might not have read the 'Weekly' this morning, oh, and now *that* might have been embarrassing." He punctuated the comment with a renewed laugh.

Giving Xavier a sideways glance, Jason answered,

"Everyone reads it the day it comes out--people want to avoid being surprised." He continued, "What in the name of Christmas were you thinking?" Jason asked as a follow up.

Xavier reached out his hand to shake Jason's. The two men shook hands vigorously and Xavier reassuringly capped their handshake with his other hand.

"Congratulations, my boy, this kind of a promotion was a long time in coming."

He motioned Jason to sit down. Jason did so, watching Xavier skeptically.

"A long time in coming? I don't have the experience to run any part of the NTA, much less all of it."

Jason, sitting, grabbed a hold of the carved bear claws that adorned the armrest of the chair.

"Well, there! You see? You need the diversity of experience to move your career to the next level!" Xavier noted, "Besides, you won't be alone, you will have a good staff working for you, and you have a well-experienced NTA veteran as your boss. Andre Leopold is an old hand at it."

Jason remarked that there must have been any number of talented, better-qualified, divisional VPs who wanted the job and asked,

"Why me, why now, why so suddenly?"

Xavier turned away to face the globe that was at his side; he put his finger just to the left of the western coast of Greenland and spun the globe. Xavier watched it as it turned, catching glimpses of the landmasses that represented that largest of the company's clientele, Europe, Russia, North America. Noting the start of the third rotation, Xavier spoke now more pensively,

"Are we an oil company, Jason?" Xavier stopped the globe, turned to face Jason and rephrased the question, "Do we *sell* oil?"

Perplexed, Jason answered, "We drill our own oil, we pump our own oil, we refine it and we use it."

"Yes," Xavier answered. "It keeps us autonomous, self-sufficient, away from outside controls, and out of reach from the rest of the world; but we do not *sell* it."

Jason thought for a moment,

"Well, we have probably given it as an unusual Christmas gift to someone … Why?" he questioned.

"Indeed," Xavier commented. "Perhaps to a president in the United States during the 1970s," Xavier quipped. "I'll have to check on that."

However, then, changing his tone and becoming very serious, Xavier continued,

"What we do at Kringle Works is world-class, our manufacturing is the best there is, but it is the Nocturnal Transportation Authority, Jason, that is the heart of what we do; it is the NTA that makes us unique, it is the NTA that fills the world with both awe and envy, it is the NTA that gives us the power we have."

Jason nodded in agreement and asked, "Yes, but why me?"

Xavier walked back around the desk and sat down. He leaned into his desk and toward Jason; then, in a quieter almost melancholy tone, said, "Jason, I have experienced talent in the NTA, but right now I do not need experience, I need someone I can trust."

Xavier leaned back in his chair.

"Take this job, Jason, learn it. Understand it. Something is happening, and it is older and bigger than me; I need to find out what it is. Help me now, as you have always helped me."

2

The Nocturnal Transportation Authority

Like the nineteenth century illustrations and caricatured portraits of company founder, Christopher Kringle, by cartoonist, Thomas Nast, helped popularize the notion that the Kringle Works company and its services was really just the activities of a single man, so too, the agreements and treaties between the company and its clients would, over time, become oddly synonymous with him. Before the turn of the century the company would move to the island and as it became uniquely capable of controlling more and more of the information that was known about it, the more and more diversionary that information would become.

As once noted in New York's The Sun in 1897 by newsman Francis Parcells Church,

"Yes, VIRGINIA, there is a SANTA Clause."

It was, indeed, the SANTA Clause that made all Kringle Works's activities possible.

Drafted in an earlier and more trusting era, SANTA referred to a document that allowed the company to exercise its--and specifically Christopher Kringle's--vision of a more commercialized and potentially profitable Christmas Holiday. SANTA, which stood for the Strategic Activation of the Nocturnal Transportation Authority, was a self-renewing agreement that outlined the logistics activities of the Kringle Works to get gifts to all participating households. A specific clause of this agreement would have to be signed individually, which allowed the Kringle Works both access to individual homes with almost complete impunity during the delivery cycle at the end of the year, and also unprecedented access to individuals' personal information throughout the year. This allowed the undersigned governmental bodies to stipulate specific behaviors for its constituency to abide by, or risk the revocation of that year's services of gift giving for that part of the population. This made the upside attractive enough to overcome the concerns of the otherwise sweeping concessions of the agreement.

Understanding that over time technology would change in unforeseen ways the Kringle Works would retain the right to adjust SANTA without prior approval from those who employed the service. By modern terms this service directly impacted over two billion people in over one hundred sixty countries across the globe in a willing partnership with the population and their respective governing bodies in each of Kringle Works's countries of operation.

Over the decades, it seemed that even those who originally sought to gain a measure of control by employing the services through SANTA would soon be controlled by it, as the service was so popular across the population that even those who signed the agreements would allow the access. And as Kringle Works withdrew behind its curtain of lore, most seemed to forget the service agreement and simply accepted its execution every year. As long as there were no ill effects, complacency regarding the treaty eventually prevailed. This complacent attitude, and the behavioral consequence of noncompliance, was forever immortalized by lyricist Haven Gillespie in 1932:

> "You better watch out, You better not cry, Better not pout, I'm telling you why, The SANTA Clause is coming to town. He's making a list and checking it twice, Gonna find out who's naughty and nice, the SANTA Clause is coming to town."

To gather information about its customers, analyze the data, define the appropriate gift level, and consequently administrate and implement the nocturnal gift delivery service without detection; that was the NTA's charter. Jason Pelham knew little about these functions; in fact there were entire elements of the NTA activities that were kept under extreme secrecy even within the company itself. Nevertheless, now that Jason had become a member of the senior management, he would be given access and even control of all of it, a thought that Jason found uncharacteristically daunting and intimidating.

Xavier accompanied Jason to his new office. The NTA was located another twenty-five minutes from the executive offices, a trip in which Jason was so caught up in his thoughts that, other than some small talk about how Jason seemed to have unusual access to the best reindeer, little was said.

Jason's new office at the NTA seemed like a strange cross between an airport control tower and a Victorian manor. Indeed, when looking out the windows that lined the walls of this top floor office, it did in fact overlook the NTA airport, railways, distribution centers, trucking lanes, and, in the distance, the harbor.

"This place is absolutely huge!" Jason thought, as he noted the view out of the windows.

He had seen it all before, but he never really looked at it. Turning his attention back inside, Jason started to take in all of the details of his new office, noticing for the first time all of the familiar objects that adorned the desk and shelves.

"The NTA already moved your personal files and effects this morning," Xavier noted. "Only then did Marcus Millerov get access to your old office."

Jason looked around, impressed with the forethought that appeared to go into the location and arrangement of his personal things. It seemed almost as though they knew how he would have done it and they did so, in what was likely less than a fraction of the time it would have taken him. It was a little eerie, especially as he had not noticed anything missing when he talked to Marcus earlier that morning.

"These guys are good," Jason thought as he sat at his new desk and tried to get his bearings.

"Ah, I heard you had arrived, yes? Jason Pelham, good to have you on board!"

In the doorway a tall, thin, elderly gentleman with thin gray hair and heavy muttonchops exclaimed with a notable Italian accent. As he entered the office, the gentleman, sporting a long, fur-lined jacket, striped ascot, and gold walking stick walked over to Xavier and whispered something, tapped

Xavier on the arm smiling, turned and quickly made eye contact with Jason. He walked over to Jason's desk, hand outstretched,

"My name is Andre Leopold; I am your new boss. You already know me, yes?"

Jason stood up to shake Andre's hand,

"Yes sir, in passing, we have met. The honor is mine."

Andre looked around inquisitively.

"The office, it looks good." Turning back to Jason, "Will it suit you?"

Jason nodded.

"Shall we take our new senior manager on a tour of the head offices, meet the team?" Xavier suggested.

Andre scowled at him. "No, first we go for some food; there will be much to do later, it will be better with food."

Jason was not sure exactly why, but he was already starting to like Andre.

Andre's build seemed to belie his love for food and as he noted that this was a special occasion, he had a small restaurant on the compound in mind, at which he planned to treat them to an equally special meal. Though the NTA had any number of high quality options for lunch, the one Andre had in mind appeared to have been created just for him. Not far from the NTA head offices there was a small cottage which, like many on the island, had a characteristically half-timbered and heavily ornamented façade and which, to many not regularly exposed to the island's style of architecture, looked like a frosted gingerbread house with the snow cover that adorned most roofs for much of the year. Inside, Andre was greeted with great enthusiasm and the party of three was led to a private dining room.

There was no ordering of food at this luncheon, but rather conversation and tall tales of business dealings gone by, and between Xavier and Andre there were some interesting dealings. As the conversations continued, the food just seemed to come out to be served at Andre's pleasure. Various dishes and bottles would be passed to Andre; if he approved of the quality, then--

and only then--was it good enough to be served to all, and the platter left on the table. Even with the multiple platters of antipasto, breads, cheeses, pasta, beef, pork, chicken, and fish dishes, goblets of drink and bowls of fresh fruit, Jason did not eat much. As the island's most common cuisine was generally more Nordic in nature, all of this Italian fare was a particular treat. The small dining area was permeated with the aroma of tomato sauce, butter, olive oil, garlic, and herbs. Still, Jason's interests lay with the conversation, which seemed to capture more of his attention than any amount of food.

The conversation meandered and as the drink flowed, so too did the stories. Of particular interest to Jason was that both Xavier and Andre had positions as sales managers in key foreign territories in their youth. Xavier was responsible for the United States; Andre, Italy and southern Europe; and both retained their citizenships in these territories to this day. Xavier, who was more charismatic and ambitious than his older brother Malcolm, seemed destined to become CEO, and as such was groomed to do so by quickly becoming part of the Kringle Works's executive staff. Andre's career moved through the more practical route in the halls of the NTA. Andre was a visionary, whose ideas would eventually lead to the largest expansion of powers associated with enactment and modern era application of the SANTA Clause. Andre and Xavier used their friendship for mutual successes, as Xavier was able to dramatically increase his clout with the staff and his father, Benton Kringle; Andre was able to lobby Xavier for easy staff approvals so as to make more significant changes to the NTA infrastructure.

Xavier reminded Andre of their combined efforts to upgrade the technology of the database storage and information gathering operations by recruiting some of the greatest minds from a few particularly prominent technology companies. These would become some of the most highly regarded and elite NTA team members, members whose true capabilities and the depth of proprietary technologies seemed to go well beyond the understanding of the system's original architects. Andre then remarked at the equally impressive evolution of the NTA delivery systems, which moved from traditional distribution hubs and reliance on road and rail access to an almost ominously stealthy aviation-based system. Jason, who had always thought that he had an extremely close relationship with Xavier, became very much aware that there was still much he did not know about him.

"We have many geniuses, yes? You will meet them this afternoon," Andre suggested to Jason.

Back at the NTA, Jason found himself in a wood-paneled conference room. The walls were lined with large, technical, logistics diagrams, roughly scrolled in black and red marker from a previous meeting, which appeared to close earlier than intended and belying the turn of the century decor of the room. These made an odd backdrop to the four divisional vice presidents, seated on one side of a long conference table. These were elite NTA managers and all were now a part of Jason's staff. Jason felt like an outsider as he alone occupied the other side of the table. Each watched Jason with a friendly but skeptical demeanor and waited for a first move. After just a few moments of uncomfortable silence, Jason, as a seasoned manager, felt compelled to take charge of the meeting he had not called.

"Eh, okay, let's first get introduced. My name is Jason Pelham." As Jason said the words he regretted them, thinking he sounded like a grade school teacher introducing himself to a classroom of students.

"We know who you are, Mr. Pelham," a curt and mildly irritated male voice interrupted.

"Indeed we do, and it's a pleasure to meet you. Your reputation precedes you and is well received here at the NTA," a middle-aged woman injected into the conversation.

She stood up and reached over the conference table to shake Jason's hand.

"I am Lorraine Barlow, vice president of data acquisition."

Her slender and petite figure was silhouetted by the light reflecting off the wood paneling behind her. With this gesture, the other three members of the team followed suit. Raymond Dunbar, vice president of gift delivery systems; Edward Grubb, vice president of data analysis and implementation; and Henry Foster, vice president of customer relations and user interface all introduced themselves.

These discussions would last the rest of the day and well past the regular quitting time. Although Jason was no stranger to long days, by the time this day had come to a close, he was beyond exhausted. He looked forward to getting home and was now regretting the walk to work that morning. Jason needed to get his sleigh and reindeer back to the southern gate and the nearby barn. Though there was a light cloud cover one could tell the sun was starting to hang lower in the sky. It was nearing nine o'clock by the time he arrived at the barn. At the desk, a patient Krystal Gardner was reading a book and eating from a small plate of smoked salmon and cucumbers; a platter of fish and vegetables on the desk with a conspicuously unused and empty plate was placed opposite her.

"Please, please, forgive me, Krystal, I'm so sorry," Jason pleaded.

Krystal pursed her lips and cocked her head, with an annoyed look in her eyes.

"I'll forgive you on one count, don't do it again!"

She folded her arms and glowered at him. Holding the stance for a moment, she broke into a laugh as she contemplated how ludicrous she might look.

"That is most likely the most impossible promise ever, so don't you ever dare suggest you would do it. Just try, okay?" she followed up. "Anyway, I assumed you'd be late today. I brought some dinner."

Krystal proceeded to take the sleigh and reindeer into the back while Jason sat down and picked at the plate.

It was only just starting to get dark when Jason arrived back at his house. Only a short few hours of darkness punctuated the night at this time of year and the dimming light exaggerated the highly ornamented facade of Jason's house. The spacious home felt oddly unfamiliar tonight and Jason found it particularly hard to get to sleep. The events of the day were running through his head and he remained restless most of the night and his discomfort was exacerbated by an overwhelming feeling of guilt which rushed over him like a cold wave when he realized that he had not spoken a word of this to his parents. Surely they had seen the announcement. No doubt Marcus would have felt compelled to have an ELF meeting with the entire manufacturing team. What perspective would Marcus have given the team regarding the changes? What would Jason's former employees think, not having heard from him at all that day? What exactly was the point of his taking the position at the NTA? Jason stared at the various objects in his bedroom, barely making out the shapes that defined it in the dark as his mind wandered. He was taking his new job seriously, he was excited about it, it was an excellent opportunity, but he had an odd sensation that he had completely lost control of his future and this was an unusual and extremely disconcerting feeling for him.

The morning came rather suddenly. Jason woke feeling more at ease. With but a couple hours sleep he was far from well rested; still his demeanor had largely improved. Jason had decided that he would steep himself in the efforts of the NTA and his new position, learning all he could. With some renewed confidence, Jason decided he would try to catch his parents before they left for work and called them that morning to talk. The excited and enthusiastic congratulations from his parents gave Jason some additional energy, as did his father's stories of a befuddled Marcus Millerov explaining the announcement and trying to answer questions about the reasons for the change and whether Jason Pelham was his new boss. Marcus was caught off guard as much as Jason was, so it was not fair to judge him. Still, Jason took a sinister pleasure from hearing about his plight.

Jason's morning was spent with Lorraine Barlow. The gracious vice president of data acquisition took her new boss through the various functions and procedures that were specific to her department, walking through the cursory and the theoretical. Lorraine then decided it made sense for Jason to see the operations in action. Together, they were going speak to the key members of her department's team.

A large, dimly lit room also known as the data hall glowed with the blue flickering from what seemed hundreds of screens. Randall Blake, the NTA's senior data acquisition manager and his team, were monitoring screens with a combination of verbal data that quickly scrolled from top to bottom and video material of people, places, and events. The team rolled their chairs from one workstation to another in an odd ballet of movement, keeping the room a flurry of activity. Looking back and forth, Randall would watch his screen with one eye and the room with the other, acting as both a musician and the conductor of this high-tech symphony. Suddenly all movement stopped. All turned to look at the two figures who entered the room unannounced. The team quickly recognized the petite figure of Lorraine Barlow. The team disregarded Lorraine's unfamiliar guest and went back to their tasks. Randall, however, remained fixated on the two and jumped to his feet.

"Right, who's this, then?" Randall asked.

Lorraine in a mildly scolding tone said,

"Randy," she paused for a moment and then continued, "this is our new boss, Jason Pelham."

Randall looked annoyed with both the tone and the shortening of his name. He hated it when people called him Randy; so much so, that those who knew him well would use this as a ploy to get under his skin. Still he felt that his reaction was in bad form. Sheepishly, Randall looked at Jason apologetically, introduced himself stressing his first name as *Randall* and shook Jason's hand.

The three wandered from one station to another watching the various operators over their shoulders while Randall described their respective activities. He noted that this was where Kringle Works acquired the majority of the information with which the company determined whether or not each member of a participating country's population was behaviorally fitting the predetermined moral, social, and political norms and to what degree.

"We have to see who's been *naughty or nice*, you know? This network is connected to every newspaper, law enforcement, and government agency computer in each of our customers' countries," Randall boasted.

He went on to suggest that if they wanted to, they could use one country's surveillance capabilities to watch another without either party knowing.

"Doesn't this violate some of the laws in a few of these countries?" Jason asked naively.

Lorraine cocked her head inquisitively, looking at Jason.

"We are not breaking any laws!" and proceeded to point out that as a sovereign entity they were not bound by another nation's laws as long as they stayed within the guidelines of the SANTA Clause. She seemed ready to cite paragraphs, subsections, and appendixes which were likely designed as an offensive onslaught of contractual legalese to thwart any disagreement with an arsenal so dense it would end the discussion before it began. Jason obediently backed off and accepted that, like so many things at the company that were steeped in the past, over time they had been made airtight.

It was with this legal impunity coupled with the fact that the company was largely out of mind, that Kringle Works was able to cement its position in the forefront of surveillance techniques. In the beginning they relied on informants and correspondence; over time, wire taps and videos, but now the technology existed to allow the company to completely disappear while it watched you. In this respect Kringle Works was unique, as they built an infrastructure with the ability to integrate data from many sources; the information merged into a single, workable database in almost real time. The truth was that even where individual agencies in a single country were unable to consolidate their data, the Kringle Works was able to do so even in different countries. The system was able to run entirely in the background, where it captured the data, encrypted it to ensure security, and transferred it to a series of servers. These remained firewalled off, while the data was translated into the Kringle Works proprietary format. These standalone servers were kept in a single location in Lapland's Korvatunturi, which was situated directly on Finland's eastern frontier and which doubled as the northern European logistic hub, where the integrity of this data could be kept safely during the process.

The magnitude of what was being said sent Jason's mind reeling.

"How is all this possible?" he inquired.

Randall welled up with pride and answered,

"Mate, the NTA has been working with various facets of the Workshop to add electronics that help us along. Circuit boards that we designed here at the NTA have been integrated into all our electronics." Randall continued, "See, we even help some of the world's largest other manufacturers and government agencies with simple electronic components that find their way into all things; computers, radios, TVs, telephones, satellites, everything! There are always electronic component shortages in the global economy, so everyone was happy when we made these available outside the Christmas holiday and outside the normal customer base. These are invisible from a functional point of view to anyone but us, who know how to activate them. The ICU chip allows us to listen in to the conversation and then use the network of chips to transfer the information to our system without anyone being able to see it happen, because we see it the same time they do. Where we do not have the chips in place, we maintain our old surveillance systems."

Jason, wide-eyed, turned to Lorraine,

"But if the ICU chips are sold outside of the countries employing our Christmas services, are we not vulnerable, being out from under the SANTA Clause?"

Lorraine smiled at him reassuringly and suggested that as long as the chips that fell outside the countries of operation were only used to assist in data transfer and not in the act of data acquisition, they were within the spirit of SANTA.

"We are not breaking any laws!" Lorraine reiterated.

Randall's face contorted with an ear-to-ear grin.

"Right, see, the NTA is the largest, legal, globally sanctioned, governmentally endorsed spy network in the world!"

Randall folded his arms with finality. Lorraine, however, shot a look of disapproval toward Randall. She fidgeted nervously and motioned for Randall to cease and desist. She was notably uncomfortable with this last comment and decided that it was time to go. In an attempt to look nonchalant, she smiled at Jason, stretched her hand out as if to say 'this way,' put her hand on his shoulder and very subtly urged him forward.

3

THE NTA STAFF

The weeks that followed Jason's starting at the NTA were a tsunami of meetings and tours that provided Jason a significant level of depth regarding his new organization's processes and practices. His days with Lorraine Barlow imparted Jason with a reasonably detailed understanding of the company's efforts to gather information about each of the countries, and their respective peoples, that employed the Christmas Services and the methods developed in the access and storage of that data. Jason learned the extent of how SANTA allowed for the subversion of an individual country's 'Right-to-Privacy' laws so as to allow for the analysis of the aforementioned acquired data and judge it against a predetermined criteria that illustrated each population's particular expectations of behavior.

Just as Lorraine Barlow was able to use the provisions set forth in SANTA to eavesdrop on the world, Edward Grubb, vice president of data analysis and implementation, was allowed to view and analyze Lorraine's data and build an annual gift-giving model for each person based on that individual's level of positive behavioral conformity and conduct. Though much of this data was continuously evaluated by an arsenal of computers which would perpetually and methodically rate every person and household on a scale of predetermined and established standards of 'goodness,' the system was often spot-checked by employing the old processes used by the company in the earliest days. These would amount to a manual review of a person's history, which would generate series of scores to be tallied and scrutinized. Edward made it his personal project to use this old method with the world's particularly prominent and powerful people.

Edward Grubb was a sullen and irritable man with an obvious disdain for the human race and the condition he perceived it to be in. It was widely thought that this was because Edward was required to look at the world one

31

person at a time and found that, all too often, he did not like what he saw. Jason, however, got the distinct impression that Edward was also significantly irritated by the dishonor of having to be subjected to the leadership of this naive interloper from ELF management.

Raymond Dunbar, the vice president of gift delivery systems, seemed to connect with his new boss more quickly than the rest. Energetic and considerably younger than his counterparts, Raymond had a generally healthy relationship and comfort level with Jason's former position and with the ELF organization as a whole. Being responsible for the implementation and delivery of Edward Grubb's gift plan, Raymond was very dependent on the timely delivery of ELF-made products into inventory. When Jason was the divisional vice president at ELF he and Raymond had crossed paths on a number of occasions but till now they never really needed to connect as, prior to the recent establishment of the senior vice president positions now occupied by Marcus Millerov at ELF and Jason Pelham at the NTA, Raymond dealt almost exclusively with ELF's executive vice president.

Prematurely gray but unusually handsome, charismatic, and soft-spoken, Henry Foster, vice president of customer relations and user interface, was in charge of a very complex and diverse group. His efforts were largely strategic and, though still firmly part of the NTA, had direct links to both the sales and marketing arms of the Kringle Works. Henry had a quiet and friendly manner which would lull you into a deep conversation that compelled you to reveal your darkest secrets while Henry, himself, remained vague and illusive. His talent was that he was able to talk at great length and in incredible detail about his department's process, charter, and team without actually telling you anything of particular substance. Most of the direct contact with the world at large was through the Kringle Works's executive staff and sales force, but Henry Foster would be the face of the NTA after a diplomatic and service relationship was established with a country's leadership, local politician, or clergy.

"So tell me about this new staff of yours," Krystal asked Jason over their first dinner together in weeks.

Jason was on a roll of cancelled dates with Krystal. His own perceived need to work at this new job was driving him to work extremely long hours. This was an entirely new position and he was determined to learn it in record time.

"Sometimes I think they are more important to you than me," she scolded him.

"Don't be silly!" he snapped back.

Undeterred, she gave him a mischievous smile while moving her food from one side of the plate to the other without eating it. She was taking a small amount of pleasure in getting him agitated. He was, after all, not being very good company.

"Well, let's see. You and I were going to go on a ride. We were going to have a small picnic. The days are getting warmer. The sun is up almost all day now. You don't want to waste it by being at the office. Right? But then … what do I get? A note, not from you, but by office courier saying, *You won't be coming*. Really, Jason? Not even a call?" she said.

"I was too busy! You can understand that?" he snapped.

"Uh huh," she responded. "So tell me about them?"

Jason dropped his fork. He leaned forward, put his elbows on the table and rested his head on his hands.

"Okay!" he snarled. "Raymond Dunbar you've met. He uses the sleighs at your barn."

Krystal felt triumphant--this was already the most conversation they had had in over a week. She was willing to declare it a victory for their relationship.

"Yes, I do! Nice guy! Young, no older than me," she noted. "Yeah, I like him."

He smiled and continued,

"Then there's Lorraine Barlow …"

She grinned at him and jeered,

"That bitch! I've met her. Kinda uptight and prissy. Not your type. Little thing, isn't she?"

Jason shook his head in irritation.

"She's very good at what she does," he defended her.

"Really? How good?" She leaned closer. "Good enough to cancel all our dates?"

He tilted his head with a look of disgust. She burst out laughing.

"Well, nevertheless. She's terrible with the animals. They don't like her much and they're very good judges of character," she snarled jokingly.

Jason rolled his eyes and went silent, picked up his fork again, and started shoveling food into his mouth.

"Okay, okay! I'm sorry!" she responded. "I'll be good. Tell me more."

He put the fork down again and continued,

"There's our vice president of data analysis and implementation, Edward Grubb."

She shook her head.

"No," Krystal interrupted, "No, him I don't know. That title, wow, that's a mouthful!"

"You wouldn't like him," he suggested, "He's not very personable, very much an introvert. He has a nasty streak, too. He has to evaluate and judge people. That's his job. I just don't think he can shut it off anymore. I feel sorry for his family."

"Oh, that's awful!" she suggested, "How do you get along with him?"

Jason shrugged.

"One day at a time is how I handle it, one day at a time," he answered, "Then there is Henry Foster ..."

"Hmm, don't know him either. Heard the name, though! He's up there on the food chain, isn't he? I thought you worked for Andre?" she interrupted.

"I do!" he snapped, "Henry works for me!"

Krystal pursed her lips and arched her eyebrows, trying to look impressed, while nodding.

"Do you like them?" she asked, "Your team, I mean."

He hesitated for a moment.

"Yes! Yes I do," he said.

She nodded again,

"That's good. I want you to be happy."

Jason looked down in embarrassment and nodded.

"I know. I'm sorry, Krystal, for these last couple weeks. It just can't be helped. It's not my fault there is just too much to do, so much to learn. There's nothing I can do," he said apologetically.

She smiled.

"So how about lunch tomorrow?" she asked, bright eyed.

He shook his head,

"I can't. Not tomorrow."

She tilted her head and put on an exaggerated pout.

"Okay then, mister senior VP. You tell me when," she suggested.

4

THE ANOMALY

It was a muffled ringing, distant and undefined, but undeniably present. Even as John Evans attempted to ignore it, the ringing was becoming more and more obvious as he felt himself ascending from the subconscious. The room was dark. The only real discernable detail was the reflected light from the side window, a blue-gray rectangle that flashed red in one corner, awkwardly placed diagonally on the ceiling; it seemed an insistent reminder of a world outside of his cocoon of slumber. The ringing became ever more insistent. Dazed, John felt his senses slowly coming to life as his mind started to wrestle with the new information like a driver on a dark and foggy street recognizing the car up ahead as he draws closer. He was only starting to make out his surroundings. The undeniable stench of alcohol still permeating his very being seemed to ooze from every pore. He was unclear about the events that had led him to this point. Last night, what was it? A Cinco de Mayo celebration? Steeped in tequila, it now seemed a distant blur and he thought it might be better left that way. The ringing now beckoned him to react, but a disquieting promise of crisis was in the air.

"Don't answer it, sugar, let it ring," an unfamiliar, sleepy, female voice added to the disturbance.

A young woman rolled over on to her stomach and fell back to sleep.

John turned to see the objects on his nightstand. A clock proudly displayed the time, 3:09 a.m. A lamp was illuminated by the glow of the clock but cast no light of its own. An empty glass and next to the clock, a phone was ringing. A phone was ringing! Clearing his voice and with a sense of foreboding, John lifted the receiver.

"Evans," he answered, his voice low, cracked, and grumbling.

The breathiness of the high-pitched voice on the other end of the phone conveyed a significant sense of panic.

"It happened again! John, the whole system seemed to blink for a moment, but when I ran a check, nothing!"

"Then maybe it *was* nothing," John said, now sitting up in his bed.

"No, there's more … listen, it's weird … look, just come in! I don't want to do this on the phone!" the caller pleaded.

John sighed and hung up the phone. He glanced over at the clock, 3:13a.m.; he sighed again as he looked over to the young woman asleep in the bed next to him. He rubbed his face with his hands and got up. Naked, he started to pick up the various bits of clothing, both male and female articles. He paused and attempted to remember the name of woman lying in the bed. He studied her shape, illuminated only by the subtle light from the window, the curves of the one leg protruding from the loosely draped sheet, the curve of her back drawing a line to her neck and to her hair which swirled in a series of "S" shapes. Like a voyeur he was fixated as he tried to piece the events of last night together. No good! He was unable to recall her name, and decided to strategically avoid its use. He started by tapping her exposed foot; nothing. He grabbed some of her clothes and gently shook her by the shoulder.

"Hey, you gotta' get up … I've gotta' go and you can't stay here. So you've gotta' go too," John whispered.

The young woman started to stir.

"What?" she exclaimed.

John reiterated, "You gotta' get out, I have to go and you can't stay here."

The young woman sat up. As she hung her head, tired locks of her hair slipped forward and obscured her face. John attempted to hand over her clothes. She looked up at him and grabbed the jumbled pile of clothes and inquired,

"What are you, an asshole? It's three in the morning!"

"Twenty after, actually. Let's go!" he corrected her and thought that this might have been a bad move, as she looked even more irritated now.

The young woman stood up and looked about the room to see if she could find more of her belongings in the dark. John started to rush her out. Naked and clothes in hand, she was reluctant to leave and protested. Pulling her by the upper arm, John opened the door and attempted to push her into the hallway outside his apartment. Her anger now overrode her modesty and she started to scold him loudly. Strangers' faces suddenly emerged and peered through partially open doors to see what the commotion was about. They curiously looked on as John managed get her whole body out the door and just as he attempted to close the door behind her, she threw one of her shoes, hitting him just as the door closed. She paused, and in an attempt to recoup her dignity she picked up a couple articles of clothing that had fallen from her hands, stood up very straight and poised, brushed her hair back from her face and, still naked, walked down the public hallway. One elderly man, whose eyes had not yet disappeared behind his apartment door, received a scornful look as she walked past toward the elevator. As the elevator door slid closed, so did the remaining apartment door.

John walked into his bathroom and splashed cold water in his face. He raked his wet fingers through his hair and attempted to clean himself up. A clean shirt, a dark suit and tie; John tugged on his jacket to straighten it. He rummaged through his pockets and found his ID badge. 'Federal Bureau of Investigation, Cyber Crime Division', John cringed at the thought of how many times he might have flashed *that* last night to show off. He poured some cologne into his hand and in an apparent effort of self-punishment slapped himself in the face to apply it.

At this time of night the traffic was light even in downtown Washington, DC and John was able to get to the office quickly. After going through security John made his way to the cyber crime division's computer lab. At the door he placed two fingers on a pad and swiped a key card. A red light turned green and the large steel door opened with a loud clunk.

Tom Bradley was a stereotypical computer geek, though he heightened the image because it was what he thought people would want and expect. His image, he thought, gave him credibility. Glasses that were too large for his face and a pocket protector were part of his image. The nervous nature that made him seem awkward in any social situation was genuine. Perhaps this was indeed the result of too much time at a computer or too much time with this night owl shift. This morning, however, he was more nervous than normal. Actually, he was truly intense.

"John! Geez, what the hell took you so long!"

"Tom, it's freakin' four o'clock in the A-M! What the hell is so important anyway?"

John sported a frustrated look as Tom Bradley pulled out a stack of freshly printed reports. Tom slapped these down with a loud thump on a table that sat at the center of the room. It seemed partially for effect, to prove how thoroughly he had checked his information.

"If you expect me to read those you're dreaming, Tom!" John suggested. He placed both hands on the table and leaned in to get face-to-face with Tom. "You pulled me out of bed in the middle of the night, and trust me this was a really bad time to do it, to tell me something. Well I'm here, tell me something and, please, give me the executive summary."

The table gave slightly as John put more of his weight on it. Its metal legs and edging bordered a worn white laminate top adorned with an old 1960s era interpretation of marble. The room was cold; three large, ceiling-mounted air conditioning units efficiently cooled and dried the room for the computers that lined the back wall in gray metal racking, but had apparently disregarded the comfort of its human occupants. Opposite the computers were four large plasma screens, all of which displayed various news programming. These were where Tom was now pointing and shaking his hand frantically to assist in pointing out one of the plasma screens. He started into a nervous, energy-driven rant that seemed like a continuation of the call John received earlier that morning.

"John, it, it, it was this screen, see? Right here, in the ticker at the bottom!"

Tom walked around the table to the plasma screens mounted on the wall. He walked up to one of them to single it out as though it had personally offended him. Tom shook his head and turned around to face John, but looked past him at the computers at the other end of the room.

"And the computers! They noted something happened. I saw it, but then when I checked to see what it was, it was gone, as though it never happened. I checked it again and again … you see the reports?"

Tom hurried back to the table, picked up the stack of paper and slapped it back down as if to imitate the mighty fallen tree that surely died to create this unreasonable tome. Tom continued his semi-incoherent rant,

"It seemed like the system saw an intrusion, or a cyber attack, or something on the system but it didn't come in from the outside; nothing was compromised, there was no malicious code, it, it, it was like it started from inside the firewall and then it disappeared, but it was there. If anything, any anomaly, *any anomaly* is recorded and logged, so it was not a question of verifying it *had* happened, it was a question of *what* happened, but then when I wanted to see what it was, the system indicated nothing, but I saw it! And see? Then all of a sudden this TV screen here noted in the news ticker, it said that there had been a brief power surge in the DC area, but the new reports are not recorded here so I went to the other room to check and the note on the ticker message didn't show up there at all. It's like it was on this one screen, the one that I was looking at and no other--"

"Whoa, there, Tom! First, calm down; second, slow down; and third, in English, please!" John interrupted.

This had the desired effect. Tom took a couple deep breaths, stopped talking and gave John an apologetic look. John motioned for Tom to sit, and the two men sat down at the table. John Evans leaned forward, folded his hands and quietly considered Tom. After a moment of silence John spoke,

"Okay, Tom, step-by-step. What happened?"

John motioned for Tom to start talking. Tom nodded both in acknowledgement and as if to say he was okay. He took another couple deep breaths and started talking,

"John, do you know how many times the government of the United States is under an attempted cyber attack? All the time! All the time, John, it never stops. Many come from hacks and amateurs; these are caught early. Others are more sophisticated; they come from foreign powers, terrorists, and even people inside who, for one reason or another, want to do harm to the government's computer infrastructure. These systems here in place are designed to watch each other. If something happens, the system recognizes it. Even if one system is compromised another will see it."

Tom paused, thought for a moment and leaned closer. He lowered his voice and started to take John through the events of this night and his view of them,

"It is my job to be sure that I do not disregard anything, even when everything around me suggests I should. This evening the computer system initiated something; nothing significant, nothing malicious, nothing more interesting than a mouse click, the opening of a directory or a window. No big deal, but I didn't initiate it. It happened by itself or by someone else. It happened once before, last week, as you might remember."

John nodded and motioned that Tom continue.

"Last week we assumed it was nothing. A lack of sleep perhaps; however, now it happened again and this time one of the other computers saw it and it notified me. Then when I went back to see what exactly happened it was not there. I checked the original computer and it also showed nothing. I checked the computers that monitor the activities of these computers and still nothing. The problem is that once one of the computers has logged the incident it can't not be there, but it wasn't. So I ran some more checks; still nothing. It's like something that cannot disappear, did. Keep in mind that all of this appeared to be happening inside the network. No, inside the computer itself, in the operating system but not using the hardware; I know it sounds nuts."

Tom stopped as if to ponder whether he wanted to go on but then felt he had to.

"It was then, after I had obsessively started running check after check, that a news report came out on that screen!"

Tom, clenching his teeth, pointed aggressively at the plasma screen he had identified earlier and continued.

"A news report, just as I looked up, not the reporter or the story being covered, but just subtly on the ticker at the bottom and only on the one screen. It said that there were occasional power surges in the Washington, DC area. None of the other programming had it and when I went back to look at the recording of the program I was watching, the ticker had some update about Afghanistan or something. I went back and forth to find it and it was simply not there."

"Maybe you *are* going nuts, Tom" John interjected.

Tom shook his head and said,

"Maybe? There's more; the message didn't just say that there were power surges, it said that there were, and not to worry about it *Tom*! It addressed me!"

With that, Tom Bradley, a seasoned FBI agent and computer programmer, took his glasses off, cupped his head in his trembling hands and started to cry. John Evans sympathetically watched as he evaluated the situation. Something happened but there was no record of it. Check. All the systems that check to make sure that there would be a record of said something, even if it was not there, *is* not there. Check. FBI agent sees a news ticker on a screen and thinks it is addressing him personally. Check. Recording of said news program reveals no such message. Check. FBI agent is sitting at table crying like a baby. Really big check.

"Okay," John thought to himself, "I think I see what is going on here."

Agent John Evans felt he knew exactly what to do. He did not like it, but it was the obvious and necessary next step. For now, John attempted to muster up his most friendly, even fatherly tone, and though he had little experience in one and none in the other, he seemed moderately convincing,

"Tom, old buddy, we've worked together for what, twelve years? Let's consider what is happening here. There is no record of what you saw, or think you saw. You know better than I that that can't happen, right?"

John looked down at his watch and continued,

"In an hour and a half Agent Jenkins will be in to relieve you for the day shift. Go home. Get some rest. Then if you don't feel better I will recommend you get some time off and maybe even a little precautionary therapy. Nothing major, just someone to talk to, okay? So, can we put this night behind us?"

Tom nodded his head in agreement but did not say anything.

John stood up, clapped his hands together and exclaimed,

"Well, okay then, we're all set! Give me a call later and let me know how you're doing."

John hurried out of the room. Leaving the computer lab seemed to be the only way to escape this unpleasant situation. Still, John's conscience would not give him much peace, which was particularly unpleasant for him as he did not normally wrestle with his conscience all that much. John had made a decision in the lab and was justifying it in his head. He supervised six agents. He could cover the needs with five if he had to. Tom was obviously having a nervous breakdown and that would leave him and the department too vulnerable, no matter how good Tom's record of service was. Tom would have to be discharged, at least temporarily. A colleague and friend, but all that needed to be pushed aside. Otherwise this could get very complicated and John was not about to wrestle with that too.

John looked at his watch again; 6:14 a.m. Coffee was now the priority. That and maybe three eggs and a chicken-fried steak. He figured his metabolism was well into gear by now and he could hit a nice little greasy spoon on his way back to his apartment. He made his way to the motor pool and started en route. Once on the street, John pulled his ID badge off of his jacket's lapel and shoved it into his side pocket. He wanted to take his mind off of the morning's events and decided to turn to his car radio. It came on, and as if to taunt him, it cut out for a moment. When the signal finally fixed he found himself listening to a talk radio discussion.

"… Okay, colonel, why didn't Army doctors diagnose such a serious and deep-rooted psychological ailment when they were recruiting the prospective soldier? The Army's own statistics show that discharges for personality disorders have increased in recent years by almost forty percent, suggesting that the military may be abusing the diagnosis because doing so is convenient."

"Well, *that* isn't helping!" John said to himself.

He switched to another of the presets in his car radio. After pushing the button the radio cut out again, just for a moment, and then the sound of a familiar song,

"You just call out my name, and you know wherever I am, I'll come running, oh yeah to see you again. Winter, spring, summer, or fall, all you have to do is call and I'll be there, yeah, yeah, yeah. You've got a friend."

44

James Taylor's 1971 version of "You've Got a Friend" started to echo in John's brain. As he sang along he made the decision to hold off on Tom's discharge and see how the next few weeks would go.

5

THE PROJECT

"We've successfully run the tests, and the new ICU2 chip works perfectly. I need for the production to change over immediately," a seemingly disembodied voice spoke from the shadowy doorway.

"You've got to be kidding me!" an irritated Marcus Millerov protested.

With his office key in hand and lights out, Marcus seemed postured as though he had been interrupted on his way out after a long day.

"Do you have any idea how much I have on my plate right now?" Marcus spoke with no effort to hide his frustration. "I would have thought with Jason as your new senior VP it might bring a dose of manufacturing realities to your organization--or is this *his* idea of a joke? Look, I've got to get home. I'm late already. I'll look at our production schedule and chip inventory and implement a running change. You'll be into the next generation by next year's Christmas delivery." He paused, "Good evening!"

Marcus moved to leave his darkened office only to be blocked by an arm in the doorway.

"I assure you this was in the works long before Mr. Pelham was put in charge, but I am also sure he would strongly urge you to comply. You will implement the change now and scrap the old chips," the voice demanded.

Marcus snarled at the shadowy figure and in an effort to prove he would not be bullied, raised his voice,

"Scrap the old chi...?! These are not sitting on a shelf! Tens of thousands are already attached to various boards ready for assembly into products! The majority of these are under the microprocessor per your design team's specs! I ... I ... I'd be throwing out the most important, most expensive part! Look, I run this operation, not you! I alone am responsible for the production lines, quota, quality, and delivery and I will not have your silly little pet projects disrupt them."

Marcus started to jab his finger into the shadowy figure's chest. His upper lip curled to expose his yellowing teeth like a growling dog trying to exert his dominance.

Undeterred, the voice answered with a measured, forceful tone and almost as though he had not heard Marcus at all.

"It will be done immediately. I will have a delivery of 4,000,000 chips at your receiving dock tomorrow morning. There is new functionality in the new chips that *must* be implemented."

Marcus felt his anger rising and allowed it to guide his follow up.

"Functionality? There *is* no functionality! In our quality checks--and they are extensive--the chips don't do anything anyway. No matter how we manipulate them. Face it, you've screwed up.... As I said, next year! And if you expect *even this timeline* ... you'd better hope that this new chip fits the exact footprint and connection points!" Marcus pushed past the figure and into the darkness. "Good ... evening!" He closed with an unusual emphasis on each of these last two words, trying to signal that this conversation was over. He started down the darkened hallway.

"Of course, I understand, you have to get home. Let me give you a ride. We have already made arrangements to return your snowmobile. My sleigh is outside waiting for us. Come, we have more to discuss; I think perhaps we got off on the wrong foot," the voice suggested.

Marcus stopped. He was overcome by a familiar and unpleasant feeling of being boxed into a corner. His choices, he thought, had just narrowed dramatically. He hung his head in resignation and turned back.

"Okay, then, let's ride to my house together; but you won't be changing my mind." Marcus asserted.

"Yes, we do have so much to talk about," the voice suggested with a strange mix of menace, condescension, and an overt friendliness. "Let us take some time to talk about our great company's history, shall we? Say, about fifteen years ago? If I recall it was a turning point for both you and Jason Pelham, wasn't it?"

Marcus's eyes widened and a very cold chill ran up his spine. His mind traveled back in time and opened a door on a number of past views and indiscretions he had hoped, and thought, would never surface or need to be answered for. He did not speak, but it seemed that his silence spoke volumes.

"Yes, *that* got your attention, didn't it? Xavier Kringle forcibly and very quietly sent a few hundred former Workshop employees to Quebec in exile, didn't he? I always wondered, Marcus, why weren't you on one of those ships?" Marcus's companion asked. "Come along now, it's already late. We can chat on the way; I think we have more in common than you may realize."

Marcus felt an arm land around his neck and shoulders in an outwardly friendly but covertly threatening gesture, and the two figures walked out. The sun blinded them as they exited the darkened building with the late day springtime brightness. As they approached their caribou-drawn sleigh, Marcus looked around. The snowmobile he borrowed that morning was no longer out front; the compound was nearly empty, with only a few people remaining as the general workday had ended. Marcus was conflicted with a wish for the comfort of a crowded active space and the desire to suffer the coming discussion as privately as possible. He was on his way home but had a sinking feeling that the conversation was not going anywhere he wanted to go.

The trip through the compound to the gates remained silent as Marcus waited for some revelation that would potentially enslave him to his traveling companion. A nugget of information about a time in which Marcus's ideas about the direction of the company and ELF had pushed him into actions that were perhaps misguided, in hindsight, would now come back to haunt him in a whirlwind of extortion and blackmail. Marcus thought he had done his time, proved his silent repentance, buried his involvement and effectively avoided suspicion. Marcus looked over at the person sitting next to him and noted a contented and self-indulgent smile, punctuated by a friendly wink as notice of Marcus's gaze was recognized.

Marcus faced forward trying to hide any outward expression of the feelings of horror and anger that overwhelmed him. The silence, now a countdown to a pending disaster, conjured up images in Marcus's tortured mind of a series of overzealous skeletons all clamoring to be the first to break down the proverbial closet door.

As they left the compound, Marcus looked around. The quiet of the late day shifts at the Kringle Works was now replaced with the bustle of the population's evening errands and recreation. Engaged in their activities and covered by the ambient sounds of the island's city limits, Marcus was comfortable that he could no longer be heard by those outside the sleigh. His presence and conversations would not be scrutinized and he would be safe to get the inevitable conversation started, as the silence in the sleigh was now becoming distressing.

"Look, I don't know what you think you know, but I'm sure you are quite misinformed!" Marcus said defensively, breaking the silence.

"It was much bigger than ELF, you know, all you needed to do was let the situation degenerate," Marcus's travel companion suggested. "Actually, it would have worked, but somehow you and your friends failed to see a young, energetic director of toy manufacturing as a threat. That was a bad miscalculation. His entire team lined up behind him. Was that naiveté and leadership, or an informed effort to thwart the plan?"

"Jason? Jason saved the day! There were just a lot of problems compounding a bad situation, but with Jason's help the company did very well that year," Marcus said with an effort to sound sincere. "We have been colleagues for our entire lives, our careers almost parallel. Anyway, he works in your organization now."

The conversation fell silent again as they left the city and started down the quiet countryside roads leading to the Millerov house. The sleigh hissed as they turned onto the long, ice-packed road that would end at his home.

Marcus broke the silence again,

"Look, I will make the adjustments you need, but get me a letter from Xavier or someone on the executive staff allowing me to scrap the chips and all the components they are already attached to, and I will deal with the timing."

The sleigh stopped, now just a couple hundred yards from the house.

"Ah, that is the rub then, isn't it? No, we cannot have an official document like that floating around, not yet. I'm sure that you can figure something out; trust me, in the long run the executive staff will support you. You have a reputation for innovation, Marcus, I have faith in you," Marcus's companion suggested.

Marcus looked ahead at his house; he would not turn to make eye contact with his companion, and in a low whine asked,

"How am I going to cover the expense? This will cost tens of millions! What will I suggest is the justification for the ramp-up of the replacement components?" Marcus shook his head, "No, this can't be done!"

Marcus's companion chuckled a little and said,

"That *is* quite the conundrum. I don't know; blame it on a catastrophic failure of quality control or something. You'll work it out. I will be there in the morning to make sure the delivery comes in as planned."

The sleigh started moving again. Marcus stopped his companion's effort to initiate the caribou and drive up the road.

"No, stop, thanks, I'll walk from here," Marcus said as he stepped out of the sleigh. "My family and home are sacred, I don't want you any closer to them."

The sleigh driver nodded and said,

"As you wish, see you in the morning. Good evening, Marcus."

Marcus started the walk up to his house, but said nothing else and did not look back as the sleigh turned around.

6

SUPPLY AND DEMAND

Raymond Dunbar, vice president of gift delivery systems, NTA, stood horrified and motionless as he listened to the synopsis of a rather devastating supply chain report being submitted by ELF management. The apparent culprit was a catastrophic failure of the conductive adhesive system that was used to put some electronic components together. It seemed that the amounts of various metals in the adhesive were not properly blended, causing inconsistent connections, or so the report would state. The problem, it seemed, was so widespread that it would bring most of the ELF electronics division to its knees, and it would be up to the NTA's gift delivery division to deal with the consequences of a shorter staging cycle and delivery window. Exacerbating the issue was that the problem was not caught by ELF quality control and as such required a rework of a huge number of components prior to assembly. Over sixty million products would be affected in this week's deliveries alone.

Sitting at his desk, Marcus Millerov was reading from an eighty-page report. Hunched over and looking through his narrow rectangular reading glasses, Marcus personally read out loud the affected products in a drone-like monotone:

- *1,550,000 laptop computers*
- *1,000,000 portable stereo systems*
- *860,000 smart phones*
- *687,000 digital camcorders*
- *580,000 video gaming systems*
- *450,000 home theater systems*
- *430,000 televisions*
- *405,000 DVD players and DVDR recorders*

- *360,000 cordless telephones*
- *350,000 cellular telephones*
- *150,000 MP3 players*
- *68,000 various talking, walking, dancing, peeing and/or vomiting dolls and stuffed animals*
- *45,000 car stereos*
- *43,000 GPS systems*

"That's almost seven million products! How much is this going to cost you?" Raymond exclaimed as he painstakingly calculated the numbers in his head as he heard them. "Jason Pelham is going to lose it! I'm sure he is going to want to know who is responsible and how you plan on enforcing accountability for this! How much will this push back our timing?"

Marcus looked up over his reading glasses at Raymond and smirked.

"At least four weeks. An estimated 20.6 million US dollars," Marcus snarled, "And you can let Mr. Jason Pelham know that three people are losing their jobs and about twenty-five are being transferred and demoted. I assume that will please him?"

Purposefully, Marcus thumbed through the massive report and flipped back to a page near the end. He tore the page from the report and handed it to Raymond. He motioned him to take it and look at it and as he did, Marcus suggested that Raymond just look at the top at Section D.

Page 63, Corrective action, Section D (continued):

Employees to be terminated, due to gross negligence:

> *- Denise Lorraine Westcott, Quality Control Manager, Electronics*
> *- Janet Rebecca Pelham, Quality Inspector #17*
> *- Charles Fox, Procurement Manager, Chemicals*

Marcus followed up,

"Take that to Jason; I think he will find it interesting. The full report is on its way to you."

Shocked and speechless, Raymond slowly folded the paper and put it in his breast pocket. He looked at Marcus inquisitively, shook his head and opened his mouth as if to say something. Just then Marcus, sitting at his desk, curtly spun around leaving Raymond with only the view of the back of his chair. As Marcus did so, he flicked his wrist so as to signal Raymond's dismissal.

Raymond stood for a moment and once he felt the sting of this unsaid insult from another division's senior vice president penetrate his psyche, he made no effort to feign decorum and allowed his annoyance to be obvious as he gasped aloud, spun around and left.

Upon Raymond's return to the NTA, he immediately rushed to the senior vice president's office to discuss the matter.

Jason Pelham slammed the telephone down.

"What the hell is going on?" he exclaimed just as Raymond Dunbar entered his office. "I have only been here for six weeks and the whole of ELF goes to hell!?"

Jason looked up at Raymond in frustration and asked,

"And what in the name of Christmas did Marcus Millerov say was going to shut everything down for a minimum of four weeks? Raymond, help me out here … can you compensate?"

Raymond Dunbar held his hand up as if to say, 'stop and calm down.' He sat down in one of the guest chairs in front of Jason's desk. Leaning closer to Jason, he said,

"Jason, I can. That is, *if* Marcus stays to his new timeline, and *if* I get regular updates, and *if* Grubb cooperates." Raymond leaned back in his chair and continued, "The four weeks are not too bad if we are in constant touch and we get continuous information on the deliveries out of ELF. Still, because we will not likely be catching up with all the products equally, it will be up to Edward Grubb to be more flexible. I have to be able to stage the warehouses globally with inventory, based on availability *and not* on his developed demand. So if 'daddy' deserves a new computer he may be getting a new DVD player based on what is available. You know this will make Grubb nuts."

"Just leave Edward Grubb to me," Jason suggested. "He and I have to come to an understanding anyway," he continued.

Raymond got up out of his chair and nodded. He offered his thanks and commitment to a clean resolution and turned to leave. Hesitating, he turned back to face Jason and spoke.

"Jason, what exactly is your relationship with Marcus Millerov? If you will excuse me for saying so, but it seems that there is a bit of tension between you two."

Jason sighed, nodded in confirmation and suggested that Raymond take his seat again. He then went on to describe how he and Marcus knew each other for a very long time. He explained how Marcus, a few years Jason's senior, had had to watch as Jason caught up to Marcus's career and then found himself competing with Jason at every turn.

However, the real conflict arose when Jason made Marcus look particularly bad fifteen years ago when Jason managed to save the Kringle Works from a disastrous collapse in deliveries.

At that time, Xavier Kringle, well seasoned in the company's business but still a new and inexperienced CEO, had only been working in this position for a year when it looked like the Workshop would, for the first time, miss all of its holiday obligations. Jason's plan, nicknamed Rudolph after the beloved character created by Robert L. May in 1939, saved Xavier and in turn made Jason a hero. It had, like Rudolph the reindeer in the story, salvaged Christmas that year.

It was early the next year that Xavier Kringle demonstrated the strength and indeed, sometimes, ruthless leadership he could muster.

An investigation ferreted out that there were some who sought to weaken the Kringle family's hold of the Kringle Works by forcing the company into a position of extreme vulnerability and make them, in turn, rash and desperate. The thought was that once weakened, the new CEO would be forced to make concessions to some of the leadership at ELF who for many years demanded an ownership stake of the company be made available to them. It seemed that elements of the ELF management had orchestrated a massive sickout at this, a particularly volatile time. However, it was a young Jason Pelham who put the manufacturing lines back into production with only half the workforce and, in so doing unwittingly thwarted the plans of these few. This also effectively exposed the conspiracy to those who knew to look for it.

The executive staff and Xavier's retribution was stealthy, swift, and complete. A significant number of supervisors, managers, and senior level management were immediately let go and several hundred ELF line workers who participated in the staged sickout were also fired. All would be forcibly deported for their participation. Some who would be evidenced to have planned the coup would be tried and jailed abroad with treaty partners. As the company was globally understood to be a sovereign entity, crimes against the management could be viewed as treasonous.

For the few who knew about it, the conspiracy was rumored to have gone deeper than those accused, but no additional evidence of this was ever found.

Marcus Millerov, though never accused of being part of the conspiracy, would loose much of his status and most of his workforce, some of whom Marcus felt were not involved or were too valuable to let go. In his mind, he thought that he had lost much to Jason Pelham's self-ingratiating opportunism and he would be reminded of it with every publicized award and promotion that Xavier lavished upon Jason in subsequent years.

Raymond was very much aware of Jason Pelham's early career, but he had not heard of the conspiracy before. Similarly, the majority of the island's population was not aware of the coup and instead most remembered the supply chain shortages, the storms, the pandemic and, of course, Jason Pelham's leadership solutions and Rudolph.

Raymond Dunbar smiled as he got up and joked,

"Well, I look forward to reading about the details when Xavier writes his memoirs after he retires."

Jason smiled at him and nodded as Raymond turned a second time to leave. Raymond then reached into his jacket's breast pocket and pulled out a folded piece of paper.

"Oh yeah, for what it's worth, Marcus gave me this. It's part of the ELF report analysis and their efforts to remedy the situation. It seems some heads will roll as a result," Raymond explained as he handed Jason the paper.

Jason's eyebrows furrowed as he looked at it. His skin flushed and he crushed the report page in his fists and pounded his desk.

"I don't believe it! That son of a bitch is firing my mother!" Jason growled.

7

I SEE YOU TOO

Krystal Gardner walked in with a huge plate of food and set it on the table.

"She makes even the most awkward and unpleasant situations seem great," Jason thought.

She smiled at him as she noticed his gaze studying her moves.

"There's something funny going on here, and I'm going to find out what it is!" Frank Pelham, Jason's father, interrupted his momentary distraction from the evening's ongoing discussion.

The room and surrounding home was in the old Victorian style that prevailed in the island's character. Modest in size but well-appointed and tastefully decorated, this was always a pleasant retreat for Jason and he made it a point to spend time there when he could. Jason's father and mother, like many on the isolated island, retained their traditional parental roles; the mother encouraging and uplifting and the father the wise consultant, though at this stage it had become more of an exercise, as there was little that Frank Pelham could tell his son that he did not already know. The light, wooden, hand-carved oval table was indicative of the island's obsession with craftsmanship and though it was set for dinner, the focus was on the two men's discussion. Seated at the table, Jason and his father had been debating that day's events. The primary topic of discussion was Jason's mother, Janet. Also seated at the table, she seemed content to lose herself in her own thoughts, though her presence was by design, as she was supposed to participate.

Because of the events of the day, Krystal had volunteered to take care of the food that evening so that the family, of which Krystal seemed to be an honorary member, could evaluate this significant shift in their daily lives.

Frank continued,

"You know your mother's friend, Trudy Fox? She has worked side by side with you mother for at least ten years and she allowed all of the same components through the quality check with no indication that anything was wrong with the products!"

Frank leaned forward, put his hand on Jason's shoulder and whispered, glancing sideways,

"I talked to Trudy's husband Charlie, who is also losing his job, and he said that the whole thing is a plot. Marcus Millerov found out about the quality issues and took immediate action; there were no double checks, no auditors to verify the report, and no one in quality saw it coming. What's more, Charlie thinks he is being set up. He thinks that the glue he was purchasing had no problems at all and that the new batch that will be used is still the same batch. It was just trucked out so they could say it was disposed of, then it could be brought back and used again." Increasing the volume, Frank exclaimed, "This whole thing stinks! It's bullshit!"

"Frank Pelham!" Janet interrupted, "All this talk of plots and conspiracies, it's getting silly. Marcus Millerov has been breathing down my neck for over ten years and it was bound to happen eventually that he find an excuse to get rid of me. Besides, I was going to retire anyway, and did you know that Xavier Kringle called me *personally* to let me know that the company would take care of me and that there would be no halting on retirement pay and that no one would be asked to leave the island?"

Janet looked adoringly at her son and continued,

"I have a feeling that we have you to thank for that Jason, even if you don't know it. Xavier is such a good man and he thinks very highly of you … what we do here at the Workshop is so important to so many in the world and …" she paused, "I'll be fine, really."

Janet smiled at Jason, as if to signal her contentment with the outcome, but Jason could see veiled pain and disappointment. She was hurt by the thought that after all the years of service this is how her career would end. It was different here from the rest of the world; life on the island was defined by your work at the company. That was the reason for your existence.

Jason also knew that the idea of a conspiracy was not in the least far-fetched. He looked at his mother,

"I can help! Even if only to clear your name of any fault."

"I know, sweetheart, you are a very important man, but I don't want either you or your father to jeopardize anything!"

She shot a judgmental look at her husband.

"And I think it would be *best* if you kept your nose out of this, if for no other reason than that Marcus Millerov is now your boss's, boss's, boss's boss."

Janet waved her index finger at her husband and continued, punctuating each word,

"Do I make myself absolutely clear?"

Dinner would change the tone dramatically, and with the edict laid down by Janet there would be no more discussion regarding these conspiracy theories, Marcus Millerov, or general shop talk while they ate. The conversation remained more wholesome.

However, it would not be long after dinner that father and son would seek an opportunity to take advantage of some time outside to talk. Frank enjoyed the occasional indulgence of a pipe, and as his wife would not allow him to smoke in the house, the two poured themselves an after-dinner drink and made their way out onto the front step.

As Jason stepped through the door, he let the evening sun bathe him in warmth. It was an unusually warm July that year and the sun, which never completely set at this time of the year, stood at the midpoint in the late day sky. The two men could enjoy what was by the standards of the island a heat wave of fifty degrees Fahrenheit, and ponder all things. Still, their conversation turned quickly again to the events at Kringle Works.

"So what else did Charlie Fox tell you?" Jason asked as he swirled brandy in an oversized snifter.

"Well, some of it did seem a little far-fetched, actually," Frank started, "but Charlie did say that he believed that Marcus chose to blame the adhesive because it would be difficult to verify. If you blame the adhesive for an *inconsistent* connection, sometimes the products would test fine and sometimes not. So if Marcus needed to produce a sample to be verified it could test fine and still be suspect."

Jason nodded in understanding. Frank leaned over toward him, took a sip of brandy and in a lower voice continued,

"There is more though. Charlie also thinks he is being targeted because he asked too many questions. He thinks that Marcus would have liked nothing more than to have him fired and then deported, but he couldn't pull that off."

"Questions?" Jason asked. "What kind of questions?"

"Well," Frank emptied his pipe by tapping it on the rail, put it in his pocket and took another sip of his brandy before contemplating his next sentence. "Here's the thing, son, Charlie is in ELF purchasing, and he found some things that didn't quite make sense. When you worked at ELF, you and Marcus both would manufacture things to the ELF design team's specifications and the purchasing team would buy materials to fit that demand. Charlie noticed that for about seven months he was consistently coming up short with some of the chemicals needed in the assembly of electronics. Conformal coatings, adhesives, stuff like that. Charlie wanted to see the design specs again and noticed that the design team's stuff was reworked by the NTA to include an upgraded ICU chip, apparently for testing, at first."

Jason interrupted,

"Yes, but that is not really all that unusual. The ICU chip is kept reasonably quiet because of the potential for misuse, and in my opinion is a little bit of a stretch for application under the SANTA Clause. The NTA is a little protective of this. In fact, I am surprised that you know about it at all. A couple months ago I didn't. Besides, the chip change shouldn't have changed the material usage that much."

Frank took another sip of his brandy, and continued,

"No, but here is where Charlie got a little weird."

Awkwardly holding his brandy snifter in his right hand, Frank stretched out four fingers and started to count down on each.

"First, the chip change was not approved through regular channels, it just kind of happened.

"Second, the new chip, marked ICU2, was not purchased with an internal purchase order from the NTA. It just appeared a few days ago in place of the old chip, and if you didn't look carefully you would never have known it changed.

"Third, the chip was not manufactured by ELF or another party. It is being manufactured by the NTA."

And finally reaching his pinky,

"And fourth ... and here is what Charlie said was using all his extra materials; thousands of the circuit boards with the new chip were assembled and purchased by the NTA. Not for the NTA warehouse inventory, or for delivery at Christmas, not for ELF products, but just for the NTA! And once they had them, they just disappeared."

A swirl of his brandy and another sip, then Frank finished his reciting of Charlie's comments,

"What's more, like the chip itself, there were no internal purchase orders cut by the NTA. They bought them outright with a *reimbursement check* to ELF from an account to which Charlie had no access. This way the books would balance and there would be no record of the transaction."

Jason looked at his father, puzzled. Frank downed the rest of his brandy and followed up with,

"I'll bet *you* have access to it! Find that account and I'll bet you find a whole lot of answers."

The front door opened and both Janet and Krystal stepped out. Janet looked at the two men and proceeded to remark about the rather significant likelihood of trouble brewing, as the two were chatting alone and unchecked. Never mind that it was obvious that Frank was encouraged to talk too much, with the abundance of brandy on hand.

Krystal, in a buff fur cap, red coat, and knapsack, looked ready to leave. When Jason turned toward her and asked if she would like a ride home, she looked over toward the street and noted the bright yellow 1956 Tucker Sno-Cat 443 that Jason had been restoring in his spare time for that last three years, and giggled.

"You're sweet, but you know me, I prefer muscle to machine and hooves to chains and treads. I'm not sure that thing is going to make it."

Krystal coyly covered her mouth as she laughed and in an apologetic offering, kissed Jason and whispered in his ear,

"I'm sorry; I know that thing is important to you. It's not that far and I'd rather like to walk."

Krystal turned to Frank, blew him a kiss, smiled and told him to take care. She then turned to Janet, hugged her and suggested,

"You just take it easy, OK? Things will work out and you deserve some time off anyway. Relax for a while. Call me, if you need me. I'm here to help!"

She stepped back, fondly acknowledged everyone again, and started walking. She turned one more time, waved and continued down the street.

As this seemed to signal the close of the evening Jason decided that he too would go home, and bade his farewell.

Jason woke up the next morning thinking about the conversations he had had with his father the night before and started to consider how he would go about finding out if any of what he had heard was true. He started that morning much in the same way he started most mornings. He opened the window and made himself a cup of tea. He sat down underneath the window and unrolled the 'Works Weekly' to scan the week's headlines.

"Hey there, mister senior VP!" A high-pitched and almost melodic voice called in from the street, "I know you're there. The window's open!"

Knowing the voice, Jason looked out to be greeted with the sight of an animated Krystal Gardner. In the middle of the ice-packed street she jumped up and down waving her arms in an over exuberant effort to be noticed.

She called out to Jason as soon as she noticed he had spotted her from his window,

"Hey, how about walking me to work this morning?"

Jason nodded in agreement, and suggested she wait by the door as he prepared to leave the house.

As Jason came through his front door, Krystal greeted him with a brief embrace and the two turned to walk down the street arm in arm.

"You and your father got pretty deep into your discussions last night. I think that your mother and I didn't see you for more than a few minutes at dinner," Krystal noted.

Jason thought for a moment and responded,

"Yes, we did. I wonder though, how much is just crazy rumors and what might actually be true." Jason pondered further and then asked, "Krystal, can I tell you something?"

The pair stopped walking. Krystal looked into Jason's eyes and fixated on them. She responded with a short but heartfelt,

"Anything!"

"Xavier thinks there is something going on that might be bad for the Workshop, something that is happening inside the NTA. He wanted me to check it out," Jason told her.

Krystal, a little surprised and disappointed as to the subject of the comment, reacted,

"Really?" her face had a look of curious irritation. "That's what we are going to talk about? Lately Jason, every time I think we can talk about us, you bring up work. I hope this promotion isn't going to take you away from me."

Still, Kystal knew that if this was what he was interested in discussing, it would be the subject, or his attention would stray and her conversation would be with herself only. Indeed, she thought if this was plaguing his mind then she owed it to him and their relationship to help. She considered for a moment and suggested if Jason wanted to find out more about the efforts that he and his father discussed last night, he just simply and perhaps discreetly ask his employees.

"You are the boss, after all," Krystal noted.

She looked ahead as they started walking again. Jason thought to himself, "Amazing -- sometimes the answer is just so simple" and wondered why he had not thought of that himself.

"Well? Is there anything else that you would like to say to me … mister senior VP?" Krystal inquired, hoping he would take her hint to talk about their relationship.

Jason looked at her, smiled and said,

"Oh, yeah!" They stopped walking and he took both her hands, looked into her green eyes and continued, "Don't tell anyone about this, okay?"

Krystal gave him an annoyed look, freed her hands, and punched his upper arm with a quick exclamation of,

"You're such a jerk!"

8

LET THE CHIPS FALL
WHERE THEY MAY

That morning, Jason was resolved to find out more about the general goings-on and if he could make any sense of the rather mysterious assertions that his father and, in absentia Charlie Fox, had made. He wanted to understand the alleged connections between the significant quality and manufacturing issues and the NTA's rumored ICU2 chip.

Jason spent some time catching up on e-mails and paperwork. It was now late morning and he decided it was time to ask some questions. He thought rather than go directly to one of his direct reports he would go down the food chain and ask Randall Blake so as to avoid any immediate suspicion. "Besides, he has always been rather forthcoming in the past," Jason thought, and picked up the phone to give him a call.

Randall Blake's phone never actually rang, but a window popped up on his main computer monitor. Intrusively, the window obscured the blue and green scrolling text and video boxes with a green-bordered black box. In it, red letters boldly read *Incoming Call*. Randall noticed this one in particular as this message was followed by an extension and the name *Jason Pelham*. He tapped his keyboard and pushed a lit red button on his desk whose color changed to green, rolled his chair to the right, and picked up his telephone receiver.

"Good morning Mr. Pelham, what can I do for you?" Randall spoke into the receiver.

"Randall, I know how busy you are, you know, seeing who's been sleeping and knowing who's awake," Jason joked. Randall, on the other end, rolled his eyes, listening to yet another version of an old joke. Jason continued and asked, "But I would like to take some of your time to go over a couple projects that I have been made aware of. I believe you are the best man to give me some of the details."

"Right, well now is as good a time as any," Randall suggested, "But can you meet me here? I need to stay closer to my station; we can use the small meeting room off of the data hall, if you would like it to be private conversation."

"That would be perfect!" Jason replied.

Randall hung up the phone. He rolled back over to his screen and with a couple keystrokes closed the incoming call message window and the activity started up again. He made a few notations and with a couple more keystrokes shut the monitor down. Randall swiveled his chair around to face the room and addressed his team,

"Right then, who has a lighter load?" Randall asked with an obvious level of authority.

As he looked around for a response, a young woman's hand went up and Randall continued,

"Excellent, Christine, pick up my feed for about two hours, I'll be back to it shortly."

Randall picked up a portfolio with a writing pad and a pen and made his way to the connected meeting room.

Smaller and lacking the standard wood paneling and heavy ornamentation that seemed common to the various meeting and conference rooms around Kringle Works, this meeting room was still well-appointed with an ornately carved round table and well-padded, burgundy leather chairs. The room was brighter than the data hall just beyond the door and obviously geared for a more high tech purpose than just a simple meeting, with a trio of flat screens set facing out from the center of the table in a triangle. In front of each screen was a keyboard. This was an area for monitoring, individual training, and presentations. On the wall across from the entrance was a larger screen, and speakers in each corner of the room.

Randall seated himself at the table and punched a few keys on the keyboard in front of the monitor that faced him. A window with a blank text box came up and beckoned for his password. Once it was entered, the screen came to life with a stream of data and a secondary window that appeared to allow Randall to monitor the activities in the adjacent room. He figured this way he could keep a loose eye on things and still meet with the NTA's senior vice president.

It was only a few moments before Jason entered the room. He took a seat and greeted and thanked Randall for his time.

Randall Blake was always proud of the incredible innovation and reach of his company, and enjoyed talking about it. He relished this opportunity to prove to his boss's boss how much he knew and sat back with a contented grin.

Jason knew that there were times when Randall spoke too much, too often, and too easily, but as Jason was an executive of the company and the leader of the division that housed Randall's department, surely he would think he could speak at will and with impunity. This was the reaction Jason had hoped for and though he knew that most at the NTA still did not trust him completely, for now, he had not stumbled into an area that would expose something too terribly perverse, and had as yet met with generally little resistance. Consequently Jason also knew that if Xavier Kringle's suspicions were founded, then it would not be long before he might find himself blacklisted and that anyone with something to hide would quickly mobilize to shut down any potential leaks. It was this reality that would guide Jason's questioning. He would edge forward and allow the situation to dictate how deep he could go before he would inadvertently trigger suspicion and have his motives questioned.

Jason paused a moment to gather his thoughts and started by asking a few questions about the day-to-day operations. Finally Jason decided to go down the path he wanted.

"Randall, sometime back you told me about the ICU chip; I'm curious, when did we implement it and can you tell me specifically how it works?"

"Yeah, the chip, that's what it's all about isn't it?" Randall answered rhetorically.

"You see, mate, when the NTA designed that chip it changed everything, didn't it?" Randall continued, "The designers had been working on it for years, but seven years ago they finished the prototypes and got immediate approval from the executive staff and Xavier Kringle himself. I think it was Andre Leopold and Henry Foster delivered the first 100,000 chips to ELF personally."

Jason, a little taken aback and confused, interrupted, "Randall, I was a senior manager at ELF; how is it that I knew nothing of this?"

Randall smiled and continued, "Well that's the thing; only a few knew of the chip, or at least, how important it was going to be. As far as most knew it was just another chip on the various circuit boards used in ELF-made electronics. It was in the rewritten design specs and it was endorsed by the ELF electronics division and the executive staff; why question it or even think about it? The truth is that unless you needed to know about it no one told you. It's not the NTA's first secret, you know. Besides, the executive staff felt there was good reason to keep this as quiet as possible to make sure no word leaked out beyond the island's borders, at least until it was either too late or the legal team had it wrapped up internationally."

Randall chuckled a little and said,

"But it never got out, did it?"

"No, I guess not," Jason answered as he leaned back in his chair.

"Right, the world never thinks much about us, do they? Not until they find their gifts under the tree, and that's good!" Randall continued, "But five years ago everything changed. It was a year and a half after I started in this post that they outfitted my department with all new workstations and … well … it was incredible! Originally only Andre, the rest of the executive staff, Lorraine, and Henry got the workstations, but once they knew it worked, we got ours. Now all we had to do was activate the chips and we saw everything, but the world didn't see us. It was amazing! No more reading of letters, the world's papers, news reports, police reports, no more need to tap phone calls, have field agents dig, or negotiate for Internet and cell phone activity records. The chip captures it all and our software lets us sort it out."

Though Jason was not entirely sure he agreed with the NTA's methods, he was impressed, and it was after all their charter by virtue of a century-and-a-half old document.

In hopes of keeping Randall's momentum going, Jason encouraged him to continue.

"It *is* incredible and how exactly does it work?" Jason asked.

"Well, it's bloody genius, isn't it?" Randall suggested.

"Almost every electronic device now has a microprocessor or CPU in it and the ICU chip is designed to attach to it. Whether it is made by ELF, Motorola, IBM, or Intel the ICU will fit under, next to, or opposite the microprocessor and it captures everything that happens in the device. It essentially makes a copy of all the data as it passes through the chip and it then sends that raw data to us. A person's phone calls, the music they listen to, the pictures they take, the e-mails they send, the chats they participate in, the texting they do, the video games they play, the television shows they watch, the places they visit, and the temperature they keep their house at ... we can see it all! The electronics go obsolete so fast, and they are so popular as gifts, the chips are in everything now! It's brilliant!"
Randall continued enthusiastically, "And to activate the ICU chip all you have to do is get to one of these workstations and input the codes."

"Really? Interesting, and which codes are these?" Jason asked.

Randall, still on a roll, "The codes? Yeah, the codes are four sequences of numbers each being thirty-eight numerals long. Once you input these, the chips open up and start to send the data. The software then looks at the data and runs all sorts of checks and filters and attaches the activities to a person."

The pride of his involvement was obvious as Randall continued to explain how his department sorted and cataloged the trillions of bytes of data into manageable packets sorted by individual for Edward Grubb's team to evaluate.

"We're not that quaint little 19th century company that Christopher Kringle founded in America anymore!" he closed with a level of permissible hubris.

"And the ICU2 chip, you have heard of it? What does that do?" Jason asked, hoping he had not overstepped.

"It's an upgrade. Stands for the second generation, I think. I'm not sure what it does; it seems to act exactly like the old chip, but the test chips have gotten into some interesting places," Randall amused himself and suggested, "Hey, you should have one of these workstations! Do you want me to set one up in your office?"

Jason thought to himself that this meeting had been most valuable and he enthusiastically nodded in affirmation.

"I have Andre Leopold's old machine; I'll have that set up for you," Randall suggested, and with a modest snicker and eye roll, "Andre's workstation is the only one that did not require the codes be input; he insisted that he couldn't be bothered to input them every morning. So our programmers hard-coded them into the workstation and had to get him a new one because the codes on his machine changed, or something like that."

"So does Andre's workstation work? Did the codes change?" Jason inquired.

"Yeah, the workstation works fine and the codes I use never changed. So it should be alright," Randall answered a little disquieted.

"So why did Andre need a new one?" Jason followed up.

Randall, looking perplexed and maybe a little uncomfortable, responded with a dismissive tone, "Well, I don't know, eh ... it must've been something else, but it works fine. I tested it! You still want it? I can't let anyone else have it. With the codes already programmed in, it would be against the rules for anyone else to take it, but seeing as you are the boss I think I can give it to you."

"Yes, Randall, I still want it. That would be great. Thank you for your time. I think I have taken too much of it already and I really appreciate it!" Jason stretched out his hand and shook hands with Randall. Jason got up and made his way out the door. He stopped for a moment and turned back to Randall, still seated, and asked one last question, "Randall, when you said the ICU2 had gotten into some interesting places, what did you mean?"

Randall looked back and now seemed a little unsure of how to react. He thought for a moment with a notable pause and responded with, "I don't know--it's nothing. Just that the new chip seems to be showing up in specific places. Clustered in test regions, I guess. It's nothing, really, I was just talking, forget I said that."

Jason nodded, thanked Randall again and left the meeting room.

Even though Jason Pelham had worked for the NTA these last few months the stealthy way in which they operated still caught him off guard. He did not recall anytime during this day that he spent any significant amount of it away from his office, not since his earlier meeting with Randall Blake, but there it was, the promised workstation from the department of data acquisition. The area was set up, and the workstation assembled and wired; it would have looked as though it had always been there if it were not for the telltale envelope taped to the screen. Jason shook his head and thought he would, yet again, have to ask Raymond Dunbar how they do it; still, he knew the answer would be the same, "Process and practice." Jason affectionately mocked his youngest vice president to himself.

Jason pondered for a moment as he noted how comfortably this new machine fit the surroundings of his office. The odd mix of modern technologies and nineteenth century aesthetics was particularly obvious here as the carved and highly ornamented wood trim offset a bank of windows overlooking a number of the NTA's transportation sites. All this made for a strangely symbiotic environment of old and new with a number of computing, monitoring, and communications devices to which this new workstation would now belong.

Jason placed a note pad and pen on his desk and walked over to the workstation. He pulled up a chair, sat down and pulled the envelope off of the screen.

Inside the envelope Jason found an owner's manual of a hundred pages and an index card attached to the cover via paper clip.

Congratulations on the acquisition of your new Kringle Works ICU Monitoring Workstation. Please note the following codes:

A36471284627456287463563847620481273921
B47857846585692154564709754649255677888
C12131342435647785869799994565782000036
D56784386002847020565735465824467647899

Please keep this card in a safe and secure place, as without them the Workstation will not operate.

With this simple and even cryptic text was a brief handwritten note.

Keep this card but remember the codes are hard-coded into this machine. Let me know if you have any questions.

Cheers, Randall.

Jason was excited and intrigued. He decided to turn the workstation on. Like so many, he disregarded the owner's manual, found the power switch and flicked it on. In an instant the screen popped to life.

The first image was a familiar screenshot of the Kringle Works logo which appeared as a backdrop for a series of icons, presumably various drivers and applications, which one-by-one appeared at the bottom of the screen, suggesting their loading or launching. The screen went blank, leaving only the pattern upon which the logo and the icons had appeared and were now replaced by a rather unremarkable textbox. In it were the four number sets indicated on the card that came with the workstation. A small flashing box followed the last number and beckoned Jason to hit '*Enter*' on the keyboard. The textbox disappeared, leaving only the screen pattern again with the exception of a small wreath adorned with a red ribbon that rotated while the machine pondered its next move.

Jason leaned back as the workstation continued to crunch whatever it was crunching and just as Jason thought he had better look at the manual, a toolbox window with a series of navigation buttons, empty textboxes, and pull-down menus appeared on the far right side of the screen. In the center of the screen the little wreath continued to rotate contentedly. Jason started to study the toolbox window at the right. The top seemed to indicate the workstation status as, *ICU Status stand-alone: Forward Processing-OFF.*

Jason scanned down and noted an icon of the globe, which spun slowly, showing off all of the continents and countries of the world. Each rotation mimicked a twenty-four hour period and took about five seconds. Below the globe was a series of textboxes and pull-down menus sectioned off as *Filters*, and buttons that seemed to be there to modify the above menus and textboxes.

Jason now noted that the little wreath stopped rotating and disappeared in favor of a new window that flashed the words, *Entering Data Feed - Unfiltered*. Suddenly the screen became a flurry of activity. Various windows started to open, text running in columns in front and behind, and within a fraction of a second the screen was a blur of colors and movement with nothing discernable save the toolbox at the right. Instinctively, Jason ran the workstation's cursor over the toolbox noting all of the 'clickable' areas.

He ran the cursor over the rotating globe and saw that when he did so it stopped moving; he pulled away and it would resume its rotation. Trying it a few times he then decided to click on it wherever it stopped the next time. He ran the cursor over the globe and it stopped rotating; beneath his cursor lay Russia and Jason clicked on it. The ever-moving and -shifting collage of color occupying the remainder of the screen suddenly lurched and the colors shifted. The screen then resumed its continuous dance of color and movement. A couple more tries, first Japan, then Canada, and every time, the screen jumped. Then he noticed that every time he clicked on a country, the first textbox showed the name of that country while all the other boxes remained empty.

He decided to try highlighting the country name in the textbox and clicked on the word Canada and started to type. *U N I T ...* Suddenly a drop-down showed several choices, which narrowed as he typed more of the name, *United Arab Emirates, United Kingdom, United States*, he selected the United States. As before, the screen lurched. Then he decided to fill in the empty textboxes, and as he started to fill them in randomly, he noticed that the random patterns of color and movement were not so random after all; they were in fact a huge number of windows with a wide variety of constantly changing content. Typing into each remaining box, Jason allowed it to offer him choices and took one; state, city, street, street number, and finally a name. As the filters tightened up the view the collage of movement and color had narrowed down to a dozen windows or so. In one was a video feed from a park security camera. In it he saw a young man sitting on a park bench, looking at a cell phone. In another window Jason saw what was presumably the text the young man was punching out on his cell phone and the messages coming back. Several windows were blank or dark. Yet another appeared to be from a police blotter, which seemed to have a record of several traffic violations and an argument which ended in a fight last weekend. Another window appeared to be the inside of a home with no one on-screen except a dog sleeping at the far corner. A couple windows showed what seemed to be satellite aerial views of the same street. Still another showed a newspaper clipping of a wedding announcement and another, an obituary. Jason clicked on the window, which appeared to show the current text messaging, bringing it to the front.

> Mike: Yes, I miss u 2 :)
> Sheryl: :*
> Sheryl: So when can I see u again?
> Mike: Maybe later 2 busy now :(
> Sheryl: Last night was incredible ;)
> Mike: Hang on
> Mike: Call coming in

The messaging paused and another window sprung to life, a white field with a black jagged line which rapidly expanded and narrowed. Jason clicked on this and recognized it as representing audio. The bottom of this window had a volume slide control. He turned the volume up.

"Hi sweetheart it's me, Sue, listen, I'm going to be working late. Can you be sure to let the dog out as soon as you get home and start dinner?" a woman's voice said.

"Sure thing, I just have to run a couple errands after work. How late are you going to be?" a man's voice answered back.

"Oh around 8:30 or so. Love you! I'll try to get home sooner, if I can. Thanks for understanding, Mike. You're the best!" she responded.

Jason glanced over at the window with the video feed of the man sitting on the park bench. He noticed the man had the phone to his ear and was just lowering it back down to look at the cell phone's screen. The audio window went dormant again and the man appeared to start texting again.

> Mike: Hey schedule opened up

Mike: Can come by after work for an hour or 2 :)
Mike: See you then, luv u :*
Sheryl: Great :) me 2

Jason, mesmerized, shook his head and talking to the screen of his workstation, exclaimed jokingly,

"Don't do it Mike! Edward is going to put a coal in your stocking for sure!"

Jason leaned back, still watching the screen, overwhelmingly impressed.

"Whoa, that is just absolutely incredible!" he said to himself.

Somehow Jason's personal sensibilities seemed compromised by this voyeuristic behavior, but he was fascinated and reminded himself that this was what people have come to expect of the Kringle Works.

Comfortable with his rationalization, Jason decided to look at a few more profiles. He knew that the people were aware that the SANTA Clause had always allowed for this depth of surveillance, but it was the fact that the Kringle Works had never used these capabilities in any other capacity and never impacted the people in any way other than to act as their conscience at the end of the year. Indeed, it would keep the public from getting too deep into the discussion of whether or not the NTA's activities as part of Kringle Works was appropriate. It seemed that the Christmas-celebrating peoples of the world were very willing to forget about these activities and instead either rejoiced in their bounty if they were good or hung their heads in shame, perhaps vowing to do better, if they had been caught behaving in a manner unbecoming of a citizen of the world. That was, of course, in the eyes of the Kringle Works's contract and their governing bodies and Edward Grubb's interpretation of it.

Still Jason had, himself, not been aware of just how intrusive, cold, and efficient the process had become, and he found it a little disquieting.

With a little typing, Jason was able to select a few more people at random.

One gentleman in Canada was obsessively playing video games while at work. A young woman in the United Kingdom was using her husband's social media profile to send subversive and inflammatory messages to various friends without identifying herself.

77

In the United States, a New Jersey news anchorman was practicing his delivery after receipt of an e-mailed memo insisting he slant a current story to make a corrupt politician look more like a victim of an unfortunate set of circumstances. It seemed that this same politician appeared to have made an unmentioned donation to the network's favored charity.

A ten-year-old boy from Atlanta, Georgia, was on line actively attempting to remove the parental controls from the family's cable television account while e-mailing friends about an impending 'Adult Movie Night' at his house.

"Not a particularly flattering slice of the human race," Jason thought to himself, and wondered how someone like Randall could spend every day immersed in this activity.

Then he noticed something that he had not realized before; on each of the windows, in the upper right-hand corner, was some text. Specifically, each window seemed, quite consistently albeit rather inconspicuously, to carry the designation ICU, however it was then he realized that a handful of windows sported the designation ICU2.

Jason started to look for patterns. He wondered if the new chips functioned differently and if he could somehow see it. Was there some kind of consistency to the types of devices in which they were implanted? Was the ICU2 any faster than the old chip? Could one manipulate the new chips? Were they geographically clustered? And what did Randall really mean when he said that they seemed to be *clustered in specific places*?

No use, it became quickly apparent to Jason that he could not pull up enough of a sample to find this particular needle in this global haystack. He had a strange sensation of being completely powerless at a time in which he felt he had just acquired the ultimate power over everyone. Indeed, he was not finding what he was looking for, nor was he sure he wanted too, or even what it was. He had now been given the power to select anyone and find out almost anything about them. Somehow he thought this had to be able to get him some answers. Randall's giving him the workstation would surely have been contrary to someone's plan, a miscalculation perhaps. Trying to spy on the NTA would certainly not be an easy task, even if he had completely infiltrated it with his management role and had the silent backing of Xavier Kringle himself.

Suddenly a feeling of panic washed over Jason as it occurred to him that he was certainly not the only one with this capability at the Kringle Works. Indeed, there were many people at the Workshop who had not only the same capabilities but were trained to be efficient at it. In fact, unlike Jason, they also had banks of computer processing power and resources at their disposal. Jason's pulse quickened and he felt himself becoming short of breath as he decided to check a very particular profile. His hands trembling slightly, he started to delete the various filters, leaving only the blank textboxes. As he did so the screen started to react with an almost violent jolt of visual activity. As he removed the last of the data that occupied the filter fields the screen had resumed the now familiar chaos of color and movement that represented the many, many trillions of bits of data vying to get his attention. In the country textbox Jason started to type, *K*. The textbox produced a drop-down menu of choices, *Kazakhstan, Kenya, Kiribati, Korea (North), Korea (South), Kuwait* and *Kyrgyzstan*. Jason continued typing *R I N G L E*, but the menu went blank and the name yielded no results. He then chose Canada and typed *Kringle* into the next textbox for territories and provinces. However, this too, yielded no results. He tried a similar exercise with Greenland and Denmark, with the same lack of results. He attempted to filter the results for each of these countries using the name *Jason Pelham*, but this yielded too many results to determine if he might be among them. He had to narrow the search to the island. His last effort was to clear all the results and attempt to pick out the Kringle Work's Island on the rotating globe at the top of the toolbox. The first two times the screen lurched and the country text box came up with *Canada*. On his third try he hit the small island right on, and once he did so, the screen went blank with only one window showing, *No Data Available*. It was obvious from this that the island was purposely exempted from the NTA's surveillance practices.

A momentary feeling of relief gave way to a more overall discomfort as the reality of what was happening started to sink into Jason's psyche. He was shaken and agitated; indeed, he felt genuinely sickened and he had lost any ability to concentrate. He stared at the screen with the one message *No Data Available* for a few minutes and then flicked the power switch into the off position.

Somehow he felt the need to get far away from this device. He went back to his desk and sat down. He made a few calls and cancelled his remaining appointments for the day, including his dinner engagement with Krystal Gardner.

Jason wanted to be alone and decided to take the remainder of this particular day and evening off. He needed the time to reflect on this and felt he could do so better at home and by himself.

9

THE MISSION

Jason fought for a night with his conscience. He spent an evening rethinking his career and life's work. His world had been shaken as it came into conflict with the values that had been generated by that same world.

The events of the morning and afternoon started to come into moral focus for Jason, who now realized the roller-coaster ride he was on. He had ascended in awe of his company's technologies and innovation only to follow down the plunge of moral and integritous despair as he wrestled with the company's use of that technology.

Jason always felt that the Kringle Works had contributed to the world in a positive way. His upbringing and education had always extolled the virtues of the peace and joy his company and the associated history had brought to the world's communities. However, the use of the ICU chip seemed wrong. The company and the NTA used these abilities to spy on people, to intrude on their lives, to make value judgments about them, and look voyeuristically at their most intimate details. Somehow this made Jason question everything.

If you started to doubt your career at Kringle Works, you doubted your life. The employees on the island grew up to be part the Workshop; they were educated to do so, they lived to do so, and they died doing so. Still, he attempted to put things into perspective. The world, after all, was a willful participant; they asked for the service, paid for it, embraced it and rejoiced in its execution. The resulting commercial success of the Kringle Works also allowed the island to be amongst the most philanthropic anonymous donors the world community had ever seen. The services brought joy to huge numbers of people. How could all this be bad? Was this not an appropriate end to the means?

No; for now, Jason was unable to squelch his disgust. It seemed foul on some level. He had always known that the process existed, but now he saw its application and its darker side, he felt a part of something filthy, vile, and intrusive. He felt permeated with it and wanted to cleanse himself of it. He resolved to approach Xavier in the morning.

Something, he thought, had to be done.

The next morning, after yet again a rather sleepless night, Jason resolved to make his way to the office, albeit a few hours early. He wrote a note and pinned it to his front door:

> *Krystal,*
>
> *Sorry I missed dinner again last night. I have much on my mind. Had to go see Xavier this morning and will have to miss breakfast and ride to work.*
>
> *Please forgive me <u>again</u>!*
>
> *Love, Jason*

He talked to no one. He was resolute. The thoughts of what he wanted to say were a swirl of comments, reactions and scenarios, which he conjured as he attempted to think through how he would communicate his concerns to Xavier and how Xavier would react to them. Jason's nerves were frayed, the result of a lack of sleep and emotional churning. He wondered whether Xavier was going to understand his stance. How would this impact their relationship? Jason has asked policy questions before, implemented new processes, done away with antiquated methods, but this seemed different. This was a strike at the heart of a new technological era for the company, a strike at the division that, in Xavier's own words:

"... *makes us unique, it is the NTA that fills the world with both awe and envy, it is the NTA that gives us the power we have.*"

"Indeed," Jason thought, "It gives us the power that we have."

Jason spent no time in his office that morning. He opened up, dropped some paperwork off, glanced briefly at his e-mail, checked his morning's schedule and left to go to the executive offices.

As Jason entered the building he repositioned his ID badge, which normally dangled at his belt line, and hung it on his jacket lapel. He glanced to the right and noted the tall and sturdy figure of Peter Sharp, the head of security, unlocking the security offices. Jason gave him a friendly nod, to which Peter smiled and responded in kind. Looking forward Jason noted the three security personnel at the reception desk currently in the process of getting set up for the day, unlocking cabinets, waking sleeping equipment, checking monitors, and generally primping both the workspace and themselves. Consequently they were a bit awkward and surprised when Jason approached the desk.

"Mister Pelham!" one of the guards said in surprise as he straightened his dark green uniform and badge as he sat down. "Excuse me sir, it's still early. How may I help you this morning?"

"Of course, no problem," Jason smiled and continued, "It is extremely important that I see Xavier Kringle this morning."

"Yes sir, I am not sure if he is in yet, but I will call up and find out. Please wait for just a moment," the guard responded.

Jason's mind wandered as the guard made his call. He looked around at the ornate surroundings of the executive offices' lobby as if to seek inspiration. The large wooden staircase behind the reception desk and gate, the wood paneling and trim work, the opalescent glass doors that led to the ground floor offices of maintenance, security, reception, and mailroom, and finally the large Kringle Works logo meticulously inlaid in various colored marble tiles which adorned the lobby floor and randomly caught Jason's gaze. Then the reception guard interrupted,

"Mister Pelham? Mister Kringle is available to see you, sir."

The guard made some notations in a book, buzzed the turnstile gate and motioned Jason to go through.

Jason climbed the large wooden steps to the top landing and looked around at the various offices of the Workshop's top echelon. In front of each office was a reception desk in a wood-framed glass surround set up for a personal assistant, which at this time of the morning stood mostly empty. Still, Jason would make special note that the office of his boss, Andre Leopold, was open and that his assistant, Natasha Cordero, was there alone, presumably getting a jump on some filing before the day started. Jason made sure to stop and wish her a good morning. Good politics, he thought; besides, Natasha was one of the most pleasant and helpful people he knew.

"And she's not exactly hard on the eyes," he mused to himself.

Xavier Kringle's office was at the end of the hall. Jason approached the reception area. Justin, Xavier's personal assistant, seemed too tired and too focused on his cup of morning coffee to pay much mind to Jason. Silently, Justin waved Jason through and greedily attempted to get another sip without burning himself.

Xavier Kringle was sitting at his desk going through a stack of reports when he noticed Jason entering. Xavier's exuberant nature, especially this early in the morning, was disarming as he jumped to his feet and exclaimed,

"Good morning, my boy! Don't you ever sleep? It seems we haven't talked in many weeks. How are things?"

"Sleep? No. Actually, Xavier, I have been better," Jason responded.

"Yes, I imagine you have been." Xavier sighed, encouraged Jason to take a seat and continued, "I know that your mother lost her job a couple days ago. I talked to her directly. Tragic, you know, just an unfortunate mistake. Very expensive, but just a mistake, so even though Marcus protested, I allowed those he deemed responsible to just retire and stay on the island. Denise, Charlie, and your mother were all close to retiring anyway and all of them had so many years of exemplary service, I thought it was only fair. How is your mother?"

"Thank you, Xavier, she will be alright. A little hurt, I think." Jason paused and then continued, "As much as I did want to discuss that particular issue with you, I really had a different subject on my mind."

Xavier looked at him, a little puzzled. "Of course, Jason, what's on your mind?"

Jason shuffled nervously in his seat and started to discuss the concerns regarding the intrusive nature of the ICU chip and its employment.

"Lorraine and Randall are topnotch, Xavier. They have gone out of their way to be sure I know most of the details of how their organization works-- and understand these are not criticisms of their abilities or the quality of their work--but I have to be honest, as I get deeper into the technology we use I have some significant moral and ethical misgivings."

Xavier Kringle was a good listener, which made him easy to talk to and in Jason's case he was also talking to both a friend and mentor. Jason continued in careful and measured terms,

"The ICU project and the technology associated with it, it seems over the top."

Xavier smiled sympathetically.

"Well, well Jason, you have been getting deeper into the NTA, haven't you?" he noted.

Jason responded,

"Indeed I have and I cannot suggest I like it. If the people of the world knew … they'd be horrified!"

Still, as Jason might have suspected, Xavier was not ready to be swayed and had some well-thought-out and thorough responses.

"You understand that the world's populations have always wanted these services. They want them, they need them, and they have spent centuries asking for them. For the Christians it was Bishop Nicholas of Smyrna, who lived in the fourth century in what is now Turkey. He was very rich, very generous, and very fond of children, people, and family. Often he gave joy to the poor children by throwing gifts in through their windows. For the Orthodox Church in Russia and the Roman Catholic Church, it was Saint Nicholas, recognized as the one who helped children and the poor. The Protestant churches of central and northern Germany knew Nicholas as der Weinachtsmann, he was Joulupukki in Finland, Father Christmas in England, and in the United States he was brought in by Dutch immigrants with the legend of Sinter Klaas."

Jason nodded in agreement but questioned the comments,

"Yes, yes but these are legendary and glorified historical figures. We are goods merchants. We build incentives. People don't really think they are being scrutinized this way."

Xavier leaned closer to Jason, punctuating his passion for the subject.

"Our founder Christopher Kringle," Xavier continued, "my great-great-great-grandfather, tapped into the growing commercialism associated with all of this. He saw the world's populations and used Kringle Works to fulfill their *need*, their *desperation* to believe the legends of gift giving and reward for being good."

"Xavier, we are reading and analyzing peoples' personal e-mails! People would be in the streets demanding the repeal of the SANTA Clause if they knew!" Jason protested.

Xavier dismissively waved his hand as to suggest Jason stop and allow him to continue making his point.

"Jason, I think you might be surprised how much they know and what they will accept if there are rewards attached. In the United States with the founding of the company in 1828, the treaty, SANTA, which would first bind the United States to our service, the document itself would eventually be adopted as the name of their legendary figure. Yes, the very document that said, *we will see you, judge you, and reward you*, would become synonymous with him. They are one and the same."

Jason interrupted, "And the Kringle Works? Xavier, the people have forgotten. That's the problem."

Xavier laughed a little and noted,

"Well, for our part, we did not discourage these practices, but we do not deceive anyone either, we simply allowed for the populations of the world to choose what they want to believe. SANTA is known to look into the lives of the people and reward those who were good and punish those who were bad. That is what they wanted. The media has access to us. They could do more to make the public aware, but please understand they, and the governments that they are attached to, choose not to."

"Yes, yes, I know, but why? Why is there no outrage? I know what we do is good and the people love you, your father, your father's father, all of them; and they love our service, but it just feels wrong," Jason lamented.

Xavier knew that he had taken Jason a part of the way, but would still need to prove that the Kringle works practices were not only understood, but out in the open. He cited yet another example,

"In 1927 on a show called Markus-sedän lastentunti, the host, Markus Rautio, called us out and noted on Finnish *public* radio that our facility, which *today* houses our NTA data acquisition servers in Finland's Lapland, Korvatunturi, is where we listen to the world. The translation from the Finnish is *Ear Fell*! They know we are listening! The world knows about us, they just *choose* to ignore it."

Like a seasoned lawyer, Xavier now prepared for his final argument.

"Jason, they not only know about the SANTA Clause, they revere it! And do you know why? It is because we don't abuse it, because we do this responsibly, because we do not overstep. That is Chris Kringle's genius, that is what has made us a 220 billion US dollar company, and that is what we *should* … no … we *must*, indeed, we are *obligated* to protect!" Xavier said as he pounded his fist on his desk.

Then Xavier leaned back into his chair. He became more somber. Xavier's face sagged; he looked exhausted, older, worn, and for the first time in Jason's memory he truly showed his age.

The two men looked at each other in silence and after a moment's pause Xavier chose to redefine the concerns he first voiced to Jason several months ago,

"Jason, the technologies we use are no different than those used by the world's governments to spy on their constituency today. In the United States, the freest of the world's nations, law enforcement watches through cameras, listens to phone calls, reads e-mail, records conversations; they don't even need a court order to do it and then they do it under the guise of *Patriotism*."

Xavier laughed, but the sound was strangely melancholy.

He continued,

"In the past we would have used these government surveillances and other resources to learn what we needed to know, but with the ICU, we have simply gotten much, much better at it. Better than anyone else. However, with that, we have also a tremendous responsibility. Jason, we must keep this technology to ourselves. Protect it so that it stays out of the hands of others. I told you in May that I thought there are others who would try to hurt the company. You helped subvert it fifteen years ago at ELF, but some element of it is still here. It has again taken root. It is starting to grow, but it remains in the dark, in the shadows, just out of our reach. We must identify it, crush it or otherwise risk compromising all that we have. Can you imagine the corporations and governments of the world with our capabilities? We must first protect the Workshop and once we have done so, once we have restored order and our control, we can reconsider things."

Jason agreed,

"Okay, I understand, but once we--"

Xavier interrupted to complete Jason's sentence,

"Yes ... once we have done so, then as the senior management of the NTA, you and Andre can decide if we need to rethink our use of the ICU technologies."

Jason nodded as Xavier followed up,

"Listen, I promoted you into this position for much more than our need to restore order. You will also be, and remain, the new face of the NTA. There is no better man for the job; there is no nobler mission. You know that!"

"Compelling to the last," Jason thought.

Jason emerged from Xavier's office energized and feeling a little better. Knowing that Xavier was open to rethinking the use of the ICU chip was important in restoring Jason's comfort. Also, he strongly agreed that the ICU technology could be extremely devastating in anyone else's hands and if that was indeed a danger, then that was a mission worth pursuing under any circumstances.

Walking past Justin, Jason acknowledged him with a nod but received only a tired grunt, which seemed to echo through his nearly empty cup of coffee, in response.

As Jason stepped into the hall, he thought for a moment as he caught a glimpse of Natasha, still feverishly working in Andre's office.

He wandered over toward her and smiled as she noticed his approach.

"Mister Leopold has not yet arrived, Mister Pelham," she anticipated his reason for coming over.

"Actually, Natasha, I was coming over to see you," Jason suggested.

Looking a little surprised, Natasha responded, "Me? Mister Pelham, whatever for?"

Jason hesitated and then spoke,

"Well this is rather embarrassing, but I need your help. I sent Andre a report with a number of conclusions and recommendations and ... well ... I realized that I forgot to consider a major piece of data and ... well ... it makes everything wrong, so I was hoping you could check to see if it was with his mail, so I can retrieve it and resend a corrected one. You understand? I don't want to look stupid or careless to my boss."

Jason looked at her apologetically and smiled.

Natasha smiled back at him knowingly, and suggested she would check in Andre's office. She put down the files she was holding and went into the office to check Andre Leopold's desk, leaving Jason to wait for her.

"I don't see anything, Mister Pelham, what did it look like?" Natasha asked from inside the office.

"It's a large tan envelope with about 30 pages in it. It would have come in the interoffice mail," Jason answered.

Natasha came out of the office and said,

"No, Mister Pelham, I'm afraid it's not here."

Ponderously Jason responded, "Have you checked the mailroom this morning? It would have gone out with the last mail run. Could it still be in the mailroom? Can you give me the key to go check?"

Natasha cocked her head, pursed her lips and sighed,

"You know I can't do that. I'll keep a look out for your report and intercept it for you, okay?"

"I really would feel better if I could be sure," Jason noted sheepishly.

"Okay, okay, just wait here; I'll go check for your report," Natasha suggested.

Natasha took off down the hall and the steps.

Jason quickly grabbed a small envelope and a pen from Natasha's desk and rushed into Andre's office. He knew exactly where he wanted to go. He went to the back of the large office and on a credenza next to Andre's computer was the ICU workstation. Looking over his shoulder, he stood in front of the machine and turned it on.

"Come on, come on ... hurry," Jason anxiously said to himself.

Slowly the familiar image of the Kringle Works logo appeared.

Jason had the feeling this was taking a lot longer than it did in his office yesterday. Finally the series of icons of various drivers and applications started to load at the bottom of the screen. After the third one, Jason looked back and tried to listen for any noise; so far so good.

"Only nine or so to go, come on!" Jason was getting more anxious and kept his finger on the power switch.

An additional two icons had loaded when he thought he heard some chatter. Jason started debating with himself as he considered a series of excuses he could use to explain why he was in Andre's office; or, perhaps abandon this likely fruitless effort.

"Come on! Let's go!" Jason thought as he continued to split his attention between the screen and the door at the other end of the office.

Another three icons loaded their respective resources. The next seemed to take longer.

"Oh come on!"

Just then, Jason heard footsteps and some more chatter in the hall. He fixated on the door. Was Natasha returning, or worse, was Andre arriving? He thought he heard two voices. Jason held his breath. He was running his finger over the power switch. Abort? He did not see any shadows or activity through the limited view of the door. Should he abort? The voices quieted. It seemed that someone had found their way to another office.

Jason let his breath go, rolled his eyes and turned his attention back to the screen.

"Come on, come on, come on," Jason pleaded with the workstation as he rolled his hand in a metaphorical effort to speed the machine up.

The final icons loaded and the screen went blank, leaving only the pattern upon which the logo and the icons had appeared.

"Finally!" Jason thought.

Footsteps? Jason was not sure. His time was running short.

Another precious moment passed as the whimsical image of a small rotating wreath, which signaled the machine's processing, taunted Jason as he felt his time slipping away.

A creak, and the undeniable sound of heels impacting a century-old wood floor echoed in the hall; now Jason was sure, he was definitely hearing footsteps, but whose?

At last! The textbox that Jason was waiting for appeared. In it were the five number sets with a small flashing box following the last number.

"The codes are hard-coded in for you, old man. I wonder, are you too important or too lazy to input them yourself?" Jason asked rhetorically.

Jason was fond of Andre, but he was getting a feeling in his gut that he could not trust him. Obviously Andre was involved in something on some level, and as he suspected, something seemed different. Five numbers, Jason only remembered four, but was not sure. Thinking the fifth number might be the difference, Jason started to write down the codes on the back of the envelope, with the last number first.

E546235498563247543547612111845690000
D567843860028470205657...

"Mister Pelham?" Natasha's voice marked her return just outside the office.

Jason quickly turned off the workstation and moved from the workstation to Andre's desk just as Natasha entered. He was caught in the office but with, he thought, no evidence of wrongdoing save a nondescript white envelope with some random numbers on it in his hand.

"Mister Pelham, what are you doing at Mister Leopold's desk?" Natasha asked with a distinct look of skepticism.

"Yes well ... actually I was going to leave Andre a message," Jason answered her waving the envelope, "but I think I will just give him a call. Thank you, Natasha."

Jason tucked the envelope into his jacket pocket, handed her the pen and hastily started to walk out.

"Mister Pelham? Aren't you interested in your report?" Natasha asked as he walked away.

"Oh yes, of course. Sorry, I have a lot on my mind. Was it there?" Jason turned back to face her.

"No, it wasn't," she answered with a mildly punctuated tone.

Jason shrugged.

"Huh ... who would have thought? Well, perhaps they caught it at the NTA mailroom? I asked them to look out for it, too," Jason answered. "Thank you for trying, Natasha!"

Jason hurried off, hoping that Natasha would forget the whole incident.

10

THE SLEEPING GIANT

The relationship with the Kringle Works and its historically largest customer had become one of mutually guarded and respectful contempt. Indeed, the United States, with nearly two hundred sixty million people who received some degree of the Christmas service, was second only to the European Union in size after its establishment in 1993.

Early in its history, the Kringle Works had managed to ride the wave of American prosperity and technology in the late nineteenth century and had also given the country a measure of stability and comfort during some tumultuous times in their mutual and respective histories. However, as the United States seemed to be more interested in making the company an asset and an institution of the United States, Christopher Kringle conversely had been making his plans to move most of the Workshop's operations abroad. Some of Chris Kringle's last efforts, in his very long and productive life, were devoted to the move of the Kringle Works to its remote location and to carefully hide it away from the world's view.

The departure of the Kringle Works from U.S. shores was never well received with the government, and that coupled with an extreme envy of the Kringle Works' intelligence gathering infrastructure would drive efforts to seize, or at least control, aspects of the company. Twice in their history-- both with a backdrop of a world war and in a time in which the political winds would lean toward a dramatic expansion of governmental powers-- would the United States attempt to exert its dominance over the Kringle Works.

In 1916 United States President Woodrow Wilson covertly attempted to gain access to the Kringle Works's surveillance network, which Wilson's administration saw both as a threat and an asset in their experiment in the progressive social reengineering of the United States. The political motivations behind these efforts seemed well in line with the seizure of the detailed information that the Kringle Works had on the American populace and with a war gaining more and more momentum in Europe, under the guise of national security, Wilson seemed only more justified in these assertions. However, sensitive to the world's perception during this time of war, the administration knew that if the United States should attempt any open or obviously hostile takeover of the Kringle Works, which at this point appeared to most as a sovereign nation and whose treaties with other countries now spanned the globe, the world community would be mobilized against the U.S. efforts. Consequently, the Wilson administration attempted to purchase its way into the company with funds made available by the raising of the new Federal Income Tax to a rate of 67 percent on the top income bracket.

Staying true to founder Christopher Kringle's vision, then CEO Bartholomew Kringle thwarted any efforts to release any assets or information to anybody outside of the Kringle Works for any amount of money. Much to the chagrin of some elements of the Kringle Works management, who saw this as an opportunity to gain quick moneys and power, Bartholomew stood fast; and in 1917 a frustrated President Woodrow Wilson attempted to use the Federal Possession and Control Act to take control of nearly all American railroads under the United States Railroad Administration. Wilson, citing the war in Europe as the reason for the takeover, suggested that the United States could now more efficiently transport troops and materials and would also attempt to quietly put a stranglehold on the Kringle Works, whose reliance on the country's transportation infrastructure was still significant.

The secret struggle between these two titans would drive Bartholomew Kringle to release and renegotiate many of Kringle Works's contracts for transport and manufacture in the United States in favor of bolstering its own capabilities. Bartholomew's systematic move away from United States goods and services seemed partially to blame for a brief but significant recession in 1920, which was punctuated by an extremely sharp decline in industrial production of over 30 percent, deflation estimated at 14.8 percent and a drop in wholesale prices of nearly 37 percent, which was said to be the most severe drop since the American Revolutionary War.

In the years that followed, while America and Europe spent their time licking their economic and war-scarred wounds, the Kringle Works continued to service its accounts by bringing the populations of the world an emotional and social refuge in its Christmas services. Still, a notably more distrusting Bartholomew Kringle continued to direct his company to further and further withdraw and cloak its operations from public view.

Another world war, and another U.S. president attempted to use the conflict as a catalyst to take charge of the Kringle Works's assets. President Franklin Delano Roosevelt coveted the information gathered under the SANTA Clause, to both gain access to information about enemies in Europe and potential sympathizers within the United States. In 1940 President Roosevelt attempted to infiltrate the company through the Employee's League of Fabricators already known as ELF. Sowing the seeds of discontent within the ELF management, the debates between ELF and the Kringle Works executive staff regarding the potential merits of FDR's solicitations would plague the tail end of Nathaniel Kringle's tenure as CEO. The debates continued into the mid-1940s and were often recounted by Benton Kringle for sons Malcolm and Xavier, having sat in on them as a young man before he took the reins of Kringle Works in 1952.

America, however, turned its attentions to a new enemy, and with the Japanese attack on Pearl Harbor in 1941, America was distracted from President Roosevelt's efforts. Noting that the Kringle Works's activities would yield minimal useful information about the Japanese, who at that time did not largely celebrate Christmas or employ any of the Christmas services around the world, the president was advised to reconsider this pursuit.

Nathaniel Kringle, like his predecessors, saw the potential dangers of Kringle Works's involvement in world affairs, even if only incidental, and further withdrew his company behind the curtain of lore. All the while America, and much of the rest of the world, relegated the knowledge of the Kringle Works to dust-covered files deep in the bowels of concrete-walled archives.

Christmases came and went quietly, with little note of the ongoing interaction. The world grew comfortable with the Kringle Works's services and for decades the only interaction between the company and its customers was to occasionally redraw sales boundaries and to meet for diplomatic and philanthropic affairs.

Operationally, the Workshop had all but disappeared from sight.

Then on a cool, late September morning more than half a century later, America was fighting a different kind of war, one waged in the world of technology, and in a small, unremarkable office in Washington, DC. FBI Assistant Director Walter Hayes peevishly thumbed through a file about the Kringle Works.

A tall, sturdy man, Assistant Director Hayes was obviously the product of many years of military service. Even in his civilian attire of gray suit, white shirt, and red-patterned tie, he wore it like a uniform. Starched and straight, everything about him was buttoned up. Tightly cropped hair and a no-nonsense attitude seemed to have worn a permanent scowl into his expression which was now looking straight ahead across his desk as his attention moved from the file to the man sitting in his office.

"Have you ever heard of the Kringle Works, Agent Evans?" the assistant director asked.

John Evans, sitting across from the assistant director, considered for a moment.

"I have never been a fan of Christmas," John suggested and smirked. "I usually don't get much, a gold pen for service to my country and a lump of coal for … well, for other reasons. I think my mother sends scathing letters trashing me to Santa Claus because she has some overly righteous idea of the kind of person I am supposed to be."

Then he chuckled a little and answered the question,

"Santa's Workshop on the North Pole, sure. Why?"

Walter Hayes slapped the file on his desk and slid it toward John Evans and said,

"Agent Evans, a simple yes or no will do. Agent, back in May your man, Tom Bradley, came to us regarding an anomaly--"

Agent John Evans sat up wide-eyed and immediately interrupted, "Whoa! Is that what this is about? Listen, I told Tom he needed to get some help before--"

"Help? Agent Evans, it seems he didn't need any, he was able to identify an issue when no else saw it. He came to us informally, but what he reported launched our investigation," Walter noted, "and Tom's information is what led us to these."

Walter dumped a handful of what looked like one-eighth-inch black squares on his desk. They were no more than one-sixteenth thick and had a series of holes along two edges. The surface was adorned with the letters *ICU2* and a serial number, which were imprinted in almost illegibly small gold type.

John was puzzled as to what he was looking at.

"What is it, some kind of a chip?" John asked, regretting the question as soon as he looked up, noting Walter's expression turning to read like a nonverbal scolding for incompetence.

"We found these in a number of computers, servers, radios, and monitors," Walter answered, "They could be in any number of other devices, but it's too hard to tell which. They don't seem to do anything and are currently not detectible, so we found these by tearing up a bunch of machines. These are glued under each CPU and mounted underneath on a circuit board. We have to guess as to which machines have them, and we pretty much destroy them to get the chip out. We can't seem to figure out what they do, no matter how we manipulate them. Even if still mounted to the host CPU, they are just there and the only reason we know they are there, is because your team saw something." Walter continued, "The real anomaly is that the chip could be observed doing something, but without a trace of its history even if it was being recorded."

"Alright, but what do you want from me?" John asked.

Walter leaned forward, looked John in the eye and answered,

"Agent Evans, your team did us a great service in finding this. You need to finish the job! Find out what the hell these things do. Find out how they got here. Find out a way for us to detect them. Confirm our suspicions and tell us where these came from." Walter paused; he stood up, placed both hands on his desk and leaned further forward, never losing eye contact with John; tensed up and sternly and loudly, he finished his thought, "And find out what the hell these chips are doing in our beloved government's computers!!!"

Walter sat back down, straightened his tie and picked up the file on the Kringle Works. He stretched forward, waving the file in John Evans's face and commanded,

"Here! This is a good place to start! Give me a progress update in three days."

John took the file and as he got up he turned toward the assistant director and asked,

"So how did you come to the conclusion--?"

"Read the file, Agent Evans! You can do that, can't you?" Walter interrupted.

Walter Hayes did not have to say the words; the message, *you're dismissed*, was clear as he turned his attention to other paperwork. John decided to take this as a cue. He tucked the file under his arm and grabbed the handful of ICU2 chips from the desk.

"Thank you, Assistant Director," John said and quickly left the office.

John, cupping the chips in his hands, wandered past a number of gray fabric cubicles and down the hall to the nearest coffee machine. He grabbed a paper cup from a stack next to the coffee machine and poured the chips into the cup for easy transport back to his office. He then placed the cup and file down to reorganize himself. He figured that he could go back to his office with a cup in each hand, so he pulled another cup for a coffee.

Just at that moment a young woman walked over to the coffee machine and stopped short in an apparent effort to allow John to finish getting his own. She was a very attractive blond woman, wearing a gray pinstripe jacket and skirt, which looked professional but still a little provocative. She appeared to be in her mid-twenties and definitely caught John's interest. He decided he would do the gentlemanly thing and allow her to get her coffee first, and gave her a motion to do so.

"Please, go ahead," John said as he smiled at her, "I haven't seen you here before, are you new to the agency?"

The slender young blond smiled and nodded,

"Thank you, Agent Evans," she started to pour herself a cup of coffee. "I'm going on my second month. My name is Katie Marks."

Adding a level of confident swagger, John grabbed a cup from the counter and responded, "Ah, so you have heard of me! I'm a senior agent, cyber crime division. Please, call me John."

Katie smiled and pointed at his chest, "Your badge, I saw your badge."

John chuckled and started filling his cup with coffee. "Of course! Well, in any case welcome to the FBI, Katie! I hope to see you around!" He gave her a friendly and confident smile.

She nodded, "I hope so, too. Thanks, John."

John watched her as she walked back into the maze of cubicles and raised his coffee cup to take a sip.

"Shit!!!" he quietly exclaimed as he noticed a number of little black electronic chips swirling in the half-full cup of coffee. "Goddamnit! This is not my day!"

John took a plastic lid from a stack, which like the paper cups, stood next to the coffee maker. He held it to the top of his cup and attempted to pour the coffee into the other cup he had pulled aside and tried to hold back the chips. He looked into the cup, inspecting the now wet and glistening chips swimming in a little residual coffee, grabbed a couple of paper towels and wadded them into the top of the cup. He took a couple more paper towels and tucked them into his file, threw out the other coffee cup and quickly walked down the hall to his office.

Once back in his office, John laid out one of the clean paper towels and started arranging the chips on it. He then laid another towel on top in an attempt to soak up and dry any of the remaining coffee. He picked up the phone and pushed an extension.

"Jenkins, I need for you and Bradley to swap shifts. Tom and I have a project we will be working on for a couple weeks," John spoke into the phone, and continued, "Yeessss, I know it would be inconvenient for you but I have no choice. Please call Bradley and make the arrangements."

He held the phone a few inches away from his ear and winced as he was apparently getting an earful from a now very disgruntled employee.

"Okay, so come in this evening and have Tom come in as soon as possible. Thanks, Agent Jenkins, I appreciate your understanding!" John said, seemingly disregarding the other side of the conversation.

He hung up the phone and started to read through the file he received from the assistant director.

The file contained various documents; letters from past presidents, politicians, and clergy, policy discussions, other historical documents, copied sections of SANTA, names of Kringle Works's executives and sales personnel, legal analysis, surveillance records, satellite images and reports from various investigations. However, the documentation that John found most relevant was of the current investigation. John read through document after document regarding tests, which were run on the chips found in dozens of electronics, analysis, and the records that suggested the reasons for the Bureau's suspicions that the Kringle Works was behind the introduction of the chips into their equipment.

It seemed that much of the case being built against the Kringle Works was surrounding the travels of a huge commercial ship named the Kringle Works Vessel Snow Globe, whose movements corresponded to the manufacture of all of the devices found to have the mysterious chip.

The K.W.V. Snow Globe, it was noted, left the Kringle Works Island about two years ago to make deliveries of an unidentified nature to several ports. She was recorded going through the Panama Canal on July 12th of that year en route to the port of Ensenada, located on Mexico's northwest corner, about a hundred miles south of the border between Mexico and the United States.

While in Ensenada, the K.W.V. Snow Globe made deliveries of several containers whose timing seemed to coincide with the manufacture of some of the devices and components in question. These were traced back from the point of manufacture in Tijuana, Mexico. Still, as records of the chips being used did not appear in any manufacturing documents, this by itself could not be suggested as a smoking gun.

However, suspicions heightened as the K.W.V. Snow Globe went on to the port of Kitakyushu, Japan, which had the most importation services in the area west to Kobe.

Evidently, sanctions imposed on Iran, which was a major supplier of oil to Japan, created an environment of hardship for the Japanese, which became a catalyst for the opening of a temporary agreement between the Kringle Works and Japan for the importation of oil. This was completely uncharacteristic of the Kringle Works and marked a significant departure from past activities and the previously consistent and predictable business model they employed.

Once a commercial relationship with Japan was struck, it would inevitably drive other agreements. These were for the sale of various electronic components, which Japan used in their manufacturing of some consumer and commercial goods. A number of these would be conspicuously timed to correspond to the manufacturing of computer equipment sold to the United States government, which were also found to house the mysterious chip.

Mexico as a *Free Trade Agreement Country* and Japan as a *World Trade Organization Government Procurement Agreement Country* were both eligible to sell their products directly to the United States government as outlined by the *Buy American Act* and the *Berry Amendments*. However, as recommended by the Office of Federal Procurement Policy, these were laws under which the Kringle Works would be barred from such activity due to the lack of transparency of their organization; as such, it was these shipments to Mexico and Japan that put the Kringle Works into the government's crosshairs.

The investigation also noted that more shipments to both Russia and China suggested a broader spread of these components and, as with all these shipments, none of the containers were definitively marked; the information recorded in the bills of lading and the ship's manifest were simply input as 'Miscellaneous Materials.'

"A little light reading?" a voice interrupted John's concentration.

He looked up to the familiar face of Tom Bradley standing before him. Tom seemed fixated on the volume of papers and reports now scattered all over John's desk. Tom scanned across the desk until his eyes stopped and zeroed in on a paper towel partially exposing a number of small, black, electronic chips.

"What are those?" he said, fascinated, as he adjusted his large, heavy glasses and leaned in for a closer look.

"Those, my friend, are the fruits of our labors," John suggested.

"Remember last May when you told me about the computers acting a little strange?" John asked rhetorically, "Well, I always suspected there was something funny going on, which is why I am so glad you chose to report the event. I was going to suggest you do so, but you beat me to it, old buddy!"

Tom decided he needed to sit down and let this sink in.

"So what is all this?" Tom asked.

"Well, this is the start of an investigation that you and I are taking over," John answered. "These chips you see here are what was found in the machine you reported. Once we found this one I encouraged Walter Hayes to step up the investigation and they took a number of other machines apart. Now I need for you to take these chips and figure out what makes them tick. What do they do, and how we can find out which machines are infected with them?"

Tom looked at the chips. He was relieved to know that he had not been going mad these past few months, but also wondered why this investigation was kept in the background--especially if John Evans was the lead on it. Still, he was excited at the prospect and the challenge.

Tom picked a chip off of the paper towel and started to inspect it.

"Wow! This thing is intense," Tom exclaimed.

"So you know what you are looking at? These were mounted under the CPU in a variety of devices."

John handed a few paper-intensive reports to him.

"Here are the technical reports and the tests run on them so far. See what you can do," John followed up with authority.

Tom held one of the chips just six inches from his face and inspected it.

"This is wild! These here are likely plug-through holes," Tom pointed at the edges of the chip, "and if the chip sits under a CPU, these are to make contacts while still allowing the CPU to plug unfettered, and presumably functionally uninhibited, into the motherboard."

Tom looked at the under side and noted all of the connections that were made using what was likely to be an extremely high tech conductive adhesive. He looked a little closer, noting the letters ICU2 and rubbed it with his thumb.

"I wonder what ICU2 stands for?" Tom pondered, "And what is this residue? It smells a little like coffee."

"Uh, I think that was one of the solvents to get the chip isolated from the host CPU," John quickly answered. "You might want to wipe those down."

Tom looked up at John a little confused, but nodded in agreement. He then gathered the chips and the reports.

"Okay, let me see what I can do. I'll be in the lab and let you know if I find anything. I have some ideas," Tom suggested as he left the office.

John stared ahead after Tom left. "Yeah, I'll bet he does," he thought to himself.

John continued to review the material he received from Assistant Director Hayes and started to write a series of notes. He arranged the papers he had reviewed into categories so that he could reference them as his new investigation progressed and added his notes to the file. He had been learning, not just about the activities of the Kringle Works as it applied to this investigation, but also about the company as a whole, and like much of the rest of the public he was dumbfounded as to how little he really knew.

Immersed in his efforts, he suddenly became aware that the activity outside of his office had gotten very quiet. Indeed, it seemed that much of the support staff had left for the day and he realized that he had been studying the file for many hours; he had completely lost track of time. This was when he thought he would check to see if Tom had made any progress.

John got up, put the file into a file cabinet and made his way to the cyber crime division's computer lab. At the door he placed two of his fingers on a pad and swiped a key card. A red light turned green and the large steel door opened with a loud clunk.

He walked into the lab to find Tom Bradley working at a desk with an old laptop; based on the FBI asset tag it appeared to be at least five years old. Tom had this laptop hooked up to a series of cables which ran to a cluster of wires. These converged at a small point on a tray. Under this cluster of multicolored wires was a small computer chip, with what John recognized as one of the ICU2 chips still attached.

Tom was so deeply involved in his work that he did not notice that John had entered the lab. On the screen, he was watching several status bars and a window in which a series of numbers and letters were scrolling randomly. Occasionally, these number and letter sequences stopped and held as the characters around them continued to change. When this happened he punched a few keys on the keyboard and made some notations on a pad of lined paper.

John took a long look at this unusual set up and quipped,

"When I was a kid, I used to build radios with stuff I bought at the local electronics store, but nothing like this set up!"

"Geezhus John! When did you come in? Are you trying to give me a heart attack?" Tom exclaimed as he jumped from his seat.

John stood back, held his hands up and defended himself,

"Sorry, Tom, I didn't mean to startle you! I was wondering how you were making out? You've been locked up in here for hours."

"Actually I have made some real progress!" Tom noted excitedly.

"Something has been bothering me since my original encounter with these chips in May. Of course, I had no idea that it was a chip I was dealing with at that time, but I always wondered; how is it that even if I could observe something, why was it not recorded by one of the other computers?" Tom paused, then continued, "Well, I believe that these chips act like a network. They communicate with each other using the technology around them to provide the infrastructure. I can't tell you why, but it seems they do and one of the basic functions seems to cover each of the other chips' tracks. Since our computers are replaced quite regularly, many are likely to be compromised. So I dug this computer out of the equipment storage archive."

Tom continued to explain how he noted that these chips, found in a variety of devices, either had to be very flexible to work in so many different operating platforms, or simply have their own.

"Unlike the material in these reports, I chose not to try manipulating the chip by addressing it through the host CPU or the motherboard, but rather the chip directly," Tom suggested.

"Not having access to the OS or a computer that might run it, I rigged up wiring to the chip and used this proprietary FBI software for cracking codes and retrieving passwords to quickly address the chip with sequences of alphanumeric content. It's been running for hours," Tom said excitedly, "And after hours of addressing the chip, I got a response. No information, no conclusive acknowledgement, nothing more definitive than a ping. Just a simple response from the chip, but it was a response!"

"Here, I wrote the number down: *A364712846274562874635638476204812739* 2," Tom said, showing the notes he had scribbled on his pad, suggesting he take a look at it.

John, looking at the pad, noticed the ten preceding pages of notes and diagrams of wiring and the chip's structure.

"Okay, cool, so what does that mean? And pretend I have no idea what you are talking about," John requested as he handed the pad back to Tom.

Tom cocked his head with a modestly exasperated expression and said,

"Once I hit that alphanumeric sequence, the chip pinged back. It's very exciting!" he explained, "It could help us identify which machines have the chip in them. Maybe even figure out what they do."

John nodded. He thought for a moment and praised Tom,

"That's impressive, Tom! In one day you figured out what our investigation team could not do in months. Great work! I'm truly glad you decided to go to the assistant director with your suspicions. Hayes will be impressed."

Tom smiled, pushed his glasses up higher on the bridge of his nose, and modestly acknowledged the reports the investigation team did which, he suggested, acted as a base to help him narrow his hypothesis.

"I wasn't alone; the investigation team built the foundation, so I can't take all the credit." Tom followed up, "I'm starved, what time is it anyway?"

"It's late, nearly nine o'clock. Come on, I'll buy you a late night cheeseburger and beer," John suggested.

They decided to meet at the Penn Quarter Sports Tavern on Indiana Avenue about halfway between the Capitol and the Whitehouse.

It was a comfortable and pleasant evening and, as such, many of the patrons at the tavern chose to sit at the tables outside. This motivated John to suggest they sit inside, away from the bar and at the foot of the stairs, which led up to the second level. He did so in the event that there would be a modest amount of 'shop talk' in such a public place.

The activity level was high, with a human conveyor of black-clad servers running trays of cocktails, beer, burgers, and chicken wings back and forth from table to table and to the decidedly louder and more animated crowd outside. John waved to one of the waitresses and with a couple of well-orchestrated hand gestures, ordered two cold beers for their table. The brick and wood interior of the tavern sported multi-colored lights, and the flicker of a dozen flat screen televisions was designed to create a casual, lively, and friendly atmosphere. Still, it seemed that Tom was strangely uncomfortable in this setting. He and John had not eaten together in many months, but the change in Tom's demeanor was reasonably pronounced as he distinctly attempted to avoid making eye contact with the television screens dotted around the room.

"Are you okay?" John asked.

"Fine," Tom answered curtly, as he seemed apprehensively suspicious of the television facing him from the upper front corner of the room.

"Just preoccupied, I guess," he followed up.

John looked at him skeptically then looked over his shoulder at the screen. The current game being televised was St. Louis versus Washington. The score was as yet unremarkable and the volume was drowned out by the ambient sounds of the bar. He looked back and leaned over to Tom and asked,

"You're freaking me out, old buddy. What's the matter, your team losing or something?"

"No, no, nothing like that. I couldn't care less about the game! You know that," Tom answered.

He then lowered his voice, looked around and leaned closer to John and said,

"I know now that I'm not going crazy, no matter how much I questioned it … there's physical evidence now, something was in the electronics we didn't expect, conceivably manipulating them in some way."

Tom looked around again, locked eyes with John and continued,

"Back in May one of the screens addressed me directly. Someone knew I was there looking at the screen. Someone knew I was running the tests. Someone wanted me to stop or at least to see my reaction. Somehow someone could see me and I think the chips have something to do with it. At the time, I questioned if I really saw it, but that flat screen in the lab, according to the reports, had the chip in it as well. I'm not going nuts! There IS something wrong with the electronics! We don't know how widespread it is, or what it is! How can we trust anything we see or hear or read on these devices now?"

Tom's voice was rising with the passion of his concern and he felt as though a few people might have started to notice them. He looked around silently for a moment. He thought he felt someone watching, but all the heads and faces were turned away. Everyone was still engrossed in their own world. He saw no one noticing or listening to their conversation. He lowered his voice again and leaned closer.

"This is huge! What if all these chips are Russian or Chinese or Islamic Terrorist--or something worse!" Tom exclaimed in a whisper.

"Really, now that's interesting!" John suggested. "You do know we are investigating the Kringle Works?"

"The Kringle Works?" Tom answered his rhetorical question, "Are you serious? I'm not kidding here! We could be witnessing the most dangerous plot against our national security in the history of the country and you are investigating Santa Claus?"

"No, I'm not kidding. You might be on to something. Yeah, that's it! Think about it, how much do you really know about the Kringle Works?" John asked him.

Tom leaned back. His brow furrowed, he contemplated for a moment. His mind tried to process this thought, but somehow it just did not make sense. John, on the other hand, looked as though a light had been lit; a light that had been extinguished for so many years and illuminated for the first time in so long that his eyes were filled with the wonder of knowing. Tom shook his head disapprovingly.

"No, that's ridiculous! What do I know about Santa Claus? I know that his company is on the North Pole. His organization writes the biggest checks to children's charities in the world. He manufactures and delivers Christmas gifts all around the world ... aaaaand," Tom stretched and emphasized the word, "he makes my sister's kids the happiest I ever see them, every Christmas morning!"

He paused, clearly still thinking about the concept, and continued,

"They're benign, friendly; an old-world institution."

"And?" John asked.

"And nothing!" Tom exclaimed.

"And? And ... 'he sees you when you're sleeping. He knows when you're awake. He sees if you've been bad or good' ..." John paused, "so? Come on Tom, you know this stupid song."

Tom sat silently, staring at John.

"So?" John continued, "... 'So be good for goodness sake!' Come on! Don't you get it, Tom? It makes sense! Think about how little we know about the Kringle Works. You and I are FBI agents. I just realized today that I know nothing about them. They have always been friendly, but out of sight. Still, our treaties have been around forever and these allow them to come into our homes and even check on us. If it hadn't been going on for almost two centuries, we'd freak out!"

Tom said nothing. He just stared back at John in disbelief. His expression harkened back to that of a little boy who has had to come to grips with the flawed humanity of his parents; an underlying sense that the world is not fair, which comes with maturity but was conveniently quieted by the gift of the ongoing Christmas service entitlement. No, he refused to accept this explanation. It was too easy, too simple. This was not the method of the Santa Claus that Tom knew. This had to be the fabrication of someone with a deep-seated hatred of Christmas--a diversion perhaps? He mentioned terrorists, yes, that had to be it.

"Jihadists, John. Don't be naive! The Kringle Works is an easy scapegoat. The terrorists hate Christmas! It's a diversion," Tom insisted.

"Yes, that is an interesting idea," John agreed, "Still, I'm going to book a flight to Canada and see if I can catch a delivery from the Kringle Works to their hub in Toronto."

"Toronto? I have a cousin there," an overly bubbly waitress interrupted, "It's beautiful up there. Okay, one beer for you and one for you. Are you ready to order some dinner?"

Tom shook his head. John looked at the waitress and suggested she come back in five minutes.

"Okay, no rush. I'll be back in five," the waitress suggested, "Oh, and I have a message for you."

The waitress pulled out a small note, which sat on the empty tray now that the beers had been delivered, and handed it to Tom.

"Okay, I'll back when you're ready," she said to the two men and darted off.

109

Tom, puzzled, looked at the folded piece of paper and opened it up.

Look at your cell phone.

Confused, he read the note a second time before he decided to pull his phone out of its holster. Apprehensively, he checked. A government-issued smart phone, it appeared unremarkable and unchanged. He studied it for a moment. Nothing. He checked the log for calls and looked for notifications of voice or e-mails. Still nothing. Perhaps this was a mistake? A message intended for someone else? He decided that he was becoming paranoid. He prepared to slip the phone back into its holster when it chimed and vibrated. Tom stopped and brought the phone to his face and pushed his glasses up on his nose. In horror he noticed the text message on the two-inch square screen.

That's right, Tom, we are everywhere it taunted him.

Tom jumped from his seat and dropped the phone.

"Easy, Tom! You can't break that! It's government property!" John joked as he took a sip of beer.

"Pick it up!" Tom commanded, looking at John intensely.

"Whoa there, Tom, you are really losing it …" John suggested.

"Pick it up! Pick it up and look at it!" Tom insisted, gritting his teeth.

John got up, shot Tom an angry look, and picked up the phone. He looked around to see a few faces looking at them. He made eye contact with Tom, who looked upset and irritated.

"Look at it and read it!" Tom commanded again.

John studied the phone and curtly asked,

"Okay, Tom, what am I looking for? There's nothing."

Tom motioned for the phone with a frantic gesture of beckoning and took it from him. It was gone. He attempted to retrieve the text message, which no longer graced the screen, and checked in the log of texts, but found nothing.

Tom regained his composure and powered the phone off and shoved it back into its holster.

"John, you find them! You find them, who ever it is! You find them and make them stop!" Tom insisted.

He sat back down at the table.

"Back in May I discovered something, something that someone didn't want me to see. They tried to distract me from the truth and now I am again getting closer to finding them out and they go after me again," Tom said, frustrated. "Whoever they are, they are trying to mess with my head!"

"Hey guys, everything okay?" their overly exuberant waitress interrupted them, "you still want to order?"

Tom shot her a perplexed look, faced John and said,

"I think I'll take a rain check. I have to go home and unplug everything in my apartment. I'll see you in the morning, boss."

John nodded and asked for the check.

The two men exchanged their goodbyes outside the restaurant and parted ways.

Walking back to his car, John felt a sense of uneasiness as he relived the last couple hours in his mind; he was disquieted by the feeling that came from seeing his friend and colleague become so emotionally unhinged yet again. His resolve hardened. He thought about finding out whoever was responsible for the chips and whatever purpose they had. Whether for good or ill, he considered, Tom might be correct in his assessment that whatever was happening, it could be most dangerous.

Upon entering his car he paused for a moment. John thought he might have the answer, even if Tom was not convinced; John thought that the Kringle Works was the most plausible answer to the question. The next move was to book that flight to Canada. He would do it first thing.

The evening did not turn out as he had hoped. He was hungry and a little put off. Still, it was a successful day. His path seemed clear to him and Tom's discovery might be enough to build some new momentum in the case, momentum lost by the original team. Why else would Walter Hayes have pulled them off? The trail went cold and they needed his department's expertise. Tom proved that to be a good decision. Indeed, until they understood what the chips' purpose was or they understood how widespread they were, they could not go further. Now that Tom was making progress, a case could be built. They would need a suspect to build a motive, a pattern, malice; they needed to see the placement of the chips from the perspective of a potential perpetrator.

"John, this is your chance, you have to find out what's going on!" he said to himself.

John turned the ignition and his car sprung to life. The sound of his car radio broke the silence with the tail end of a commercial. There was a silent pause just before the station started playing the familiar song by the Beatles "Let it Be."

"Yeah, fat chance," John mused, responding to the radio as he pulled out of his parking space.

John arrived at the bureau offices early the next morning. At nearly thirty minutes before his scheduled arrival time, he was surprised to hear the exasperated moans from Agent Bob Jenkins.

"Bradley is supposed to relieve me; I can't leave until he gets here," Jenkins bemoaned, "With these hours, I hoped I could at least see my family for breakfast!"

"Okay, relax," John suggested and asked, "When did Tom get here?"

Agent Jenkins dropped a folder on John's desk and answered,

"He hasn't yet, but now that you're here, I can leave."

Stunned, John did not say anything. The pause in the conversation gave Agent Jenkins his opportunity to go. He looked up expecting a moment to respond, only to see the now-vacated space on the opposite side of his desk. He shook his head and gave it no more thought as he proceeded with the task he had laid out for himself that morning.

John started to work on his computer. He used various secure databases and websites that allowed him to view flights going through Toronto's Pearson International Airport and shipments going through the Port de Quebec. His intention was to isolate which of these were destined for delivery to the Kringle Works's warehouse on the outskirts of Toronto. The product that was housed at that location would later be staged for deliveries to both Canada and the northern United States in December of that year.

John thought that the best way to determine if there was any Kringle Works involvement in the placement of these chips, he would need to seize product that came directly from ELF, the manufacturing arm of the Kringle Works. Ideally before it reached the warehouse and after it was removed from the NTA's own transportation, in hopes of gathering information and products without immediately alerting the Kringle Works of the investigation. This would be the only opportunity. Once the product arrived at a local Kringle Works warehouse, it would never again be transported by a third party, as all logistics were handled by the NTA's own fleet from that point on.

Fortunately, the FBI had the ability to place pressure on the Quebec Port Authority, whose partnerships with terminal operators specializing in the handling, movement, and storage of cargo would allow them to interrupt the supply chain in any number of transfer points. In this case the most advantageous point would be prior to leaving the port via the Canadian Pacific Railway. Similarly they could leverage local authorities to seize shipments once removed from NTA aircraft in Toronto.

The customary mode of operation was for FBI headquarters in Washington, DC to use their legal attaché office in Ottawa, Canada to facilitate and support the investigative interests as it pertained to threats against the United States. The legal attaché staff would become directly involved in specifics of the investigation, but have no law enforcement authority in Canada and, as such, it would require that the investigation be conducted jointly with local law enforcement agencies in accordance with laws and procedures. John would have to leverage the FBI's relationship with the Canadian Security Intelligence Service, or CSIS, for collecting, analyzing, reporting, disseminating intelligence, and conducting covert and overt operations on perceived threats to Canadian and United States national security.

John had determined that there were two shipments coming in to Toronto via air and one was already en route to Toronto via the Canadian Pacific Railway. He thought that the CSIS and the FBI's attaché could intercept all three shipments and hold them. He planned to join them for the product seizure and analysis. Their office in Ottawa would handle the details associated with activities that could have a potential impact on the conduct of US foreign relations and, as such, would be coordinated with the United States Department of State. His counterpart, Teresa LaChapelle at the CSIS, would manage the investigation.

John picked up the phone to call CSIS Agent LaChapelle and explained the situation, requesting that she open up an investigation. John would send a secured e-mail that would both give some of the latest details and attach some documents to act as support to ask for a court order that allowed them to stop the shipments and seize the product for analysis.

He typed out a number of forms and gave a general synopsis of his intentions. He wrote up a cover letter with his anecdotal findings based on yesterday's discussions, with Tom Bradley's progress included. He added the shipments he hoped the CSIS would target on the FBI's behalf and the supporting information. Finally, he would need to include the evidence, which the original investigation had generated to implicate that the Kringle Works might be involved, though this was as yet mostly circumstantial.

John walked over to his file cabinet and retrieved the file he had been working on yesterday. He laid out those documents that he felt were most relevant. He also pulled out his notes regarding the reports he had given Tom Bradley. John noted the catalog number of each document on a piece of paper. An envelope containing a flash drive was stapled on the inside of the main file folder, which he pulled out and plugged into his computer. Scanning through the directory on the flash drive, he retrieved all of the documents that matched those he noted and attached them to his e-mail. John gave his e-mail one more thorough look and prepared to push send. The screen of his computer seemed to flicker for a moment as the e-mail embarked on its trip through cyber space. John watched the status bar on his computer screen and upon its completion, picked up the phone to call Teresa LaChapelle back.

"The file should be in your hands, Agent LaChapelle. Please confirm your receipt of it," John spoke into the receiver with an unusually professional tone.

Stern and low yet unusually feminine, the voice of Agent Teresa LaChapelle answered with a modest accent,

"I have received it," she paused, then followed up, "Agent Evans, the file is blank and there are no attachments."

John moaned in frustration.

"I'll send it again, hang on," John suggested.

He retrieved the e-mail and confirmed it was still intact. He attempted to send it again and the familiar status bar chronicling the progress of his e-mail's journey popped up.

"Coming right at you, Agent LaChapelle," he said more casually.

A moment passed and Teresa spoke,

"Agent Evans, I'm afraid this is the same. The letter is blank and there are no attachments. Is there anything else you can do?"

"Let me try it again," John responded as he repeated the effort.

Albert Einstein once suggested that the definition of insanity was to attempt the same operation over and over with an expectation of a different result. That was the thought that crossed John's mind as he watched the e-mail status bar for the third time. Still, one might think an operation is identical only to find that other influences might alter this outcome inconspicuously, and so it seemed here. Upon the third effort to send this e-mail the status bar on John's computer screen did not complete its journey, but stopped half way only to be covered by a new status window.

I'm sorry, but the sending of this particular file failed and sending it will not be possible.

This text was followed by a frustratingly singular option of clicking *OK* to close the window, leaving no other recourse.

John was confused. He felt he had never encountered this message before. Something about the language was not consistent with what he had come to expect from his computer.

"Damnit!" John exclaimed, "God, if Tom was here he would suggest it was …"

John went silent, his mind processing an idea, a thought that had not quite matured yet.

"Teresa, how old is your fax machine?" John asked hastily.

"I do not know, perhaps five or six years? We hardly use it anymore. We do almost every thing by e-mail or FTP. Why?" she answered, confused.

"I'm going to make arrangements to have one of our administrative personnel contact you to send this to you by fax. Don't receive it in your computer. Please use that fax machine, but I'm warning you, it will be about a hundred pages long," John said.

"Okay, but why--" Teresa questioned.

John interrupted,

"I can't explain it now, I have to go and track down one of my agents. Thank you, Teres ... eh ... Agent LaChapelle."

11

THE DOWNWARD SPIRAL

He was not sure of how he ended up in this cell. He huddled in one corner and eyed his five cellmates carefully. He did not have his glasses and squinted to make out their features and body language. Uncomfortable, exposed, and vulnerable, Tom Bradley was wearing nothing more than a pair of boxers, a t-shirt and a pair of worn and faded blue plaid slippers. He did not understand why he was there.

The morning was a blur. He remembered barely getting to sleep when he was jolted out of bed by the sound of his apartment door breaking down. The vision of blue and red strobe lights flashing alternately through the window and illuminating the walls of the otherwise darkened second-floor apartment seemed to be his first memory. What was it? 2:00 a.m.? He was yanked out of bed by three men dressed in black body armor and wielding automatic weapons. They simultaneously yelled questions and orders at him. He could not make out what they said. They were all talking on top of each other. He was tired. He tried to show them his FBI badge, but they forced him to the floor. Tom thought they were police officers but did not remember if they identified themselves. He told them he was an FBI agent, but they just continued to bark orders at him. He felt a sharp pain in his arms and back as they forced his arms behind him. One of the men was holding him down by placing his knee across Tom's shoulders. They cuffed him and lifted him up by the arms. Before he could get his feet under him they forcibly dragged him out of his apartment and into the back of a police car. He was being taken to a police station for processing, but he did not remember much about the drive and he was not sure which station they drove to.

Tom remembered hearing his Miranda Rights and something about an imminent threat. Someone said something about a text message, a computer programmer gone bad, and that they take things like this seriously. Again he identified himself as an FBI agent, but he was not a field agent. The DC Police would not recognize him as they had never crossed paths. He spent most of his career in the computer lab at the FBI headquarters, usually at night.

"They will verify it," he thought, but that was hours ago.

He was chilled and tired. His head and body ached. He felt the dull pain of an acidic gurgle from his stomach into his chest, reminding him that his last meal was breakfast the day before.

"Bradley, Thomas!" an officer yelled from outside the cell. "Come with me!"

Tom walked toward them and the cell door. He saw the slightly blurred figures of two uniformed officers. One of the officers had his hand on the cell door and the other stood back a few steps with his hand resting on his sidearm, at the ready as Tom approached them.

"I'm Tom Bradley. I'm an FBI agent," Tom said as he stepped forward.

"Yeah, yeah, yeah, so you say," The first officer said curtly, "You're coming with us."

Tom heard the alert buzzer of the electronic lock on the cell door and then the sound of metal bolts releasing their grip. The cell door slid open, mimicking the sound of a freight train as it passes through a tunnel. It echoed loudly, exaggerating the whole operation in the stark, nearly unfurnished room that housed the holding cell. They handcuffed him and the two officers escorted him out. He heard the cell door slide closed.

They approached a windowed steel door whose light tan color matched the walls and sparse trim of the room, making its edges nearly indiscernible to Tom's compromised vision. Another buzz signaled the door lock releasing and they entered a nondescript hallway. The silence of the surroundings made him acutely aware of every step. He thought about the events that led him here, trying to understand. His mind wandered as his senses, deprived of input, focused now on the sound of the soles of the officers' shoes authoritatively striking the linoleum floor. Tom tried to orient himself. He noticed the glowing square shapes of florescent lights along the ceiling passing overhead as they walked. He looked around and watched as they passed door after door along the wall.

They stopped at a door and one of the officers opened it. The lights flickered as they turned on. Immediately across from the door they entered through was another door. A large window next to this door gave a dim view of the adjacent room; a row of five chairs were set up to allow a view through the window. They entered the second room. It was a small room with an imitation wood table with metal legs and three chairs; two on one side which faced the other. This single chair was opposite the window, which from inside this room looked like a large mirror. One of the police officers unlocked the handcuffs while the other forced him into the single chair, and with one quick movement Tom found himself seated and cuffed to the table. Without a word the two officers left him there.

It was nearly an hour that Tom found himself sitting in this room. Finally someone entered; a bald man sat down on the other side of the table, slapped a pair of glasses down and slid them across the table toward him. Tom recognized these as his and grabbed them with his free hand. He fumbled for a moment before he managed to open them and put them on. His vision restored, he studied the man opposite him at the table. Bald, worn, the man had an intense expression that seemed intent on staring Tom down. He was in his mid-fifties, dressed in an older sport coat and partially loosened tie; a police badge hung from the breast pocket and he sported a three-day-old goatee on an otherwise shaved head and face. Tom assumed him to be another police officer. They said nothing and for another five minutes no verbal communication transpired. Still, there was communication of another sort; Tom distinctly felt the level of contempt this man seemed to have for him. Tom chose to break the silence first.

"Thanks," he said sheepishly, pointing to the glasses on his face.

There was no response.

Tom continued, "I'm Tom Bradley, programmer and analyst for the FBI Cyber Crime Division. Why are you holding me? What is the charge?"

"Yes, I've heard that bullshit story already, and we found your fake badge and ID. Who are you really, and where is it?" the policeman finally spoke.

"Where is what?" Tom said agitated and confused.

"Listen pal, you've been read your rights, you don't have to talk to me but we have you on a number of charges; impersonating a federal agent, threatening the police department, attempted terrorism, and about twenty other charges based on this little stunt." The officer continued, "Did you think we wouldn't track down where the message came from? So tell me now and make it easier on yourself. Is this a hoax, or where did you put it? We've scrubbed the building and turned up nothing, so if it's here, you're not leaving, so this just turned into a suicide mission. Capisch?"

"Suicide mission!" Tom exclaimed. "Okay, I'm not saying anything else until you tell me what you think I've done and who you are!"

"Who am I? Police Lieutenant Joe Marino and who are you, really? Listen, the evidence is pretty clear. Your credentials are fake, obviously to help you gain access to buildings like this one. Your apartment, yeah it's textbook terrorist hang out. So don't play stupid, innocent, or me as a fool."

Lieutenant Marino continued, "About a dozen computers, half of them dismantled, books on Islamic terrorism, Chinese politics, right wing extremists' literature, eco terrorism, books about the Russian Mafia, dozens of books on computer hacking and computer viruses. Yeah, you're the real deal alright; if not now, you're on your way."

"Good God! I told you I'm an FBI agent! I use those books to do my job!" Tom exclaimed.

"You're NOT an FBI agent! We checked! Our computer ran through all the databases and YOU are NOT an FBI agent!" the Lieutenant stressed. He continued, "We received your little text message at midnight and I think the words '*I hid a bomb! BOOM you're dead*' said it all. We traced it right back to you! You're much too dumb to be an FBI agent."

"Text message? OH MY GOD! Your computer is wrong! Don't you see--?" Tom started to scream, when Lieutenant Marino interrupted,

"It's not wrong! It's brand new, a little gift from the federal government via economic stimulus, and you are not an agent! Just come clean!" Marino pulled out some stapled pages from a folder. "You are a computer programmer with a history of over-the-top activism. Yeah, we looked at your rap sheet; assault with a paint gun against a business executive, a slew of vandalism charges. Oh, here's a good one … do you remember holding five people hostage in a military recruitment office in Boston?" Lieutenant Marino leaned closer, waving the paper at Tom, "Check this out! You planted a smoke bomb under a state police cruiser in New Haven! Smoke bomb, huh? So ... stepping up to the real thing now?"

Tom's frustration grew. He was now certain that his suspicions from last night were true. He was also no longer capable of restraining his anger and yelled at his interrogator,

"Marino! You incompetent idiot! I'm being set up! I never did any of those things! Don't you get it? Listen, if you're not going to listen to me, give me my lawyer and phone call!"

Lieutenant Marino nodded and stood up. He said nothing else to Tom and walked over to the door. The door had no doorknob on the inside. He had to call to the outside to be let out. He pushed a button on what appeared to be an intercom and spoke into a round speaker,

"This is Marino. We're done here."

The door opened and a uniformed officer walked in, holding the door.

"Throw this scumbag back into lockup!" Lieutenant Marino commanded as he left.

The uniformed officer nodded at someone outside the door, and the two policemen who brought him to the interrogation room entered. They walked over to him and each took a position behind Tom. One held him down while the other uncuffed him from the table and in an obviously well-rehearsed maneuver, forced him up by twisting his arms. In a mere moment he was handcuffed with his arms at his back. Tom felt the strong grip of each officer on his upper arms as they pushed him forward into the hallway. He recognized it, though the new detail he perceived with his glasses on seemed to exaggerate the stark nature of its architectural aesthetic. The officers moved him forward aggressively. Tom had the sensation that he need not walk along, as his feet barely seemed to touch the floor. They arrived at the door to the holding cell. With a buzz the door unlatched and they entered the room. Up ahead was the holding cell; metal bars reinforced by crossed wire. It was painted the same light tan color as everything else in the room. It seemed to heighten the colorful nature and variety of the five other occupants. Tom saw this as some sort of perverse and intimidating circus sideshow as he now approached the cell door. He had not realized the weight of the stench in the room until he returned to it. Indeed, it was the unseemly combination of alcohol, cigarette smoke, vomit, and sweat, which seemed to betray the sins that landed each of them behind these bars. He eyed his cellmates apprehensively as the door slid open and he was shoved back in. Just past the door's threshold one officer released him from his handcuffs and the door slid closed.

"Hey, where's my phone call? I want to call an attorney. Call the FBI and they will verify my employment!" Tom yelled after the two officers as they walked out.

"The phone system is down, pal. You'll have to wait. Enjoy the hospitality." One of the officers said as they walked out.

Tom hung his head and groaned, frustrated and depressed, as they left. It became obvious that this police department was completely convinced of his guilt and were going give him as hard a time as they could.

"Hey, FBI Agent Poindexter!" Tom spun around as one of his cellmates addressed him contemptuously with a slight chuckle.

Tom was getting the sinking feeling that his day was about to get worse as he noted the man who was now speaking to him. A thin, younger man, perhaps in his mid-twenties, wearing black jeans and a black tee shirt covered by an untucked and open flannel plaid shirt, glared at Tom. The young man was tattooed, pierced, and unshaven. His long hair added to the overall unkempt appearance. He glared at Tom with a thin smile which harbored a degree of malice as he continued his questioning.

"And what'd they getcha for, gettin' to the Star Trek convention too late, or was it indecent exposure?" the young man asked, noting Tom's assertion that he was an agent, with his heavy glasses and his lack of proper dress. The question was followed by a snort. He glanced around, smiling and nodding, with an expectation of approval from the other cell occupants.

Tom was awkward in his dealings with strangers in a friendly environment. Caught off guard, he shuddered at the potential disaster of a bad response in this context. Still, before he could stop himself, he blurted out the truth,

"Impersonating an FBI agent and domestic terrorism. They're charging me with trying to blow up this police station." Tom nervously pushed up his glasses as he addressed the man.

Stunned into a momentary silence, his cellmate nodded and with a more respectful demeanor replied,

"Right on, dude! Hard-core!"

Realizing that a follow-up professing his innocence would be counterproductive, Tom quietly reclaimed his corner of the cell and warily sat down. He felt that somehow, without a real understanding of why, he had, for now, managed to defuse this part of his situation. He was not sure whether it was his manner or his words but he did not question it.

For the moment he felt more secure and he closed his eyes in an effort to transport himself to a friendlier place in his mind.

"This is like a bad dream," he pondered silently.

Why would no one listen to him? How could he convince them that they could not rely on their information? He was tired. He felt himself drift and jolted himself awake. No, he could not sleep, not here, not like this. It was too dangerous, too disarming. I will sleep when this is cleared up, he thought. He kept his eyes closed and tried to relax. He felt the cold hardness of the painted concrete on his back and shoulders. The rumble of chatter from his cellmates echoed off the walls, making them sound as cold as the surface they bounced off of. Tom allowed it to disappear into a monotone of white noise, disregarding it as communication, refusing to listen to it in a manner that would engage him. He kept his lids closed; it felt good on his burning eyes. They were tired and dry. The darkness allowed him to cloud the gravity of his situation. He faded, and though he tried to avoid it, he drifted off to sleep.

"Do you have any idea how difficult it is to get a court order to investigate the Kringle Works in Canada, Agent Evans?" the stern and irritated voice of Agent Teresa LaChapelle transmitted the frustration she felt as she talked to John Evans on his cell phone.

"There is a long history between Canada and the Kringle Works and there are few government officials willing to even talk about action against them," she followed up.

John frowned. He was standing under the canopied entrance of a DC apartment building trying to understand the distorted and broken signal. Between the traffic and the sound of rain hitting both the street and the canopy above, he found that he was having a particularly difficult time and spoke in response artificially loudly as if he would hear her better.

"… but did you get an answer? What did they say? Is anyone willing to help us?" he questioned.

He hunched over, holding the phone to one ear while plugging the other with his finger in an attempt to isolate the sound of her voice.

"It's not politically viable for officials to take them … here. No one is willing to believe they … ever do wrong and … know that … very popular … public. It's political suicide," Teresa suggested, her voice breaking up more and more.

"Have … idea … will … …" Teresa's voice broke up to the point of being completely unintelligible.

John was not sure if she could still hear him but shouted,

"Okay, agent, I can't hear you, just do what you can!"

John holstered his phone and looked ahead. The door to Tom Bradley's apartment building was at the end of the fifteen-foot canopy. The colorless light of the sun filtered through a gray, overcast sky, adding an odd red glow which was cast over the doorway as it penetrated the red canopy above. Behind him, John heard the sounds of the traffic as it splashed through puddles gathering on the street. The rain was getting heavier and even under cover he felt the wet around him. He approached the door and entered into the foyer. The dark-tiled floor looked shabby with the light from the doorway reflecting the water that had been tracked in. Four gold-toned elevator doors, two on either side, and between them a worn Jacobean patterned chair on either side, adorned the foyer. John noted a mailman who was just in the process of filling the bank of mailboxes at the far end. His keys rattled as he unlocked each brass door, slipped the day's mail inside, relocked the box and moved on to the next.

John pulled out his cell and looked at the screen. No signal was available. This was curious. He could not recall a time when he did not get even a weak signal in this area of town, even in the worst of weather. He lightly slapped the phone into the palm of his hand several times as if to loosen it up. He looked at the screen again and shook his head. Nothing. Holstering his cell phone, John looked for a public or maintenance telephone. He saw one at the far end sitting on a small hall table under the mailboxes. Wandering over, he gave the mailman a friendly nod. The mailman smiled back and went on with his task.

John picked up the receiver, and following the guidance of an adhesive label stuck to it, he dialed the building's section prefix and then Tom's apartment number. The phone rang a few times when his answering machine picked up. John attempted to leave a message but the machine hung up almost as fast as it picked up. He tried again with the same result.

"Not a good day for phones," he thought to himself.

Security at this building did not allow for John to use the elevators without an apartment key or a 'buzz in' from one of the building occupants. It was this security that had attracted Tom to this complex in the first place. John thought he could use his FBI credentials to get in, but that would take too much time and too many calls for what might turn out to be his employee and friend lying on the floor drunk. It did not sound like something Tom would do, but then he hadn't been himself, John thought.

John hung up the phone and gave another friendly and casual glance to the mailman. He grabbed a newspaper sitting on the table and walked over to the chair nearest the elevators on Tom's side of the building. He sat down and casually opened the paper and started reading.

A moment later a well-dressed younger gentleman walked in from the outside. He was drenched, second only to the newspaper, which had apparently borne most of the rain, acting as a makeshift umbrella. John watched him as he quickly made his way to the gold-toned elevator doors across from where he was sitting. The man took out his keys and slid one into a keyhole under the elevator call button. An illuminated upwardly bound arrow indicated the man's intention and the building's acknowledgement of this person's legitimacy. John did not move; he just watched. Another resident of the building entered and once again made their way to the side opposite him. Again, John made no moves. Finally, an older woman came in, her bright red umbrella soaked. Recently closed, the umbrella dripped from the pointed end and left an unbroken trail of water squiggling out a rough trail of where she had walked. John was waiting for someone to enter via the elevators on this side and was relieved when she started toward the elevators where he sat. He got up casually, slipped the paper under his arm and addressed the older woman politely. While chatting, she slipped her key into the keyhole under the elevator call button, pushed the button, and the up-arrow lit up in obedient response. The elevator door opened and John politely held it for her to enter as she managed her keys and umbrella. He engaged her in some small talk and walked in behind her as the elevator door closed.

John got off of the elevator on the second floor and started down the hall. As he approached the door to Tom Bradley's apartment, he started getting a sense of just how bad the situation was that had kept Tom from work. The front door had the signs of forced entry and a large 'X' in yellow caution tape marked the apartment as a crime scene. To further discourage intrusion a sign stating, *Crime Scene - Do Not Cross*, was taped to the door and more caution tape was wrapped around the doorknob. John peeled the tape off of the doorknob and opened the compromised door of the apartment. He pulled the tape off of the lower left corner of the doorframe and cautiously stepped in, ducking under the remaining caution tape. The apartment seemed intact but disturbed. Most of Tom's books were removed from the bookcases and stacked on the kitchen table; some seemed to be missing. His computer had been taken. Almost every cabinet door was open and almost every drawer was placed on the floor in front of the furniture it came from. Tom's bed was unmade and the sheets and blanket appeared as though they had been pulled off hastily.

"This was a systematic search," John thought, "Not a violent intrusion; an arrest perhaps, but not likely a kidnapping."

John was puzzled; if this was indeed the case, why had the department not heard anything? Why were they not immediately notified? What could Tom have done or what was he a part of? Which police department might have more information? He pulled his phone out and looked at the screen again; nothing, no signal. He was going to have to go back to the office and work from there.

CSIS Agent Teresa LaChapelle stood quietly with the FBI's legal attaché while receiving a long dissertation and mild scolding from Judge Bernard Paquette an old family friend. They were in the offices of the Ontario provincial courthouse in Mississauga where she had recently stated her request for a court order to seize the Kringle Works's product. She sought to leverage her relationship with Bernard Paquette, as she had been woefully unsuccessful with others thus far.

Completely gray, Judge Paquette's age seemed to have worn an austerity onto his manner and face that comes from years of political and legal pragmatism. He was not given to the petty concerns of many, but he was a stickler for process and procedure. He addressed them with a professional yet mildly angry tone. Still, Teresa felt he had a way of sounding fatherly. She had known him since she was a young girl. Bernard Paquette was a friend of her father's and had stood by her family when he was killed in the line of duty as an officer in the Royal Canadian Mounted Police. Indeed, it would be these two men who had inspired her to seek a career in law enforcement as a young woman.

Asking Bernard was a little desperate, she thought. She had hoped not to have to do so and she knew that she was going out on a limb for the FBI. Still, the more times she stated the case for the court order, the more she had the feeling that there was something that needed their attention, that there was more to this story than any of them knew. She had, like John Evans, her counterpart in Washington, DC, felt the subtle beginnings of an epiphany that she had not quite gotten a hold of. One she felt she had to pursue.

"Teresa, I don't think that any laws have been broken! Think about what are you asking me to do?" The judge suggested, frowning at her.

Teresa started to talk, but Judge Paquette cut her off and motioned for her to stop.

"No, don't say it." The judge continued curtly, "If I do this, there will be some ground rules."

Teresa stood silently and obediently. Then she nodded to acknowledge that she would agree to his terms.

"This will be done discretely! It will be done respectfully! I am signing this order to allow the United States to satisfy their suspicions. This is not a

Canadian effort, and we are just stepping out of the way. You will go out of your way not to disrupt Kringle Works's operations," said Judge Paquette.

He turned, faced the FBI's legal attaché and continued,

"And I expect that the United States will have their lead agent there, no Canadian law enforcement officer will be directly part of the action. We are there only to support. Finally, I expect the United States to apologize to both Canada and the Kringle Works, officially, if nothing is found. This will not be a circus, not on my watch; I expect that you will make sure that this is executed as I wish. Do I make myself clear, Agent LaChapelle?"

"Yes sir, you do," she said respectfully.

Judge Bernard Paquette signed a number of documents and handed one of the pages to Teresa. She bent over and grabbed the paper, but he did not release it. Now locked together by a single piece of paper in a personal tug-of-war, he looked at her intently and said quietly,

"Do not make me regret this, Teresa."

She nodded and he surrendered his grip of the paper to her. She stood up straight and thanked him. Teresa LaChapelle and the attaché walked out.

Back in his office, Agent John Evans was getting increasingly frustrated as a combination of technological failures, a lack of specific information, and what appeared to be a lack of cooperation created an information cocoon around anything involving Agent Tom Bradley. He found his smart phone and computer were no longer reliable and if he used his office line he was still at the mercy of the computer systems of the various police departments, which today seemed particularly incapable of looking up or sharing information. This task might be cumbersome even when everything was working, but this was not the case today.

The most obvious direction was to pursue the Washington, DC Metropolitan Police Department, which required calling each of seven districts, and since a runaround of one and a half hours confirmed only that the district local to Tom Bradley's apartment was not involved, this would prove to be a potentially very, very long day.

John lamented that though some departments were more likely to be involved than others, he would have to consider a long list of policing agencies with jurisdiction in the DC area that could potentially be involved in an arrest or questioning of Tom Bradley, if in fact he was arrested at all.

Beyond the Metropolitan Police Department, John had started discussions with the Metro Transit Police, Naval District Washington, Secret Service Uniformed Division, Federal Protective Service and several others. He was grabbing at straws. What was worse, he realized that if all of these agencies were having similar technological challenges to his, he could be talking to the one holding Tom but they might not be able to see that they had him in their system. To further complicate the issue it seemed that the Metropolitan Police Department's new phone system was not working in at least two districts.

John's frustrations grew but so did his resolve; he felt that this unusually problematic activity might be the result of his and Tom's efforts getting closer to some significant discoveries. All of these issues could be the result of the chips, he thought. They still had no idea what they did. Could this be part of the problem he was having today? He pondered this question. What was it that Tom said last night?

"There's physical evidence now, something was in the electronics we didn't expect, conceivably manipulating them in some way."

Manipulating the electronics in some way? That sounded ominous, John thought. Indeed, if that were the case they only needed to control a handful of devices and people to cause the issues he was having and it seemed as though it was becoming worse as more pieces of this puzzle appeared, even if they did not fit together, yet.

John's thoughts were interrupted by the intercom on his office phone,

"Agent Evans? I have a message for you from the CSIS." The voice of Aaron Lynch, a member of the FBI's support staff, addressed him via the speaker.

John excitedly asked, "And?"

"CSIS Agent LaChapelle called. She said to tell you she has good news. She said you have your court order and to make arrangements to fly up to

Toronto as soon as possible. Shall I make the arrangements on your behalf?"
Aaron followed up.

12

THE PROPOSAL

Jason Pelham was working through a manufacturing report on his computer; it seemed that Marcus Millerov had completely caught up with the shortages created due to the electronics division's quality issues last summer. Indeed the output was quite impressive. Good thing, as October was a particularly busy time for the NTA and it seemed that the amount of electronic components increased with every gift-giving season. It seemed that the lines between the two largest manufacturing divisions had started to blur as more electronics were classified as toys and more toys were classified as electronics. Shipments were going all over the world, landing at staging locations and warehouses across the globe. It was the issue of the electronics that had Jason's mind wandering. He thought about the millions of people who would be receiving electronics this year and all those who had already received electronics in the past few with the ICU technology on board. He had gotten so engrossed in the running of the day-to-day business that he had spent very little time in the last month thinking about the concerns voiced by Xavier, his regarding the ICU technology, and the conversations he had had with his father months ago.

Jason spun around in his chair and eyed the ICU workstation contemptuously. He had not turned it on since his first experience some months ago. He decided it was time to follow up on a hunch. He walked over to the workstation and turned it on. He watched for a moment as the machine entered into its start-up cycle. He pulled out the envelope from under the workstation's keyboard with the owner's manual and the card with the start-up codes. He placed the owner's manual back into the envelope, slipped it back under the keyboard then took the card to his desk and sat down. He studied the codes for a moment.

A3647128462745628746356384762048127392
B4785784658569215456470975464925567788
C1213134243564778586979999456578200036
D5678438600284702056573546582446764789

He opened the center drawer of his desk and dug for a moment. Finally, he retrieved a small, white, folded envelope and placed it next to the card. It was the same envelope he had used to take down the code he had retrieved from Andre Leopold's office some months earlier. He compared them.

E5462354985632475435476121111845690000
D567843860028470205657

"That's it, I knew it!" he thought.

Jason recognized the numeric sequence that following the letter '*D*' as matching the last of the sequence he had for his own machine. It seemed to him that this was too much of a coincidence. He had too much of this sequence written to suggest the numbers were all different. However the sequence that was preceded by the letter '*E*' was different altogether. This was a new number, and that seemed very intriguing.

Convinced that he understood how his discovery would work, he transcribed the new number onto the card, writing it more carefully than the hastily written version on the envelope. He took both and walked over to the ICU workstation. By this point the machine had proceeded through the start-up process and was displaying the four codes that had been hard-coded into this machine. The machine obediently waited for the user to hit the enter key. However, instead, Jason started to enter the additional code. The lengthy sequence made him realize why Andre insisted his machine was to be hard-coded, and as it was this little breach in policy allowed him to discover the new code in the first place, he was grateful for it. Dutifully he continued. Once he finished he pushed the enter key.

Jason waited as the workstation started its loading of the interface. The toolbox window with a series of navigation buttons, textboxes, and pull-down menus appeared on the far right side of the screen. In the center of the screen the familiar little wreath rotated as it processed. The toolbox loaded. The status at the top was as he remembered it, *ICU Status stand-alone: Forward Processing-OFF*. The little wreath stopped rotating and

disappeared, a new window opened with the words, *Entering Data Feed –
Filtered – Restoring last session.*

"Restoring last session?" Jason pondered, "What was my last session?"

The screen became a flurry of activity. Various windows started to open,
text running in columns in front and behind, and within a fraction of a
second the screen was a blur of colors and movement with nothing
discernable. The toolbox at the right, however, reminded him of exactly
what it was he had last had up on this screen. In an instant Jason not only
knew where he left the machine but he thought he understood what this new
code added to the functionality.

His jaw dropped and his heart jumped into his throat as his worst fears
seemed realized. The window which graced this screen last before he turned
it off, had the words, *No Data Available.* He remembered that his final
search on this machine was to determine if the ICU technology was capable
of gathering information about the Workshop itself. It was not, but it seemed
that with this fifth code that capability had been added.

With tremendous discomfort, Jason felt compelled to test this capability. He
started typing the name *Jason* and the drop-down menu started with a long
list of names starting with *J* then *Ja* until it narrowed to a handful of names
with the first name as *Jason.* He continued typing until the drop-down menu
showed only two names, *Jason Pelham* and *Jason Pelter.* He selected his
own.

As Jason filtered his search, the workstation's screen reacted to the activity,
slowing to a manageable number of windows. All that graced the screen
now was six: a satellite image of the island, which seemed to have his
neighborhood in sight; an audio window for his home phone; another for his
office phone, both with a flat line indicating no current activity; yet another
window for Jason's mobile device, which acted as the island's version of a
cell phone; and his computer, on which Jason could see his e-mail inbox and
the manufacturing report he had been working on. The final window showed
the title *ICU Workstation SN5214662*, the five codes he had entered, and
name *Jason Pelham* in a text box at the base.

Jason frowned, walked back to his desk and picked up the phone, dialing the
extension for Randall Blake.

"Randall, answer me truthfully!"

Jason was distracted by an echo of their conversation as the ICU workstation broadcasted it with a modest delay. Looking back at the machine, Jason noted the window for his phone had sprung to life. The flat black line that had sat lifeless was now animated, rising and falling with every word they spoke. He stretched back while holding the receiver and slid down the volume bar in this open window. He continued,

"Do you monitor any Kringle Works personnel?"

Randall, stunned by the question, answered, "No, we don't deliver the Christmas Service on the island do we? What would be the point?"

Jason followed up, "How many codes do you input into the ICU workstations?"

"Four, it's always been four. Why?" Randall had a tone of concern in his voice. "What are you asking about? I don't think I understand. You sound a bit odd."
"Don't worry about it Randall, everything is fine. One last question, do you recall telling me that in your view, you thought you saw the original ICU2 chips clustered in specific places. What did you mean? I know it was just an observation but it seemed to make you uncomfortable. What was it?" Jason followed up.

Randall was silent for a long pause and finally gave in,

"It's just that when the program started, almost all the ICU2 chips were in various countries' capitals and their government buildings. I might not have noticed if it weren't for the fact that the chips started to give us information about countries where there was very little Christmas Service. You know, like China and Saudi Arabia? It was just a little strange, but they're all over now, more and more. Even before the holiday delivery season more seemed to show up every day, but it's all good, isn't it?"

Randall seemed to want to reassure himself as he spoke.

"Sure it is Randall; it's fine. You're doing a great job and you better get back to it; Edward is going to need your final reports to finish up the gift schedule," Jason said.

"Right, best get back to it then. Cheers," Randall said, and then hung up.
Jason looked back at the ICU workstation with a level of contempt and loathing, but it faded as he felt his mood slip into a sense of futility. Knowing now that he could see anyone on the island was interesting, but this was again a dubious capability, as he knew that he was not the only one with the ability to do so. He stared at the workstation for a moment longer. Did Xavier know? He knew that Andre did, but Jason was not sure of what that meant. Not yet.

Jason got up and stood before the workstation. He would have to give this some thought and determine what his next step should be.

Should he tell Xavier? This concept scared him. What if Xavier did know? That thought disquieted Jason. Who else knew about this and who else had this access? Andre Leopold was a brilliant man, but this was not his personal crusade; he had to have enlisted others to work out the technology. Was he the tip of the spear or just a part of the equation? With every answer, Jason seemed to find five more questions. His head was reeling.

His thoughts were interrupted by the sound of a slow clapping which was coming from the doorway of his office. It seemed as though it almost harbored a level of mockery toward him. He turned.

The tall, slender, and handsome figure of Henry Foster stood at the threshold of Jason's office. He was leaning on the doorframe casually but with a level of elegance, a mix of attitudes as only Henry was convincingly capable of pulling off.

"So, how did you find out about the additional codes?" Henry asked.

"Codes! How many are there?" Jason replied.

Henry's attitude seemed friendlier, his response quick,

"Jason, I knew you would figure it out. That's why Andre was so uncomfortable with Xavier's announcement of your promotion to the NTA management," Henry smiled as he responded.

Jason was a little puzzled and looked for clarification,

"Figured WHAT out? And how did you know that I…"

"Be careful of the workstation. It will tell you a lot, but it will also betray you," Henry replied and continued, "You can see me, but I can see you too. Please Jason, please, turn it off, we have things to discuss."

Jason turned around and shut the power on the workstation off. He noted the card with the codes and slipped it into the envelope. He felt uncomfortable leaving them unattended now, so he slipped them into his jacket pocket. He turned back to face Henry and with a little skepticism said,

"Okay then, let's discuss. Tell me what you think I have figured out."

"Not here, not on the compound," Henry said, thinking; he paused and then continued, "Let's have lunch! I know the perfect place. It's a bit farther out but you are the boss, so we can't get into trouble. I'll meet you in front of the building; I want to get my coat. Your vehicle or mine? Wait, you have that cool antique Tucker Sno-Cat 443 … you drive," Henry quipped.

The two men met in front of the building and walked around the side where Jason had parked his four-track Sno-Cat. The two men climbed inside. Jason situated himself in the driver's seat and Henry made himself comfortable and looked around at the parts of the vehicle with the fascination of a patron looking at the display of great art in a gallery. Jason made some adjustments, pulled the choke and primed the fuel line. He started the old vehicle up. The engine sputtered and rumbled. The cabin did little to shield them from the sound of the engine but with some fine-tuning, a push here and a twist there, Jason was able to tame this great yellow beast into a steady purr. With a bit of a lurch, the vehicle started to move forward. The lights flickered as the Sno-Cat started down the snow and ice covered path. The sound of the old treads, one at each corner of the vehicle, chattered almost as loudly as the engine. Henry had an ear-to-ear grin as they drove through the compound and out the western gate. The island streets seemed much darker than the well-lit space of the compound, but at this time of the year the sun would cast long shadows just after noon and duck out of sight by three.

"I love the feel and smell of an old vehicle like this," Henry casually shouted over the sound of the Sno-Cat, "The old metal, the wet canvas, the vinyl, and fabrics; it all has a smell. It smells wise, simple. It actually smells of ingenuity. Not like modern technology. We no longer have to solve problems today; it's just pushing the technology. Today it's a matter of code and software. Most of the creativity is gone. You already know you can do it. It's just a matter of how much code and time it will take."

Keeping his eyes on the road, Jason responded,

"Henry, technology is your job! You and your team are responsible for some of the most innovative technologies the world has ever seen."

Henry laughed in response.

"That's why I think I reject it. I think it has gotten very dangerous," Henry said. "I think that we might have gone too far too fast," he followed up pensively.

"Oh, that's it, turn here. Go down this path," Henry pointed out Jason's path with a more exuberant voice and continued, "Your friend Krystal, now there is someone who rejects technology. Don't get me wrong, she's one of the most charming people on the island, but I think that if she had her way, we'd be living like we did when Chris Kringle first moved operations here."

"The way I understand it, Christopher Kringle never actually set foot on the island," Jason followed up, hoping to divert the conversation a little away from Krystal Gardener. This always made him uneasy, as he was not sure how to define his relationship with her, even if the rest of the island seemed to know how.

"Indeed, he did not. It seems a little sad, actually," Henry replied.

This was a common experience for people who spent time with Henry Foster. He was an excellent conversationalist and always seemed to know more about them than they did about him, but he had a way of engaging that generally put one at ease. The conversation went on and Henry continued to give direction for Jason to take. The snow and ice covered roads seemed to get narrower and lonelier as they went on. For a while they just followed the same road for miles. Finally, Henry indicated the trek was coming to its conclusion,

"There it is! Pull in there," Henry said quickly, and completed his earlier thought, "From a technology standpoint, when Chris Kringle decided to separate us from the world, the fear was that we would be left behind, but that didn't happen. It is we who left the world behind. Well, more on that later. Let's get inside."

The two men got out of the vehicle. As Jason started to approach the lonely old building, Henry grabbed his shoulder, held him in place and said,

"Stop, before we go in, leave your mobile device on the seat. I'll do the same."

Jason was a little skeptical, but complied.

"These devices only sleep, at least until the battery runs down. I want to be alone to talk. Truly alone," Henry explained.

Before them stood a lonely cottage. They had driven for over forty minutes out from the edge of the island's commercial centers to get to this lone spot. The features of the old, half-timbered building were fading into silhouette as the afternoon moved to the island's twilight, but one could still see the age and modesty. Exposed to the severe elements of the island, it was beaten and worn. The extreme pitches of the roofline and imperfect angles gave one a sense of suffering and hardship. In this context, Jason thought for the first time that he realized how significant it was just to have the wood to heat the building on this island as he noted the cords and cords that almost cocooned the structure. It seemed to act as both a barrier and a resource.

"What is this place?" Jason asked.

"Well," Henry responded, "you are looking at the first permanent structure ever built on the island."

Jason looked at Henry stunned, and asked,

"Really, and why did we come here?"

Henry responded,

"Well, lunch of course." He smiled at Jason with a look of a grifter who had just scored a deal and could not contain his excitement.

"As for the building, a solid ten years before Charles Francis Hall led the tragic Polaris Expedition toward the North Pole, Chris Kringle sent a contingent to this island to start the movement of operations out of the Americas. You know the story? Kringle sent hundreds of loyal employees to scout out land for his company and they kept moving north until he felt the icy grip of politics and government intervention relinquish its hold in favor of the icy grip of the Kringle Works's Island. The story is taught as history but glosses over the human cost. Still, if you send hordes of people to one location eventually they will accomplish what you want even if you loose fifty percent of the population in the process."

Henry smiled proudly and opened the door for them to enter as he continued his dissertation,

"This building is not only the first, but it's the former home of my ancestors. My family has lived here longer than the Kringles themselves."

They entered the building. It was sparse and rustic but its casual nature seemed unusually comfortable. Much of the interior was part of a single room all heated by a huge fireplace. The air was thick with the smell of aging building materials, wax, food, and the smoky fire that snapped and roared in the fireplace beyond. It was a pleasant scent, one of a time gone by, Jason thought. It felt unusually warm. All the lighting was by candle and oil.

In the far corner was a bed. The view was obscured partly by a privacy screen adorned with a hand painted floral motif. It was dark in both the lighting and the color. The wooden wall panels were stained by countless years of open fires. The corner nearest the door had a long, narrow wooden table with five chairs on either side. Behind the table was an open kitchen area, whose large black stove sported two glass windows giving a fragmented view of the wood fires inside. On top, a pot bubbled with what appeared to be fish stew. Everything seemed old and worn but maintained with care. So it was with the elderly woman who stood by the stove cutting some herbs into the pot. She, too, was old and worn, but proud and friendly. Hunched and modest but not broken, she fit these surroundings as though she had been here upon its building. She did not appear to want for a more lavish or modern a household. She just seemed to belong in this place as though she had been forgotten by time along with this cottage.

Taking off his coat and laying it on one of the chairs, Henry spoke,

"Good afternoon, Aunt Gwen."

The woman, without turning around, answered the salutation,

"Hello Henry! I hope you are staying for some stew. Who is your friend?"

She turned with a bowl in each hand as she approached the two men standing at the table.

Jason turned toward the woman politely and introduced himself with a modest bow,

"I'm Jason Pelham."

Gwen studied him silently for a moment, shrugged and answered,

"Gwendolyn Foster; I think I have heard your name before, haven't I?"

She placed the bowls on the table. Henry sat down and smelled the stew, closing his eyes to heighten the sensation. He answered her rhetorical question,

"Of course you have heard of him; Jason is a very important man."

"Well of course he is. He is a friend of yours, isn't he?" she adjusted her gaze to see Jason with a cock of her head. She did not turn toward him but met his eyes and smiled mischievously at him in a way that only a woman of her age could do without looking disrespectful, "Mister Pelham, do you know how important my Henry is?" She responded trading gazes between both men.

"He's my boss, Aunt Gwen," Henry jumped in, hoping to take control of the conversation before it gained a life and path of its own. He motioned for Jason to take off his coat and sit down at the table.

"You two want to talk business, don't you?" Gwen said plainly. "I'll leave you to it then, help yourself to more stew. I'll just sit by the fire."

She smiled at Henry as he looked back at her apologetically. She proceeded to make up a bowl for herself, grabbed a cup and poured herself a drink from an old brandy bottle. She moved slowly but deliberately and unhampered to the large fireplace where she sat down in a chair and placed her food and drink on a side table.

Henry leaned forward across the table, looked at her and then Jason.

"I come to help her when I am not working, but make no mistake; she hauls the wood and maintains this place herself. My Aunt Gwendolyn is almost a hundred years old." Henry stated proudly, "She's cut from the same stock of those who first arrived on the island, when they built homes like this one or lived as the Inuit do across the bay, in ice buildings. Their job was to survive first, and then to build a company where no one would have ever thought to do so. That's why so few believe we're actually here today. The world can't conceive of it!"

Henry leaned back, "But look at us now! An island smaller than the Republic of Cyprus with an economy the size of Australia!"

"The stew is excellent and the conversation is fascinating, but why did you drag me this far out? This is not the conversation we were going to have, is it?" Jason asked, watching Henry inquisitively.

"No, it's not," Henry responded "Look around you. There is nothing here. You cannot be heard or seen. You cannot be monitored. With ICU technology, the system finds you by what you do, what you carry, and how you use technology; and with the fifth code it can be done here on the island, but in this house there is nothing, no technology. The best the ICU can do is monitor our computers and phones in our homes and offices. That, and, in this case, listen to the inside of your Sno-Cat, where we left our phones, or look at this house from a passing satellite. But no one will hear what I have to say to you and that is the way it has to be."

Jason looked over at Gwen who was now sitting back, reading at the fireplace. Henry's eyes followed his and as he turned back to face Jason, he said,

"Don't worry about Gwen; she doesn't trouble with such silly matters of business or politics. This is her world, separate from the technologies that have come to enslave the rest of us, and from those who move to exploit us through those technologies. No, she doesn't care about such things. She has food to prepare, a home to heat and work to be done. I envy the simple honesty of it."

"Okay, Henry, so tell me more; what are you trying to say?" Jason asked.

Henry lowered his voice, if only a little; his face became stern and serious as he leaned closer to Jason,

"You have to watch Andre. Not with the ICU workstation but in the old-fashioned sense. The electronics that we produce all contain the ICU technology, and we produce all of our own electronics on the island. All of the equipment on this island produced in the last seven years has it. Why pull it off line? Why raise suspicion by suggesting we should be exempt? If you do it on all things it is questioned less. For my part, I always knew that we could easily shield the island with software, like a firewall, so to speak. The fifth code, the '*E*' code, shuts down that firewall and allows us to see ourselves. Andre was obsessed with this capability and used some of the people in my department, loyal to his hidden agenda, who created the code for him. I don't know who they are, so we must be extremely careful. You mustn't use the ICU workstation unless you feel you absolutely have to. You can get caught if someone is watching you and if you understand why Andre wanted this technology for his use, you will understand that he has reason to watch all those around him. As long as he thinks he is still safe and anonymous, he will remain confident and betray himself by continuing to act on his plan."

Jason's eyes widened with interest, his expression that of a man attempting to hide his anticipation without being successful at doing so. Henry stopped as he noticed Jason's interest. He had a feeling that Jason was somewhat aware of the subject. There was no shock, but an extreme attentiveness. Henry smiled, holding a pause that lasted only for a moment, but it was enough for Henry to study the reaction.

"Plan! What plan?" Jason asked, as he thought that this might be the very plot that Xavier had been trying to uncover.

Henry continued,

"Jason, there are people who owe their entire lives and careers to the Kringle family; still, those same people resent that the family has retained power and control of the business and the lands that make up the Workshop. There are people who feel that they are entitled to a part of the Kringle Works even though they do not bear the family name. There are those who would use the mechanics of the Christmas Services and the information we have because of the provisions afforded us by the SANTA Clause and sell them as separate services in exchange of assistance in removing the Kringle family from power in favor of their personal ascendance. I believe that Andre is at the head of that effort."

"Andre *is* up to something, but to push the Kringle family from power? He and Xavier have been friends forever!" Jason interrupted. He watched Henry's face inquisitively.

"Yes, that's just it. Their careers have been largely in parallel. They, together, have made great strides for the Workshop, but Andre always knew that only Xavier would be given the chance to lead the company and that he wouldn't. There are some who feel that the Kringles have not always done what's best for the business, and Andre will find kinship and support from those who harbor resentment and jealousy. They are out there," Henry suggested.

Henry was about to continue when Gwen interrupted them,

"Henry? That big yellow sled you came in is playing strange music and making some very odd noises," Gwen said, holding some wood she'd just gathered from outside.

The two men jumped up and stepped out the door to check on the Sno-Cat. Without their coats, the cold felt angry as the wind needled them through their clothing. A step closer revealed the chaotic symphony of sounds as both their mobile devices vibrated and rang with contradictory ringtones. Jason opened the door and grabbed both devices from the front seat and handed Henry his then looked at his own.

"It seems all hell is breaking loose back at the Workshop!" Jason exclaimed, "I have a message from Andre, two messages from Natasha, and one from Lorraine. We better get back immediately."

Henry nodded as he noted that he, too, had two messages from Natasha.

"Could they have heard anything?" Jason asked Henry.

"No! No, that was the point of coming here. No, there's something else going on," Henry responded.

The two men darted back inside and grabbed their coats. Henry gave his aunt a hasty and apologetic goodbye as they swung their coats around them and ran back out.

The road was dark and the trip back to the NTA offices gave Henry the opportunity to check his e-mail and listen to the messages he had received from Natasha. In the simplest terms, it was to suggest that a customer was unhappy and that they needed to regroup to discuss the next steps. Henry sighed and chuckled to himself.

"Well, it's been sixty years since the United States has rattled its saber. I suppose it's about that time again," Henry said as he and Jason continued the drive to the Kringle Works compound.

When the two men entered the NTA offices, they were almost accosted by Natasha Cordero, who immediately led them down the hall toward the first-floor conference room. She seemed distressed and burdened with a sense of foreboding that was uncharacteristic for her usually upbeat demeanor.

"Where have you two been? Andre was looking for you! He said that a situation has come up that would require an immediate meeting," she said breathlessly.

She opened the door to the conference room and with a level of open respect but an unusual sense of urgency rushed the two men inside, closing the large wooden door behind them without entering herself.

Three heads already engaged in discussion stopped suddenly and their gazes turned to the door, where Henry and Jason stood, feeling as though a spotlight was illuminating them for review. Seated at the table were an astonished Lorraine Barlow and an accusingly mocking Marcus Millerov. Pacing in front of the ornately trimmed wood-paneled wall was Andre Leopold, who after a moment of awkward silence, spoke,

"Jason! Henry! I am pleased that you can join us on such short notice. I am certain we have dragged you away from very important business."

The two men nodded quietly and took their seats at the table. Lorraine gave them both a brief nod and turned back to face Andre. Marcus fixated on Henry for a moment as he watched him contemptuously, and did not acknowledge Jason at all.

Andre cleared his throat as though it were a gavel pounding a bench. It seemed to be an effort to get all attention back on him and served as a moment to regain his thoughts.

He resumed pacing back and forth. Andre was not dressed as a modern business executive. He, as many on the executive staff, embraced a more old-world fashion aesthetic. This was publicly expected on the rare glimpses when the general populations saw members of the Kringle Works's executive team. Almost as one expects ceremonial attire of a monarch when publicly viewed. His long, dark blue, embroidered jacket moved gracefully as he walked the span of the room. It exaggerated his movement as the tail nearly swept the ground. It gave him an air of elegance not commonly seen in the modern world. The Victorian roots of the company had never completely released their grip on the people of the island.

Andre pondered his words. He had the demeanor of one whose confidence was not shaken but has had to allow for a significant miscalculation in a grand vision. His tone authoritative, he started his discussion again with a fact that sounded like it should evoke gasps from the team he had assembled.

"We have been the subject of an investigation, and our accusers are on their way to enforce their laws," Andre said, and paused after a moment. It seemed to be designed for a reaction that never came.

"We are loved by the world." Andre stopped in midstride. He put his hand to his chin and contemplated for a moment. He gathered some thoughts. Slowly he restarted his pacing and in turn his words continued,

"We are *truly* loved by the world, and more so by the populations than the countries that lead them, but it is those leaders that are our customers and we must remember this. Still, it is because the people love us that gives us leverage over our customers. We make the populations of their countries content, complacent, and eventually, *compliant*."

Andre unnaturally stressed the last word of this thought and continued stressing the first of the next,

"*This* is most important to them. That is why they pay us to do it. Yes, they pay us. They pay us very well, because we do it very well. *But* ... we must do this from the shadows. Yes? The world will do what our customers ask, but only if they do not realize that it is they who are asking. We must do this for them with a silent nudge and a little push. So we hide. We remain as transient as a fairytale. As inviting as the smell of freshly baked gingerbread, but we are the aroma only. They cannot touch us. They cannot taste us. We are only what they perceive. The thought of the gingerbread, sweet and spicy, is better than the actual tasting of it. That is why they love us, because we are the gingerbread that they perceive but have not tasted. So we sell this love to those whom the people do not love ... our customers. Our customers, who trade their money for the love they could not buy without us. But sometimes our customers forget this. Sometimes our customers think their money is more important than the love that they buy and our relationship becomes strained. When this happens, they come back to us. They challenge our relationship. They try to take the upper hand in it. It has happened before and it will happen again."

Rhetorically, Andre asked the question,

"Is it a problem?"

He continued,

"Yes, but only if not handled well. If it is handled well, it is an opportunity! Sometimes, it is an opportunity that we have waited for. It is an opportunity *because* our customers come to realize how much the love we sell them is really worth. With every Christmas song, Christmas book, Christmas play, movie, and show, the great SANTA Clause tells the people how to be and how to act. And so, they get rewarded and they do so happily because they believe that it is good. But they forget that what we ask of them is a translation of what their governments want them to be and how they want them to act and it is the governments who forget that if they ask without us... *they will not get it*! That is because the government is the gingerbread that the people *have* tasted and it is sour and bitter."

Andre stopped again; staring ahead and seemingly oblivious to the world around him, said quietly,

"We must remind them. We *must* remind them how little power they really have without us and when we do, we can strengthen our relationship and gather more strength between us."

The team sat quietly, listening intently. The silence seemed an indication of the efforts of each to try to understand or draw out a call to action. Andre started pacing again and continued softly, measured and thoughtfully precise,

"The United States is our largest customer. It is the country the Kringle Works was first founded in and it is a country that has always felt it had a stake in and a hold on our company. We must remind them that their stake is in what we have and that it is our hold on them in what we can give or what we can take away. *Then* we can improve our relationship."

Andre stopped pacing again and approached the table. It seemed as though, until now, he had been talking to himself and would finally be ready to address them directly. He placed both hands on the tabletop and leaned toward them. His eyes touched on every member of the assembled team in turn. He started talking with a quiet intensity and conviction,

"Think of it; the most powerful country in the world forging an alliance with us, because they ... " Andre stopped; long moment of silence passed. He smiled and with an almost whimsical nature said, "But for now, we address their concerns only. Yes? Still, I should like to speak to them myself."

He sat down at the table with them. His demeanor became more even and passive. He then addressed each of them individually,

"They will want to talk to the management head of the Employee League of Fabricators, Marcus, but I think we know how to answer their questions from ELF's point of view."

Andre made eye contact with Lorraine. He smiled at her and in a soft tone addressed her,

"Lorraine." He seemed to put an unusual and lengthy emphasis on the saying of her name, "You are the keeper of the data. You are the acquirer of the data. They will surely want to know by what right you gather it. You will have to let them know that it is they who agreed to it. Our methods are secret but sanctioned, and they will want to know that the data is secure. You should tell them why and what, but not how and not where."

Lorraine nodded and in an almost inaudible whisper, as if only to say it for her own personal gathering of justification and strength, she noted,

"We are not breaking any laws. We have the legal precedent." The words broke slightly as she said them.

"Henry!" Andre said confidently, "You will know what to do."

Henry acknowledged the comment with a nod and as if these simple words had a lengthy and complex meaning, Henry pondered these with a moment of silence.

Andre watched Jason for a moment almost as if to decide what to do. He then looked apologetically at him and said,

"You have been only with the NTA for a short time; less than one year. Your talent is great and you will be required at this meeting. They will want to talk to the head of the Nocturnal Transportation Authority, but for this you must let me take the lead. Please understand."

Andre looked around at each of the senior managers in the room again. Sitting up and smiling, he said in conclusion,

"Take some time. Gather your thoughts and paperwork. Be prepared. I will talk to you individually in the morning. We will each learn our part in this dance. Yes? They will be here tomorrow evening."

Henry and Jason left the conference room together. Jason felt obligated to get to his office quickly, as he needed to prepare for this meeting and felt a rather desperate need to recapture the day, which at this point, had gotten completely away from him. Henry followed him, though neither spoke as they walked. Henry stopped him at the door of Jason's office, looked around and spoke softly,

"Listen Jason, we are not so different, you and I. If I can prove to you that Andre is leading a conspiracy against the Kringles, will you trust me and help me to thwart his plan?"

Jason studied Henry. He did not speak and for a moment attempted to read Henry's face, peering as deeply as he could. He tried to understand Henry's motives, to get a sense of his honesty, to see his soul. He was not sure, but felt that perhaps they both had the same mission.

"Okay, Henry. You prove it and we go to Xavier himself. He will have to be the one to thwart the plan," Jason suggested.

"No!" Henry said intensely, "No, there are too many of them." He paused and continued after gathering his thoughts, "If I prove Andre's intentions, you and I must expose the whole plan, all those involved, otherwise it will be for naught. They will simply hide and rise again after we have let our guard down, or worse, they might get desperate and become dangerous and even violent. So far they have been hiding; but if they get partially exposed, who knows what they might do. We have to find out who else is involved, all of them. We have to see how far and how deep the tunnel goes. Then, and only then, do we notify Xavier. We have to be sure! Will you help me? Can you trust me?"

13

KRYSTAL CLEAR

Jason was looking out at the darkness that shrouded the landscape of the island. His plate of food seemed of no interest as he looked around for inspiration to guide his thoughts.

"Aren't you going to eat anything?" Krystal said with a level of concern.

Jason looked up at her, not quite seeing her, as his mind was wandering in a distant land. His eyes moved again to the window.

"Jason? Where are you?" she asked.

"Huh? Where?" Jason's gaze turned to her and he appeared to have been jolted into reality, "I'm sorry, I was just thinking."

"About what?" she asked.

He looked around at the familiar surroundings of his house and then across the table at Krystal,

"I don't know … a lot of things … it's this meeting tomorrow, it's Andre and Henry," he paused, "I don't know who to trust."

"You can trust me," she said quickly, "What's going on; you have been so distant lately."

She chuckled a little. The sound was amused but it seemed to harbor an element of deepening concern. She paused for a moment and continued,

"Well, I mean more than usual. Especially tonight, I don't think you have been here all evening. Where are you? Let me help you find your way. You seem lost."

For the first time that evening he looked at Krystal and truly saw her. She had a sincere look, wide-eyed and focused. She was watching him intently. A modest cock of the head indicated that she was trying to read him. Her expression was inquisitive, though it seemed that she was genuinely trying not to ask too many questions out loud. Then as if to confirm the look, she followed up,

"You don't have to tell me, if you don't want to."

"No, it's okay. It's just that things are not what they seem anymore and I'm just not sure what the truth is," Jason said with an air of frustration. He looked up at her, not making complete eye contact, and focused instead on the glint of her earring as she shook her head.

He watched it for a moment and looking past her, his eyes moved back to the black of the window.

"Okay so tell me, what truth? Why are you so conflicted?" she asked.

"I'm just not sure of my relationships. Are people telling me what I need to hear or want to hear? Are they sharing their secrets or diverting me from them? Are they asking for my trust or leading me astray? What do I do now? Where should I go? Whom can I confide in?" Jason was speaking with his teeth slightly clenched, his hands tensed, his gaze out the window and distant.

Krystal frowned,

"Oh God! Are you talking about us?"

Again his eyes shot toward her, his head snapped to look at her directly,

"What?" He paused again, trying to grasp the situation, "No! No! It's not that at all."

"What is it, then?" she asked, voice low and trembling.

"It's just that things are not what they seem, *that* I know, but what they *are*? That's what I'm not sure about," Jason started.

"Xavier has told me there were things happening that must be found out and stopped. Henry tells me the same thing, but Henry would have me believe that Andre is the one trying to hurt the Workshop for his own gains. Xavier would have me trust Andre."

Jason thought for a moment and continued,

"Still, Andre talks as though he wants nothing more than to protect the company, but has some convictions that make me uncomfortable. The whole thing makes me uncomfortable. Andre seems to want to exploit the company's power, it almost seems sinister and Henry seems to want to stop it, yet he designed the systems that make it possible in the first place."

"Who do I trust?" he asked her.

"Is there someone else you can ask?" she asked him, "Is there another way to find out what they're up to?"

Jason looked at her and watched her silently. His eyes fixed on her as he contemplated her last comment.

"Yes, there is," he said, "I can ask them; I can watch them through the ICU station."

"I thought you hated that thing?" she said quickly, "Besides, I thought you said it can't see anyone on the island."

"I found out today that Andre can," he said.

"Really? And you can, too?" she asked.

"Anyone who knows the fifth code can," he suggested.

"Fifth code? And who else knows this code?" Krystal followed up.

"I don't know … Henry and I do." He stopped, thinking, and continued, "It seems Randall doesn't."

"But isn't it Randall's job?" she asked.

"Yes, but I don't think that it was meant to be part of the job. Andre wants it for other reasons. Henry says he can prove it."

"What other reasons?"

"Well, Henry thinks that Andre wants to take over the Workshop. To take it away from the Kringle family," he suggested.

Krystal laughed, "Why? He's Xavier's best friend, he's practically in charge of it now. I've never seen him be denied anything. And Henry suggests he is against him? I always thought that Henry and Andre were very close. I think Henry owes his career to Andre."

She thought for a moment and then said,

"Well then, use that infernal machine to spy on them."

"That's the other part. Henry told me not use the machine. He said that it could give me away," Jason noted.

"Or it could give him away," Krystal stated bluntly, "So then, have him prove it. If you won't use the machine?"

"I suppose," he answered.

"So anyway, how would it give you away?" Krystal asked, "Does it tell the other machines?"

"No, I don't think so. I think that Henry is just worried that Andre is watching me, and if so, then he would see me watching him."

"Well then, I could watch him. He has no reason to watch me; right?"

Jason looked at her intently. She was wearing a mocking smile and leaning toward him across the table.

"Huh? Well … maybe," Jason suggested.

Krystal sat back into her chair and took a sip of tea. She gave Jason a sideways glance and looking quite pleased with herself, she suggested,

"See, I'll bet I can help you!"

"So tell me, mister senior VP," she spoke with an almost mocking voice, "Do you ever watch me on that device of yours?"

"What? No!" he said in a moment of shock.

She laughed at him, "Pity, I wouldn't have minded if you did."

"Really? Are you serious? Why would you want that? Who would ever want that?" he asked.

"Well at least that would give me an indication of your interest in me. Ever since your promotion, you have been more and more distant. You were hard to read before, but now I have no idea what you're thinking. It seems like you are shutting me out, but it's not just that, it seems like you are shutting everyone out. Maybe that's why you are confused and frustrated? You need to trust someone, and you have not allowed anyone to be there. You haven't been able to see whom you can trust, even though you can see anyone you want. I've been here all along," she paused, "Jason, you can trust me, but you can't see it. That machine has made you blind. You are so afraid to use it you have shut your eyes even if you aren't using it. I want to help. We can do this together."

"Krystal, why are you doing this? Can't you see that if I get you involved you could get hurt? I'm just afraid that this could get ugly and I don't want you to get wrapped up in it. I've probably told you too much already. You already know too much. I don't know how dangerous these people might get. If they find out that you know anything, they might come after you. Listen, Andre is talking about putting his thumb on the United States government. Henry thinks there is a conspiracy to topple the Kringle family. If either or both are true, these people are serious. They're not fooling around. God, I'm just scratching the surface and it's like there is some huge monster just beneath it." Jason shuddered for a moment and continued,

"As it is, if anyone suspects anything, well … then they are watching me and they might be watching you, too.

He shook his head in frustration,

"You might never even know it but some people, who are not friends of the Kringles or anyone who would support them, might be watching you. Every e-mail you send, every time you walk past a camera, every time you make a call or use the Internet, they might be there, watching you. I can't risk you or my family of becoming suspect. What little I have already learned has made me realize how vulnerable we all are. I think you should stay out of this. Henry suspects that Andre has reason not to trust me! That being the case, he will watch anyone who is close to me, and that includes you!"

"Jason, I can take care of myself, you know that! Whatever you think can happen it can't be as bad as you excluding me!" she exclaimed.

"Besides, maybe I really can get more information. You know that I hear things at the stables. People talk. In fact I was talking to your mother yesterday, and she was telling me about some of the crazy rumors your father was bringing home. I could ask some questions as I hear things."

Krystal paused, hoping for an acknowledgement that did not come. She continued,

"And as far as being watched, well you know me; I'm not really one to use a lot of technology. In fact, when your mother called me yesterday, I told her that as far as I'm concerned, I almost wish we could go back to the way things were back when the island was first settled. You know, without all of these gadgets everyone relies on."

Jason stood up suddenly and whether driven by frustration or concern, his tone and manner became forceful and emotional,

"Just stay out of it! Can't you understand that? I'm not sure where this is leading and I will not have you mixed up in it! Just stay the hell out of it!"

"Fine," she said curtly, "Wallow in your self-pity alone. Call me when you get past it."

Jason looked at her with an intensity that quickly melted into an expression of shock, and finally, regret. Still, he said nothing more. No justification, no apologies, he simply dropped into his chair and stared into space with an exasperated, exhausted, and pathetic expression.

She was not sure why, but with his mild outburst she was sure it was a sign that he cared. Krystal became more confident or, at least, her insecurities were masked by a mild level of anger and irritation. She picked up her jacket and scarf and with no further discussion chose to go home.

Krystal Gardner was not the kind of person who would knowingly defy those she loved, but she was also not the kind of person who would be stifled by them either. She felt that Jason was asking for space, even if it was indirectly, and she would be willing to give it to him. Jason's mood made him hard to deal with and she felt no desire to try.

The next morning Krystal left her house earlier than usual. Emotionally churned up, she had trouble sleeping and decided to leave for work.

"The animals always make me feel better," she said to herself. For reasons she could not explain, she felt that being in their presence gave her clarity of thought.

It was dark much of day by the end of October, and it would take a number of hours before the sun would make a feeble attempt at warming the icy rooftops of the island. Was it three or four o'clock in the morning? It did not matter anymore. Daylight was a luxury of the summer months here. She entered the barn from the back, wandering quietly and whispering to the caribou, reindeer, and the occasional Icelandic Pony as she checked in on them. One by one she walked from stall to stall making her way toward the front of the barn, reassuring each of her animals that breakfast would be coming soon. Some of them stood back and watched her; others approached her looking for attention, which she gave freely. She walked past the last of the stalls with animals and walked by those that housed the sleighs and motorized snowmobiles. She always felt that the building seemed longer once she passed the animals, though she knew that was not the case. She walked silently forward, listening to the sound of the occasional snort from one of the stalls and her footsteps, which crunched as she stepped on a combination of wood, ice, and straw. She heard her own breathing as she walked. It seemed to give her an audible sense of the cold as the warm air of her breath hit the cold air of the barn. It swirled past her face like smoke illuminated by the low lights above. She stopped near the door, which lead to a storage room that housed the tack. She made some adjustments to a control panel next to it and flicked a few switches. The lights to the front office flickered to life. She then turned up the heat, which was signaled by the sound of a blower behind the walls and doors of the storage room and the office.

Krystal entered her office but chose not to open any of the wooden shutters or the front doors. It was too early and she thought it made sense to conserve the heat and her privacy for now. She was used to being one of the first to arrive on the compound but this was early even for her, so it was a complete surprise when she heard voices outside her office window. It was still shuttered, and those outside would have no reason to believe their anonymity would be compromised as she had entered from the back and many hours too early, which was why no one would have been aware of her presence. Curious, she quietly pressed her ear against the closed window of the front office.

"… and now the United States government is coming to ask questions!" Krystal, recognizing the voice, heard the agitated whisper of Marcus Millerov outside her office as he continued. She listened more intently.

"You used to make these yourself but since I took over all of ELF, I have been doing it for you, no questions asked. I am not taking the fall for this. You have to protect me or I will produce the paperwork that shows the production schedules of the boards and who ordered them. It won't absolve me but it will implicate you. So keep that in mind! I have the evidence and if I get into trouble, I will drag you with me … straight to hell if I have to."

She pressed her ear closer; but as she did, the shutter creaked and the voices stopped. She held her breath. A moment passed in silence. Then she heard footsteps and the sound of someone attempting to open the front door. It was still locked. She heard a knock on the door, which agitated some of the animals. "Be quiet!" she thought to herself. Her heart was pumping; she felt as though it would burst from her chest and throat, but the two wandered off, satisfied that the sound of the animals was all they had heard.

14

THE INQUISITORS

Getting to the Kringle Works Island was not an easy task. There were no commercial flights that would take you there if you did not have the benefit of an NTA aircraft at your disposal.

They had come up the day before. The contingent from Washington, DC consisted of three people. Walter Hayes, assistant director of the FBI, would represent the United States' concerns from a legal point of view. He was joined by Secretary of Commerce Brenda Willis. She was an overweight woman with an overtly pompous attitude which was painted over her face, giving her the look of one with a perpetual pout. Even though the connections to the country's interest with regards to commerce might have been obvious, she was not sure why she had been asked to join in what was obviously more of a law enforcement venture. Still, she accepted the invitation quickly. She assumed that if successful, though she did not understand what success should mean in this context, it might be a good opportunity to get some publicity which she felt was woefully lacking in her current position within the government. Brenda regretted agreeing to the trip on a couple of occasions when the reality of the climate and temperature in Canada, at this point in the year, became apparent. She was not shy about letting her travel companions know how she felt about it. Dressed in a navy blue suit and covered in a long, gray, down-filled jacket which exaggerated her distorted figure, Brenda clutched her coat tightly, holding it closed from the icy wind upon her arrival in Toronto. She loudly declared that the last bit of genuine warmth she felt had been at the terminal in Ronald Reagan Airport in Washington, DC.

"It's going to be a whole lot colder up at the Kringle Works, Madam Secretary," A mocking and whiny voice behind her suggested as they stepped off of the aircraft and onto the tarmac.

Dressed in a camelhair overcoat, black gloves, and gray suit, the slender figure of Holden Mealy emerged from the aircraft, following Brenda. Holden was a Washington insider and a longtime friend of some key members of the current administration. As such, he landed one the most unessential jobs the country had to offer. As the administration's Christmas Czar, he did not have to deal with the irritation of a proof of performance since his position was neither elected by the people nor vetted by Congress. His job, it seemed, was to watch the appropriated moneys go to the Kringle Works and then take credit for the execution of the service they provided. Occasionally, he liked to remind people he also worked with the White House staff to select a new Christmas ornament for public spectacle. He reveled in the notoriety of his position's façade of public service and the generally positive public view of his office's activities. An otherwise unremarkable man, he had a contemptuous and cynical manner which seemed inappropriate for his charter. So much so, that even in his effort to appear in the spirit of the job, his habit of wearing a garish red and green, holly berry-adorned tie year round seemed to be mocking those who appointed him.

"I hear that if you are bitten by a polar bear outside of Santa's Workshop, you do not have to tie off the wound, because the blood will freeze instantly," Holden taunted Brenda as they walked toward the glass-enclosed bus stop to await transport to the main terminal.

The party was greeted at the main terminal by FBI Agent John Evans, CSIS Agent Teresa LaChapelle, the FBI's legal attaché, and two CSIS security personnel. With immediate nods of greeting and respect, the two security men flanked the new arrivals, one on each side of the group. The remaining three stood before them like a formal reception line. As the Canadian representative, Agent Teresa LaChapelle spoke first, welcoming the Washington team to Toronto.

Agent Evans and Agent LaChapelle then escorted them to their vehicles and suggested they would meet at the hotel to go over the information they had gathered and the plan to present it to the Kringle Works.

They left the next morning, leaving from Toronto Pearson International Airport with an 8:10 a.m. flight. The trip would take them all day, hopping from one airport to the next. Their arrival at Ottawa/Macdonald-Cartier International Airport would be approximately an hour later and would act as their starting point in a series of flights that would take them to the remote and icy world of the Kringle Works.

It seemed to them to be more like an artic expedition than a commercial flight to see a multi-billion-dollar vendor to the United States government. Being treated as VIPs, the Canadian authorities had sent a party to meet them at each stop, shuttling them from aircraft to gate for their comfort and their safety, but not as participants--as was demanded by the Canadian government--suggesting that this was and would remain a United States effort alone.

"I don't understand why we are being herded around like cattle from airplane to airplane," Brenda whined, "Why couldn't we get the FBI to request a United States government plane?" she continued loudly, hoping the two agents would hear her.

"Cattle, huh?" a mocking laugh came from behind her.

She looked back and saw Holden staring at her with a smirk.

"Well, you should know," he said contemptuously as she shot him a look of extreme irritation, "Because of your recent endorsement of the new livestock bill, I mean, Madam Secretary." Holden bowed his head with an almost too polite a gesture.

"Besides, we don't rate with law enforcement," Holden Mealy snarled.

Overhearing the comments, John Evans rolled his eyes, choosing to ignore them; he was surprised to hear the measured voice of Walter Hayes interrupt them,

"We do not have the funds to charter Air Force One whenever the need arises, Ms. Willis. You, of all people, know that. Besides, Mister Mealy, we did not want to attract too much public attention until we know more. This is a simple fact-finding mission, an inquiry, in which you two might be of value! Bear in mind that the Kringle Works does not allow for large government aircraft to fly in, nor did the Canadian government want to allow us the opportunity to do so at the risk of their relationship. If it turns out that we have nothing to go on, this would be very embarrassing, so the less attention the better, for now."

Agent Hayes found his annoyance getting the better of him as he had little patience for most Washington bureaucrats and followed up,

"Still, I would be willing to reduce this to a simple FBI matter at your request. Would you like to remain here?"

John grabbed him by the shoulder,

"Walter," he said quietly, hoping to stop him. Walter gave him a nod.

"Mister Mealy, Madam Secretary, please accept my apologies," Walter said reverently, "Understand we have our reasons for doing it this way."

They left Ottawa at 10:00 a.m. for Iqaluit and as if to punctuate their distance from their world, the weather at each airport became more and more treacherous as the locations became more and more remote. The flight took them deep into the territory of Nunavut. Nunavut, or "our land" in the Inuktitut language, had been home to Inuit people for millennia and part of Canada for more than a century, and it seemed to mark their passage through a gate into a harsh, unforgiving, and punishing world. Brenda Willis frowned as she studied the landscape outside of the aircraft from her first-class window seat. It was the capitol city of Nunavut, but it seemed to her that there was little to see in what appeared to be endless ripples of snow as they approached the southern side of Baffin Island.

For its modesty, the city of Iqaluit appeared as a last oasis in a desert of snow and ice. Their landing at Iqaluit Airport was to be at 1:00 p.m., but the complexity of a trip to the Kringle Works was second only to its unpredictability as at this time of the year weather was always a concern. So they hurried to catch their next flight to Igloolik at 2:30 p.m. The accommodations on the next flight grew sparse and Brenda yammered about her discomfort, first in the seating and on to the lack of an opportunity to have lunch. Her frustration gave way to a feeling of a cold triggered not by the temperature but rather a sense of foreboding as the trip to Igloolik took them over Foxe Basin. The nearly completely ice-covered body of water made her dread the thought that they were still relatively south of their final destination.

"There is nothing but ice out here! How can anyone have a business anywhere near this place?" Brenda blurted out as she looked over at Holden Mealy.

He either did not hear her over the sound of the engines or he chose to ignore her. Brenda was not sure which. She watched him for a moment. Holden spent his time on these flights writing up talking points. He thought that, as the Christmas Czar, this would be a tremendous opportunity. Soon he would be one of the very few who had ever set foot on the Kringle Works Island from the outside world. His efforts were to have clever comments ready so that they might be quoted later in the papers. He carried an air, an attitude that attempted to look to the others as though he was not only the most knowledgeable about the Kringle Works but almost as though he had been there before. He had not. None of them had.

Brenda looked around and noticed the two men of the FBI in deep conversation in the back of the aircraft. She wondered what awaited them at the island. The large number of empty seats that adorned the fuselage of this aircraft highlighted the desolateness of the locations to which they needed to travel to get to their destination. Scientists, meteorologists, and fishermen, she thought, but not a business executive or a politician; why was it that the Kringles chose to go to this extreme place to build their business?

She looked out as they approached the island of Igloolik. The city had the only features she could make out as the darkness fell. The lights were few and the whole of Igloolik seemed to be no larger than the airport that served it.

They touched down at 4:20 p.m., and as with the other airports, they were met by a representative of the Canadian government. Unlike at the other airports, this man was not dressed in a dark suit and tie, he seemed to speak very little English, and his appearance was distinctly traditional and ethnic. The handmade leggings and caribou leather boots peeked out from underneath his modern made hooded and fur-lined jacket. He was well-groomed but had a weathered face. Quietly he rushed them off of the aircraft and into the modest airport's facility. Once they entered the building, the Igloolik emissary handed them each a hot cup of broth, encouraging them to drink it.

John Evans was the first to give it a taste. The hot liquid felt good going down; it had an unusual taste that he could not identify but he was hungry enough not to care. He gave their guide a nod and smiled.

"I'm not touching that!" snarled Holden, "It's probably whale or seal piss or something."

Brenda had a look of shock and put her cup down sharply.

The dark, leathery face of their guide smiled at them and he shook his head in disbelief.

Walter Hayes shot a look of irritation at them and then, like John Evans, raised the cup to his lips and drank. He smiled, raised the cup in salute. The man smiled approvingly and nodded back in acknowledgement.

Their aircraft was readied for their next flight taking them to the airport at Pond Inlet. They would be sharing the flight with a small number of students and their guides, two research scientists who planned on a week of polar bear study.

Their 5:15 p.m. flight left as scheduled, expected to arrive at Pond Inlet an hour later. Staring through the ice-covered window of the aircraft, Brenda lamented that she had never seen a landscape this dark. She was not sure why, but it continued to unnerve her.

It was a bumpy landing at the Pond Inlet, but their arrival was otherwise uneventful. Tired and exhausted, they knew they were on the last leg of their trip.

Before being given a chance to deplane, a handsome young man boarded, asking for their party. He had dark hair and was wearing a fur-lined black leather bomber's jacket. Sporting tightly cropped hair and clean-shaven face, he had an air of military discipline in his manner. With what seemed to be a mild Australian accent he introduced himself as their pilot to the Kringle Works Island.

They left the aircraft, with all the other remaining passengers held until they had gathered everything. Immediately the pilot pointed out a smaller aircraft on the tarmac, which would be their shuttle to the Kringle Works. Their bags were taken from them and moved to another location, presumably for checking. They saw the aircraft; a single engine turboprop, it was the smallest plane they would use but likely the newest and most luxurious with its executive level additions and appointments.

Upon their entrance they noticed the interior, which though small and restricted in height, had plenty of room for the four of them once seated. The wood-trimmed cabinetry, flat screen video panels, and leather seating made this aircraft interior seem more like a fancy conference room. Four of the chairs were situated to face each other across two wooden tabletops, and recessed lighting comfortably illuminated the cabin. Walter Hayes, as a private pilot himself, noticed the 'glass cockpit' which replaced all the traditional mechanical and gyroscopic gauges with three large, electronic screens. These could display a larger array of instruments and information including weather and traffic in addition to the electronic versions of the standard altitude, airspeed, compass, attitude, and climb gauges.

Once each of them had taken a seat, they were immediately served a welcome and fresh cup of coffee. Quick apologies were made about the cold due to the open cabin door as their luggage and other supplies were loaded. The treaties between Canada and the Kringle Works made it unnecessary to do much paperwork for their arrival on the island, but the pilot sat down with them in the cabin of the aircraft and conducted what seemed to be a general interview and debriefing, before stepping to the front and into the left-hand pilot's seat. The lights dimmed and the cabin door was closed. They all felt a moment of relief as they heard the sound of the powerful engine of the aircraft ignite.

Sitting in the cabin, Walter made note of the pilot's calls,

"Pond Inlet ground, Caravan Charlie Golf Sierra Zulu Whisky departing runway to the Northeast. Expecting heading zero six five for the Kringle Works, NTA Main, full stop. See ya tomorrow afternoon. Have dinner ready for me!"

They had not realized how much they had forgotten and disregarded the sounds of the engine that drove the turboprop, until the sound changed. The steady hum that penetrated the well-insulated cabin seemed to draw back into the distance of their minds like a meaningless element of a complex soundtrack that now rose to the front of their brains, alerting them to a milestone in their odyssey. The growl of the engine slowed and grew not quieter, but lower. The change in pitch seemed to highlight the sound of the cold air that passed over the plane's fuselage as the difference in these grew more distinct. The aircraft seemed to grab a hold of them as their bodies felt the sensations of their personal speed slowing down with an aircraft that had already done so and was physically reminding them to do the same. The pilot made several calls, talking to an unseen and unheard entity, which he addressed dutifully as 'NTA Tower.' Realizing their approach to the island was imminent they felt an unrelenting curiosity and looked out of their cabin windows anxiously hoping to glimpse that which so few had seen.

The sight of the Kringle Works Island stunned them. Their day's travels had taken them from one sight to the next, each growing smaller, colder, darker, and lonelier, desensitizing them to it; but what they saw now jolted them into a new reality, a reality that in an instant suggested the cost of the world's want for a Christmas that was focused so on the receipt of gifts. The price they all paid for their entitlement. This was not a small, dark factory, which produced wooden toys of a bygone era. It was not a fanciful palace whose sole source of illumination was by way of candles on a decorated pine tree. No, it was a modern metropolis whose purpose was designed for the production and delivery of billions of goods to billions of people. If there had ever been homage to be paid to the visions of Christopher Kringle's dream of a global, modern and commercial Christmas Holiday, then this was its altar to him. Sitting in the vast darkness of Baffin's Bay, the island shone like a bright sun in a nighttime sky.

The aircraft turned and its speed increased as it banked tracing the outside edge of the island.

With their altitude dropping, the details and features of the island became clearer. Like a cluster of golden-colored lights showing the unnatural impact of man's technology, they contradicted the organic edges of the coastlines. The lights were arranged with a mathematical precision of straight lines and perfect curves which defined homes, warehouses, office buildings, factories, roads, harbors, docks, rails, and airports. They sat quietly in awe when Holden shrieked with delight.

"Look at that!" he squeaked loudly, pointing out the three large, lighted squares which stood unevenly spaced several miles off shore on the north side of the island.

"Are those deep-sea oil-drilling platforms?" he said with astonishment, allowing a crack in his carefully crafted façade of omnipotent disinterest.

The aircraft banked again and slowed as it started on the downwind to the NTA runway. The pilot gave them a reminder to stay buckled up and banked again to enter the left base, and then made final approach, lining up with the lights which would indicate their path from here to the ground. The aircraft engine now sounded more erratic as the minute corrections in speed and altitude punctuated the well-rehearsed dance between aircraft and runway. The engine went idle as they neared the ground and with a modest raise of the nose, the aircraft released its defiance of gravity and fell gracefully to its wheels with a subtle double chirp of the rubber tires.

Much to their astonishment, upon exiting the plane they did not feel the extreme cold winds they had expected and had experienced at the last few airfields. The air seemed to hit them more like a warm springtime breeze.

"Why is it so warm?" asked Secretary Willis.

Holden Mealy shrugged, unable to offer an explanation when she turned to him expectantly.

"The NTA Main Airport runways are heated, Madam Secretary," the confident voice of Henry Foster answered her from the edge of the tarmac, his voice raised in an effort to overcome the sounds of the airport in the background.

"They are kept clear of weather at this time of year. It allows us a more predictable take off and landing schedule. It's an unfortunate paradox that our opportunity to bring your people the extravagant holiday celebrations of material goods they expect must happen at the most inopportune times of year for delivery." He punctuated the comment with a light chuckle.

They all noticed the tall, handsome, gray-haired figure of Henry Foster coming toward them, and he acknowledged them with a friendly gesture as he approached.

He stopped, just for a moment, and made note of the aircraft's Canadian registration number on the fuselage. He held up his mobile device and entered the number into it. He watched the screen, and it seemed to recall some specific data about the aircraft. He noted the information, smiled and put the device back into his pocket. Looking up at them again, he finished his stride toward them and once reached, he stretched out his hand in greeting.

"My name is Henry Foster; I am the vice president of customer relations," he said, shaking their hands, each in turn.

"You see, at this time of year, this particular airport is the busiest in the world. It is of course almost entirely cargo and not people that comes in and out. We have little need for passenger transport," he noted as he pointed to the lines of huge black airplanes that seemed to occupy every gate. They looked more like large military transports than airliners, with tails open, as not passengers but boxes were driven onto each by small, custom-designed, flatbed vehicles. The gates all attached to buildings that were obviously warehouses, not traditional terminals. There was an odd sense of daylight, as everything was so brightly lit; but with the black of the sky above them, it all seemed very surreal.

Brenda looked around at the continuous activity, not quite believing her eyes. Everywhere was the movement of aircraft taxiing in and out, cargo being loaded with the precision of a Swiss clock, people driving vehicles, signaling, loading, unloading, and fuel trucks and cargo trucks moving about like the ordered chaos of the most energized ant hill.

"There are so many people here," Brenda whispered sounding almost like a gasp, "Where did they all come from?"

The words slipped from her mouth almost as an involuntarily reaction to the overwhelming reality.

"Well, what did you expect," snarled Holden arrogantly, turning toward her, "Elves?"

She shot him a look of contempt.

Henry smiled at them and said,

"No, the elves are in our manufacturing plants, Mister Mealy. You should know that." Henry smiled at Brenda, almost with an implied wink.

"The Employee League of Fabricators, or ELF, is our manufacturing brotherhood, Madam Secretary. You will be meeting their representative shortly," Henry commented.

The pilot emerged from the aircraft and gave Henry a knowing nod. Henry responded with a nod back and excused himself for a moment, walking over to the pilot.

"She's a beautiful bird, isn't she?" Henry said to him pointing at the aircraft. "Is she as new as she looks?"

"Thank you, Mister Foster. Yes, brand new, the latest of everything," The pilot said proudly, and then looked at his passengers standing on the tarmac. He smiled at them and looked back at Henry.

"Well I'll just leave you to it then. Let me know when your meetings are done. I'll be bringing them back to the mainland tomorrow afternoon. Let me know if you need me, you know where I'm staying," the pilot continued.

Henry patted him on the back and nodded. The pilot picked up a bag and went off in his own direction, leaving the group in Henry's charge. Henry encouraged them to follow his lead to the nearest building.

As they walked from the tarmac toward the building, they noticed the airport control tower and, further beyond, a remarkable skyline of buildings and smokestacks. It seemed odd; everything had the feel of a modern facility but with a notably old-world aesthetic. Just beyond the airport all the buildings looked like perfectly preserved antiques, half-timbered and handcrafted in wood and stone that seemed uncommon in most modern cities of the world. What was not obviously industrial or technologically-based was ornate and decorative like the architecture of a past age.

They felt a strange sensation of the air around them cooling as they approached the building. The structure they entered was one of the few with windows and a traditional door. Most of the other buildings at the airport had large loading docks. Once they entered, they were asked to join Henry up an elevator which brought them to the main level. Through a number of large windows they saw the snow covered streets of the Kringle Works compound.

Henry pointed out the windows and said,

"There, across the street from the NTA Main Airport, you see the Nocturnal Transportation Authority headquarters building. You will be staying the night at the inn on the left and NTA personnel are currently moving your luggage from your aircraft to your rooms. So follow me to the NTA building; I will introduce you to our team. You haven't eaten, so you will have an opportunity to freshen up and then you will be having dinner with some key members of the Kringle Works staff. I know that you have concerns to cover with us and we will address these with you in the morning, but for now, let us show you a little portion of the facility and the teams that run them. Welcome to the Kringle Works!"

Walter Hayes leaned over to John and in a whisper said,

"Talk about putting the mice in charge of the cheese. I don't like them taking control of our agenda so quickly and I don't feel comfortable about them taking charge of our bags. Our evidence and case files are in there! And how does he know that we didn't have a chance to stop for lunch? Did you notice how he never asks any questions? Who is who? How was our flight? He just seems to know. I don't like it. It all seems a bit too cozy."

Though the thought had not occurred to John, he nodded in agreement and once reflecting on it, became somewhat curious if not a little unnerved.

Henry opened the door to the street. Brenda and Holden gasped as they looked at the sight around them. The street was snow-covered and the buildings were brightly lit. They saw a number of vehicles from commercial snowmobiles designed to move across the snow with a large payload of products and materials, to the fanciful quaintness of a single-person, caribou-drawn sleigh.

Henry noted that the activity was high considering the time of night, reporting that there were multiple shifts on the logistics side of the business at this time of the year. December was only a little more than a month away.

"Mister Foster, is it?" John interrupted Henry, "Who stays at the inn if you have so few visitors?"

Henry smiled.

"Agent Evans, but we do have visitors. Lots of them. It's just that they don't usually leave," Henry said.

John gave him an uncomfortable look as he pondered this thought.

"The inn is used to house new recruits for the NTA. We sometimes need to get new talent from the mainland, and until they are trained and have been officially assigned a job, they have no place to stay. The inn becomes their temporary home. Once they have been assigned they can move into a more permanent residence. As they earn their living they are put in contact with our real estate people to see what kind of housing is available to them. Based on their position and pay, they may choose where on the island they want to and can afford to live," Henry told them. "It's not unlike the capitalist system you live by in the United States, except here, we all work for the same employer."

"How can you call that a capitalist system?" Brenda questioned, "There is no competition."

"Of course there is," Henry replied, "We have shop owners who serve the work force. They compete for the business by having the best quality or the best price. We have restaurants that try to appeal to the island's population by offering styles and atmosphere, price, or convenience. We have people who leave a job at the Kringle Works to go into business for themselves helping other businesses that serve the people of our island. We have nearly half a million people who live here. Consultants, ad agencies, security and fire departments, stores, builders, radio and television studios, theaters, and concert halls--the only thing we do not have much of is politicians."

Henry looked at both Holden and Brenda with a level of amusement before finishing the thought,

"That task is managed mostly by the top executives who also run the primary company. I think, Madam Secretary, this seems to be more of a capitalist system than any other on the globe. Don't you agree?"

"But if you don't have politicians, this is not a free capitalist system," Walter interrupted.

Henry answered,

"Sure it is. The island's functions are run by the company and within that context the people can choose their careers, recreation and lifestyles. They may not have the opportunity to elect their leaders, but when was the last time you held an election of your boss? If you do not like working for one, you always have the choice to change jobs. The only thing you have to be comfortable with is that you are committed to the world's need for their Christmas service. The people of the island do not pay taxes. Municipal infrastructure and security are paid for by the profits of the company. Its towns and cities are run as part of the company's infrastructure just as one of your own private companies might maintain a series of facilities."

Later that evening, John and Walter met in the drawing room of the inn as they remarked on the brief tour they had received earlier. They were fascinated by the NTA technologies in both the front-end and back-end logistics of information-gathering, and the NTA delivery systems left them speechless and in awe. They amused themselves recalling the disgusted look of pain on Secretary Willis's face as they moved across the street in what Henry suggested was the seasonal norm of minus twenty degrees Fahrenheit. Though they were not expected to be ready for dinner for another thirty minutes, the two law enforcement professionals enjoyed a moment away from both their political colleagues and the presence of their hosts. The inn allowed them access to a quiet place to chat and share a drink. Both had been given a snifter of fine brandy as they made themselves at home in the plush surroundings of the room.

"This place is cold," John remarked, "I don't know if I could get used to it, but it's amazing how at home I feel once I'm inside."

He glanced around at the room and punctuated his thought with the sweep of his hand. He then held his glass up and looked at the fireplace through the translucent snifter, watching the flames flicker through the dark amber liquid.

Walter nodded,

"It's remarkable. My room was set up with my phone charger set on the night stand on the side I use it at home, my computer was plugged in, my clothes were arranged in the closet and my travel toiletries were arranged in the bathroom. I mean, not just in a way that makes sense, but in a way that makes me comfortable, the way *I* would have done it at home," he said in wonder.

"And the evidence and case files?" John asked.

"Carefully placed next to my computer, complete and unaltered," Walter replied with a shrug.

John, in answer, suggested an anecdote,

"Well, consider that you are back in the States and you go out shopping in the middle of December, set the alarm to your house and lock everything up. When you get home you unlock the house and shut off the alarm. Nothing's changed, but then an hour later you are wrapping a gift for your mother or father or something at Christmas, and then you notice the new boxes under your tree or in a stocking, marked *'From SANTA'* but you never ask *'How did those get here?'* you just accept it as normal, it's just what they do."

"I suppose," Walter conceded, "It's just a little unnerving to see it put into practice outside of Christmas. We spent our lives seeing and getting used to it around Christmas, but when you see it used in a different context you realize just how ominous it can be."

Walter pondered for a moment as he eyed his snifter of brandy.

"They seem open and willing to share their operations with us but I have heard nothing about how they do it. This Henry Foster seems to tell us a lot about the *why* things work but somehow I can't figure out *how* they work."

"Trade secrets, I expect," John interjected.

"Oh boy, I could sure use one of those!" the overtly flamboyant voice of Brenda Willis broke the relative quiet of the room as she entered.

Brenda was eagerly and furiously pointing at Walter's snifter of brandy. She looked around the room in hopes that someone capable of getting her a glass would hear her. She was smartly dressed, looking as though she had prepared for this dinner as a major international event. Appropriate and of fine quality, she looked the part of a diplomat with the one exception that the outfit seemed just a little too tight to look as impressive as she had apparently intended.

Like a charging bull, Brenda broke through the two men's conversation toward the fireplace. She reached it and turned around, and as if on cue, noticed the proprietor of the inn holding a snifter for her. The dapper but small-framed man almost seemed to flinch as Brenda screeched, raised her finger and stormed back to grab the glass he had stretched out in her direction.

"Ah, there you go! Thank you, my man!" she exclaimed, taking the glass and a quick swig.

Turning around to face her two travel companions, she raised her glass and stated,

"It's insanely cold on this island, but boy, they sure do know how to make one feel comfortable!"

She smiled eagerly at them waiting for a response.

"Certainly, Madam Secretary. Agent Evans here was just saying the same thing," Walter answered her.

After about ten minutes of small talk, Holden Mealy joined them, remarking how hungry he was. Then, with uncanny timing, Henry Foster joined them as well.

"All together?" he asked rhetorically, "We are eating at a small restaurant about one city block from here. It will take very little time but we are going by open sleigh, so bundle up since you're not used to our weather."

Henry motioned for them to leave the drawing room.

As they approached the front door he said,

"You will be dining with some of our top executives this evening: the head of the NTA, Jason Pelham; the head of ELF, Marcus Millerov; myself; and from our executive staff, Mister Andre Leopold and our CEO, Xavier Kringle. I apologize that Mister Kringle will have to leave early, but at least you will have the opportunity to meet him. Please, the sleigh is just outside the front door. Take one of the seats behind the driver's seat. Try to stay warm," he chuckled and smiled as he opened the front door for them to exit the inn.

Krystal Gardener was closing down the barn and her office. It was late and she had been preoccupied all day. Her mind was on a conversation she had overheard very early that morning. She was thinking about an unpleasant evening she had spent with Jason. Somehow she felt the two were linked.

"Production schedules" she thought to herself, recalling that early morning conversation. She did not know what to look for but Jason would, she thought, if she could make copies he could identify what was so incriminating.

Though Krystal had completed a very long day and thought longingly of home, she readied a sleigh and instead drove deeper into the compound.

The sleigh ride took about fifteen minutes, and just shy of the ELF manufacturing building, she removed her heavy coat and hat and tucked them under the seat. She then completed her ride to the front of the building. She jumped out and approached the front door, addressing the nighttime guard,

"Holy Christmas, I'm freezing!" she exclaimed.

"Ms. Gardener, what on earth are you doing, riding around like that? Please step inside the door," the guard suggested.

Krystal stepped in, rubbing her shoulders.

"Thanks!" she said gratefully, "It was so warm in my office and I was so preoccupied by my promise that I completely forgot to grab my coat. By the time I realized it, I was halfway here."

"That is the most foolish thing I have ever heard. What promise?" the guard inquired.

"Oh well, you know Mister Pelham is having dinner with some important people from America. Well, he made me promise to pick up his father this evening because there would be no way for him to do it," she explained.

"Yeah, I heard about the meeting with the folks from America. The whole compound is talking about it," the guard agreed. "So, what are you going to do now? Can you call someone to get your coat? You can get really hurt in that cold!"

"No, I just need to get warm and then I can make it back. I think Frank Pelham will have an extra jacket I can borrow," Krystal suggested.

The guard shook his head,

"Suit yourself but it sure sounds crazy."

"There is a favor you could do for me," she said coyly.

"Ms. Gardener, I can't leave my post. You know that."

She cocked her head and smiled.

"No; nothing like that. I was just wondering if you could let me go through the offices here and get to the Workshop's factory floor from there. I'll bring him back to my sleigh this way."

"Ms. Gardener, you are supposed to go around to the back of the manufacturing wing. I can't let you through here," the guard said.

"Please, the building is so huge and it will take me forever to get to the back entrance. Just let me walk through and have a chance to warm up and get back to my office to pick up my coat. Frank won't let me freeze, and you'll be doing Jason Pelham a big favor."

"This is the stupidest thing I have ever heard!" the guard snapped, "Okay, because it's you. Hurry back. I am going to call Peter Sharp just to let him know I let you through."

"I won't be long, I promise," Krystal said.

Krystal quickly dashed past the lobby and empty reception area and up the stairs to the ELF executive offices.

The night guard watched in stunned silence as she disappeared up the stairs. He shook his head as he got on his mobile device to call Peter Sharp, head of security.

Krystal knew exactly where to go. She headed for Jason Pelham's old office at the end of the hall. On one side at the end of the hall was an expanse of windows that overlooked the interior of the main manufacturing facility and a set of stairs that led down to it. On the other side was the closed and locked door of Jason's old office. The name on the ornately carved door read 'Marcus Millerov.' She looked through the window at the brightly lit factory floor of the Workshop and casually checked if anyone was looking up at her. No one noticed her; they all busily worked on their end-of-the-year manufacturing quotas. She tried to open the door, but could not. She glanced back down at the factory. Still, no one had noticed her. She started to reach around the frame of the door and felt for a small hole at the top corner.

"Ah, it's still here!" she said.

As though she was pulling a coin from behind a child's ear, like a simple magic trick, Krystal pulled a small key from the side of the door frame.

Krystal wondered if it would still work; have they changed the lock? She only knew about the key because Jason had showed her where he kept it. In years past, during the day when the building was open, he often had morning meetings with his manufacturing team, sometimes before he had made it to his office. All too often these meetings would go longer than expected and if Krystal was to meet Jason for lunch he wanted to be sure she would not be standing in front of a locked office door for twenty minutes.

Krystal slipped the key into the lock and slowly gave it a turn. She felt it resist when it gave way with a click. The sound was jarring in the quiet of the hall. With a last quick glance through the window at the Workshop, she slipped into the office and latched the door behind her.

Her idea was to find what she was looking for and go back, suggesting she looked for Frank but must have misunderstood. She knew his shift had already ended and he would not be there. A weak plan, but if anyone could pull it off it would be her, she thought.

She groped along the wall seeking the light switch.

Depressing the old-style switch, the light assaulted her eyes with a blinding flash. She clamped her eyelids shut involuntarily. Cupping her hands around her face, she slowly opened her eyes and started to look around the office. The large window that looked out over the manufacturing floor had a heavy curtain drawn.

"Good!" she thought to herself.

Jason always kept it open but it seemed that Marcus valued his privacy from the line workers more. In this case it was a benefit, as it kept her presence in the office concealed. Along with this manifestation resulting from the difference in behavior, so too, the office itself seemed familiar but different. She had spent many moments sitting in the guest chair watching and waiting while Jason took some ill-timed call or was wrapping up some report that he had estimated would not interfere with their lunch date, but did. She knew the room, the walls and furniture, but it was everything else that had taken on a character she did not recognize. Indeed, it seemed many things had changed. She wondered for a moment what drove her to come here and when, if ever, did she have an interest in lying to the security team.

"Okay, focus ... production schedules," she thought to herself.

She knew her time was short, so once she oriented herself she quickly went to the file cabinet looking for something that might be of value. She rifled through the files looking for documents that might be helpful. Rummaging through the top drawer she found nothing of interest. When she reached the second drawer, she noted the files and subfolders were marked alphabetically by category and by year. As she fingered past each one she whispered the names to herself,

"Annual Business Plans ... Finished Goods Reports ... Inventory Management, Issues: Supply Chain, Issues: Product ... Product Reports," she hesitated and said with a quiet enthusiasm, "Production Schedules!" she chuckled lightly, "This is almost too easy!"

She grabbed the contents of the current year and walked over to the desk; placing an inch-high stack of paper in front of her, she flicked on the desk lamp. Standing at the desk with her back to the door, she started to thumb through the various reports and though she did not know what she was looking for, she figured a comment in a margin or an additional note might indicate a document had more than the normal level of interest or value. Perhaps something that looked like it might be incriminating. She continued to fold back the papers of each report, studying each for what might be anomalies. Engrossed in her task, it took her a moment to react when she heard something. She turned and looked at the door of the office. She had not locked it, but it was still closed and latched. The office of senior manager of ELF, it was a large room, so she scanned it carefully. As she looked around she heard another shuffle. A nondescript sound, a movement, but still she saw nothing. Her eyes panned to the large curtain. Movement? She watched closely but now everything was still.

"Marcus?" she whispered, "Are you in here? I was looking for you. Marcus, I was looking for something and hoped you'd help me. I could really use your help. Marcus?" She wracked her brain, trying to think of an explanation, hoping that if he had entered, she might talk her way out of being caught.

There was no response. It was quiet. She focused on the room for a long while, but remembered that her time was running out. Though it seemed that there was no one here now, if she waited too long, there would be. Again, she reengaged her task and went back to studying the reports.

Suddenly, just as she stretched out her arm to fold over another page, someone grabbed it. She felt them yank her back away from the desk. She cried out in panic. She was trying to struggle loose when her assailant cupped her mouth from behind and pulled her close and off balance. She was unable to move. Her head was now pinned between his chest, shoulder, and the crook of his arm, which was wrapped across her mouth. She felt his breath on the lobe of her ear as he leaned closer and whispered,

"Find what you're looking for, Ms. Gardener? Maybe I can help point it out to you? You know we are prepared for things like this? This is bigger than you!"

Krystal felt a jolt as her arm was released and she tried to pull her head free when she felt a prick at the base of her neck. Her body shuddered. A sharp pain shot through her skull, and in an instant her body chilled, weakened; she became dizzy and her vision blurred. Then …

Everything went dark.

15

THE CONSPIRACY

Henry Foster, charged with the relationship between the Kringle Works and their customers, was up early that morning setting up the conference room, which was to be used for that morning's meetings with the delegates from the United States. He had ordered assorted teas, coffee, juices, pastries, and fruit. A team under Henry's direction set everything up against the back wall of the room with an eye toward perfection, the kind of attention to detail you would expect from the finest resort hotel. The gleam of the large chrome coffee urns acted as sentinels in the center of the long credenza, which was draped with a red tablecloth and held baskets of food and condiments. On each end were two expertly carved ice sculptures of reindeer, which punctuated the table's elaborate fare.

Henry looked everything over carefully and then took a document from his team's lead and signed it, indicating all was delivered and set up as ordered. With a nod Henry released his team.

Now alone, Henry looked at his watch and then looked around the room. He took a small computer tablet which he had laid on the conference table and placed it inconspicuously behind the food and drink on the credenza. He ran a power cord and plugged it in and propped it up.

He looked at the conference table and noted the cold-water pitchers, empty glasses, and the pens and note pads at each seat. All was ready and in order. He looked again at his watch and decided to lock up the room and head back to his office for the next twenty minutes. The meeting was to start in half an hour.

When Henry returned he found that Jason and Lorraine had already arrived. He bade them a good morning and unlocked the conference room door.

They entered and each took a spot at the table. Moments after, Marcus Millerov entered and with a grunt of acknowledgement sat down also. He snarled at Henry,

"So, where are they? Let's get this over with!"

Henry smiled politely and answered,

"They are on their way, Marcus. Don't worry. Andre is bringing them over."

Marcus sat back and grunted in response.

Henry got up, walked behind Marcus, put his hands on the back of Marcus's chair, leaned down toward his ear and said quietly,

"Have a cup of coffee, Marcus. You're not your usual, friendly self this morning, or worse, maybe you are."

Marcus smirked but did not respond.

Jason decided he wanted a cup and asked Lorraine if he could get her one as well.

Henry jumped forward and said quickly,

"I'll get them for you, stay seated, I'm up anyway," he smiled at them and turned to Marcus, "And you? Extra sugar, I assume?"

Peevishly, Marcus jeered,

"Black! No sugar! Thank you."

"Pity, already as sweet as you can be?" Henry responded sarcastically as he siphoned four cups and customized them for each, to their taste. He distributed the cups, the last one for Marcus. As he placed the cup on the table for him he said, teeth slightly clenched,

"Don't make this stink, ELF! This is bigger than you."

Jason interrupted them loudly,

"Gentlemen! Please! What is wrong with you?"

Henry smiled, inclined his head and sat back down. As he did, he answered Jason's call for civility.

"Of course, boss. You are right, of course," he suggested sheepishly.

"Andre will be here any moment with some important guests. Marcus Millerov is a senior member of the Workshop's management and my counterpart. That display was embarrassing at best."

He looked at Henry with bemusement and followed up,

"Disparaging ELF is disparaging me. It's where I grew up."

Marcus glowered at Jason and started,

"Listen, Jason, I don't need you to def--" Marcus's sentence cut short as Andre entered with their four guests.

Graciously, Andre started,

"Madam Secretary, Mister Mealy, Assistant Director Hayes and Agent Evans, you remember our management team from dinner last night? Ah, and here is a modest breakfast. Please help yourselves. I think you will find everything quite excellent."

Andre motioned for them to take what they desired.

Each took a cup and small plate, filled them and sat down at some of the open positions at the conference table. Walter put his cup down and pulled a large file from his briefcase. He placed it down with a slap and looked back at Andre inquisitively.

Andre reacted,

"Well, yes, I know that you have concerns that you would like to discuss, but I think it would be wise to first understand things from each other's point of view."

"Point of view?" Walter interrupted, "With all due respect, Mister Leopold, we have found Kringle Works's components in just about every electronic device manufactured in the last five years!" John Evans watched as Walter Hayes launched his verbal attack,

"We are having trouble finding products that do not have your electronics in them. The United States government does not like to be made fools of, Mister Leopold."

"I assure you, Assistant Director, we have no intention of making fools of you," Andre answered defensively, "Indeed, we abide by all international laws and the terms of the contracts we have signed with the various countries around the world. As we have with yours. The electronics you speak of are simply components we manufacture while fulfilling the terms of our commitments in providing goods as part of the Christmas Service."

Walter Hayes started to pull several documents from his file and followed up,

"But these components are not in products that were provided by the Kringle Works during the Christmas Holiday, but in everyday goods."

"The world has its problems, Assistant Director," a low and slow drone came from Marcus Millerov. He continued as all heads turned toward him, "Inefficiencies, capacity constraints, supply shortages; for the last ten years it has been the practice of some departments of the Employee League of Fabricators to offer our capacity to close some of these gaps and leverage our capacity and manufacturing prowess to regions beyond the normal Christmas Service."

Jason shot a bewildered look at Marcus. Glaring back, Marcus drew a narrow, contemptuous smile and continued,

"In fact, ELF has used its electronics division to supply many countries with various circuit boards and processors to maintain the world's demand. In other cases we have sold our resources such as raw materials, fuel, and even some logistics when needed."

"Yes, all to help in maintaining the public good across the world. We have kept many countries and companies from defaulting on their promises and this has allowed us to extend our reach," Andre said and smiled warmly, "much like your companies and your country. Yes?"

"Yes, but we are finding these components in our government's equipment, our computers!" John Evans said in a frustrated whine, pounding his hand on the table, "These components are not allowed; it's against our laws!"

"We are not bound by your laws under the terms of SANTA. We are not breaking any laws, Agent Evans."

John turned to her and responded,

"We have reason to believe that these components are potentially compromising our country's national security. We suspect that it is Kringle Works's technology that is a potentially hostile threat to the United States! Do you understand what that means, Ms. Barlow?"

"Agent Evans, we have never been a threat to your national security. In over a century we have never exercised any action against any sales territory due to any knowledge acquired through our technology or day-to-day business. We have always remained true to our contractual obligations and well within the constraints of international law," she refuted.

The nasal whine of Holden Mealy's voice interrupted them,

"We are the United States government, Ms. Barlow. We do not abide by international law. We write international law!"

Stunned by this comment, all eyes shifted to Holden. Suddenly aware that this was his opportunity to grab the attention, he continued,

"I have a list of demands from the president of the United States himself."

Holden puffed up his chest and pulled a paper from his jacket inside breast pocket. He shook it open with an unnecessarily flamboyant wave and after almost ceremoniously putting on a pair of reading glasses and clearing his throat, started reading out loud,

"The president would like to make the following items part of the official naughty behaviors list: eating too much salt, complaining or demonstrating about paying your taxes, driving an SUV or large truck, owning more than three guns, feeding your children fast food after six o'clock at night, chewing gum and blowing bubbles while on a White House tour--the first lady asked me personally to include that last one," Holden looked up at everyone and continued, "keeping the temperature in your house too hot or too cold--"

Holden Mealy was abruptly interrupted by a loud laugh. Looking up, he noted Andre Leopold staring at him with a big grin. Andre spoke,

"Of course, Mister Mealy! But you are setting the bar way too low. We will do all this and more. Let us start with the negotiations. Yes?"

"Negotiations?" Walter interrupted, "This has nothing to do with negotiations! We are defining a legal precedent and whether or not our laws have been broken."

"Your laws, Assistant Director, are always our concern and never compromised unless explicitly superceded by the mutual agreement of both the United States and the Kringle Works," Lorraine said confidently, jumping back into the conversation.

"I think you will find the legal implications of your concerns are quite unfounded under the technological elements of the SANTA Clause," she continued.

"Ms. Barlow, with all due respect, our laws do not allow for you to sell product to the United States government. Still, the evidence suggested that your product is in our government's electronics," Walter argued, as he pulled out some close-up photos of the ICU chips accompanied by a list of devices used in government offices. Lorraine looked at the photos intently.

"Indeed, if they are there, then their presence is covered by the SANTA Clause. How they got there is a concern you have to bring up with the manufacturer of the electronics," Lorraine rebutted and continued, "We have not manufactured any devices and products directly for your government. If the products you are discussing are Kringle Works products, then they came to you through regular commercial channels; if they are a component within another manufacturer's product, then your problem is with this other manufacturer."

"What do they do?!" John interrupted the discussion abruptly, "What do the components, these chips, do?"

Lorraine cocked her head, turning to John and responded to his outburst,

"For technical questions, I think you may want to address Marcus Millerov from ELF, Agent Evans. They are the ones that build it."

John looked at Marcus and asked,

"What do they do?"

"I can't tell you that, Agent Evans," Marcus snarled slowly, talking past his hands which were touching each other at the fingertips to form a triangle, giving him a quiet, pensive look, "The designers, Agent Evans, only the designers, can tell you that. It seems that they enhance the functionality but I have never been able to see a specific functional attribute in my tests and quality checks. Isn't that right, Henry?"

Marcus turned to Henry Foster.

Henry smiled. He looked John Evans in the eye and said,

"They are part of a shadow network that allows us to see the machine. You know, if we need to service or refurbish it. It has other functions also, but these are all very legitimate and covered by the terms of our contracts with you."

Andre jumped back into the discussion with authority,

"There you see? All legally acceptable; Lorraine and Jason, please take our friends from the FBI to see our legal team. I think that they will find their concerns are quite unfounded. Please allow them to voice any charges, and the legal department will certainly address them appropriately."

Henry Foster jumped to his feet and suggested,

"Andre, I'll join Jason and Lorraine to be sure that Agent Evans and the assistant director are well accommodated and all questions answered."

"Of course, Henry, please do," Andre agreed.

Jason, confused, got up as Lorraine and Henry did. Henry motioned for Lorraine and their two guests to exit as he held the door for them.

Lorraine, taking the leading stride, started down the hall while Henry and Jason followed her, John, and Walter.

Henry held Jason back a little and called out to Lorraine,

"Lorraine, please take our guests and go ahead without us. Jason and I have some additional paperwork to gather from my office. We will join you in a few minutes."

Henry stretched out his hand, motioning Jason to go toward Henry's office. He got somewhat frantic and hurried Jason along.

As they walked, Henry said with a sense of urgency,

"Jason, quickly! I don't want to miss anything. I think you might find this interesting. That is, *if* my suspicions and timing are correct."

Upon entering Henry's office, Jason noticed the ICU workstation fully powered up and set to view the island. Henry quickly closed the door behind them and sat down at the station, encouraging Jason to join him at the screen.

He typed in the name *Andre Leopold* and the feverishly active screen quickly settled to a few quiet and inactive windows with two that appeared to be functioning in the foreground. One was of a video feed which looked out at a conference room framed by the blurry, dark edge of a croissant on one side and the gleaming chrome leg of a coffee urn on the other. Just beyond a short strip of red cloth were Marcus Millerov, Holden Mealy, and Brenda Willis. Pacing back and forth in front of them and the conference room table was the slender figure of Andre Leopold. The other computer window showed the undulating sound bar of an audio feed. Henry used the curser, slid up the volume bar and Andre's voice came to life,

"We too have an underclass of law enforcers, our own version of paid, heavy-tusked walruses to keep order, but they can sometimes think too much in the terms of their training, too much in terms of black and white. Yes?"

Holden and Brenda nodded their heads in agreement, but looked a bit bewildered.

Andre continued,

"The Kringle Works has for too long been suffering from the archaic idea that our technology and resources are inappropriate in the hands of any government. That it would inappropriately alter a balance in the world. Yes? However, this is an old idea, one that needs to be rethought. Still, it will never happen as long as the people who insisted on this notion remain in control of it."

Marcus quietly watched as Brenda and Holden followed Andre's pacing figure.

"Give me that list, Mister Mealy; the one with your president's requests," Andre politely demanded.

"So then can I tell the president you will agree to his requests?" Holden smiled and asked.

"Mister Mealy, do you know what I see when I read this list?" Andre asked.

Holden did not answer.

"No? No thoughts? I see a president who wants his people to get out of his way to make things happen. I see a president who is weak and unable to move. I see a president who has been beaten by his own country." Andre stopped pacing and leaned across the table and continued, "I see a president who is the most powerful man on Earth, but he cannot consolidate his power. You understand me now, yes?"

Holden looked at Andre. He turned to face Brenda Willis and turned back to Andre and spoke sheepishly,

"I think so."

Andre looked both Brenda and Holden in the eyes. He alternated glances between them and began again,

"Do you wish to have your president to win his next election?"

189

"Well, yes. Of course!" Holden answered.

Andre smiled at them and looked at Brenda,

"And you, Madam Secretary, would you like to be able to hand that election to the president?"

Brenda nodded.

"Yes, I thought so," Andre suggested and continued, "I can help you hand it to him. I can make your president the strongest in your history. I can make him the president who can make the changes he desires."

Andre started pacing again, held up Holden's note and waved it in the air and said,

"Real changes--not just petty issues born of a president who has been frightened from action, but real changes with substance. Yes?"

Holden seemed more interested, more confident, and raising his voice now asked,

"What are you suggesting, Mister Leopold?"

Andre stopped pacing and looked at him and said,

"What I am suggesting, Mister Mealy, is that if you want to change what your people do, you and your president must stay in power long enough to change things. To do this you need to know what your voters are thinking about, what they do, what motivates them. Then you know how to talk to them and get them to elect you again and again. That is how you do it. Yes? I can offer you this ability. I can put the power of the Kringle Works technology in your hands, but only if it is mine to give you."

Stunned, the two Washington, DC insiders tried to process the implied offer from this Kringle Works executive. After a moment Brenda spoke,

"So what do we need to do?"

Andre smiled.

"Tell your president that if he will help me take control of the Kringle Works then I will sell him access to the information that is the byproduct of the Christmas Service. If he uses it correctly, yours will be the last political party to control your White House. You will be able to offer your leaders something that they have wanted for as long as we have both existed. You give me the sword of the United States and I will give you the eyes and ears of the Kringle Works."

An excited look washed across the faces of Brenda Willis and Holden Mealy. They were about to answer when the screen that Jason was watching went silent and black. Henry had turned it off and was getting up.

"Come now, we can't take any more time. Someone might get suspicious," Henry said, and hurriedly continued, "Jason, you wanted proof, now we have both heard it from Andre directly. Let's go!"

"We have to go see Xavier!" Jason exclaimed.

Henry shook his head,

"No, not yet! We can talk about this later, but at least now we know a lot more."

The two men started out the office door and up the hall to meet Lorraine and the legal team at their offices.

The look of frustration and displeasure on the faces of John Evans and Walter Hayes was almost as obvious as the look of self-indulgent triumph on the faces of Holden Mealy and Brenda Willis when they met again outside of the conference room an hour later.

"This isn't over," Walter grumbled under his breath, "I will not let their insidious legal double-talk win this war. The day and this battle, but not the war. This isn't over."

"Oh, but we have won the war," Holden Mealy interrupted quietly, hearing Walter's comments, "I think that this has been a most successful and productive endeavor."

Holden's face contorted into a mischievous smile and he turned to Brenda Willis, giving her a knowing nod.

Jason was now both confused and a little panicked as the feeling that with every new bit of knowledge and every new development, things seemed to get further from his control and understanding. He looked around at the assembled group. Andre, Holden, and Brenda seemed content, while by contrast John and Walter shared a look of frustrated dissatisfaction. Lorraine and Marcus stood to the back and Henry had that look of omnipotent knowing that seemed to grace his visage most of the time.

The overwhelming desire to share some of this morning's events with Xavier preoccupied Jason to the point that he was almost oblivious to the conversations and events taking place at that moment. Xavier was always so close to Andre, how could he not have seen this? A feeling of uneasiness washed over him at the thought that perhaps Xavier was part of the conspiracy, but then he was the potential victim of its ends. It was all very confusing. Still, Henry was always so sure of himself, maybe he was right to wait and gather more information. It seemed to be the best course, at least for now.

"It was a pleasure to meet you, Mister Pelham," the voice of John Evans jarred Jason from his thoughts. "I admit the developments are not as I had hoped or expected, but I did enjoy both meeting your team and my stay. Will you let me call you with some questions? I still have a lot of questions."

Jason nodded.

"Sure, Agent Evans, it would be my pleasure," he responded.

Andre was already making arrangements with some NTA personnel to gather their guests' belongings and then proclaimed that he would take them back to meet their aircraft personally, citing that he wanted to take the remaining minutes to discuss some additional details with Holden and Brenda.

"You have a plane to catch, yes?" Andre pointed out and with a natural flair and authority, he ushered the Americans on their way.

"Well I'm glad that that pile of reindeer dung is out of here!" snarled Marcus upon their exit, "Still, Andre seemed to be able to defuse that situation." Marcus chuckled contemptuously and followed up, "He's not as dumb as I thought. I'll be in my office catching up, if you need me."

192

He threw his coat around himself, turned abruptly and left.

Lorraine nodded at Henry and Jason and suggesting that she too needed to catch up on the work for the morning, bade them a good day.

Jason then turned to Henry and said,

"We should talk to Xavier. We really shouldn't let them leave."

Henry shook his head and reassured Jason,

"We need more information. You can see that this is just part of the equation."

"But the Americans! You heard Andre's offer!"

Henry smiled at Jason and suggested,

"I don't think they will be able to act on their information; I know these people, trust me. Haven't I proved to be right so far?"

Jason nodded and acknowledged,

"Yes, but we are taking risks here; we should act soon."

Henry agreed and looked at his watch,

"Okay, Jason, soon. We will act soon, but for now I, too, have a plane to catch!" He paused and smirked, "You know ... delivery schedules!"

Agent John Evans was visibly vexed while he watched Holden Mealy and Brenda Willis as they seemed to be having a particularly jovial and animated, yet private, conversation near the back of the aircraft. Walter's frustrations seemed to make him pensive. He quietly stared out the window as their plane started its take off rotation. The sound of the engine made it impossible for John to make out the conversation just six feet away, but he felt he knew that somehow the United States was being swindled. Tom had been right all along, not about whom, but certainly what. The ICU chips were watching them. That much he figured out, but there was more to it. Perhaps even more than they could have imagined; but for now, the investigation was halted. Halted, all because a couple of Washington bureaucrats seemed to get something they wanted and an ancient document that was full of legal loopholes designed for the purpose of the Kringle Works's exploitation kept them at bay.

His frustrations were gnawing at him as they seemed to turn to anger. He looked back at the odd couple leaning into each other, still talking and laughing.

"These two couldn't stand each other a day ago!" John said to himself; he shook his head and decided to look out the window instead.

He watched as they passed over the frozen streets of the island's oddly developed metropolitan areas. It was even more difficult to believe the sight of the buildings, infrastructure, and technology of this arctic landmass in the daylight. All points north, east, west, and a significant area to the south of the Kringle Works was almost uninhabited, but here in the middle of it all was this island with as much technology and population as any similar-sized areas of the United States. This place was truly surreal, he thought, as the aircraft climbed further.

John was now allowing his mind to drift as he looked out at the partially frozen waters of Baffin Bay. The sun seemed to have just attempted its rise only to remain low in the sky, already conceding to its setting in just a few hours. The light cast an odd amber glow over the white frozen details of the bay. Every ripple, every iceberg, expressed its features in bright orange on the sunlit side only to succumb to the darker shades of blue on the other. The almost black waters below contrasted the frozen sections and landmasses while a large, dark gray mass ominously blurred the horizon to the north in an otherwise crystal clear sky.

"It's a very strange world the people of the Kringle Works live in," he thought to himself.

John was never a fan of the Christmas holiday. It seemed more trouble than it was worth, and for his part he knew that between his family's disapproval and the now-apparent observations of the Kringle Works, he was never going to live by a standard that would earn him the yuletide rewards that others so coveted at the end of December. Still, as fascinating as this brief visit was, it seemed to have savagely stripped him of some dear childhood memories of the season.

"Of course the Kringle Works would be huge," he contemplated quietly to himself, "Look at all they do around the globe. It's just that no one really thinks much about it."

Now for a brief moment that same childhood would flood back into his body, forcing an involuntary smile to punctuate another thought,

"But, I got to meet Santa Claus face-to-face." As he remembered the events of the evening before, "I had dinner and drinks with him and I have seen a part of his workshop. I got to meet Santa's helpers. How many people can say that?"

John's smile turned into a subtle laugh as his mind drifted past this concept. He considered that he might have been willing to kill his own puppy for this chance as a child, maybe he could even have been persuaded to kiss a girl.

Still, it was a harsh reality that one has to grow up. This was never more obvious to John as he thought about the business-like efficiencies of how the Workshop operated and that when he actually had the opportunity to meet Santa Claus, it would be to accuse him of illegal practices.

"There is a spot of severe weather to our north and though we will be staying well south of it, the clouds will be gathering around us as we approach the mainland. It may get just a little bumpy, so please keep your seatbelts fastened for the remainder of the flight." The voice of their pilot on the speaker yanked John from his thoughts.

His frame of reference back to the present and sitting closest to the cockpit, John became more acutely aware of the pilot's radio calls.

"Caravan Charlie Golf Sierra Zulu Whisky, climbing to twelve thousand feet, squawking IFR, one-zero-zero-zero for Canadian Airspace. Thank you, Kringle Works, have a g'day!"

The pilot completed his maneuvers and as predicted, as the flight continued the clouds started to obscure their ability to see the landscape below.

Between the short days and the gathering clouds, the view out of the aircraft became considerably darker and John now noticed that he could make out snow flying past his window, illuminated by the aircraft's lights.

Undeterred and unfazed, the pilot went about his business, when for just a moment he seemed to lose Canadian Flight Service's communications. He repeated his call and heard a different voice come on line to give him further guidance. He speculated that Canadian Air Traffic Control might be a little busier than he would have thought, perhaps due to the weather, and did not give it another thought.

The new voice on the radio gave him a corrective heading of two-seven-zero. The pilot acknowledged the heading and looked down at the avionics screens. Suddenly his heart jumped as all three electronic screens went momentarily blank before coming back on line without issue. Making a call to alert Canadian Flight Service of this, they responded by suggesting he hold his course and check his instruments. He acknowledged and said that all seemed to be in order.

"Maybe a faulty fuse," he suggested, "I'll have everything checked after we touch down."

Canadian Flight Service acknowledged and repeated his heading of two-seven-zero.

The pilot acknowledged and shut off the autopilot to manually compensate.

With visibility nearly gone he made the correction watching his instruments and turning slightly to the right. He noted that during the turn he seemed to gain too much altitude and adjusted for it, getting back down to twelve thousand feet.

After holding his course for a few minutes, Canadian Flight Service indicated that the weather system coming from the northwest was pushing him off course to the south and slowing his progress. He would have to adjust his heading to three-zero-zero.

Acknowledging the correction, he turned the nose of his plane further to the right. The turn seemed to take much longer than he would have guessed. More alarming was his continued gain in altitude as he made the turn. Again, he made the correction and dropped his altitude until his instruments indicated twelve thousand feet.

The flight was getting significantly bumpier and visibility was now down to a dark gray backdrop to the white streams of snowflakes that flew at and past the aircraft.

Becoming a little uneasy, the pilot called Flight Service for a weather briefing, as he thought that he should be closer to his destination by now and should start his descent.

Flight Service agreed but for the significant increase in wind slowing his progress, and commanded he adjust his heading to three-two-zero.

It felt wrong, but between Flight Service, the flight instruments, and his GPS screen it seemed he was making the correct adjustments and slowly crabbing his way toward the airport at Pond Inlet, Canada.

The flight became even bumpier and he glanced back at his passengers to be sure they were buckled up. They had all grown very silent but did not appear particularly concerned. He gave John an apologetic look and started making his next course correction. Three-two-zero. Again, he corrected for a significant altitude gain during the turn.

A moment later the plane suddenly and very violently lurched.

"Bloody hell!" the pilot exclaimed, which was punctuated by a collective gasp from the passenger cabin.

Now everyone looked more panicked, and the pilot felt he would have to make an announcement to keep everyone calm.

"The weather seems to have come in much quicker than we anticipated," the pilot suggested on the aircraft's speaker system, "Please remain calm, and be advised that we are only a few minutes from our final descent into Pond Inlet. Chin up! Everything will be fine." He paused and continued, "The bad news is, I don't think you are likely to get back to Toronto today."

Maintaining course, the pilot decided again to ask for a weather briefing but this time received no answer. The aircraft was now consistently bouncing around.

The plane lurched violently, highlighted by the panicked scream of Brenda Willis.

He steadied the aircraft again and made another call to Flight Service,

"Caravan Charlie Golf Sierra Zulu Whisky, we are getting our bloody asses kicked up here. Please verify heading and wind direction!"

There was no reply.

"Shit!" he exclaimed in a moment of frustration.

"This is Caravan Charlie Golf Sierra Zulu Whisky, is there anyone there? Please verify heading, wind direction, and location! Please respond!" the pilot anxiously requested.

There was no reply.

"Hello! Hello! Hello!" he called, tapping his headset's microphone.

Still, there was no reply. He tried a number of other frequencies but none generated an answer. He looked down at his flight instruments and the brightly colored GPS suggested he was still on course and was now no more than ten miles east of the airport.

Convinced that he was having radio problems, he reset his transponder to seven-six-zero-zero to signal Air Traffic Control of his loss of communications and proceeded to make a cautious descent. Eleven thousand, ten thousand, nine thousand; flying over the waters of Baffin Bay and with thousands of feet of altitude, he was reasonably comfortable that he was safe. If only he could get under the weather then he could orient himself visually. He dropped their altitude another thousand feet. He watched his instruments carefully. He switched his GPS into weather mode only to have the screen go blank. He quickly attempted to go back to GPS mode but it seemed the screen had shut down.

"Shit! What in the bloody hell is going on?!" the pilot rhetorically questioned.

John looked over suddenly as he heard the audible cry of frustration from the cockpit.

Trying to stay calm, the pilot disregarded the blank screen and watched the others for his avionics. He dropped another thousand feet and thought he might be nearing the cloud ceiling. Then without warning, all of his avionic screens went blank save for one new status window, which he had never seen before.

I'm sorry, but this screen is no longer receiving data and restoring will not be possible. Goodbye.

The pilot's eyes widened with panic as he was now completely blind. His mouth dropped open as words failed him, reading the almost mocking text that now graced the screens where his trusted instruments were to be.

Regaining his composure, the pilot quickly tried to calculate his rate of descent.

With the aircraft still dropping in altitude, he determined the time it would take before he would be in danger of being too low, based on his last altimeter reading of twelve thousand feet.

Then, a moment of relief as they emerged from the clouds, but this moment was fleeting.

The pilot's brief second of relief turned to extreme panic when he realized that not only was his altitude much lower than he had anticipated but he was now facing a wall of rock and ice, as he had descended into the Treuter Mountains of Devon Island many miles north of their expected location.

His eyes growing wider and he recoiling into his seat, the pilot mouthed the words, "Oh, my God!" but no sounds came from his clenched, dry throat.

He throttled up and pulled the yoke back all the way into his chest, desperately hoping to climb enough to scale the mountain ahead of them. The engine whined and the aircraft's nose rose abruptly. Papers, books, laptops, and briefcases went flying through the cabin. Holden cried out when an open computer hit him, inflicting a two-inch-long gash on the side of his head. The motion was so severe that Walter's seat reclined without warning, knocking his head back so hard, a sharp pain shot through his neck.

The aircraft shuddered as the nose continued to rise and a wall of snow-covered stone sailed past the belly of the plane.

Brenda was now screaming in terror. This sound was obscured only by the squeal of the stall-warning horn of the aircraft. The plane buffeted, signaling what the pilot had hoped to avoid. The aircraft had aerodynamically stalled. The nose dropped sharply. Flight had ceased. There would not be time to regain full control of the plane before they impacted the side of the mountain.

The left wing dipped as the aircraft started to spin, but before it was able to complete a full rotation, the wing hit a protruding ledge. The wing ripped from the fuselage, with a fireball accenting the moment as the windows on this side shattered.

The lights went out.

The smell of smoke, melting plastic, and aviation fuel permeated the cabin as the cold belied the flames that left a trail behind them. Snow somehow managed to find its way into the cabin.

The nose and prop lurched to the right as the blades hit the snow-covered rocks. Pieces of the prop broke loose and large fragments broke through the cockpit windshield and shot through the cabin, taking parts of the cockpit and pilot with them as they ricocheted from left to right, making the horrific sound of metal chunks clunking and clanking as they indiscriminately hit and shattered parts of the interior.

The plane flipped and Brenda Willis's seat broke from the floor and fell to the ceiling with her hopelessly strapped inside. Flipping again, the right wing broke free and with a loud crack, the back half of the fuselage separated and rolled off to one side. The open back half of the cabin filled with snow and ice as its momentum on the snowy surface had the effect of scooping and packing the snow into the tail section like a macabre version of a giant snow cone machine. The front half of the aircraft spun along the snow-covered surface and flipped over as it came to rest against a sharp incline leading up the mountain.

Then, as if nothing had happened, the mountainside was quiet.

He was shivering when John Evans opened his eyes. He was unsure if he had been there for just seconds or much longer. It was dark. The silence of the mountain was broken by the sound of the wind whistling through the shattered aircraft's broken body. He was disoriented and it took him a long time to understand that he was hanging upside down, still strapped into his seat. He looked ahead and recognized the back of the pilot's seating, but everything forward of this point was a combination of debris and snow. The snow took on a shade of dark gray as the overcast sky's light dimmed with the setting sun. He turned to his right and saw the seat in which Walter Hayes had sat. The seat was intact, but there was no sign of the occupant. With a sharp pain in his shoulder, John turned to look behind him but saw nothing but the open landscape. Some areas were illuminated by a small series of fires still burning as the sun continued its descent. Still shivering, he felt the warm trickle of blood running from his left ear to the top of his head. He looked up to see the snowy ground and a puddle of blood below him.

Finally, after a long pause, John freed himself from the belts that still tied him to his seat and he fell into the snow below him.

16

THE VULTURES CIRCLE

Krystal Gardener's eyes were burning as she opened them, which added to a discomfort she felt from a hollow pounding in her head and the subtle feelings of nausea. Her throat felt swollen and dry.

Taking several deep breaths, she tried to focus on the room she was in. Lying in a bed on a luxurious down comforter, she attempted to sit up and look around. It was a well-appointed room, ornately trimmed and tastefully decorated. She thought that were it not for her physical distress, she might have awoken quite comfortable. The room smelled of pine and spice. Clean and bright, the room belied the dark that would appear outside the windows at this time of year. Still, she thought it ominous that all the room's windows were curtained and drawn closed. Ahead was a beautiful curtain of decorative fabric; it was sheer to a point, allowing her to see the rest of the room beyond and the door at the end, but in so little detail that she could barely discern the shapes of the furniture. She lifted her hand to find that she was chained to the wall behind the bed. The chain would allow her freedom of movement from the bed to the bathroom behind her, but not to the long floor-to-ceiling curtain ahead.

She sat for a long while. Her head was heavy, and placing her elbows on her knees, she rested her head in her hands, slumping over and hoping the feeling of sickness would pass.

Krystal took another deep breath and coughed. She put her head down and closed her eyes. For another hour or so--she was not sure how long--she was left alone.

Then the sound of a lock turning, a door opening and a number of footsteps, then as if by design she recognized a male figure appear at the front of the room, disguised by the curtain. Krystal tried to make out a face but could not.

"Who's there? Marcus?" she questioned abruptly, "Where am I? What do you want from me? What happened? Tell me who you are!"

The room stood silent for a moment after her inquiry. Then a quiet, slow and measured voice answered,

"Who I am is not important now; I came in to check to see if you were awake and to give you this."

The figure walked to the edge of the curtain and tossed a bottle of fruit juice from behind it and to her on the bed.

"Drink it! You will feel better," the voice instructed sympathetically.

"I feel like crap! What did you do?" she responded.

"I'm sorry about the aftereffects of the tranquilizer; they should pass soon. Think of it like a hangover. We had to subdue you. You see, we knew that eventually people would get hurt, but we do try to keep this to a minimum. Still, you gave us no choice."

Krystal grabbed the bottle and looked at it skeptically. She noted the intact seal on the bottle and decided it might be safe to drink. She cracked the seal on the cap and being parched, she took a couple of cautious sips. Feeling better after these, she drank greedily and too fast. She coughed and gagged. Her throat tightened and she hunched over as she choked up some liquid, which she involuntarily allowed to drip from her mouth. Still, after a moment she felt better, the cool drink rehydrating and rejuvenating her.

"You see, Ms. Gardener, you're a very hard person to keep track of. No social media, extremely little use of landlines or mobile phones, almost no e-mail and Internet usage, no web cam, no television, your house is a virtual black hole; but no matter, we can see you when you are at work or in public areas and I dare say that makes you a bad girl, a very, very, very bad girl," the voice suggested.

The events that led to her being in the position she was in notwithstanding, she shot him a bewildered look and in an unnaturally drawn out tone, defiantly said,

"Why?"

"What, you don't think so?" The voice paused for a moment and then answered with a question,

"Well that's the rub, isn't it? Good or bad, it's all a matter of by which person's interpretation you are to be judged and since I am the one in control here, you're going to be judged by my standards," the voice continued.

"You see, that's the flaw in the system. It's only as good or as moral as those by which you are judged."

"So!? That's the way it has always been," she snapped back with venom, "Who are you to judge? What makes you a good moral barometer; are you suggesting you are any better? Look what you've done to me!" she held her hand up to make the chain more obvious, "You've chained me up like a zoo animal, you drugged me and you've given me no opportunity to explain myself--"

He responded firmly, interrupting her impending rant,

"We know what you were doing!"

Then more calmly, he continued,

"And no, Ms. Gardener, I am not suggesting I'm any better, but at least I'm aware of my potential corruption," he said and continued, "Indeed, in my own way, even my most sinister efforts would bring about a world of peace and order."

The voice paused, thinking before continuing. Krystal saw the figure take a seat behind the curtain and thoughtfully watch her through it. Then he answered with his own question,

"Did you know that the Kringle Works gave a huge bounty of gifts to a small group of people because of the *good deeds* they did by killing a number of their enemies, who had the audacity to live in their community? There's a group in China whose Christian beliefs are considered unpleasant by the government, so they are rewarded at *Christmas* for publicly denouncing their religion and for pointing out their own religious leaders to the government so that they can be held accountable for preaching it. Don't even get me started on the contradictions in Ireland. The way things are now, our résumé is full of these foul and rotten examples, and we just obediently carry them out for these corrupt and unworthy customers."

Krystal could not see his face but she could hear the carefully restrained and hidden anger beneath what sounded like clenched teeth. The man took a deep breath and followed up calmly,

"No ... No, the problem with the whole system is that it is the wrong people who are judging what is right and wrong, what is good and bad. The governments we have served for over a century have proved themselves the unworthy masters of their populations. The only way to make things work, to make things right is for a better, new set of leaders to tell *the governments of the world* what the standard should be. They won't listen and cannot be trusted to control their people. So, we will have to control them as they use us to control their own."

The man got up and started to pace behind the curtain when he continued,

"You see ..." he paused, "The people are just the unwitting slaves of their representative governments, the best of which are like insatiable leeches that suck the lifeblood from their populations. The people then foolishly and euphorically rejoice when the body politic belches up a modest excess of their own blood for them to take back. And you know what, Ms. Gardener? We are just contributing to that effort. We are just another entitlement that the body politic uses to appease the population in its effort to hide its true motivations to simply continue to feed itself. It's ugly and sloppy and unsustainable. And the final result? Each of these governments will eventually need to feed on each other when they have sucked their people dry. And in so doing, will destroy the world one war, one treaty, one negotiation at a time."

"No, Ms. Gardener, we cannot allow that to go on! It must be stopped before they destroy the world!"

"You understand Ms. Gardener? We can change all that, we alone have the ability to control everything, we alone can save the world from itself and they would never know it happened."

Krystal watched the pacing figure for a moment and then with a tone that was almost contemptuous and slow she questioned,

"Really? How?"

"Ah yes, well let's just say that for years we have been organizing numbers of like-minded people, and we are ready to stretch out our hand to some of the most powerful people in the world."

He stopped pacing and looked at her through the curtain. He seemed to consider his words again and started his pacing once more.

"You see, Ms. Gardener, we here on the island are the smartest, the most innovative and the most visionary, but we are not the strongest. No, our founder was good at creating a global business but not at creating a global power, something our current leaders have neglected; but we believe that this was not far from Christopher Kringle's mind. We think he felt that eventually we would be a global power, and as such, be able to improve the world because we can improve man's own fundamentally flawed behavior."

'A man's ability to give is dwarfed by his ability to take. Those who profit by fulfilling man's need to take by giving will be the most powerful on earth.'

"You see, he said that when he opened the doors to his fifth US factory, and now, a couple centuries later, we are ready to fulfill his vision because we *are* fulfilling the need, and are in a position to be the most powerful, but we will need to exploit those who are the strongest by partnering with them."

Through the curtain, Krystal saw him stop pacing and retake his seat. He leaned forward and continued,

"While some of our senior management have been content to improve the status quo, we have been maneuvering to get to the next level and expand on what it can do. They have been happy to just listen and evaluate; in the words of Chris Kringle,"

'Our success will be based on listening and knowing our customers when they are not aware we are listening and learning.'

"However, *we* have been rethinking the application of the technology. Perhaps, to sell it to the most powerful governments, indeed to the beast itself; then we can work within the belly of the beast to expand our ability to reach back and influence it. Yes, then we can gain the power to control them from within and reshape them to lead the world as we would have them lead it. Do you understand me?"

"No, I do not! Do you really think I'd have any idea what you're talking about? You're talking in circles; and why in the name of Christmas are you telling me this?" Krystal questioned defiantly.

The voice responded quietly and measuredly,

"I am telling you this because I am hoping you can help us. We are so close to executing the first stages of our plans."

"Great! You are quite mad, aren't you? You do realize that? Still, in your mind, it sounds like you have everything well in hand. Trust me--there is nothing I can help you with. So why don't you just let me go? I promise to stay out of your way. I'll even get a home computer so you can watch me!" she sniped back.

"Ms. Gardener, you know I can't let you go. Not yet," he said quietly and continued, "You have forced us into action and I think that you might be a valuable asset to us, once you understand us, but for now you will have to remain here."

'Do not lament the suffering we have to endure to fulfill the dream but rejoice in the courage with which we will face it.'

"Spare me the history lesson," Krystal snapped, rolling her eyes, "You want me to suffer? Bring it on; I'm not going to be useful to you."

"Ms. Gardener," he said with a hint of condescension, "we don't want you to suffer. If that were the case, you would be in a much more unpleasant situation now, but you intruded on us, and we do fear what led you to look and what motivated you. So a degree of suffering will be at hand; for now it's your incarceration with us, but like Christopher Kringle, we are looking to fulfill a dream, a better world. So, this is a quote that I find quite appropriate. You see, he said it to the many pioneers who were to go to the island knowing that their journey and settlement would be one of sacrifice. Yes, I do believe the quote, it applies here quite well," the man behind the curtain suggested calmly.

"You see? Most of the people who might want to stop us don't know enough to look. Some look but don't know what they are looking for. We can watch these and divert them. Those who are getting too close can be neutralized. Still, there are those who have slipped through our fingers or are too close, key people, and must be dealt with in different terms. People like you, for instance." He continued, "I hope you are feeling better. You may not have noticed, but there is a phone on the nightstand. It will not let you dial out but it will allow you to call one of my associates should you need anything. You may not feel like it, but you should eat something. Let us know what you like. Good day, Ms. Gardener."

Krystal saw the figure get up, take a polite bow and quietly open the door to exit.

With the sound of the door latch, she groaned in frustration and then fell silent, the singular sound of a clink of the chain at her wrist a reminder of her situation. She placed her head in her hands.

Flowers were a luxury that the majority of the population on the Kringle Works Island could not afford, which is why Jason Pelham was extremely upset when his effort to apologize by having Krystal Gardener's home filled with them seemed to go completely unacknowledged.

Raymond Dunbar went out of his way to give his boss an opportunity to make things right between him and his girlfriend, and like any NTA gift delivery system's operation, it was reportedly perfect in its execution.

Krystal was to notice a few flowers in her foyer with a card that simply suggested,

I'm sorry! I love you and my only concern is for you!

-- Jason

Words that Jason had a hard time with but felt he needed to say them now. Besides, this was the easy way to do it; romantic and extravagant, but easy. No face-to-face, but rather a heart-to-heart without any awkwardness. Simple.

Just some flowers in the foyer and a note to bring a smile back to her beautiful face;, but then, to drive home the point and depth of his feeling, this display would be followed up when she entered her main living area where the number and variety of flora was to be so extravagant and so spectacular, it would be awe inspiring. Yes, that was the way to show off his feelings.

Jason was not given to these outward displays of wealth, but he was certainly a man of means and thought that because of his normal conservatism this would be all the more poignant. Still, Jason had not heard from Krystal. Now with several days having passed after their minor disagreement, he was starting to get uncomfortable, disappointed, or angry-- he was not quite sure which--but definitely one of those, he thought. Why was she ignoring him? Did this not warrant some attention?

Jason had been avoiding Krystal these last few days, driving his antique Sno-Cat on to the compound. He was purposely avoiding the barns at the entrances to borrow a vehicle or sleigh and staying away from areas where he would normally have run into her. This made him feel foolish and guilty, so he avoided her even more. He rationalized that he was too busy, too distracted, but that only made this downward spiral worse. If she was not ready to talk to him after receiving all those flowers, how then could he face her now? He would have to wait a little bit longer; he thought she would come around, she always did.

Marcus Millerov approached the half-timbered structure, driving his snowmobile with a level of reckless aggressiveness and speed as he pulled it into the open barn door. Coming to a jerky stop he leaped off and called out,

"Eric! You incompetent slug, where the hell are you?"

A bundled young man emerged from the office and sheepishly asked,

"I'm right here, Mister Millerov, what seems to be the problem?"

"This piece of shit snowmobile won't start consistently!" Marcus snarled, holding two of his fingers in the young man's face, and continued, "Twice this thing didn't start for me! It made me late for a very important meeting!"

Marcus glared at the young man. Marcus's upper lip quivered, baring his teeth. Breath swirling like smoke from a fire-breathing dragon's mouth and the amber light from the office reflecting on his winter goggles all made him appear unusually menacing. His eyes narrowed as he leaned forward. The man reactively recoiled and with a stammer defended himself,

"I ... I ... I'm sorry, Mister Millerov, but I am not a mechanic. I don't know which machines are working or not. I'm sorry you had a problem, but it is twenty-five degrees below zero and fixing these is not my job."

"It is your job!" Marcus spat back, poking his finger in the young man's chest, "You are supposed to make sure that the animals are healthy and fed, and that the snowmobiles are running and fueled! Before! Before lending them out to use on the compound! Where the hell is Gardener, on vacation during our busiest season? Typical!"

"I don't know she's gone, I was just told to fill in," the young man responded.

"Yeah, for how long? She's your boss, isn't she?" Marcus snarled back.

"I ... I don't know. I was just told to fill in; it came from high up, and I was just told to fill in for a while. She's gone for a while, family or something. I'm sorry!" the young man whimpered.

"Yes, you will be sorry if this ever happens again! I was almost stranded at my office. Do you think that anyone in their right mind would try to walk any kind of distance at this time of year? You know it's dangerous!" Marcus completed his tirade and grunted in frustration. He shoved the young man at the shoulder, pushing him off balance and almost knocking him to the ground.

Pulling the hood up and clenching the collar of his coat, Marcus proceeded to the parking lot at the compound entrance.

He approached his vehicle and climbed up on the tread to enter the cabin door. Looking inside he stopped, inclined his head and slumped his

211

shoulders and after a brief pause looked up and climbed into the driver's seat.

"You people at the NTA just have no appreciation for the sanctity of private property--and locks, for that matter," Marcus said to the bundled figure sitting in his vehicle's passenger seat.

"Well, it's just what we do. Go ahead and start the engine, I won't be long." The shadowed figure suggested, "You know, I have that production schedule you threatened me with a week ago."

Marcus snapped his head to face the figure sitting beside him and growled,

"I knew someone had gone through my office! Damn it! What gives you--?"

The figure interrupted him,

"IF!" he snapped, then paused and continued more calmly, "If ... if I had arranged to have your office searched, trust me, you would never have known anyone had been there. No, you had a different intruder who inadvertently brought the schedule to us. Think about it, any idea who it was?"

Marcus shook his head, though he did not speak.

"Krystal Gardener," the man in the passenger seat said, "We caught her going through your office. So, now we have the production schedule and we have her, too."

"ARE YOU INSANE?! Do you have any idea how dangerous that is?" Marcus exclaimed.

"Oh yes, I am quite aware of how dangerous this is," the passenger suggested, "In fact, it seems she knew what she was looking for. Do you know how dangerous *that* is? She knew that you had compromising information; where do you suppose she got that information and worse, who close to her might know more than we think? You know of whom I speak. No, Marcus, this is your mess and you will help me clean it up."

Marcus frowned and nodded in response before saying,

"You weren't there, but I suppose you know that Andre has already reached out to the United States government; who knows about the plan may be of little consequence in the near future."

"Andre is a fool!" the figure snapped back, "Still, maybe you're right. You will help me deal with Gardener. Here, take this folder; I've left instructions for you to help us move her to a more secure location. I suggest you commit it to memory and burn it. You seem to have a problem with keeping information out of the wrong hands."

Marcus took a folder reluctantly and reached behind his seat to slip it into his briefcase's side pocket. The passenger opened his side door and got out and turned to Marcus,

"Good evening, Marcus. Have a good ride home."

He shut the door and walked into the darkness. Marcus started to back his vehicle out of its space.

17

FINDING THE SKELETONS

He was mesmerized by her. Indeed, Tom Bradley refused to allow her to stray from his gaze. His eyes were burning, swollen, and filled with tears, which even through his glasses blurred his vision slightly, adding to an almost angelic quality of the young, slender, blond woman who stood before him. She might have been the most beautiful woman he had ever seen--or at least so it seemed at this moment.

She repeated herself again,

"Agent Bradley? My name is Katie Marks. I'm here to take you home! I've found you!"

Katie took a seat at the table across from Tom and studied him. A disheveled man in an orange prison uniform, he simply did not look like he belonged here. His glasses sat low on his nose, one lens was cracked down the center, and his face was bruised with a reasonably fresh cut on his upper lip and over one eye.

"Agent Bradley, did you hear me? I'm here to bring you home. And how in the world did you end up here in Charleston, West Virginia?" the young woman asked and continued, beaming with pride, "Agent Evans said I had to find you before he returned, and I did!"

She smiled brightly.

Tom looked her in the eyes but still found no words to say. Something was different. Tom had not been treated this cordially in some time and he noted that he was not handcuffed to the table.

Breaking the brief silence, she continued,

"I've filed all the documents and taken care of all the clerical work but most importantly, I was able to track you down!" Katie said exuberantly, "Do you realize that even though everyone knew who you were, if you looked at the computer systems, no one had you by your name in their archives or in any of the records that were transmitted to us? Well, I was thinking that if I started to cross-check your name with statements made by prisoners or with doctors and patients at hospitals, someone might have noted your name in a statement. And you know what? I actually found you because of statements you made ... huh ... it was really strange, but it's almost like every time they transferred you, your name and records would disappear. Kinda like someone erased them once they were archived. You know, it's like someone wanted to be sure if someone called a clerical assistant they couldn't pull your name up, but some of the detectives you spoke with remembered you, but you weren't in their computer system ... who knows how many different prisons you were in?"

He looked at her and seemed to want to speak, but Katie continued, scarcely taking a breath,

"Well ..." she chuckled lightly, "I suppose you do, but wow, do you realize that the charges filed against you changed from one detective to the next? I checked with a printout in DC and whoever checks those, but found that by the time you got here they might have been ready to ship you off to Guantánamo Bay detention camp--"

"What day is it? What's the date?" Tom interrupted her.

"Oh ... uh, November sixth," she answered.

Tom nodded.

"I've been locked up and hidden away for over a month?" Tom grumbled quietly.

"Yeah, I've been looking for you. The police department had one hell of a big misunderstanding, I'll tell you what, but I got it all straightened out. Agent Evans told me just before he left to make absolutely sure I helped find you. He said it would be my big chance to show off my ability to investigate and mine data ... and I did it!" she proclaimed proudly.

"Agent Evans? John Evans? Where did he go?" Tom asked quickly.

"I'm not sure. Canada, I think … we can find out at the office," she answered.

"When can we leave?" Tom inquired feverishly, "If my misunderstanding with the police is what I think it is, John may be in an unbelievable amount of danger. Especially if he is getting closer to figuring out who is responsible."

Agent John Evans was trained in survival techniques and though he had never needed to apply them before, he had done about as well as could be expected considering his circumstances. He gathered as many provisions as he could carry from the aircraft's wreckage; food, water, and blankets. He found two small pillowcases, one which served to carry a few items, and the other he tore into strips and used them to soak up some fuel which he found in the remaining portions of one of the aircraft's wings. He wrapped these in plastic to carry so as to be able to make fire easily.

He knew to survive he would have to get off of the mountainside, and as he descended he traced the path of broken aircraft parts hoping to find more provisions to aid his survival. He was too far from any populated areas to expect a quick rescue and felt he would have to find his way toward the bay's shore and he resolved to make this his goal.

He was bundled, but the cold bit through the layers, reminding him that these were likely the worst conditions for a survival situation he might have found himself in. He walked along the plateau to the edge of the mountainside. John consciously made note of what appeared to be their impact point; a few thousand feet above the foot of the mountain. He wondered how they could have been so low. How could the pilot have allowed them to lose so much altitude? For now, he was happy that his trek down the mountainside would be a little less difficult than it might have been.

Finding the crumpled remains of the tail section, John used a broken panel from the fuselage to dig out the snow that had been scooped up in the tail of the aircraft. He remembered that just a few feet back was the luggage and storage section of the plane. He might find more useful items, some additional food and provisions, perhaps.

To his horror but not to his surprise he found the broken bodies of Brenda Willis and Holden Mealy. He had not known them for long, but felt he owed them the respect of pulling them from the wreckage and taking some of their personal identification to present to authorities later. He freed each from their frozen tomb and dragged them out and placed them next to each other. He stood for a moment in a courteous attempt to bid them farewell and passage into the afterlife, but with a modest level of guilt, found that by virtue of both his situation and his experience with these two representatives of his country's government, he felt little for them. Still, it reminded him of the loss of his colleague Walter Hayes and the stroke of chance that enabled he himself to survive. He did not linger for long.

John started digging again. He had planned to take what he could and then to use the wreckage as a brief shelter from the elements. He pulled out the blood-stained grey down coat which Brenda Willis had worn during their ill-fated flight. It was large enough to fit over the clothing and blankets he had wrapped himself in, and as it had a hood, this jacket would also help him retain his body heat and cover more of his face and head.

He layered his dress to conserve heat and mentally made a plan to ration his food and water, which he kept in a bottle inside his jacket to keep it from freezing, thinking that he would be in greater danger of hypothermia if he had to rely on eating snow for hydration. Trying to remain goal-oriented, he continued the excavation of the snow-filled cabin. Reaching the inside wall he cleared the snow to partially open the luggage and storage compartments. He found a few candy bars in a box of snacks but decided it would not be worth the effort to try to pull the luggage from below his position. He placed the bounty in his pockets and took a few minutes' rest to recoup his strength in the sheltered rear of the aircraft. He allowed himself a few bites from one of the candy bars in celebration as he did so.

Aware of how little time he might have, he did not linger long and after an hour or so he got up again and, feeling a bit stronger, he continued down the mountain.

As he approached the base of the mountainside he was able to find shelter in a rocky crevice. He felt a strange sense of exhilaration with the hitting of this milestone and as he again rested, he gave little thought as to the likelihood that this was the last opportunity to take advantage of a rest sheltered from the elements. The terrain ahead was remarkably dry and desperately barren. He had reached the foot of the mountain after twenty-four hours, and overlooking the terrain ahead it was strangely flat. Once off of the mountain he found almost no snow. There was no visible plant life and no animal activity. There were no materials to build a shelter or irregularities in the terrain that would serve as one. It was cold and rocky; that was all. With the nearly continuous night he knew that he might not survive, because even if John found shelter in these temperatures he would barely be able to avoid hypothermia, even dressed as he was. In fact he knew he had little real chance of survival, a thought that surfaced from time to time and one he tried to bury.

Still, for now he was feeling lucky. He had escaped death in the crash, which none of his companions had been able to. He had not been badly injured. A couple hours of what seemed to be twilight gave him a feeling of optimism and with no real hope of finding anyone, he continued, the mountains at his back.

The temperature dropped to forty below zero and with the temperature, so did his mood. Now at the darkest point of the everlasting night what little exposed skin he had, the air seemed to burn more than freeze. John began to obsess on the pain brought to him by the cold. How could he be so cold? He was dressed with so much clothing he could barely move. With the sun barely breaking the horizon he never felt much of its warmth nor did it offer him a direction or visibility. He started to become acutely aware of his lack of direction and the depth of his predicament. He looked ahead at the darkened and desolate landscape. Realizing that he could no longer see the mountains, he lamented that everything looked the same in every direction. He stopped looking to the sides in the hope of avoiding accidentally moving in circles. He focused on a large boulder up ahead and made this his next goal.

He felt he had to keep moving. Though he was not certain of his location, he knew that a chance of a rescue finding him was unlikely.

"I'm breaking one of the primary rules of survival," he said to himself, "but I'd have died if I stayed at the crash site."

He reached the boulder and set the next goal, hoping to keep his path straight and his motivation up.

As John walked, he ran the events of the hours leading to the crash through his mind. Could the weather alone account for their crash? The few-hour flight was almost entirely over water, so how did they end up here? He wondered again about their altitude. How could they have been so low? There was no indication of engine trouble. They had not lost altitude due to mechanical problems. The pilot, though agitated at the time, was clearly surprised before putting the aircraft into the extreme climb that marked the beginning of their crash. Their pilot appeared to be seasoned. How could he have been so wrong, so unaware?

He pondered and realized he had just passed his last goal. He stopped and looking into the dark landscape, he set his sights on another.

Figuring that it had been about forty-eight hours since he left the crash site, John had a sense that his mind was starting to shut down. Perplexed by his dilemma and losing some coordination, he feared that he was becoming hypothermic. He had to keep moving, even if only to keep his body temperature up.

He quickened his pace.

His coordination continued to degenerate. He was now barely able to walk without tripping on the rocks. His vision was blurred no matter how much he tried to focus it. He was no longer shivering and though he knew this was a bad sign, he took some solace in the fact that he recognized this to be the case. He dropped to his knees and curled up on the ground. It hurt him to breathe as every breath bit at his lungs like icy fangs.

How did he end up in this situation? John was barely able to remember why he had been in this part of the world. Just a few weeks ago, he might have been sitting at a desk in Washington, DC. He wanted to rest. No, he had to keep moving. His singular focus driving him forward, he had to keep moving.

He wanted to build a fire to warm up but did not have the energy, and with nearly nothing to burn he could not sustain the fire long enough to help him. He thought that if he could find his way back toward the waters of Baffin Bay then nearer to the shore there might be some dried grasses. He could burn that. He rested and a few minutes later he struggled to get up.

His knees were weak, but he started walking again; his legs quivered, not from the cold, but from the exhaustion.

Clumsily he moved forward, now with less of a walk and more of a stagger; he continued looking for a new feature in the landscape to make his next goal.

His watch gave him little clue as to the time. He was not sure if he had walked for twelve, twenty-four, or forty-eight hours since he last checked. The second hand seemed to have stopped also, so it was not likely to be accurate anyway. So too with the sun, which gave him little clue, and he resolved not to care and focused on a large pile of rocks that reminded him of a large turtle.

"The turtle--that's my next goal then I can rest for a minute," he said to himself in an effort to self-motivate.

John could not feel his body anymore, save a tingling in his fingers that felt like a cell phone vibrating. He stopped, and with a sense of optimism pulled out and looked at his smart phone. It was not working. Whether by virtue of the crash or the cold, it would not turn on.

Mindlessly, he focused on the rocks ahead and pushed forward.

The cold seemed to sap him of his strength and he collapsed again. Sitting on his knees he would have wept out loud, if he could muster the energy to do so.

Then, eyes burning, he saw something that did not seem to belong; something man-made. He could not make it out, but it was there.

Yes! This would be his next goal.

John stretched out a leg and attempted to stand again. His joints were stiff and seemed to protest his commands. Struggling to lift himself up, he finally managed to get to his feet.

Looking at the object in the distance he attempted to identify it, but could not. Still, it was worth the effort to find out what it was and so he pressed on.

It looked bigger from a distance. He had dared to hope that it might be large enough to act as a shelter of some type. However, as he approached the object he noted that it was no larger than a trash can.

White and cylindrical, the metal object was fastened to the ground on a heavy metal pole. A cluster of wires protruded from the side, which mimicked a small rainbow as it arched to the ground. Opposite the wires was a large numeral *4*. Some smaller lettering was also present but in his condition he could not make out the words. A single object amongst the rocks, its mission was unclear. Rivets adorned each side making it obvious that this was built purely for a functional purpose and not aesthetics. It was scarred by the elements but showed no corrosion. It was too dry here. Still, the white paint had lost its luster where it had been blasted by the wind. He found a modest level of comfort in this object as it signaled that someone had been here. He scanned the landscape but in the darkness he could not see anything else. He found no other signs of human activity, just a countryside carved by glacial imposition. Flat and covered by the rocky refuse which the glaciers left in their wake, the landscape was strewn with chunks of stone ranging from the size of a fist to boulders the size of a small automobile.

Dropping to his knees, he again studied the object. Then in a moment of frustration he picked up a rock and with as much energy as he could draw he started to smash the rock against the cylinder. Twice he hit the side, denting it. Then dropping on his hands, he tried to catch his breath.

Eyes closed and on his hands and knees, he rested again. Then, with all his remaining strength, he picked up another rock and struck the object on the protruding cluster of wires. He broke two wires and sheared the plastic housing off of a number of others. There were no sparks, no flashes of light to indicate a short circuit. The object just stood there, broken. Dented and forlorn, the object seemed to mock him. The rock fell from his hands and he dropped completely to the ground. He could no longer move. Just maybe, he thought, if he broke this thing, someone would have to come to fix it. It was a futile effort, he lamented. He would only have an hour or so before he would succumb to the environment. Maybe, just minutes. His eyes closed and he moved no more.

John seemed to regain partial consciousness as the feeling of being jostled from side to side in the back of a vehicle jolted him awake. Limp and without any strength, he bumped around like a rag doll in the back of a pickup truck, but this was like no truck that John had ever seen before. It had six large, black tires that moved up and down with the terrain independently. The cab was open and an array of pole and dish antennae protruded from all sides. He was certain that he was hallucinating since the driver looked like a space traveler fully suited with oxygen pack and helmet. They drove down into a valley and with his vision still compromised, he saw them approaching a small structure. It was illuminated at the top and cast an almost blinding light their way. Similar to the object he had found, it was cylindrical, white, and riveted together; it bore a large numeral *4* on one side. It reminded John of a water tower. It stood about fifteen feet from the ground, suspended atop four legs with a ladder that reached a hatch at the bottom with an additional ladder that ran up one of the legs and the side. Some smaller, clear plastic domes surrounded the structure. The vehicle slowed and then came to an abrupt stop near the ladder under the cylinder.

The person in the spacesuit climbed up the ladder as quickly as he could. John saw the figure disappear into the hatch only to reemerge holding a large line with the far end coming from the hatch. The spaceman pointed at John, showed him the line and then pointed up at the hatch. John nodded, assuming he was being told he would be brought inside. The figure in the spacesuit then affixed the line round John's chest and snapped it closed behind his head and with a push of a button on the spaceman's wrist, John felt himself being lifted up.

Guided by the hand of the spaceman, John's suspended body was maneuvered from the vehicle to the ladder. Dangling at the foot of the ladder, the spaceman steadied John and then by apparent command from the remote on the spacesuit's wrist, proceeded to slowly hoist John up through the hatch above.

John felt as though he was barely maintaining consciousness. He dangled above the hatch opening inside the structure; as he watched, the spaceman followed him through the hatch, closing it behind him. With a turn of a wheel on the hatch's interior, the spacemen had it presumably safely sealed.

He turned his back to John and fumbled with a control panel on a wall. John looked around at the surroundings, which looked very much like the interior of a submarine, but clad in white rather than the steel gray he might have expected. It was a small space full of equipment. Two additional spacesuits hung inside a closet and a small door stood closed on an interior wall in a ninety-degree angle from the closet. The outside wall was curved in conformation of the exterior cylindrical shape of the structure. A bench followed the curve of the wall.

John felt himself being lowered and guided to the bench to sit down.

The spaceman undid a latch and with a quick turn and the hiss of releasing pressure, he removed his helmet and hung it in the closet.

The man in the spacesuit smiled at John and eyed him inquisitively.

John looked up at him. He was a relatively young man with a freckled face and red hair. He had a kindly expression and fine-featured face, which was exaggerated by the heaviness of the spacesuit.

John's head dropped looking at the floor.

The man knelt down in front of John as quickly as his suit would let him and started snapping his fingers near John's face.

"Stay with me now," the man in the spacesuit said as he attempted to keep John from passing out.

John looked up again.

"Where am I?" John inquired slowly.

"Brilliant! You speak English!" the spaceman noted excitedly in an English accent, "I could have done French or German, but my Inuit is miserable. Now stay still. I have set the temperature up to help you warm, but we don't want the blood from your arms and legs to rush to your body's core too quickly. I don't want you to go into cardiac arrest," he chuckled lightly, "So stay calm."

"Cardiac arrest?" John mumbled.

"Right, I suspect you are quite hypothermic," the spaceman suggested and continued, "Now don't move; I will get you some hot water."

The spaceman got up, turned to the closet and with some effort slipped out of the spacesuit and hung it up under his helmet. He was a fit man, wearing a tan jumpsuit with pockets everywhere and an emblem on his upper arm. He pushed a few buttons on the control panel and turned back toward John,

"I will be right back."

He exited through the side door, leaving John alone.

John was too tired to get up and slumped over on the bench.

It was just a few minutes before the spaceman returned with a cup of hot water.

"Here, drink this; it will help warm you up." He handed the cup to John and continued, "I can offer you some food and tea, but for now the water is the best thing for you."

"What in bloody hell were you doing out there?" he followed up.

Quietly John spoke as his body started shivering as he drank the hot liquid,

"P ... Plane crash ... Wu ...Where ... am I?"

"Ah, right! Well then, welcome to Mars," the spaceman responded, "Euro-Mars 4 to be specific, the name's Mike O'Connor."

John took another sip of hot water and inquired,

M ... Mars?"

"Euro-Mars 4, in the southeastern part of Devon Island to be precise, cheers," Mike responded, "The fourth European Mars Analogue Research Station and habitat, this unit is my home for eighteen months. It's funded by the United Kingdom and operated by a consortium of European Mars Society chapters. I conduct geological and biological exploration, because this area is similar to the conditions on Mars, or at least that is what they tell me. Honestly, I think they are really just trying to see if I will go mad. So, who are you? And tell me about your plane crash."

Mike took a seat next to John.

"John, my name is John Evans. Thank you for bringing me in. We were on our way back to the mainland from the Kringle Works when we got caught in a storm."

Mike's eyebrows arched and eyes widened in interest.

"We?! Did you say *we*? Are there any other survivors?" Mike asked quickly.

"No, no one else survived," John answered.

"Well, you're lucky I found you or you wouldn't have, either. I suppose that's why you tried to smash up one of the perimeter's thermal heater control modules. I will have to go out there tomorrow to fix it or one of my botanical growers will fail. I guess I will log that as a meteor strike simulation. My team in Manchester would be very irritated with me if I called it an alien attack."

Mike pulled a device from his pocket.

"I'm going to take your temperature."

He stuck the device into John's ear and after a quick beep he pulled it out to look at a small LED screen.

"Right, you're getting better. Your temperature is near normal." He put the device back in his pocket and followed up, "I'm going to have you lie down in the infirmary and put you on a saline drip. You are probably extremely dehydrated, too."

He got up and walked toward the door and turned to address John again,

"While you're resting, I will make a call to the mainland and let them know you're here. I was not supposed to unless the situation became extremely anomalous, but I think this qualifies. When you feel strong enough, come on out and I will get you fixed up."

John nodded.

CSIS Agent Teresa LaChapelle had been trying to gather as much information as she could about what happened to Caravan Charlie Golf Sierra Zulu Whisky, its passengers, and pilot, for several days. Still, she was getting little more than,

"The aircraft left the NTA Main Airport and Kringle Works airspace uneventfully when, without warning, communication and the transponder signal stopped."

She had been trying to retrace the aircraft's expected path with Transport Canada but still had found nothing.

She attempted to use her connections to both the Canadian government and law enforcement to put particular pressure on Transport Canada. For now, Canadian authorities had hoped to keep this information out of the hands of the United States until such time that they had a little more definitive information as to the fate of the flight and its passengers. She knew, however, that the time frame in which Canada could keep silent was closing fast. Accidents do happen, but this would be a terrible embarrassment for the Canadian government just the same. Unfortunately the window of opportunity to find out more slammed shut rather abruptly when the FBI's legal attaché contacted Teresa, suggesting that the FBI had particular reason to believe the contingent from Washington, DC was in potential peril and they wanted a follow-up from them. She would have to work fast.

Teresa's efforts regarding the missing aircraft would generate a lead from the unlikeliest source of information, as she would find herself in a telephone conversation with the European Space Agency who apparently contacted Transport Canada about an incident involving an unidentified aircraft and a single survivor at one of their affiliated research stations.

"Agent LaChapelle, we were given your name by Transport Canada when we inquired about any recent aircraft accidents in the Northern Territories. You see, we were contacted by one of our research scientists, and he spoke of a plane crash and a survivor who stated his name is John Evans," a voice with a British accent said on the phone.

If the discussions she was having about the charges the United States was putting forth against the Kringle Works were not already unbelievable, this information concerning the whereabouts of John Evans was becoming strangely surreal.

"This incident has ruined our mission and is costing our agency a tremendous amount of money," the man told her, continuing curtly, "We will not be able to extract Mister Evans for at least four weeks, and we are not in a position to go to the crash site. We have been given assurances that there were no other survivors."

Teresa LaChapelle acknowledged and asked if she could make arrangements to have him picked up.

The man on the other end of the phone was silent, suggesting that this was a solution he was either considering or not comfortable with.

"You will have to wait for two weeks to allow Mister Evans the opportunity to recover and our man at Euro-Mars 4 to make preparations," he finally answered.

Then after a pause the man followed up, "This mission was costing us several million pounds and it's already compromised, so please make sure the extraction of Mister Evans is as undisruptive as possible. You will not be able to talk directly to the research facility, so your communications regarding the timing and transport arrangements will need to be coordinated through my office. We will communicate with our man on the ground."

She agreed.

Tom Bradley was relieved when the news that John Evans had been located alive reached him. Still, he was unnerved by the news of the crash. An accident due to a level of pilot error and bad weather was the premise of the report drafted by the Canadian authorities. Tom, however, was insistent that this was not the case and asked that the FBI use its authority to get access to the communications records, the crash site radios and instruments, and the flight recorder.

His suspicions were enough to compel the department to investigate both the crash and his erroneous arrest. The FBI was making the local law enforcement quite miserable in an unofficial effort to punish them for their mistakes.

Due to the length of his ordeal, Tom was given the option to take a couple weeks of paid leave but refused, and during the weeks that he waited for John's return Tom continued to work on the strange electronic chips that had been his last assignment.

He was now making rapid progress based on some of his earlier work and the implementation of some concepts he had thought through while sitting in jail.

His efforts yielded some important results, as he was now able to address the mysterious chip consistently with a signal composed of the long series of numbers preceded by the letter A that he discovered back in September. He also became aware that he could address the chip through the host device's electronic infrastructure. Soon Tom modified a computer tablet that he could use to communicate with the chip if it was present.

Tom had gotten no closer to discovering the chip's purpose, or at least proving his speculations, but he had been able to figure out if it was resident in a device by addressing the chip via hard wire or wireless network, radio frequency, Bluetooth, or directly through a USB port.

Tom spent little time at his apartment, due to a combination of discomfort resulting from his arrest and the fact that much of his computer equipment was still in the hands of the local authorities and much of it likely ruined in their efforts to gather evidence. So it was very late when he returned home one night with his prototype tablet. This evening he plopped himself down on the couch and turned on his television and started to watch the news. Noting the ticker at the bottom, he thought of the incident that had first given the department an indication of the chips' existence.

He looked intently at the DVR above his television and noticed the USB port on the front of the device. He turned to look at the case, which sat casually next to him on the couch, and pulled out the tablet. He plugged it into the DVR and addressed it. To his dismay, the device acknowledged the code. The chip was present. Tom's jaw dropped and he started testing other devices in the apartment. The television, his programmable thermostat, clock radio, microwave oven, and most every device that was manufactured in the last few years had the chip.

"And those devices that don't have the chip communicate and are linked by some that do!"

He started to panic when he realized that his building's wireless systems were all affected. The security system was too old, but the cameras in the lobby were not. Indeed, it appeared that any systems that might have been or would be frequently upgraded would be systematically compromised.

The next day, Tom started to randomly test devices all around him.

The internet access at the local coffee shop, and indeed the vast majority of the computers in the FBI's offices; the chip was everywhere.

"It's a surveillance network, to help Santa Clause, eh ... I mean ... the Kringle Works monitor who is being good and who is being bad," John told Tom on the phone that afternoon.

"Apparently it's all very legal," he followed up.

"It's good to hear your voice, John!" Tom said, speaking into the phone, "Are you alright? When'll you be back?"

John did not answer definitively and just indicated that he would be back soon.

Tom hesitated but then asked,

"John, what do you think happened to the plane?"

"I don't know," John said, voice cracking, "The weather, I guess."

"Yeah, I'll figure it out for you. I promise. I am requesting that parts of the plane be brought to me in my lab. Take care of yourself!" Tom closed the conversation and hung up the telephone.

18

THE DELIVERY WINDOW

It was an unassuming black van, remarkable only because of the quiet suburban surroundings of this small town. It was dark and though the lawns had a fresh dusting of snow, the streets were clear and quiet. Around the vehicle, three men clad in black uniforms conducted themselves with military precision. They were fast and though no one was there to see them, they seemed to be focused on speed and stealthiness.

The operations leader was focused on a handheld device that seemed to stream information vital to their operation and his command and control. He watched and received his confirmation. He gave a silent signal to his comrades.

Like clockwork and with a glance around, two men opened the back doors of the black van. They quickly lowered a large container onto a wheeled platform and proceeded to the nearest house. One of the men turned to watch for the signal from their leader holding the device, and with a nod they sprang into action. Using a key, they opened the door to the house and entered. The man who had unlocked the door pulled a device from his pocket and quickly proceeded to a lit keypad that was beeping in the foyer. Putting an electronic device near the keypad and pushing a button, a series of numbers appeared on a screen. He entered them in and the keypad stopped beeping. The screen above the keypad displayed a status of *Disarmed*. With the snap of a couple latches the container opened and the two men pulled out a number of wrapped boxes and with a glance at a handheld device, they made their way to a decorated Christmas tree and, in this case, to a series of stockings hung from a mantle. The boxes marked with the recipient's name and the acronym *SANTA* were left. Next to the gifts from friends and family there were always some from SANTA. Then, as quickly as the two men entered, they left; with alarm set and door relocked. They proceeded back down the driveway.

The two watched again for a signal preparing for the next house, but this time they received a shake of the head and a series of hand gestures signaling, *negative, go to the next house*. They skipped this house and went on to the next; they would have to come back another day when the time was right.

Quietly the two men approached the front door of the third house. Their operations lead gave them a silent signal to hold. He checked his device and tapped the name and address in his device, launching a window displaying a video signal which had apparently come from inside the house. He was allowed to view a small image of a woman reading a book and drinking coffee at her kitchen table. The woman looked up and a small colored square caught the image of her face. In a moment the device confirmed her identity via facial recognition. With another tap on his device the video switched to a view of the house's floor plan. A number of red markers indicated the location of people in the house. One more tap on the device and the screen switched to a different camera showing some children playing in another room. The ICU technology was largely implemented in homes with more security features, allowing the NTA to dramatically speed their operations, taking advantage of a smaller margin of error, because this allowed them to enter homes with the residents still at home and active by tapping into these systems to monitor them. The team waited for the signal. Some hand gestures indicated what his team already knew. *Enter. Subjects in view and occupied. Deliver packages. Door unlocked. Make haste.* The two men entered and set a few boxes under a tree and on a deacon's bench in a large foyer. Less than two minutes had passed and they went on to the next house.

On this particular street, the team made all deliveries in less than two hours with only three homes skipped. Operations like this were now happening all over the country and in other parts of the world. Throughout November and the first part of December the Kringle Works would distribute packages from key warehouse locations and with an execution model not unlike the most sophisticated parcel post service, NTA aircraft, vehicles, and personnel would deliver packages on all days of the week and at all times of the day and night, though in the early years of service, it was these nighttime deliveries that became the namesake of the Nocturnal Transportation Authority, and the document that marked its strategic activation.

The actual implementations of the NTA deliveries had, over time, become very similar to a military or law enforcement operation. All of their activities were based on a precise schedule in which they would enter either when a resident was not home or not in a position to see them deliver their Christmas service. Each delivery took less than five minutes, and in most cases residents would not even be aware of the delivery until days had passed.

Tens of thousands of these black vans would rush around hitting houses, condominiums, apartments, community centers, churches, and other buildings, delivering the Christmas Service with the inventory that had been building up for months in accordance with the contracts and expectations of the local and federal governments.

By now, Jason Pelham was appropriately pleased with the progress of SANTA this season. The NTA had made up time enough to compensate for the shortened delivery window brought on by the forced scrapping of millions of units of the most popular electronics and the subsequent delays in product deliveries that stressed the supply chains of both ELF and the NTA. All was progressing well, all the more because this was Jason's first gift delivery season at the NTA's helm.

Still, Jason was preoccupied. Krystal Gardener, as the story went, took some time for herself and decided to retreat for an unspecified amount of time. Some close to Krystal suggested that she went to Alaska to study animals with some well-known scientist. She had done so before.

At first it seemed as though no one knew what had happened to Krystal, but then within a few days everything started to fall into place. Documents that appeared to be from Krystal herself started to appear; a letter requesting the leave of absence to the director of facilities management, a work schedule for the care of the animals, work assignments for the management of the barns at the main Kringle Works compound, all seemed to corroborate the narrative that was starting to emerge. What appeared to be a rash and impulsive decision suddenly seemed to have been a well thought-out plan. All of the evidence suggested that she had been planning this for some time.

This was perplexing to Jason at first. How could Krystal have been planning all this without even mentioning it to him? This was not like her, but as time went on he started to think that maybe she was purposefully trying to send him a message. Their relationship was currently a little …

"Undefined," Jason said to himself.

If Krystal was trying to help him understand what it would be like without her, this was a way to do it, but she was not usually this manipulative. Still, every time Jason attempted to look, the information turned up to support the idea that she had planned to get away for a while and told only a few. Perhaps to keep the information from leaking to him, he thought.

He was worried. He did not like the fact that he had not heard from her in weeks. Still, perhaps as a coping mechanism, Jason started to defiantly immerse himself deeper into his work. Yet the preoccupation lingered no matter how he tried to ignore it.

In a moment of particular anxiety, Jason decided to wander over to the ICU workstation which sat at the back of his office. He removed the cover he had placed on it to hide it from his view and minimize any temptation to use it. He considered it a loathsome machine and he felt using it was hypocritical. He stared at the machine and its dark screen.

"Be careful of the workstation. It will tell you a lot, but it will also betray you," Jason said to himself, remembering the words of warning he'd received from Henry Foster some months back.

Jason turned away, walked back to his desk and pulled a small folded, white envelope from the top drawer. He opened it up and placed it on his desk and pondered it for a while. He looked up and walked to the front door of his office and quietly shut it.

He walked back, grabbed the envelope and took a seat in front of the ICU workstation.

He turned it on. In an instant the screen popped to life.

The familiar screen adorned with the Kringle Works logo appeared and then a series of icons loaded the various applications and drivers needed to run the station's functions. Then the familiar textbox with the four number sets appeared. Jason unfolded the envelope and entered the fifth code, which he knew he needed to view people resident on the Kringle Works Island. He hit 'Enter' on the keyboard. The textbox disappeared, leaving only the screen pattern again with the exception of a small wreath adorned with a red ribbon that rotated while the machine pondered its next move.

Jason leaned back as the workstation continued to load the various windows and menus.

ICU Status stand-alone: Forward Processing-OFF. The little wreath stopped rotating and disappeared, a new window opened with the words, *Entering Data Feed – Filtered – Restoring last session.*

The screen now loaded, the filtered search of his last session graced the workstation's screen. Six windows loaded. A satellite image of the island which showed Jason his own neighborhood, an audio window for his home phone, another for his office phone--both with a flat line indicating no current activity--yet another window for Jason's mobile device, and his computer on which he could see his own e-mail inbox and another window which showed the title *ICU Workstation SN5214662*, the five codes he had entered and name *Jason Pelham* in a text box at the base.

Jason cleared the text boxes of his name and the screen reacted violently, becoming the familiar flurry of activity. Windows started to open, text running in columns in front and behind and as before within a fraction of a second the screen was a blur of colors and movement with nothing discernable.

Jason started typing the name *Krystal Gardener.*

In an instant the screen lurched and a handful of windows appeared. However, unlike those he had seen before, these contained very little activity. Most were dark and compared to searches Jason had done in the past, there were fewer. This was not a surprise as Jason was well aware of Krystal's open rejection of technology.

Just at that moment, when Jason was going to sort out what he could, his office door opened as someone burst into the room.

Jason instinctively and quickly shut the ICU workstation's power off and shoved the envelope into his jacket pocket.

He got up, spinning around to see who had entered.

"Jason! I'm so sorry to interrupt you, but I have some extremely important information for you!" Jason noted the breathy voice of Henry Foster, "You are wondering what happened to your friend Krystal, aren't you? I think I know, and I ran down here as fast as I could to tell you. I think we have to move fast!"

Krystal Gardener slowly slipped on her change of clothes with an unnatural level of quiet pensiveness. It was becoming common and familiar, the degrading feeling, twice a day, of changing clothes and washing up while a hooded figure stood outside the bathroom door holding the chain that would be hers to burden the rest of her day and night.

She could never identify the people she interacted with but she had a sense that there were a significant number of them. She was not dealing with the same people every time. Her captors were not just one person. Still, on the days in which she had the ability to converse with anyone, it was always the same person, always the same subject; a discussion on politics and the flawed nature of the world, the solutions that this group of people had been planning on imposing on the unwitting populations. The discussions were designed, she thought, to convince her of the 'good' that they were doing. It seemed to make sense at times. She could almost believe in the concepts.

"No!" she thought, "They are just programming me," and Krystal would rebuild the barriers in her mind for the next discussion.

She scrubbed her head with a towel and leaned closer to the mirror as she brushed her hair straight. Her thoughts wandered when she was interrupted by another familiar sound. The knock, knock of an impatient hooded figure outside her bathroom door suggesting she was taking too long for their comfort.

"I'll be right out!" she exclaimed, contemptuously rolling her eyes.

"You're not the one who is going to be chained up for the rest of the day," she followed up under her breath.

She finished up and stepped obediently through the door. She stared at the hooded figure, and with a passive but defiant resignation looked to the side in disgust and stretched out her hand in anticipation of being shackled.

"You have an important visitor coming in, so you'll want to behave yourself," the hooded figure suggested.

This news surprised her and she turned suddenly to face the hooded figure, but in the absence of a discernable visage she was unable to get a sense of what this might have meant by virtue of his expression.

He finished snapping closed the handcuff which kept Krystal confined to areas of her room and loosely tethered to the wall.

"What good is having an important visitor if I don't know who it is?" she grumbled.

He released her hand. She felt the chain fall and she let her hand drop.

"Actually, I think you know him. He'll be here shortly. I believe you are going on a road trip today," he told her as he walked behind the curtain and out the door.

"So, behave yourself, as I said," he followed up before closing the door to her room.

Krystal stood motionless for a moment. She was strangely excited. She was looking forward to meeting with someone she knew.

She had been treated well, but she was still a captive. She liked to refer to herself as a zoo animal in her conversations with the one man with whom she interacted most often. Defiant at times and resigned at others, she was fed well and treated cordially save the fact that she was kept captive and chained. She thought back on the weeks of her incarceration, the days that she would scream and curse her captors, demanding her release. She spent a number of days destroying the room breaking everything she could, only to have hooded figures come in to repair and replace the damaged goods, leading to a conversation regarding behaviors and the nature of humans to be self-destructive. Other times she took advantage of the odd hospitality and found that her captors tried to make these circumstances as comfortable as possible, given their own rules of her captivity.

Often she would invoke the name of Jason Pelham in hopes of either evoking respect or fear, she was not sure which. She wondered what Jason might be thinking. Did he realize she was in trouble? She spent a number of nights crying herself to sleep, questioning what her friends and family might be thinking happened to her. She had been told that no one would wonder about her, that they would not come looking for her and not to worry. She had been told that she would eventually be released when the time was right, though she had trouble believing this. Still, slowly she resigned herself to this environment and spent more of her time asking when she might be released on the occasions that she met with her conversational companion who remained safety tucked behind the curtain when they talked.

For the moment she felt safe. They had not hurt her and she had no reason to believe that they had wanted to do her any harm. If they did, they would have done so by now. She thought that if they wanted to harm her they would not have kept her here this way for this time. Still, Krystal had a sense that they were not sure of what to do with her. It seemed that they had been keeping her there until they figured out what to do next. Perhaps she had a part to play in their plan, but it was more likely they had not planned on her being here. One thing was sure, they were confident that if they achieved their goals, however they might be expecting to do so, the single person's dissension, such as hers, would not matter.

She went back into the bathroom, dragging the chain that allowed her access to all sides of her room, closet, table and chairs, books, entertainment center, but not the curtain and exit beyond.

Krystal stood before the sink and looked into the mirror to assess herself. She splashed water into her face and dabbed it off with a towel in an effort to refresh herself.

"Who could it be?" she thought to herself.

If they told her that she would know who it was, then it stood to reason that they would be willing to show themselves to her. She pondered this and stepped back into the main room. She walked over to a small table and chairs. Making small adjustments for the chain she dragged with her, she sat down, lifting a book she was reading this past week. Her concentration, however, did not allow her to read; she was too focused on the aforementioned visitor. In this moment she realized how desperate she had become to have some interaction with someone other than the faceless captors she had been dealing with.

It was about thirty minutes later when she heard the door to her room open. Instinctively, she looked to the door though she knew that she would not have been able to see any detail past the curtain at the far end of her room.

She saw the outline of a figure approach. But before they might have made their way to the curtain's edge, the figure stopped.

"Ms. Gardener," a strangely familiar voice said, "I assume they are treating you well."

Krystal stood up and hesitated as she pondered the voice.

"Well? Eh … if you consider being caged like some poor zoo animal as good treatment. Yes, stellar!" she proclaimed defiantly.

"Bear in mind, Ms. Gardener, that this situation is of your own making," the voice suggested.

"Marcus? Marcus Millerov?" she inquired, the voice suddenly triggered in her memory.

The figure did not respond verbally but instead started to walk toward her to the edge of the curtain.

Her heart stopped. When the figure of Marcus Millerov appeared from behind the curtain and stood before her, her mouth dropped open. She would not have known how much she craved seeing another's face. Even if, as in this case, it was not one she might have hoped to see. She resisted the urge to giggle, to embrace another human being; she paused to regain her composure in hopes that her exuberance at the thought of face-to-face companionship did not expose her moment of weakness.

"What!? No hood?" she mocked, trying to sound measured and defiant, "Marcus, how did you get involved with these people?"

"These people?" Marcus snapped, "These people have an agenda."

Krystal looked at him a little bewildered,

"But that agenda, it isn't yours too?" she looked at him with a look of sympathetic concern, "Is it? Marcus, this isn't your style. You're an executive at the Kringle Works, a senior manager at the Employee League of Fabricators. You are an integral part of all of the happiness the Kringle Works brings to the world."

Marcus looked down and sighed. He looked at her with an apologetic look.

"I've done things, things in my past, things I'm not proud of. Now I'm trapped in a nightmare with a number of people who think I still believe what they do, but I don't, not all of it, but they won't let me free. Now I'm so deep…" he paused.

"Marcus, help me. Help me escape. You know that Jason will support us. He will go with us to tell Xavier." She looked him in the eyes and clutched her hands in an almost prayer-like pose. "Help me, and Xavier and Jason will set us both free!"

"Help me," she followed up in a whisper, and the room fell silent for a moment.

He reached out and ran the back of his fingers down the line of her left cheek. It was a tender touch. One of caring, but not an appropriate element of their current relationship; it made Krystal uneasy and she involuntarily recoiled.

"Marcus?" she questioned with a sense of disquiet.

He followed her movement as she backed up, and with his advance she continued to edge back until she could move no further. Her back against a wall, Marcus moved closer, pinning her against it. He moved closer and she could feel his breath on her face and right ear. His lips open, she could hear nothing but his breathing. Her heart pounded as her throat tightened. She whimpered slightly, but could not seem to say anything. She shut her eyes. He reached around her head and gently ran his hand along her hairline and behind her ear. She felt herself trembling and found it hard to breathe in anticipation of what might come next. Marcus's hand continued down to the nape of her neck and he grabbed hold of a handful of her hair. She could feel the hair in his hand as he tightened his grip, and with a sudden jerk and increasing malice he pulled her head back. She felt a sting in her neck as her head shifted and the skin stretched. He yanked her head back as far as she imagined it could go without breaking her neck. She squealed briefly, just a chirp as the air burst from her throat. She felt herself starting to hyperventilate, her breath fast and shaky as a tear ran down her cheek. Marcus leaned even closer.

He snarled and in a whisper said,

"You have embarrassed me one too many times!"

She could feel the moisture of his breath in her ear as he spoke.

"You will not do it again!"

Marcus released her, pushing her away with enough force that it knocked her to the ground. Shaken, Krystal sobbed. Emotionally drained, she did not get up as Marcus growled,

"That's what it feels like to loose control of your situation."

"Why should I help you? Neither you nor Jason has ever been my friend! Neither you nor Jason can help me! Xavier can't help me! No one can. You will join them, either because you believe as they do, or because there will simply be no alternative," Marcus continued.

Then bending down toward her he reached over, placing his hand under her chin; he lifted her head so their eyes could meet. She watched him with tear-filled eyes but did not move, paralyzed by fear and confusion. He looked back at her focusing on her swollen eyes, arched his eyebrows, shook his head slowly and quietly said,

"They're always watching. They're putting their technology into every corner, every crevice, every hole, every shadow, behind every door and in every window; they will be watching and if they get their way they will sell this service to every government. They will dismantle the Kringle Works and resurrect it as a global government sitting in the shadows just under the surface of those governments everyone sees. They'll start with the United States and they've already reached out. Trust me, I know. I was there."

Marcus stood up again, looking down at her and followed up,

"No, no one can help. This will be the way of the world, the Kringle Dynasty will fall, the power of the governments of the world will fall with them and, who knows, maybe it really will be better? I never believed in the Kringle family vision. It's just as self-serving as anyone else's. These people, at least their vision is for a better world."

Marcus turned and took two steps toward the curtain, then swung around again looking at her,

241

"The world can't be much worse. Can it? Eventually we'll all be like you, living comfortably and provided for, even if caged like *a poor zoo animal.* Or like one of your beloved reindeer perhaps?"

He chuckled nervously and tossed a key to Krystal, which landed on the ground just in front of her collapsed figure.

"Unlock yourself. Get up, we're leaving," he barked.

Disappointed with herself for her own perception of not remaining as strong as she would have liked and for the unpleasant nature of their visit, Krystal remained silent as she got up and unlocked the cuff and chain. She took a small amount of pleasure in letting the chain fall at her feet. Then with great apprehension and still emotionally churned up, she slowly followed Marcus toward the curtain that bordered her world these past weeks.

At the door, Marcus stopped and handed Krystal a heavy coat and bade her to put it on. As she did, he followed up with a hood that would act as a blindfold for their journey.

She slipped it over her head hesitantly, knowing that she should have expected this but had hoped that she would have been allowed to see the outside world. It seemed that the courteous requests and apologetic nature of her captors when she was asked to do something in the interest of security was in stark contrast with the vexed and curt manner in which Marcus snapped out commands. Still, though she was anxious to leave this room, she allowed Marcus to lead her with tremendous reluctance. This made her acutely aware that she had not been given a choice. She had no reason to trust him.

Krystal felt Marcus's tight grip on her upper arm as he pushed her along.

Deprived of her sight, she focused on the sounds as she walked down a hall, stairs, and then the blast of cold as they apparently exited the building and entered a vehicle.

With the start of the engine she noted the sound of the engine, the heat from a dashboard vent, vibration, and the hint of exhaust in the cold air as they embarked on their trek.

She sat silently for a few hours before she worked up the courage to address Marcus again,

"Who?" she said, clearing her throat, voice cracking and shaky, "Who reached out to the United States?"

There was no response.

"Marcus? It's still you, isn't it?" she followed up.

Still there was no response and after another twenty minutes, Marcus spoke,

"He who knows everything controls everything. Remember that."

"You can take that hood off now, there is nothing to see," he continued.

Eagerly she pulled the hood off. Her eyes seemed to express a joy at the new sights. The dashboard lights of the track-driven vehicle, the desolate snow-covered road ahead illuminated by the vehicle's lights, and Marcus Millerov sitting stoically at the driver's controls.

She looked around, sat silently watching the dark road ahead for a while longer and then broke the silence again,

"Who, Marcus? Who reached out to the United States? Who is that well-connected?"

He did not react, focused on the task of navigating the dark and desolate road ahead.

"Marcus?" she inquired again, "Who was it? Andre Leopold?"

Krystal pulled the name from her memory, referencing the last conversation she had had with Jason. Thinking about that evening with him might have caused her to drift into a melancholy walk through their relationship and thoughts of what he might be doing and thinking right now were it not for the reaction she noticed in Marcus. It was subtle but she noticed it nonetheless.

Marcus had inadvertently shuddered in surprise and accelerated the speed of his vehicle upon hearing the name. Leaning forward with a look of panic in his eyes, Marcus silently scolded himself for the reaction. He said nothing. He refused to acknowledge the question and stared straight ahead. Still, he continued to quicken the pace. He was now hoping that his reaction went unnoticed and that this task before him would soon come to an end.

Then his fears were realized when she responded to his feeble attempt at covering his reaction,

"It is! Isn't it, but why? Come on Marcus, why would he want to?"

He refused to acknowledge what she had decided she had figured out already and simply suggested again,

"He who knows everything controls everything." Marcus paused and continued, "That's something the Kringles never understood."

"But that's why people love the Kringles so much!" Krystal jumped in enthusiastically, "Because they have the power to see everything but only use it to bring Christmas to the world. You know that!"

Marcus abruptly stopped the vehicle. He turned to her and impatiently barked,

"They would be loved anyway! Don't you get it?" Marcus shook his head in frustration, "If they wanted to they would be able to control everything and no one would be the wiser because they could use the information to keep things under their control, in their favor. Who would know?"

He paused a moment to try to make out her expression in the dimly lit cabin before continuing,

"Listen up, Gardener, there are four kinds of people in the world: Those who want to profit off others without changing anything, like the Kringles for instance. Those who want to profit off others and would try to improve the world, like those who have been holding you. Those who want to profit off of others and are willing to destroy the world to do so and finally those who don't care to profit off others and are the inevitable victims of the other three. The trick is to know which one of these people you are."

Krystal did not respond and the discussion seemed to end as abruptly as it started.

Marcus grunted with exasperation and leaned back into the driver's seat.

After a few moments she spoke again,

"Which one are you, Marcus?" she asked again, "Which one of those four kinds of people are you?"

He turned toward her again and watched for a moment.

"Do you see that light up ahead?" he asked her, changing the subject.

She looked ahead, focusing on a light that seemed to indicate a small house at the end of this desolate road.

Marcus continued,

"There is a small house about five minutes ahead. In it are some friends of ours. They have been given instruction to take you in and keep you safe. Remember, not everyone wants you safe," he suggested, looking at her through his brow, "I've also been given instructions. I am supposed to offer you a choice."

He paused and then while motioning with his hand, barked,

"Give me your coat!"

She scowled at him in bemusement and asked sharply,

"Why?"

Nervously and curtly he repeated himself,

"Just ... just give me your coat!"

Her heart started to pound. She was not sure of why he would make such a request, but reluctantly and with an emotion between fear and anger started to pull her heavy coat off of her shoulders.

"Hurry up!" he commanded.

Shifting awkwardly in the confines of the vehicle's cabin, she finished taking her coat off and tried to toss it at Marcus in an effort to silently voice her protest. The large coat landed partially on his head and he quickly pulled it away from his face and balled it up in his lap before tossing it behind his seat.

"As I said, you have a choice. I'm going to set you free if that's what you want." He paused for a reaction, but heard nothing and continued with a condescending tone, "In these temperatures, at your age and health and dressed as you are, you'll be able to make it to that house. However, if you'd like to escape, now's your chance, and you are likely stupid enough to try; you can go anywhere you want. Just keep in mind it's about forty below, you have no transportation and no light, and there is nothing around for miles. So if you choose to run, you will die in the cold and you will solve many problems for everyone. Most would die in thirty minutes or so, but I'd say you'd last forty-five. Personally, I hope you run," he snarled at her, and turned away.

"Now get out!" he snapped, turning away.

Her expression of horror was lost to him as he barked out a last,

"Get out!"

She needed not speak, her disgust was communicated in her silence and she opened the passenger side door.

As she stepped out she felt the cold stab through her body, like icy blades cutting her face, chest, and arms. The cold made her focus quickly on the light ahead and she gave little thought to the belching sound of the engine of Marcus's vehicle as he started to back away from her, the chatter of the treads in the snow, and the grumble of the engine as he turned around and started on his way back. She clutched her self tightly to fend off the cold as she thought just how sinister and evil the choice he gave her seemed. She had to decide voluntarily to face her incarceration or her own death. She took a step toward the light. Hesitated and stopped. A deep breath of crisp air did not refresh, but burned the inside of her sinuses. The darkness now fell silent as she tried to force herself forward. Frozen by indecision, the cold was already causing her to shiver uncontrollably. She took another step forward. Her joints already felt stiff. She stopped again. Then in the dark she heard someone. Her pulse quickened.

246

"There she is! Grab her now! Get her before she gets too close to the house! This will be our only window of opportunity!" a voice in a low, menacing and assertive whisper commanded.

"I'll go after them, you go get her!" the voice continued.

Then a grunt of acknowledgement from another person was followed by a sharp whine of two snowmobile engines starting up. Lights on either side of the road blinded her when she looked toward them, and she realized one set was coming closer. The other appeared to go down the road in the opposite direction.

Krystal started to run. Her throat went raw as she gasped for air, breathing the icy cold through her mouth. She started down the road toward the house. Realizing a set of lights was catching up to her, she ran faster. She was having trouble keeping her balance as the snow caused her feet to slip. Uncontrolled, her momentum thrust her forward in lurches and she started to fall to the ground, her hands impacting the hard, frozen snow. She could feel it scraping the skin from her palms as the whine of her pursuer's snowmobile came closer. The air started to stink of oil and gasoline. She tried to get up and run further, but just as she regained her balance the snowmobile pulled up beside her and the rider jumped off and tackled her like a roped calf in a rodeo. The rider threw a heavy blanket over her, forcing her back down to the ground. She struggled, but the weight of her assailant kept her pinned under the blanket.

Marcus did not hear the engine of the snowmobile approaching him as he drove down the dark road, but rather only saw it as the lights pulled up next to him. Shocked by the presence of the snowmobile and its rider, he watched it intently as the rider signaled to him to pull over. Marcus had no intention of doing so and instead accelerated and pulled away. The snowmobile whined as it caught up again. Marcus looked down at it through the side window and steered toward it in an effort to run it off the road.

Chunks of plastic and fiberglass flew through the air as the treads on Marcus's vehicle impacted the snowmobile's side. It swerved and erratically steered off the road and fell back. Then with a whine the snowmobile came back undeterred, its motion shaky as elements of it had been damaged and pushed out of alignment. Marcus tried again to force the snowmobile off the road, but this time the rider was able to maneuver out of his way and push forward. Marcus accelerated and ran into the snowmobile again. He saw its lights flicker off and on again and then drop back. Marcus pushed on. Then to his surprise the half-cocked, cross-eyed headlights of the snowmobile started to catch up again. He steered into its way, but even in its compromised state the snowmobile was still more nimble and pulled up on Marcus's passenger side.

From the driver's seat, Marcus had trouble keeping track of the snowmobile and he hardly noticed that it was pulling ahead. It happened too suddenly for him to react, but the snowmobile seemed to have lost control as it accelerated past him. Whether by accident or in an intentional effort to stop Marcus's vehicle, the snowmobile turned in front of him suddenly, cutting him off.

Marcus struck the snowmobile broadside. His vehicle lurched as his windshield was showered with shattered pieces of fiberglass and metal. A flash lit up the darkness and the broken snowmobile rolled in front of Marcus's vehicle as it was pushed forward. Then in a moment the snowmobile rolled under him. Marcus's vehicle's nose jumped skyward as the crumpled snowmobile entangled itself with his undercarriage. Now straddling the snowmobile, Marcus's vehicle's nose dropped into the snow and ice, bringing the two machines to a tangle stop. Marcus's head struck the steering wheel. The engine went silent and the lights dimmed.

Marcus lifted his head, looking out and scanning the area illuminated by the beams from his headlights. He felt blood trickling from his forehead and grunted in frustration as he violently flung open the door to his incapacitated vehicle.

It was nearly impossible to see all the damage in the dark, but Marcus looked under his vehicle anyway. The nose pointed into the ground, it resembled a seesaw with the crushed body of the snowmobile as the pivot point.

He stood up and scanned the dark landscape as he stepped out in front of the still-glowing headlights. He was suddenly pushed to the ground by a tall, heavily dressed man in a helmet.

Marcus struggled as the man pinned him down on his back with his knee. Marcus could not see his face, as the reflection of the headlights and the wreckage of the two vehicles obscured any features. Marcus saw as the figure's silhouette drew back his right arm. Then with a jolt, Marcus felt a gloved fist cross his face. Pain shot through his cheekbone and nose. The padding of the glove lessened the blow, but Marcus felt blood filling his sinus.

He saw the man's arm draw back again. Instinctively he reached toward the wreckage and grabbed the first object he could. Getting hold of the twisted remains of one of the snowmobile's front skis, Marcus struck the man hard on the side of the head and broke the visor off of the helmet he was wearing. In so doing, for a moment Marcus saw his face illuminated by the headlights.

"You!" Marcus exclaimed as the man stumbled back, stunned by the blow.

Marcus, still on his back but free, now drew back his legs and kicked the man in the chest, sending him to the ground. Marcus stood up, still wielding the ski, and struck the man in the arm and again on the head. Writhing in agony, the man attempted to block the blows with his arms and shoulders as Marcus struck him again and again.

Crawling on the ground, the man tried to escape as Marcus hammered him with the ski.

Then stretching out his hand, the man grabbed a hold of the ski before another blow could hit him and pulled hard, throwing Marcus off balance again and Marcus released his grip on the ski.

The man swung around and with a long, defensive swing stuck Marcus in the head. The sound of bone cracking horrifically evident, Marcus staggered for two steps and like a marionette whose strings had just been cut, fell to the ground, lifeless.

The man, wiping the blood from his face, injured and exhausted, stumbled toward the vehicle's hood and leaned against it, catching his breath. Just then a set of headlights came rushing toward him and came to a stop about ten feet away.

"Henry!" a voice called out, "Holy Christmas, what happened?"

The figures of Jason Pelham and a bundled Krystal Gardener got off the snowmobile and hurried over. Jason wrapped his arm around her in an effort to keep her close and to help keep her warm as they came closer.

Henry Foster removed his cracked helmet and mopped more blood from his face with the back of his gloved hand.

"I'm afraid this got totally out of hand," Henry said, falling back against the tattered vehicle.

"Marcus tried to run me off the road and almost ran me over!" he followed up.

"And Marcus?" Jason asked breathlessly and wide-eyed.

Henry shook his head and said simply,

"Fatally injured."

"Henry!" Jason exclaimed with agitation, "Now we have to go to Xavier!"

Henry inclined his head in silent agreement.

19

The Government Intervention

It was perplexing. Whether by virtue of the misalignment of the data captured by the flight recorder on Caravan Charlie Golf Sierra Zulu Whisky and the actions and recorded responses of the pilot, or the quick move to judgment by both the Federal Aviation Administration and Transport Canada that pilot error was entirely to blame for the ill-fated flight, Tom Bradley was mystified by the dismissive nature of the official channel of investigation. Tom had consulted a number of aviation experts to advise him in his investigation, but had a biting reservation about all the conclusions that were drawn.

He had had a chance to study components of the aircraft which had been retrieved for him at the behest of Agent Teresa LaChapelle. Still, he wanted to have the avionics and flight recorder, which were with the National Transportation Safety Board under the oversight and jurisdiction of the Transportation Safety Board of Canada and would have to be moved back to the FBI offices for further study in his own lab in greater detail. Reluctantly, this was taken under advisement with the understanding that it would be done only after the initial investigation by the NTSB and TSBC was completed.

On the surface Tom agreed that it appeared as the investigators had suggested,

"Pilot error, that's all."

However, he decided to look at those questions and anomalies that, when asked, made the NTSB investigator stutter and wave off dismissively without reasonable explanation.

How was it that we have recorded voices of the pilot's radio calls and reactions to commands of an aviation controller even though our records showed a loss of communication a short time into the flight?

Why did the pilot's responses suggest he was attempting a particular maneuver but the flight recorder's data suggested a different execution of that same maneuver?

Why and who would have given the pilot the direction to fly the aircraft so far north and to what purpose?

Why would a seasoned pilot not have questioned the prudence of the course and altitude?

Indeed, it seemed that with every questionable response from the pilot to a command, presumably from air traffic control, the corresponding execution seemed even more problematic. The list of discrepancies went on as he dug deeper, but that only managed to distance his collaboration with the other two government agencies.

Tom had started to formulate a hypothesis. To him, once he considered it, it made everything fall into place, though he also felt that articulating it without further evidence would be waived off as ridiculous and fraught with fanatical conspiracy theory-generated paranoia. Still, Tom thought the obvious explanation was that the pilot had no reason to question the commands and had no information to suggest the perilous nature of his execution. Perhaps the pilot was not getting accurate information from either air traffic control or his instruments. This would explain everything, Tom thought, and the investigation had already yielded a couple absolutes that might support his theory:

Though the pilot's reaction and lack of judgment might suggest impairment, there was no evidence of drug or alcohol use, physical, psychological, or even ideological factors.

Though the weather conditions on route were starting to degenerate and visibility was compromised, the aircraft would not have had any significant problems until it turned north and into the oncoming weather pattern.

Still, the final and official explanation of the circumstances that led to the crash was noted as *'pilot error'* and the report closed.

This was an unsatisfactory conclusion for Tom and Teresa, who then followed up on the request to have the avionics and flight recorder returned, and used the clout of their collective offices at the FBI and CSIS to get the permissions needed for Tom to completely disassemble the components, once the NTSB and TSBC had finished their reports, in his own lab at the FBI.

A week later the battered radios and the flight recorder arrived.

Tom was tired, as he had been working into the early morning every day this week, disassembling parts of the flight recorder, avionics, and other radio components.

The flight recorder yielded nothing of particular interest beyond the recorded account of the flight. However, the avionics, screens, and radios of the aircraft which, according to the logbooks, were added after the original manufacture date of the aircraft as an elaborate upgrade before delivery to the charter company, piqued Tom's interest in particular.

Tom had powered up the screens a number of times and found that one still worked though most of the electronics that fed it did not. He rubbed his eyes and yawned. Then, before he called it a night he decided he would take the face off of one of the nonfunctional screens. One had a long crack down the center. With a thin blade he parted the face and plastic frame of this screen from the rectangular box that housed the additional components. He loosened a corner and started the separation. He became more impatient and more aggressive with the task and then, without warning, the screen popped loose. One half of the screen broke away, exposing the green circuit board beneath. Tom turned it over and unplugged the ribbon of wires that held on the other half of the screen. He carefully examined it. Then with a moment of both vindication and horror he gasped as his expectation was fulfilled. Behind the screen on the board he found a small chip marked *ICU2*.

It was now nearly two o'clock in the morning when Tom started to prepare to leave the building. Motivated by curiosity and determination, Tom had managed to find five ICU and ICU2 chips amongst the aircraft's cockpit components.

"There will be more," he thought.

As he would have more trouble disassembling the nearly indestructible casing of the flight recorder, he chose to test it with his own device as the flight recorder was still working. It appeared clear of chips. Tom considered this result as inconclusive, but acceptable for now.

His heart pounded as he considered what this circumstantial evidence suggested to him. Could the flight have been sabotaged by someone through the chips? And if so, was this a wanton act of premeditated murder of some US government officials? He hurriedly cleared his table of the materials and locked them up. Though it was normally common procedure, for these reasons he chose not to document his investigation via digital camera but rather with an older video device. He feared being seen, not by anyone at the office, but through the devices. He was starting to feel uncomfortable and vulnerable. The prospects now seemed even more terrifying. He would consult with Teresa LaChapelle in the morning. For now he would have to go home, even if for only a couple hours.

On his way home Tom eyed every camera, every scanner, monitor, radio, cell phone, and computer with suspicion. He was starting to feel quite paranoid.

The air was humid and heavy and though it seemed unseasonably warm, large snowflakes fell to the ground, melting quickly into the wetness of the streets. Illuminated by the lanterns on the walls of his building, the dry pavement of the path to the front door under a long red canopy beckoned him to get inside.

It was mid-December and the presence of the Christmas decorations in the lobby of his apartment building did not help Tom's demeanor. He glowered at the lobby cameras and dragged himself to the elevator, now more concerned about getting to his bed than his discovery of the chips in the airplane's electronics. He slipped his key into the keyhole security panel under the elevator call button, pushed it, and the up-arrow lit up. The elevator door opened and Tom entered.

He got off of the elevator and started down the hall to his apartment.

Tom entered his apartment after running through a series of new locks which adorned a new door. The doorframe, however, still bore the scars of the police's forced entry a couple months before.

He entered, head bowed and hardly awake. Then something caught his attention and with a shriek like the squeal of a pig being stuck with a pitchfork, he recoiled in terror at the sight of three beautifully wrapped packages adorned with colorful paper, pine boughs, holly, a tag marked SANTA, and tied off with gold ribbon. The presence of these packages filled Tom with dread. They sat there mocking him and his feeble attempt at security. He backed away from them, refusing to allow his gaze to stray. Fixated, he moved backwards into the darkness of his apartment until he felt his bedroom door behind him. He opened it without turning, backed in and slammed the door shut.

Tom leaned hopelessly against his closed bedroom door. Illuminated by a small nightlight, he looked at the telephone and clock radio. He scanned the room and his gaze stopped at the flat-screened television in the corner opposite his bed. Turned to the wall, silent and unplugged, it was a testament to Tom's discomfort with the situation that was unfolding in his mind. He remained there motionless for a few moments before sliding down to the ground and settling at the base of the door. His face contorted and he started to weep in frustration. He would spend the night there.

He woke with a jolt from a disturbed sleep. His neck and back ached from sleeping against his bedroom door, a briefcase full of paperwork and equipment still slung over his shoulder. Stiff and groggy, he got up and started unplugging, removing the batteries, and disconnecting everything in his apartment. He pinned closed the curtains and inspected all of his light fixtures. He was determined to try to create a safe zone. Then as he prepared to leave that morning and approached his front door, he decided to deal with the packages in the front hall. Strangely unwilling to touch them, he pushed them to the outside hallway by moving them with his foot as though they were a foul-smelling and decaying carcass. He had always enjoyed receiving gifts from SANTA, but now these seemed dangerous and toxic. He shuddered at even the thought of opening them and had a distinct feeling of relief once they were completely out of his apartment.

"I will mark these as trash when I return tonight," he thought to himself as he went through the ritualistic process of locking his door.

He was tired and his nerves frayed, but he wanted to be sure that he contacted Teresa LaChapelle that morning and then get back to his lab to gather the aircraft components he'd reviewed last night.

"All channels of communication may be compromised," Tom suggested to Teresa in his phone conversation that morning, "We must talk face-to-face. Someplace where we can't be heard and can't be seen by anyone or anything! Can you come to Washington, DC to discuss my findings?"

"I'll catch a flight out of Toronto tomorrow morning," Teresa responded.

Tom felt a sense of relief in the knowledge that she was coming. She would be a sympathetic ear and one who would look at his theories with an open mind; she had already been involved in the investigation with John Evans. After making some arrangements to prepare his office to receive her he went back to the aircraft's electronics.

He pulled out a tray of broken cockpit components and the battered flight recorder and pulled back a sheet, which covered them. Now exposed, the components were like the remains of a started and opened cadaver in an autopsy. He pulled some lights closer and mounted an older video camera to record his progress in removing the parasitical ICU chips from the remains of the radios and screens. Tom grabbed his bag and pulled out a small tape and loaded it into the camera.

Now that he knew the chips were present, he set is mind to finding evidence of tampering in the aircraft's operation of that fateful morning.

Tom had already started to understand how the chips could be addressed and that they would respond. Still, he found it difficult to reverse engineer this very proprietary technology.

However, with these aircraft components, he theorized he would be able to use the flight recorder's data to detect anomalies, because in this case the data had been recorded but, before the chips might have been able to erase their own digital impact on that data, the systems went off-line in the crash. Consequently he might be able to discern how they did it. This would also lead to the evidence he needed to implicate the chips and the Kringle Works in the crash. This was the information he needed to tune the direction of his investigation, which would have eluded the NTSB and TSBC in their more results-motivated inquiry.

The idea that the chips were part of a monitoring network was now established. With confirmation from John Evans, who was still in the Washington Hospital Center nursing the loss of six toes due to frostbite, the

Kringle Works had all but admitted their connection to the chips. John had also suggested that prior to the crash, he thought that the Kringle Works had implied some type of future agreement with the United States government which would be somehow connected to this monitoring network, but this was conjecture on his part as he suggested the preliminary discussions were held with Holden Mealy and Secretary Brenda Willis in his and Walter Hayes's absence.

Holden Mealy and Brenda Willis's recovered bodies had just been buried at Arlington National Cemetery two weeks earlier and a direct confrontation with the Kringle Works in light of the NTSB and TSBC reports seemed unwarranted and imprudent at this point,

"At least to the outside observer," Tom thought to himself.

Indeed, in the time it took to regain access to the aircraft components, it seemed that motivation to dig any further was faltering even more and if this incident and the now somewhat unsupported investigation was to be kept from disappearing into the archives with most every other interaction with the Kringle Works, it would be incumbent upon Tom and Teresa to find compelling evidence of malice, and quickly. It was, after all, politically unpopular to accuse the Kringle Works of wrongdoing and this politically inconvenient investigation had now been neatly closed up in the eyes of the current administrations of both Canada and the United States. In fact, it was not lost on Tom that at this time of year specifically, support would be waning. A fact made even more obvious when the United States suddenly and almost prematurely issued an official apology to the Kringle Works for the direction the FBI's investigation had taken. This served as a precautionary measure so as to avoid any potential disruption in the scheduled delivery of the Christmas service.

"… Or any other service, for that matter," Tom said to himself aloud, "Merry fucking Christmas!" he followed up, shaking his head as he soldered some wires to one of the circuit boards.

He knew that the media attention that would follow the disclosure of the crash to the public would lead to potential exposure of their investigation and would desperately hurt the FBI's credibility and popularity. The investigation's progress would be in imminent danger once a successor to Assistant Director Hayes was named. Tom felt that it was likely that the new assistant director would opt for political expediency and suggest that the quiet closing of the investigation might be preferable to any 'truth' they were pursuing. Especially considering the 'potentially rogue interests' of Walter Hayes's motivations in pushing for the original investigation.

To save face, the FBI was already distancing itself from Walter Hayes's leadership. This left Tom particularly uncomfortable and saddened as he also knew the real truth was that Walter Hayes's motivation was nothing more than to identify and plug a security hole which Tom himself had first witnessed.

Time was becoming a luxury that they no longer had and he focused on the effort.

"I have to do this for John and Walter!" he said to himself as he proceeded to power up a part of the aircraft's electronic instrument display on a new screen.

The idea that the chips might have communicated to someone at the Kringle Works what the aircraft was doing and where it was going did not explain how that might cause the airplane to crash or how the events that led to Tom's false arrest in September might have been precipitated. For the ICU chips to impact the flight or the computer check of his criminal record they had to be able to not just read and relay information from a device but disseminate it back as well. This, however, was still a theory unique to Tom and he would have to prove it, even to Agent Teresa LaChapelle.

He had gotten a late start that day. A good deal of time had been spent talking to Teresa LaChapelle and making arrangements with her. His mind was slow; he had not gotten more than a few hours sleep for several nights and this last night, he thought, did not really count as any. It was under these conditions that he had his next major breakthrough.

Tom discovered a small flash memory chip that was integrated in the screens' support electronics and remained undamaged in two of the three screens. This memory chip was designed to allow a pilot to be able to switch display modes quickly and without a delayed response as graphics loaded. Storing these graphics, which were the elements that built the digital versions of the gauges and which kept the pilot informed, made the switching of screen modes perceptibly instantaneous. It was also meant to act as a backup to allow the gauges to come back online quickly if there was ever a momentary loss of power or fluctuation to the system, or if an engine restart was needed.

Tom was able to tap into this memory and with it, see the data that would have been displayed in the cockpit just prior to the crash. He was able to pull two different images from one of the chips.

The first was ominous and perplexing. A blank screen with one single window, which stated an almost silly sounding message,

> *I'm sorry, but this screen is no longer receiving data and restoring will not be possible. Goodbye.*

Tom shuddered at the thought of a pilot that would have had to manage an emergency in the air with this message on his cockpit screens.

The other image was of the avionics instrument cluster displaying the familiar gauges for heading, pitch, compass, and altitude. It was here that Tom noticed a major discrepancy.

He noted that the altimeter on the screen image indicated an altitude of 11,945 feet, yet the data sent from the same sensors to the flight recorder indicated an altitude of 3,945 feet. This perilously low altitude was arrived at by a consistent descent at the pilot's hand after the flight recorder's last audio recording in which the pilot was heard to acknowledge an altitude of twelve thousand feet. This information from the flight recorder was a part of what led the NTSB and TSBC to assess the decision making of the pilot as flawed and at fault. Only, Tom now knew that the pilot, who was at the mercy of his instruments, was receiving dramatically erroneous information leading to one of the circumstances that would manifest in the catastrophic crash which killed the pilot and three of his passengers.

For the next hours Tom pursued this line of inquiry further. It yielded some additional information which, he felt, gave compelling evidence of tampering, and noted them in his findings. Specifically, even though the aircraft sensors transmitted data that appeared correct when compared to the physical evidence gathered from the plane and the crash site, it did not match the information displayed on the pilot's digital instruments. As it seemed that the electronics, which appeared to be in working order, displayed completely different information versus the data sent from the aircraft sensors, Tom theorized that the data was correct but stopped at the point of the ICU chips, where it was either altered or alternative data was created and passed on to the displays. Furthermore, after careful review of the manufacturer's documentation and the avionics technical information, Tom also determined that the error message displayed on the other screen image was not one that could be generated by any part of the electronics on board the aircraft and suggested, in Tom's mind, evidence of an external influence.

Tom had found what he wanted. The evidence was still largely circumstantial but compelling enough to reconsider the investigation. Maybe this was even enough to motivate the department to act on it when considered with the material gathered by agents John Evans and Teresa LaChapelle. Certainly the charges were serious enough.

Tom felt energized and was comfortable that he would now have a productive meeting with Agent LaChapelle. Excited, he emerged from his lab only to realize that he had once again worked past the normal daily hours.

He packed up and decided to head home. He gave a nod to Agent Jenkins, who fired back a resentful look as he continued the overnight shift of monitoring the nation's computer security, which he was pushed to take on since September and that had been Tom's burden to bear prior to his special assignment.

When he returned to his apartment building, the feeling of accomplishment resulting from his breakthroughs for the day seemed to carry him through the familiar ritual of locks and security procedures now common to his building and apartment.

He had a confidence that was a little foreign to him, but he liked it. He knew what he was doing. He had always been a brilliant mind and had been recognized for it, but still he had always felt a little meek and powerless in his life. Now he was on to something, something that had been weighing on him for most of the year, something whose implementation put him through the worst month of his life. He was feeling a sense of power over something that seemed to be a metaphor for a lifelong feeling of powerlessness. This was big, this was dangerous, but this was something that he might be able to rally those around him to help overcome.

There was a sense, in Tom's mind, that his comfort with numbers and technology, his affinity for analysis and logic put him at odds with the society around him. A feeling of oppression that came from an unknown, unseen, and lifelong enemy that came from deep within and seemed to take a physical form when he started to be taunted by the technology around him. Clearly, someone wanted him to diminish and cower, but he was starting to understand them and this would allow him to reclaim a measure of control.

A smile broke across Tom's face, which signaled an unfamiliar feeling of personal triumph.

However the glow of euphoria would fade quickly upon entering his apartment.

He could see it illuminated by the light of the hallway through his front door. It filled Tom with dread as he was reminded of the gravity of the situation, the depth of the conspiracy and the strength of his nemesis. His heart jumped into his throat and a shiver ran up his spine as he caught the reflection of his own silhouette and the bright outline of his doorway across the room. In the past he would have shrieked in delight, but now it was grim and intimidating.

A brand new laptop computer with an additional large screen sat in his living room. Presumably to replace the one he lost to the investigation of his potential terrorist activities, the Kringle Works had apparently provided him with a Christmas upgrade. The screen was turned off and the glossy face, in which his reflection stood and was interrupted by a diagonal ribbon and a bow in the upper right corner, seemed to look back at him. In the darkness of the room he felt its presence and its unyielding interest in watching and listening to him. He viewed this computer as though it was a person eyeing him with malice and ill intent.

He closed the door behind him and the room went completely dark. He took a deep breath and turned on the light. He allowed his eyes to adjust and apprehensively he walked toward the machine.

He stood quietly and thought of taking a hammer to his new computer. The idea that he could destroy it allowed Tom to regain a level of control but it also reminded him of just how vulnerable the population was to this new foe, one that was the result of an unconscious trust with the people and their nations, which had never considered the potential for abuse should that trust fall into the wrong hands. The people always knew that Santa was watching, but he was always benign, positive, and inspiring. No one had ever considered Santa as a threat, but the depth of the surveillance, the evidence of manipulation and the alleged malice of recent actions showed how dangerous and overreaching their practices seemed to have become.

Depriving it of power and proximity, Tom unplugged the new computer and screen, took out the batteries, boxed them up and shoved them into a closet. Then he checked around the apartment again to be sure he had eliminated as much of the potential for monitoring in his apartment as possible before he retired for a restless night.

The lack of sleep was starting to catch up to Tom. Still, early in the afternoon of the next day he enthusiastically received Agent LaChapelle.

It turned out to be another long day, but after review of the original investigation under Walter Hayes, the follow-up investigation by John Evans and Teresa LaChapelle, Tom's data and discoveries were starting to build a reasonable case for a rather disquieting scenario. Consequently, Agent LaChapelle agreed that though this was a Canadian aircraft that crashed, the case should be followed up on by the United States, as it was their diplomats who were killed.

They spent the next two days drafting up the case and appropriate paperwork. Early the following week they presented their findings to a reluctant FBI Director Patterson. Still, once presented, Director Patterson had a rather strange and almost enthusiastic reaction. One that Tom did not quite understand, but took it as a good sign when he and Teresa were asked to present it again to a White House-appointed liaison by the name of Nancy Otis. However, Nancy's reaction seemed even stranger, as a rather odd and excited look crossed her face. In fact she seemed strangely delighted at some of the conclusions drawn and enthusiastically took the case materials and suggested that they would be presented to other elements of the Department of Homeland Security and the White House Chief of Staff. Indeed, she suggested that it might be appropriate to include the Pentagon in their discussions. Then she inquired about John Evans' condition and whether or not she could talk to him.

"I would be most honored if I might be able to have a word with this Agent Evans. I should like to get his understanding of what exactly happened on the island. Thank you, agents LaChapelle and Bradley. Your contributions are appreciated. I think we have enough information to further pursue this issue on our own. I will make sure you are recognized for your work. We'll handle it from here," she noted in a friendly but rather dismissive tone.

20

FOLLOWING THE MONEY

Xavier was pacing the floor in a most agitated manner before he stopped and addressed the two men in his office.

"Gentlemen! How could you be so completely irresponsible? Do you have any idea of how complicated the last couple weeks have become?"

Henry sat silently with his head bowed as Jason attempted to address Xavier's rhetorical question.

Xavier stopped and raised his hand to signal Jason to stay silent.

"No, I have heard your story! I understand what you thought you were doing, but honestly, we have law enforcement on this island and no matter what Marcus was involved in, they and only they are at liberty to pursue it!" Xavier scolded the two men and continued, "I have a great deal to mop up as a result of your escapades and this is going to be very difficult for all of us!"

"Peter Sharp is personally debriefing Krystal Gardener and we will have to see what information she can give us. In the meantime you two are going to have to lay low until I sort this out!"

Xavier started pacing again and followed up,

"As it is, I still have a fair share of diplomacy to follow through on, with the United States trying to sink their greedy little teeth into our affairs again."

Henry looked up and then at Jason,

"That's part of what we needed to talk about!" Henry noted quietly.

Xavier stopped and turned toward him, cutting him off,

"It's being handled! Andre personally volunteered to take on this latest burden and has been quieting the wolves at the gate."

Xavier wasn't sure who cried out first or which was the loudest, but he was startled by a collective, "NO!" from both men.

Stunned he responded,

"Silence, gentlemen! I assure you these last weeks would have been a disaster if Andre had not been working with the mainland these last few weeks. He has been successfully calming the rhetoric and defusing the situation since our meeting some weeks ago and he has been doing so at my direction," Xavier paused, "The circumstances surrounding the United States' investigation of our humble company have made things very, very complicated."

He stared at the two men grimly,

"Which is more than I can say for you! You! You two have made things here very complicated. He shook his head in frustration and continued, "Your effort to rescue Ms. Gardener may have been motivated by good intention but this should have remained a law enforcement issue, which by taking into your own hands, has resulted in your involvement in the accidental death of one of my executives! Are you even slightly aware of what this means?"

He started pacing again.

"I will get a report from Peter Sharp regarding his conversations with Krystal Gardener, but she too, exhibited some questionable behavior. What was she thinking, breaking into Marcus' office in the first place?" Xavier stopped and sighed, "Peter is not happy; he is rightfully suspicious of the whole situation."

"Just because you are a victim, it does not make you innocent," he followed up. "For now you're all lucky that Peter thinks highly enough of all of you not to ask my endorsement to have all three of you locked up while he investigates what has happened."

"But Xavier!" Henry exclaimed, "Andre…"

Xavier raised his hand to stop him from completing the comment.

"Henry! I will follow up with you shortly. Andre is of no concern of yours for now," Xavier interjected, "Not until we have cleaned up this mess you have created." He paused and asked, "Do I make myself clear?"

"Yes sir," Henry mumbled.

Xavier nodded and followed up,

"You are both free to go. I will follow up with both of you later."

The two men got out of their seats and started to leave.

"Jason!" Xavier broke the silence, "I think you and I should talk *right now*. Stay here for a minute."

Jason and Henry looked at each other for a moment in silence before Jason turned to Xavier. Henry humbly nodded a quiet farewell acknowledgement to both men and continued on his way.

Xavier walked up to a painting of Christopher Kringle and with his back turned to Jason spoke,

"So, this is where your investigation has led you," he sighed and turned to Jason, "You have been a little reckless and I'm not convinced that you're looking in the right places, but I will do my best to resolve this. Know this, even as an accident this won't be easy. Now tell me what you think you know."

Jason looked at Xavier apologetically and took a seat.

"Xavier," he started, "there is a lot that we haven't told Peter Sharp and there is a lot that we haven't told you. I wanted to come to you sooner, but the truth is that we are not sure who is involved and we were afraid that if we came to you, you would be forced to take action, which would have driven those involved underground. We know very little."

"We, Jason? We?" Xavier interrupted, "Is 'we' Krystal and Henry?"

Jason nodded.

"Why, Jason? Why would you involve them? Were you so sure that they could be trusted?" Xavier questioned, "Were you so comfortable exposing them to the dangers? You see what happened."

Jason shook his head and answered,

"No! No, neither was supposed to be involved. Krystal was just trying to help though I asked her not to. Henry was already digging and came to me to try to find out more. Still, I do trust them, Xavier, implicitly."

Xavier eyed him skeptically but then nodded in acknowledgement and took his seat behind the desk.

"Okay, then tell me what you've found." Xavier folded his hands together, leaning on the dark wooden surface of his desk.

The mid-February sun was casting a golden glow in the late afternoon sky and over the tarmac at Dulles International Airport in Washington, DC. The runway was accented by some melting piles of snow, remnants of a season of past storms now starting to give way to an early spring.

A lone aircraft stood at the end of the field with a limousine and a black SUV parked at the nose near a set of roll-up stairs leading to an opened door. At the base were four men in dark suits and the well-groomed and excited figure of Nancy Otis, anticipating the emergence of their special guest. She watched eagerly as two men in uniform appeared from the aircraft, carrying a number of suitcases and an old-world styled trunk. They arranged to have the luggage loaded in both the SUV and the limousine.

Now all eyes fixated on the fuselage door.

A moment later the men at the base of the steps started to mobilize, responding to instructions transmitted through earpiece communicators.

Another second passed and the elegant, tall, and slender figure of Andre Leopold emerged from the aircraft door at the top of the steps. His gray thinning hair, muttonchops and long embroidered coat harkened to a bygone age, as did his manner. He slowly descended the steps with his eyes focused on the smiling face of Nancy Otis. At the base of the staircase they spoke briefly, shook hands and then disappeared into the limousine, the doors closed behind them by the dark-suited men, who then moved quickly to enter the SUV. The two vehicles drove off.

As they left the airport, Andre sat back for the ride. He watched the landscape go by for a moment and then politely made eye contact with Nancy, who was watching him. He clasped his hands on the top of his walking stick. A wry smile crossed his face before he spoke.

"We have much to discuss Ms. Otis," Andre broke the silence with an even, quiet, and controlled voice, "I hope your president has empowered you with an appropriate amount of authority to negotiate with me."

"Indeed, Mister Leopold," she answered coyly, "Perhaps not me, but those who will be joining us."

Andre nodded and his gaze turned back to the passing landscape.

The interior fell silent again. For a while Andre watched out the window, with the only sound being the muffled hum of the engine and the passing road.

"Mister Leopold?" The apologetic tone used by Nancy Otis seemed to indicate the delicacy of her charter, "I hope you do not think me too forward, but after you check into your hotel, I should like the honor of your company at dinner."

Andre shifted his gaze to her. He inclined his head and answered,

"The honor is mine, Ms. Otis. You are, after all, my guide and host, yes?"

A schoolgirl-like grin formed on Nancy's face and she responded enthusiastically,

"Oh yes, Mister Leopold. Yes. That will do quite nicely. Thank you!"

The sun had set in the time it took for the two vehicles to arrive at the Watergate Hotel.

It was a long night but nothing Andre was not accustomed to. Still, the need for sleep was growing as his age advanced and it was not until the next morning that he felt rested and ready for his mission, barely recalling the evening before and when he actually fell asleep.

Seated in a chair in the sitting area of his suite, he pushed aside a wheeled, chrome-based cart which stood before him and his chair. It blocked his way. It had a white marble top that protruded from under a white tablecloth. The bright bouquet of flowers and silver-domed dishes looked largely undisturbed until the cart hit the wall with a small, unintended jolt. With a jingle of clattering silver, glass, and porcelain, a splash of coffee swamped over the lip of a gold- and silver-rimmed porcelain cup, staining the white table linens.

He grabbed a black case and assembled a file of documents that had been laid out on the bed before room service brought the breakfast cart. With a quick look at his watch and a confirmation glance at the clock radio, he got up to leave. He stepped in front of the mirror and straightened his gray suit and collar. He draped a long coat over his shoulders and left.

Upon exiting the hotel, Andre was greeted by a driver and limousine. Behind it was a black SUV flanked by a number of dark-suited security personnel who were watching him intently from the curbside. The limousine driver looked at a note then looked up with an expression of confirmed recognition. He moved to the back and making eye contact with Andre opened the back door and motioned for him to get in. Once he did, the men in the dark suits started to scurry and jumped into the SUV. Together they pulled away.

It was not a long ride to their destination on Pennsylvania Avenue. They would have a meeting in the administrative office at the White House. Andre paid little attention to the security and logistics of getting him to his location, allowing his handlers to do as they had been instructed. Instead he chose to take the time to think. He calculated his moves, considered his options and anticipated the outcome.

The door to the limousine opened and a voice streamed in. Sounding like a police siren with an obnoxiously cheery disposition and a song-like flourish at the end, came the words,

"Good morning!"

Leaning forward into the limousine toward Andre, with her hand outstretched in an effort to aid his exit, was Nancy Otis.

He stood up and they started to walk.

"How did you sleep?" she asked him politely, "was the room adequate?"

He answered as they walked,

"Of course, madam, quite comfortable; but I find that you keep the temperatures in your buildings quite a bit too warm."

Nancy stopped cold. Sympathetically, she gasped and in a voice with a hint of panic and indignation, she responded,

"Well, that cannot stand! I will have that taken care of immediately! Please accept our apologies!"

Andre chuckled to himself, amused at the thought that she might have the entire building's temperature lowered on his behalf.

"Such a society of excesses," he mused quietly.

Her chest puffed and exuding an air of self-importance and pride, Nancy walked the halls as Andre's guide, nodding at various staffers and personnel as they went through the maze of passages.

They arrived at the door of a well-appointed conference room with an adjacent sitting area. In it were two men; both stood up as they entered.

The younger of the two men jumped to his feet with the immediacy and exuberance of youth. The other slowly got up, suggesting that years of wear had put an irreversible brake on every movement, manifesting itself as an unapologetic lack of a need to impress those around him.

"Good morning, Mister Leopold, my name is Jonathan Casper," the younger gentleman stretched out his hand to shake Andre's, "I am this White House's public information czar."

Andre pursed his lips and looked him in the eye,

"So then you are responsible for the information that is distributed to the public. Yes?"

Jonathan laughed,

"No, no. Mister Leopold, I'm responsible for gathering information ABOUT the public, not to disseminate it!"

Andre eyed him knowingly and a smile grew across his face.

"Indeed, well then we have much to discuss," Andre suggested as he firmly grasped the young man's hand.

The elder statesman now approached Andre.

With a head of thick, white hair, being broad shouldered, heavyset and hunched, he had a gruff dignity; a duality that was accentuated by his learned speech and grumbling voice.

"Mister Leopold?" he said, preparing to shake Andre's hand, "Jacob Vanderberg. It's a pleasure to make your acquaintance. Call me Jake," he followed up.

"I am the acting White House chief of staff. Mentor, friend, and confidant to the president, and the only bum who can keep that ignorant idealist from self-destructing."

Jake grasped Andre's hand and shook it vigorously.

"Don't get me wrong; he's a good man, full of ideas, but just like my friend Johnny over here, not very politically viable, if you understand me?" Jake followed up pointing at Jonathan with his thumb.

Andre nodded and caught the perplexed look Jonathan was giving Jake at this comment.

"Our youth ... Jake, they are an impetuous lot, yes? Please, call me Andre," Andre suggested, winking at the senior statesman.

Jake smiled and nodded.

"Thanks, Andy, yes they are ... something that only men of such long-lived experience, such as ourselves, can appreciate." he paused, taking wheezy breath, "As I said, I'm the *acting* chief of staff; the last one was caught up in a scandal. He was shooting his mouth off at a convention as a guest speaker. Oh and believe you me, he got lots of applause, talking about free federal housing and income equality. Everyone was cheering him on, but he forgot that all these events are recorded. Then it hit the twenty-four-seven news cycle and now everyone is up in arms about some new movement to trying to maximize freedoms." Jake took another deep breath, "I gather you can help us with things like this."

"Andre, please call me Andre," Andre noted and continued, "Indeed, I think I can."

"Sure thing, Andy," Jake continued, "We can do more for the people if they are not so aware of what we are trying to do or, at least, be more aware of what they are hearing. It eliminates those unfortunate... well... misunderstandings!"

"Excuse me, gentlemen!" Nancy broke in, clearing her throat to get their attention, "Perhaps we should carry this conversation into the conference room and sit down?"

"Quite right, Nancy," Jake turned to her and smirked, "My knees are getting a mite sore anyway. Lead the way, my dear."

She shot him an indignant look, which he seemed to relish. The party started to enter the conference room and took their seats at various points around a long, mahogany table. The room was paneled, with a large portrait of George Washington hung at the far end.

Nancy pulled the double doors closed and proceeded to take her own seat at the table.

She positioned herself and started to talk,

"Gentlemen, honored guest, I have been empowered--"

"So, as I was just saying, Andy," Jake interrupted her; and with little concern for protocol, chose to lay the groundwork for what he thought he needed. "The president and his young, new administration have some good ideas, but they lack the experience to understand how the people think. It's like they are surprised again and again when the people disagree with them." Another deep and wheezy breath followed by a light cough gave Nancy her opportunity to reclaim the conversation.

"Excuse me, Mister Vanderberg, but the White House and the president have set a very specific agenda aside and--"

"Listen, sweetheart, I *am* the White House!" Jake interrupted her again. "Don't you understand that? This president, and most of those around him for that matter, haven't pulled their noses out of the political science books long enough to tie their own shoes, much less run the country! Andy here is going to help us open our eyes to what the public thinks and help us accomplish what we promised to accomplish."

Jake leaned over the table closer to Andre,

"The people of this country love an idea when you present it, but once you start to implement it, they start to whine about government overreach or archaic elements of the Constitution. The people want the government to provide for them, just as you have done at Christmas, at our request, over the years. They want it to be Christmas all year around. They just don't want to know about it."

Jake sat back into his seat, folded his hands and looked directly at Andre.

"The president received a text message from his old friend Holden Mealy just after he took off from your island. The crash was a tragic loss, truly! Still, I think he and Brenda Willis had laid the foundation for a new relationship. They have served their country and purpose, and between your discussions with them and our own intelligence, I think we are on to a tremendously mutually beneficial relationship." Jake took a breath and coughed before continuing, "So tell me the details, Andy. I think I know what you're offering, though you haven't given us your sales pitch; blow the minds of my two colleagues here. Give us your terms. I can tell you we are in the market and we are prepared to buy!"

Jake leaned back almost slouching in his chair and with a wheezy laugh punctuated by a cough, he motioned for Andre to speak.

"Well, Jake, it is true that I started to outline my proposal and we have discussed some of the assistance I expect from my partners in this effort, but we have not outlined my terms financially. I shall then… *'Give you my sales pitch,'* Yes?" Andre responded.

The room fell silent and Andre knew this was his time,

"America, do you love your president? Do you love this political party? Do you need more time to create the laws to govern your lands the way you believe they need to be, even if it is unpopular? If you do then I can hand you the information you need to do all this and more, yes?"

Andre turned to Jonathan and started to speak directly to him,

"Mister Casper, you could become one of this administration's most important people. You would like this, yes? When voter sentiment turns, you will know it. When your president makes a speech, you will know how the public reacts. When the people speak in private about your administration you will know what they are saying." Andre got up and leaned on the table, pivoting himself forward toward Jonathan, "And if your opponents make mistakes, you will know this, too. You will know if they have been bad or good. You will know. What you do with that knowledge will be up to you. You want this ability, yes?"

Jonathan jumped to his feet almost involuntarily and in a volume just shy of a scream,

"YES! Mister Leopold, yes! But how? How will you make this happen?"

Andre smiled and sat back down, looking at Jonathan, who now stood in the room eyeing all of his comrades. All of whom were now staring at him after his near outburst. He looked around and slowly sat back down.

"Ladies and gentlemen, I present you ICU," Andre suggested with an almost carnival like flair, "For years the Kringle Works through the SANTA Clause has used and developed the ability to access, to watch, and react to the peoples of the world. We have done so to reinforce the societal norms the governments of the world have asked us to encourage in their respective populations. In this effort we have had the opportunity to perfect the technology to make Christmas better for the world, but the technology we now have could make the world better, yes? It could be used directly, all year, and everywhere. Over the years I have personally recruited the most brilliant technological minds and we have developed a surveillance network that can see almost anyone at any time in, as you say, *real time*."

Andre pulled a file from his briefcase and tossed it on the table. It slid toward Jake and as it did, photos, transcripts, video stills, and letters spilled out across the table.

"Here are some examples of the information you can have access to. It is intriguing, yes?"

Andre grabbed another file from his briefcase and placed it on the table in front of him. He placed his hand on it.

"This is a brief summary of how ICU works. It is over two hundred pages." He tapped the file folder distorted by the huge stack of paper inside. "It is like a sophisticated computer virus, but it's not a virus; it is resident in the machine, hidden in the electronics. It cannot be removed or easily detected. It talks to us and lets us know what a machine is doing, and because we know what the machine is doing, we know what the person using the machine is doing. ICU operates on its own and it can broaden its ability by talking to other machines that are connected to it, even those with no ICU technology on them. You have seen how we can see you through the SANTA Clause, yes? We can see you anywhere in the world."

Jake jumped in,

"Andy, this is remarkable, but are you lying? With all due respect you can only see into countries who celebrate Christmas, correct?"

"No, Jake," Andre responded, "The technology is everywhere."

Andre tapped the folder he had laid in front of him.

"The Kringle works has been manufacturing electronics for many companies, but not just for Christmas but to fill other needs. When Mexico needed components for cell phones we sold them the screens and circuit boards. When China had a shortage of silicone to make computer chips, we sold them the chips and motherboards. When Japan lost three electronics manufacturing sites to an earthquake, we supplemented their supply. When Dubai built their last island resort we exchanged oil for televisions, computers, and telephone systems. When Russia built a new communications satellite and did not want to use American technology, we sold them ours. The ICU technology was on all of them. The technology is everywhere. You understand this now, yes?"

"Very impressive," Jake noted, "and how much would this cost us?"

Andre hesitated, sat up straight and started to outline the program,

"We would have to set up with several hundred workstations locally. You will need at least ten of our special servers dedicated to your specific tasks and we would have to supply three hundred technicians to work all of them. For a short time we will run the program through our servers, but you will need your own. We will continue to administrate the program and aid in filtering the data. The data will be global and it will require a great deal of equipment. The Kringle Works will remain in charge of the data and the equipment, which we will lease to you as part of the service, but we will have control always. Though these activities will mirror what we do to lay the annual groundwork for the Christmas service, it will be separate, yes? How you follow up on the data will be your own choice."

Andre sat back and paused. Then leaned forward again and said,

"The program is expensive. I will need one trillion of your US dollars in the first year. It will cost five hundred billion annually after that--"

In another outburst, Jonathan interrupted,

"One trillion dollars!? Have you lost your mind?"

He grabbed a number of the documents and photos that had slipped from the file showing the fruits of the system's labor and held them up, waving them at Jake. He stood up and addressed him directly,

"Good God, Jake," he snarled, "This is information that any one of my sources could produce! It's all very exciting--but one trillion dollars? It's an outrage, we can do this ourselves!"

Andre sat quietly. As Jonathan ranted, Andre pulled a handheld device from his briefcase, and tapping on the screen, started to gather some information which he noted on a pad before interjecting himself back into the conversation.

"How was your steak last night, Mister Casper?" Andre asked calmly and then continued, "You asked for it medium-rare, did you not? I believe you had also asked to hold the mushrooms, which were on the menu, and instead had them add crumbled blue cheese, yes? You told your companion, I think her name was Christine, that the mushrooms give you gas. It was a joke; she laughed, but was sorry that you would have to work after dinner as she was having such a good time. But this was a lie, because you actually met two of your colleagues at a bar after dinner."

Andre looked at the screen of his device and appeared to scroll down.

"This morning, perhaps due to the vodka," Andre continued, "you were running late; you had six shots. At 6:15 you stopped on 1916 M Street Northwest to pick up an Egg McMuffin and coffee, just one cream and two sugars. You wanted to make up time so you rushed and where you could, your General Motors car was driving as much as twenty-eight miles an hour faster than you should. It was good that it was early and there were few other vehicles on the road as you drove past the Lafayette Square, yes?"

Andre scrolled a little further and continued,

"Currently you are in a meeting with me and it appears that you have cleared your schedule for this meet as you did not know how long it might go. Your secured calendar has this meeting marked as '*VIP Meeting.*' VIP, I am honored, Mister Casper."

Jonathan stood silently, staring at Andre. He had a forlorn expression, dropped the documents on the table and fell back into his chair.

"You see, yes?" Andre looked around the room and continued, "You see the information we can gather at an instant?"

Andre held up his device and waved it in the air. Then placing it down, he addressed Jonathan,

"Mister Casper, this device is little more than a sophisticated smart phone, a small computer tablet. It is, however, attached to one of our ICU workstations and with that I can find information about anyone. Where they are, what they are doing, yes? It is the way our technology works, every one person is like a package and like our own delivery services we track that package at all times and ICU allows me to see its status."

A grumbled, wet laugh followed by a light cough interrupted him, and Jake spoke up,

"Hey Johnny, you see what Andy here is tryin' to say to you? Can you imagine what would have happened in that last midterm election if we had information like this about our new senator? How many millions did we spend to try to keep him from getting elected? It was just like throwing money out the window, but with information like this we would have known everything he was doing and that would have given us an edge. Even better, we could have seen the public reaction and countered the perception of our candidate, not through polls but right from the horse's mouth. Isn't that right, Andy? So tell me, how do we track everyone at once? How do you do that for Christmas?"

Andre nodded.

"Yes, Jake. You would have access to conversations, meetings, correspondence, and much more. You would have likely been able to see a campaign strategy in the work and known how to react before it became public. More importantly, you would have seen the public reaction as it happened. We do this now with servers and workstations designed to process and filter activities by the public in mass. We set up criteria and parameters and the machines process the data and return results, which then are reattached to a person. We can then manually filter the data and spot-check anyone. For example, the criteria might be, *lying*. The system gathers data; just like I have about you, Mister Casper; judges it against behavioral patterns and builds a model on this one criteria. The system then tells us the number of times anyone has lied in a particular time frame. If we want to, we can then go into the data and see what it was about. The system judges the United States population against over nine hundred thousand specific behavioral criteria for their Christmas service."

A loud cackle erupted from Jake like an uncontrolled belch, bursting forth before an exclamation,

"Fucking unbelievable!" another laugh and cough followed as he looked around the room, "I knew there was a reason Santa has been ignoring my wishes every year," and he drew a deep, wheezy breath. "Okay, Andy, two hundred billion dollars annually and no sign-on bonus for you."

Andre shook his head slowly, but answered affirmatively, "You will have your service and you can pay only two hundred billion, but I will have my trillion US dollars," Andre focused on Jake, "It is a global service; you will share it with the next country, they will pay to make up the difference. They will have access to the same information but you can share the cost and the information, yes?"

Jake slapped the table with both hands and got up, leaning toward Andre, "What?! Share in the information? What do you mean?"

Andre smiled and leaned back into his chair, looking relaxed, "You are our first country. My price is one trillion US dollars and five hundred billion annually. I then provide the service to the world. It matters not to whom. You are our best current customer and I have come to you first."

Wide-eyed and pale, Jake sat down slowly and responded,

"Wait, you mean to tell me if you sign other countries they would have access to our county's information?"

"And you theirs," Andre responded calmly, "If you choose to share the service you would have to draw up agreements with the other participants as to how you use the information, we will just provide it. How you use it is up to you. You understand, yes?"
"But that could impact our national security!" Jake said sharply.

"Then I suggest you choose to build reportage with the others as I offer the service to them, or choose to keep it to yourself," Andre answered calmly and continued, "The service and the information will be the same."

"Wait; if we have the service to ourselves, then we can see the goings-on in other countries also?" Jake asked abruptly.

"Of course," Andre responded with a measured demeanor as though this fact had never been in question, "I cannot concern myself with local borders or politics. I must deal with the logistics of gathering and providing the service.

You will see every point on the globe that ICU can reach, with the exception of the Kringle Works Island."

Jake slapped both hands together and enthusiastically responded,

"Hot damn! I think we have a deal there, Andy old boy!"

Hearing this, Jonathan jumped in,

"Good God, Jake! You can't just accept this deal! A trillion dollars?"

Jake waved his hand dismissively,

"Hey, Johnny, think about it. We can slap a five hundred dollar tax on every household in America and there is your trillion dollars. If that is a little too much we can easily pull money out of Homeland Security and Defense. This will be the best intelligence-gathering product we have ever had."

"Five hundred dollars per household?" Jonathan inquired.

"Sure, why not? We'll call it the … eh … *Digital Communications and Information Enhancement Act*. We'll tell the people it is a federal program to pay for the building of information and communications infrastructure. It's not even a lie. Yeah, we'll announce that it created a couple thousand new jobs for hard working Americans." Jake winked at Jonathan as he sat back looking devilishly proud of himself and continued, "It's brilliant and this is way too good to pass up."

"Andy, I think we have a deal!" Jake got up and stretched his hand out to Andre across the table, "I will have some of our legal eagles draw up our side of the agreements for you to review. In the meantime we will need further demonstrations of the system and some time to evaluate the product. I assume this will be no problem?"

Andre smiled casually and got up, reached for Jake's hand and shook it.

"Then I believe we have an accord," Andre responded. Then after a small pause, Andre continued, "There is a small matter of preparation of the service. As I have suggested to your colleagues on our island, the initial one trillion US dollars are designed to assist me in starting up, partly to …" he paused again, "*realign our management*. I will need to do this to make the

281

product available. I may also need some military assistance. I have an outline of the operation with me. This should not be a problem, yes?"

Andre took a binder of documents with a combination latch on it out of his briefcase and reached it over the table toward Jake. Jake eyed him for a moment and then, burst out laughing,

"Andy, that is the one thing that will be easy to do. The money, that will take work; troops, no problem," he took the locked binder from Andre and followed up, "We look at your plan and draft it into the '*Year One*' part of the contracts."

Andre released the binder.

"Thank you, Jake. Once you have drafted your side of the contract I will have it incorporated into SANTA, our general service agreement, as an addendum and update. When will you have this ready for review?"

"Andy, something this important takes priority; tomorrow morning!" Jake answered with a wheezy gasp and continued, "Now we will be talking about a United States exclusive. Understood?"

Andre nodded and responded with a smile,

"Of course, I would wish it to be no other way."

Jake got up and pushed his chair under the table.

"Well, I think we have some significant work to do," Jake held up the binder, "You will send me the combination?" he turned to Nancy, "Nancy, dear, please show Andy out. Set him up with whatever he needs while we draft up our proposal for tomorrow morning." He turned back toward Andre, "An office perhaps? If you will excuse us, Johnny and I have a great deal of work to do to prepare. Andy, it has been a pleasure."

He motioned for Jonathan to get up.

"For me also, Jake," Andre responded. Nodded at Jonathan, "Mister Casper," then turned to Nancy, "Ms. Otis, my hotel will be fine."

The group left the conference room and Andre followed Nancy Otis into the hall.

Silently for a moment Nancy led Andre through the halls. Then almost as though talking to herself, she broke the silence,

"I find Jake Vanderberg to be an extremely unpleasant person; I'm sorry for him," she stopped walking and turned to Andre, "but I'm very excited about the pending agreement."

She smiled at Andre, who responded with a nod and they started walking again.

"Mister Leopold, may I ask you a question?"

"Of course, madam," he responded.

They continued walking.

"ICU, that's cute, like *I see you*, is that what it means?" she inquired.

Andre laughed,

"*Integrated Communications Unit*, actually. This makes sense, yes?"

"Yes. Yes it does," she agreed, "Does this communication only go in one direction? I mean, is it possible to send communications back so that *I see you too*?"

Andre stopped, somewhat disquieted by the familiar-sounding double entendre.

"Why? Why would we want it to do this?" Andre gave her a perplexed look, "It would make the unit detectable, yes? The genius is that it is mostly invisible, unless, as you have, you take the machines apart. Besides, it is one matter of taking data from many different technologies and translating them to one system. It is quite a different matter when going the other way, translating from our system to many different ones, yes?" he answered, and started walking again.

"I can imagine," she agreed, "It's just that our investigation at the FBI suggested it did go both ways."

Andre shook his head, searching his brain for something he may have missed, but then answered confidently,

"No, this we cannot do. They are wrong, yes?"

She smiled and nodded. Then after a moment's pause,

"Mister Leopold, would you like to join me for lunch? I know a great place near the Capitol that I think you would love; it has a great view--"

Raising his hand, he interrupted her and responded affirmatively.

It was not a late night, and the next morning Andre got up feeling strong and refreshed. He set foot on the granite steps outside the hotel lobby. He noted the black limousine at curbside ahead of him. Then stepping out from under the canopy, he allowed the mid-February sun to hit his face and he stopped walking. He closed his eyes to let it warm his skin and took a long, deep breath. The air filled his lungs; it felt unusually warm and humid to him as he was used to the temperatures of the island, and this February morning in America felt like summer. He thought about the success of his trip and with this glorious weather as a bonus, he was looking forward to working out the details with his new trading partners. He opened his eyes again and moved toward the black limousine and the driver. He was a different driver today, but he seemed to be there to meet him and nodding at Andre in recognition, he opened the door for him to enter. Andre smiled and he nodded in response. Then his eyes shifted to a large black van which was parked behind the limousine. Andre had not noticed it before and a chill ran up his spine. He watched the van cautiously as he approached the limousine door. Andre hesitated and turned back to the driver who was still holding it open,

"Please, Mister Leopold," the driver suggested, while motioning for him to enter.

Andre smiled politely at him and stepped into the vehicle, sitting down in the back seat. The new driver smiled in response. Then through the open door Andre said quietly,

"I still love him, you know? Tell him, this was..." he hesitated, "strictly business, yes? Nothing personal. You understand?"

The driver smiled and said,

"I will pass that on, Mister Leopold."

The door closed and the driver got into the front seat and started the vehicle. Together the limousine and the van pulled away.

A frantic group of men in dark suits were talking on communication devices, holding a hand to one ear. Another man appeared to be scolding the driver of another limousine across the street from the hotel. Quickly, three of the men jumped into a black SUV and with the chirp of the tires, took off after Andre and the black van.

21

THE TRIP

"It's making you crazy, isn't it?" Krystal suggested.

Jason nodded. Sitting across from her in the comfort of his kitchen at a characteristically open window, he unwrapped the latest issue of The Works's Weekly and with a sip of tea from a small, white porcelain cup, he responded without looking up,

"I feel like I'm locked up while Xavier gets things resolved."

"Uh huh … so … let me tell you what locked up feels like … really, what took you so long to find me?"

Jason rolled his eyes.

"Do we have to go through this again? Krystal, the whole world thought you went on a trip," Jason defended himself, "I thought you had planned it all along, you've done it before…"

"Not without telling you! I was locked up for weeks!" she responded with a now all too familiar irritation in her voice.

"Krystal, the first week everyone was just finding out that you were missing; the second, we realized you had planned it, or so it seemed; the third week I tried to find you, and if it weren't for Henry, I don't know if--"

"Henry, yes. I know," she interrupted, "There is something strange about him; how did he know? How does he always know? In all the years I've managed the animals, I've hardly ever seen him, yet he seems very familiar to me."

287

"Henry helped me save you!" he reminded her, "and yes he seems to make everyone feel like they have known him forever. At least he seems to know everyone."

"I think he killed Marcus! I don't think that was an accident," she whispered.

Jason hesitated,

"Look, he's okay and you're safe now; besides, Marcus had all but attempted to kill you. You seem to have forgotten that. He was into some bad stuff. We still aren't sure about all of it."

Trying to divert the conversation, Jason untied the gold- and red-twisted ribbon from around the rolled newsletter and pulled a parchment-colored paper from around it.

"What now?" he questioned rhetorically.

The text, "Directly from the desk of Xavier Kringle," and the company logo adorned the top. Jason read it aloud,

> *"Directly from the Desk of Xavier Kringle, CEO & Owner, Kringle Works:*
>
> *It is with an extremely heavy heart that I must announce the accidental death of Marcus Millerov, senior vice president, ELF. In his long and distinguished career Marcus had spent years working toward the betterment of the Employee's League of Fabricators and has left a lasting legacy of achievement. Until a successor is named, all ELF management issues will report directly to me and the executive committee.*
>
> *We wish to extend the company's most sincere sympathy and pledge of assistance to the Millerov family. Please join me in offering the social support that they need in their time of sorrow.*
>
> *With respectful regards,*
> *Xavier Kringle"*

"Really? No mention of the circumstances? No mention of an investigation?" Krystal responded, "What's wrong with this place?"

Jason shook his head.

"Must be how Xavier is trying to smooth over what happened," he pondered for a moment, "This might be how he is trying to make sure that some who might have been working with Marcus don't just go underground. It makes sense, I suppose."

"I suppose," Krystal agreed, "Listen to me." She paused, and then in an elevated and regimented tone continued, "I will never go anywhere … anywhere," she repeated again with additional emphasis before continuing, "Without telling you."

He looked at her apologetically.

"Anywhere," she repeated, "Got that?"

Jason put down the paper and got up. He walked around the table to her side and motioned for her to move over in the chair she was sitting in and he awkwardly sat down next to her.

The chair barely accommodated them both, but he moved closer and wrapped his arms around her.

"Yeah, I got that," he whispered into her ear.

She struggled a little.

"No, I'm still mad at you," she taunted him.

"Well, I'm not letting you go," he told her, "I mean it this time. I have taken you for granted too long. I almost lost you."

A chime rang at Jason's front door and they both stood up, startled.

Jason answered to find Peter Sharp, head of security, standing at the front door. Peter's six-foot-five-inch tall frame and dark green uniform made him look authoritative, and though his demeanor was quite friendly, Jason still found his presence, under these circumstances, rather disquieting.

"Peter?" he stuttered, "What can I do for you?"

"Mister Pelham, Ms. Gardener," he responded politely.

"Well, ask him in, Jason," Krystal demanded, "Don't just stand there like an idiot. Ask him to come in." She smiled at Peter Sharp, "Come on in, Peter, would you like a cup of hot tea?" She turned as if to signal they should follow her back into the house. She looked back, "For such a brilliant man, Jason can be a little slow sometimes."

Peter smiled and acknowledged her with a nod, but remained in the doorway.

"Thank you, Ms. Gardener; no, I am only here to ask for Mister Pelham to join me," he responded kindly.

"Join you? Where?" Jason jumped in.

"I have been asked to bring you to the executive offices to talk to Mister Kringle. He has asked that you join me now," Peter said stoically.

"Finally!" Jason responded, relieved at the thought of renewed action.

"I'm coming too," Krystal demanded against Jason's effort to signal 'no.'

"That's fine," Peter suggested, "I think this may be of concern to you, also."

Krystal picked up her coat and walked over to them. She grabbed Jason's coat from a peg near the door and handed it to him.

"Let's go," she suggested while shooting a sharp and meaningful look toward Jason before continuing, "Me too, Jason. I'm never letting you go, and I mean it, too," she said, referring to their earlier conversation.

They arrived at Xavier's office and Peter Sharp left them with Justin, Xavier's personal assistant.

"Go right in. Henry Foster is already here," he thumbed back at the office door.

They entered to find Xavier and Henry in an animated conversation, which ended abruptly with their arrival.

"Jason! And what a delightful surprise, Krystal Gardener! I'm glad you're joining us," Xavier said exuberantly, "Please sit down."

Krystal did not spend time in the executive offices, though she thought she had been in Xavier's office before, as a child on a school field trip or tagging along with her father delivering a package to the CEO's office, perhaps. She could not remember when.

She looked around in awe at the huge space as she took her seat. She focused on the room and the embellishments, the antiques and the paintings of each of the dynastic CEOs. She stopped and lingered for a longer moment at the image of Christopher Kringle. She considered that this image of the founder of the Kringle Works was the only portrait that had not been painted on the island and how he, with his long, white beard and rather odd trademark dress, would set the stage for the legend that would personify Christmas for the world. Every CEO since, now endured the same dress to maintain the image.

"Funny!" she thought and she scanned the high ceiling, hand-carved wood trim, highly ornamented furniture, bookcases, and wooden file cabinets.

Then, suddenly jarred from her daydream, she became aware of the figure of Xavier Kringle watching her with an ear-to-ear grin.

"There's a great deal of history within these walls. I think that some of us who spend our time here forget that," Xavier suggested in a very fatherly tone, "Thank you for your subtle reminder, Krystal."

Krystal looked back and in a moment of uncommon modesty, gave Xavier a sheepish smile. She inclined her head and refused to look Xavier directly in the eye, but her face betrayed her effort to disguise her embarrassment and he chuckled lightly before continuing,

"Krystal, Jason, I have only just become aware of some details of our technology that was neither sanctioned nor developed with my knowledge."

He paused and shot a disapproving look toward Henry, who sat quietly hunched and forlorn, a posture not usually associated with him. Xavier continued,

"There is an element of our technology that was designed to compromise my position. Indeed, to help build an agenda of betrayal against my position. A technology that I should have been made aware of, even if the direction had come from the executive committee." His normally calm attitude was starting to show a level of anger trying to get out.

With a deep breath, Xavier continued more calmly, "Nevertheless, the time has come to mop up. Jason, you were right. The ICU technology has become a liability. It's with a heavy heart that I must admit that it appears that Andre has betrayed me and now I am going to ask you, Jason, to assist me in undoing some of the damage that has already been done."

Jason nodded.

"What do you need for me to do?" he asked.

Xavier silently acknowledged the quick willingness and continued,

"Thank you, Jason," he leaned across the desk, "I need for you to go to America, to Washington, DC. You will need to determine what exactly Andre has promised, and try to renegotiate with the United States government on our behalf and to put this to rest. We have to contain this now. It should never have gotten past our borders. Once we have done so, then we can deal with the insurgency here on the island. You must help me in this."

"I'm going with him!" Krystal interjected.

"No, I'll join him," Henry followed up.

Xavier raised his hand to calm the conversation.

"No, Henry, I need you here. We have work to do," he noted.

Krystal gave a determined look and repeated herself,

"I'm going with Jason! I'm not letting him go to America alone and besides, I need to help keep him out of trouble."

"… or help him to get deeper into trouble," Xavier suggested.

Krystal shot him a rather indignant look and proceeded to present her defense. She was not going to stay here wondering what was happening to Jason. He had been too distant lately. She would not be sentenced to another open-ended separation. Then she endured the trauma of being locked away-- no, she had been kept in the dark and away from him far too much these last months and she was not willing to stand for it. Besides, it was only now that she felt they were starting to define themselves to each other. No, it would not be Xavier who would keep them apart this time. Not now.

"He needs someone he can trust in America with him," she insisted, trying to keep her voice from becoming too shrill, "Xavier, I was abducted. Marcus was willing to let me be killed. Now, Andre has betrayed you." She took a deep breath in an effort not to sound emotional and continued, "I think the only people you're absolutely certain you can trust are right here in this office with you. If Jason gets into trouble it would be best if you had someone there to help follow the evidence, to watch from another vantage point, to alert you or sound the alarm. Xavier, we no longer know who to trust; I won't raise suspicion if I travel with Jason. Remember, most who know him, know me. In America I wouldn't seem like a threat, but I'll be there watching."

Xavier nodded, taking in the argument, looked at Jason and said,

"Jason, the decision is yours. Will Krystal help or hinder your progress? I do not suggest she join the negotiations, but if you have need of her at your side…"

Krystal watched Jason's face, trying to decipher his thoughts. Her heart pounded. He may not have realized it but this had become a test for her. One moment, one question, would now define her position in his life. She had unwittingly set up the parameters to gauge their relationship from his point of view and now that the stage had been set, she became afraid of the answer. In her mind, she knew that Jason's first thought would be to say 'no' in a desire to keep her from harm, but to allow her to be left alone again, to willingly accept another separation without considering her desire to join him seemed too easy. She would not be tossed aside again, even if under the guise of safety; she could not bear it. She just told him she wanted to go, and her desires made known, he had to choose for her to go with him. Anxiety flooded her body in an instant that felt like an eternity. She needed to give him a hint. Quickly, before he made the wrong choice, she had to let him know. She had to be sure his decision was not made flippantly; just a hint to let him know how pivotal this moment had become for her.

"I'm not letting go," she whispered, holding her breath, allowing no air to escape her throat to make the words audible. She did barely more than just mouth the words, but still, Jason's expression seemed to change and she thought he might have heard her.

"With your permission, Xavier, I'd like for Krystal to join me in America," he responded, "She's right, we don't know who we can trust. If she joins me, she can watch for suspicious activity."

Krystal's heart seemed to jump into her throat and she snapped up a deep breath, the first in what seemed to be an eternity. As she exhaled again she felt a rush of exhilaration wash over her. She closed her eyes and allowed her body to slump slightly in relief. It was just a moment, a split second in time but she felt as though she had just run a marathon.

"As you wish, Jason," Xavier agreed, "The choice is yours."

Krystal's heart raced on the ride back to Jason's house. Though she kept her thoughts to herself, Peter seemed to notice her heightened mood. He brought her back to gather some things on Jason's behalf to prepare for the trip to America. She would then head home to pack her own things while Jason stayed behind with Xavier. They were going to go over the details of their negotiations with the United States government and the last information they had about Andre's visit.

Though similar to Andre Leopold's arrival nearly a month earlier, Krystal and Jason's appearance by private NTA aircraft was met with considerably less activity and fanfare upon touching down in Washington, DC. They were greeted by a single border control official who simply checked their paperwork on the tarmac before heading back to the main terminal. A black van with two local Kringle Works NTA representatives, dressed in black jumpers and ball caps, assisted them with their luggage and would then shuttle them off the airport grounds. On the tarmac the noise of the aircrafts and the speed of the transactions made verbal communication nearly impossible and the whole of their arrival seemed to take place with just a few unintelligible words and a series of handshakes and nods. Still, all seemed to go smoothly and once they were seated in the van, the two travelers felt a quiet relief overcome them as the door slid closed and the driver took his route to the highway.

Jason was fascinated and peered out at the passing traffic and landscape.

"It's been a very long time since I've been in the United States," he stated pensively.

Krystal, exhausted, leaned into him, placed her head on his shoulder and squeezed his hand, locking their fingers together as if to create an inseparable bond.

"You could've joined me in Alaska three years ago," Krystal answered him rhetorically, "But I seem to recall you were too busy making toys back then, ELF."

"I know, but that was then," he said quietly, nodding.

She smiled at him and gave his hand another squeeze.

"We're going to be about twenty minutes outside the city, Mister Pelham," the man in the front passenger seat called back to them, "That's where our southeastern distribution center is. The NTA has some executive offices you can use and we have a number of condos for visitors like yourself. By the way, my name is Vic Clifford and our driver over here is Mike Hector."

Vic stretched his hand back for them to shake. Mike, keeping his hands on the steering wheel, looked back and winked.

"Thank you, gentlemen, I'm pleased to meet you. This is Krystal Gardener."

Krystal offered a smile and nodded.

"Yeah, we know. The pleasure's all ours. We don't get a lot of visitors from the island here, but now we have both you and Andre Leopold! Wow, who would've thought?" Vic continued, "You'll be wantin' to talk to him, I suppose, huh, Mister Pelham?"

"Eh … yes. Yes! Of course!" Jason answered with a moment's hesitation.

"Yeah, well he's been cooperative, but I don't think he's very happy," Vic responded, "The distribution district manager, that's our boss, told us to keep him comfortable but locked up. Yup, it came straight from the executive committee. Guess it sucks to be him?" Vic chuckled.

Krystal looked at Jason with concern and as their eyes met she saw in his face that he was as troubled as she.

Upon their arrival at the distribution center compound, they were given a chance to freshen up and a brief tour of the facility. It seemed that the NTA team in this particular US location was particularly excited to show off their operation to Jason.

"We don't show the facility very often, Mister Pelham; most of the surrounding area has other companies' distribution sites and the vast majority don't even know who this site belongs to," their guide suggested, elbowing Jason lightly in the ribs, "You know, to keep things undercover. We wouldn't want people to think Santa Claus is getting too much help going down those chimneys," the tour guide snorted with a loud chuckle.

It became quickly obvious that the majority of the Kringle Works NTA's US-based employees enjoyed a significant amount of amusement at the hands of the fanciful legends surrounding their operations, and the jokes seemed to pepper the majority of their conversations. There was also a note of lonely isolation about their manner, as he knew that they were largely asked not to talk too much about their jobs publicly.

After the tour and some discussions regarding the operation, the two travelers were brought to their adjoined condos and as one might have expected from a segment of the NTA, found that their belongings had been brought in, unpacked and arranged in a manner that would best suit their needs. Krystal found this unsettling. She was not sure why, whether it was because she did not like the idea of a stranger unpacking her personal belongings or because it was done with such a knowledge of how she might have done it for herself.

Shortly afterwards, Jason received a call from Vic asking if they would like to join him and the district manager for dinner. Jason respectfully declined, intending to have dinner with Krystal alone. Vic agreed and suggested that there were, 'some nice, romantic restaurants' not far from their site and followed it up with the news that they had a car for them to use just outside the condo door,

"The keys are inside. It's the blue Town Car. It's all yours to use, Mister Pelham. You do know how to drive, right?"

Jason hesitated but then said yes, with his thanks. Indeed he knew how to drive, but had not done so in many years. Not on dry pavement, anyway.

Perhaps it was because he was so tired or that he was so out of practice, but Jason found himself quite perplexed by the car and found his ability to drive this huge vehicle was nothing short of an embarrassment. It seemed so stiff, so grounded and so heavy; it was incredibly hard to maneuver, curves took a tremendous effort and he seemed to have an affinity to running the vehicle against the curb as he compensated in the turns for a slide that would never come.

His frustrations were heightened by an almost ruthless barrage of taunting from Krystal at the restaurant, which punctuated the whole experience. She did so playfully, but seemed to feel a need to reach out apologetically after each comment, beckoning for his hand across the table. Several times they locked hands. She would look him in the eyes softly and, with a tilt of her head, she followed up with,

"I'm just kidding; you know that, don't you?"

He nodded in response and focused on the dinner menu.

"Wow, they seem to eat a lot of red meat here!" Krystal noted with surprise as she discovered the variety of fish that was a more significant part of their diet at home was in the minority on this menu.

"Nope, and no whale meat!" Jason responded then suggested that he would gorge himself on a variety of salads, since fresh vegetables were such a luxury on the island.

Krystal quipped back with a comment about being what you eat.

As the evening started to wear on, Jason became more at ease. He started to remember just how much more he enjoyed himself when he was with her.

She was fun and had a good sense of humor. He wondered why this seemed to elude him in the past couple years.

Once they made their selections and their waiter took the orders, Krystal inquired about the evening's plans and why they were given the opportunity to dine alone.

"Well actually, we were invited to have dinner with Vic's boss," Jason told her.

She leaned back into her seat and in a moment of both shock and pleasure, she demanded to know more.

"Jason, you probably shouldn't have declined," she noted.

"I've been so focused on work, too focused on work. It was everything to me. I'm starting to realize that," Jason told her, "I felt I owed you the time. Besides, I suspect dinner with one of the US district managers was likely to be a bore and …" he paused, "I'm trying to change. I promised, remember?"

A rare moment of speechlessness overcame her and she sat there just watching Jason with a bright smile and eyes wide and glistening.

He was not sure if it was the dim lighting in the room or if her eyes moistened, but she had gone uncharacteristically quiet.

"Krystal?" he asked, "You okay?"

She shook her head silently and then in a low voice said,

"Perfect."

She held her napkin to her face to cover a slight giggle followed with subtle dabbing of one eye.

He watched her for more clues as to what she was feeling, but he knew this was what she was yearning to hear. He had done well and sat back, looking pleased.

"I'm not letting you go," he said again reaching for her hand across the table.

"Nor I," she responded, grasping his hand. She cocked her head and watched him for a moment and with a more characteristically mischievous smile she said,

"… but don't you dare get cocky. You have a lot to make up for."

And Jason nearly lost the mouthful of water which he had just drunk as the two chuckled with this last comment.

Once the food arrived, Krystal pushed the conversation.

"So tell me about your discussions with Xavier. What are you planning to do, now that you're here?" she asked.

Jason shook his head,

"Okay, so this is a trap! I'm not talking workshop business with you!" he stated.

She smiled at him with an apologetic look.

"No really, I want to know," she quickly responded to the accusation, "Work is your passion, I want you to share it with me. Actually, what I found most frustrating is not that you worked so hard, but you didn't share it with me."

"Okay, okay, there isn't that much to tell," Jason noted and continued, "He and Henry had some conversations and based on what we found out, Xavier now agrees that we have to shut down the ICU workstations."

"Does that make you happy?" she asked.

"Yeah! Actually, that's what I wanted all along. I didn't like the technology, I told Xavier that a few months back. It's scarily intrusive," Jason suggested, "and now it seemed as though Andre was going to sell it to the Americans. He also wanted to ask them for help to depose the Kringle family from rule of the Kringle Works."

"So he wanted power over the island?" Krystal asked, "Is that what you believe?"

"Yes, I think so. Andre all but admitted it when the Americans came to visit," he responded.

"Just the Kringle Works?" she inquired.

"Well, yeah. The Kringle Works has a lot of influence over the world, so I think that would be enough, don't you?" he responded.

"Yes, I do, but then I'm not trying to take it over, either. Am I?" she reminded him.

"No, I suppose not," he agreed.

"It's just some of the things I remember in the discussions I had with my kidnappers. Things that Marcus said on the day he was killed," Krystal's voice broke a little as her nerves churned at recalling some of the time she spent in captivity, "There was a whole lot of self-righteous talk about improving the whole world. Changing the whole world for the better. Taking it over without anyone knowing that it was happening."

Jason thought for a moment.

"Changing the whole world?" he asked, "How?"

She attempted to recall some of the discussions she had had.

"They're always watching," she said, "They're putting their technology into every corner, every crevice, every shadow, behind every door, and in every window; they will be watching and if they get their way they will sell this service to every government. That's what Marcus said!"

Krystal thought for a moment longer.

"They will dismantle the Kringle Works and resurrect it as a global government sitting in the shadows just under the surface of those governments everyone else sees," she followed up with a mild hit of panic.

Jason grasped her hands.

"He was trying to make you feel powerless," Jason said sympathetically, "They were being forced to keep you, and they had hoped you'd just give up."

"I'm not so sure that was it. There was a lot of this kind of talk," she interrupted, "What did Xavier or Henry tell you?"

"Well for the most part, they know what I know. Andre wanted to take over the island and needed the help of the United States to do it," he answered her, "There are those who supported Andre and some of them, as Henry admits, are in his own department. He has been trying to ferret out who they are for some time. Xavier has been suspicious for years, but had no proof. Just a feeling."

Jason looked her in the eye and decided to end this conversation. It seemed to be upsetting her and he had to admit it was making him uneasy also. In closure he suggested,

"We'll have a chance to find out more tomorrow. Okay?"

She nodded.

"I was never really scared. I think it bothered them. Well, okay, I was … but I didn't show it!" she said defiantly.

"They had no idea what they were getting into," he quipped.

"You look terrific! You know that?" Jason interjected, trying to force the change in subject again.

Now Krystal smiled coyly.

"Do you?" she asked him.

He looked at her in confusion.

"Do you? Know what you're getting into?" she clarified.

He sat back smiling.

"Not a clue!" he said, "but I'm willing to risk it."

"Really? Why, mister senior VP?" she asked with curt defiance.

Jason drew a mischievous smile and pondered artificially for a moment.

"Well, I don't know. You give me a warm feeling all over," he suggested playfully while tapping his index finger to his cheek.

"That's the heat," she laughed, fanning herself, "This place feels like the middle of summer and it's still March! Look at the coats people wear in this heat around here. I can't stand it."

Their discussions lasted for a short while longer, meandered and ended with a struggle to decide if they should share a dessert.

If both had not been so tired, Jason might have suggested they let the evening run longer, but it seemed the time had come to go.

To his surprise, Krystal suggested she drive back and seemed reasonably competent at doing so.

"When you fly to Alaska to study animals with an old hermit of a scientist, you have to rent a Jeep to get out to his shack," she noted slapping him on the arm from the driver's seat as they drove back.

"What? No dog sleds?" Jason quipped.

"Well, sometimes ... but not on the highways. They plow those," she noted.

"I should've gone with you," he mumbled as they approached the chain-linked electronic gate of the distribution center grounds and made their way to the condos.

"Krystal ..." Jason said sheepishly as they exited the car.

"I know, I know, you want some time to yourself to think things through," she answered, anticipating his request to remain alone this night.

"No, actually," he suggested, "I was going to ask if you would join me when I talk to Andre in the morning. I don't know why, but I think it's important to have you there."

Surprised, she immediately responded enthusiastically,

"Of course!"

"Still ..." Jason followed up.

"Yes, I know, you do need the time tonight," she interrupted him again. "I'm tired and want to do a little reading anyway. Just get me in the morning."

Jason nodded in response.

The next morning Jason seemed a little desperate, anxious, and preoccupied. Krystal tried to determine what had him so agitated but it seemed even he did not know exactly why. He was planning on meeting and interrogating his boss that morning. He was not sure what he was going to discover and he was not sure he wanted to know. As such he felt a little uneasy and very unprepared. Still, he was equally determined to follow through and after a brief phone conversation with Vic, they made their way to the executive offices.

The office area of the facility was attached to the main warehouse. There was little to identify who owned and operated the building in the reception area, just a dusty, faded, gold-toned plastic Christmas wreath which was hung unapologetically all year long and above, some simple block lettering which stated 'Nocturnal Transportation Authority.'

Jason picked up the phone in the unattended reception area and dialed Vic Clifford's extension, which he found on a list of phone numbers hung next to it. His brief conversation alerting Vic of their arrival was followed by a buzz at the door opposite the glass-fronted entry.

Beyond this rather unassuming reception area was an equally unremarkable span of pale green, fabric-covered cubicles, in which people were dutifully taking and making calls, entering information and corresponding. There was a cadence to the operation, a rhythm that seemed constant and mechanical. Jason felt as though he could tear away the walls in a dramatic, fiery sweep and the rhythm of the office would continue unencumbered. These people were the part of the NTA that executed the delivery of Christmas to their part of the world, but for all their efficiency and dedication, they seemed to lack a passion that Jason thought was inherent in the Kringle Works's charter.

Jason assessed the area. Against the back wall was a line of offices separated by a set of double doors that led to the warehouse. He made his way toward them with Krystal at his side. There was a hint of gasoline exhaust in the air, whose source became obvious only when someone walked through the double doors, which was highlighted by the momentary sound of forklift engines, back-up alarms, and the run of conveyer belts. The sound interrupted the consistent drone of the office. Still no one but them seemed to notice the disruption as the doors swung open time after time.

The area was clean but worn and looked as though the decor had not been significantly updated for a couple decades.

As they approached the offices along the back, the scent of fresh paint and a slight mismatch of the eggshell-colored wall betrayed an effort to hide the scuffs and scrapes along its lower half. It suggested a history of packages on hand trucks being shuffled back and forth.

Jason looked around, making note of the office doorways and the signs that adorned them.

"Clifford, Victor," Jason noted aloud, "Here it is," he indicated to Krystal.

He entered the doorway to an enthusiastic response from Vic,

"Mister Pelham! Come in, come in!" Vic jumped to his feet and motioned for them to come in and sit down in his twelve-by-twelve-foot office.

The office was the same eggshell color of the area outside it. There were no decorations on the wall except a large corkboard, which was covered in various papers pinned up in columns. Stacks of paperwork covered most of Vic's desk with room only for a modest work area and his computer and screen.

"So!" Vic said eagerly, "What do you think of our facility? It's been a 'Gold Wreath' facility for the last eight years, you know. Yes sir, jumped right from Bronze to Gold! Betcha' we'll be the first to become a *Platinum Wreath* facility!" he suggested, puffing his chest.

"We do all the tracking and order entry right here," he continued, "You saw the warehouse and staging areas yesterday and the gift prep and wrapping area is on the other side just before you reach most of the trucking bays. I understand that Mister Dunbar himself is quite proud of our record."

Jason thought for a moment and could not recall if Raymond Dunbar had ever actually mentioned the facility to him, but it seemed that Vic was looking for validation from his honored guest.

"Of course, he has commented on it a number of times," Jason suggested.

A smile crossed Vic's animated face and he nodded enthusiastically.

"Well!" A now even more confident Vic Clifford followed up, "I suppose you'd like to see Mister Leopold now?"

Jason acknowledged and then Vic explained,

"Along this wall, in the far right corner is our planning and conference room. I have a guard from our security team standing at the door. He'll know who you are. Mister Leopold is being held there for you. Once you're finished, let the guard know and he will open the door for you. Mister Leopold will then be escorted back to his condo unless you want me to do something else. I have been told to hold him there and to keep him as comfortable as possible ... until, 'further notice.'"

Vic motioned quotations with his hands to highlight this last instruction.

"Jason Pelham and Ms. Gardener!" Andre said standing up. "Jason, I had expected you might come to see me on Xavier's behalf, but Ms. Gardener, you are a pleasant surprise! It is nice to see such a fresh and radiant face as yours, yes?"

Jason was surprised by the friendly and disarming tone displayed by Andre Leopold when they entered the conference room and the door shut behind them.

Andre sat back down and continued,

"I must admit, that you are here also may answer some questions for me, yes? Perhaps you, Ms. Gardener, were his greatest miscalculation. I assume then you know of the fifth code, Jason? You have been watching, yes?"

Krystal felt a cold chill wash over her, though she was not sure why, and she quietly grabbed Jason's hand.

"Yes, Andre. We know of the fifth code," Jason responded.

"Then, this explains much. Then you know everything, yes?" Andre said sounding more somber, "It seems, Jason, you and I have crossed paths on the same road again, but you were part of ELF then. I knew that I would need to watch you as you grew these last fifteen years. It was easier to keep things hidden then, but it was also harder to know who was going to get in the way. Then it was just you and your skill, but now you know. No doubt, Ms. Gardener, you opened many eyes, yes?"

She clenched Jason's hand tighter, trying to hide her anxiety.

"His miscalculation?" Krystal asked, "Whose miscalculation?"

Andre turned his head sharply. He gave Krystal an uncomfortable stare.

"Perhaps, we do not know as much as we think?" Andre responded quietly. He chuckled nervously and continued, "You have the code, you can see everything on the island, yes? I am of no use to you; I will say nothing more."

Andre leaned closer to Jason,

"The condo, she is okay, the food … eh … is not so good, but it is more comfortable than I will be soon, yes? He is my friend but he is not kind to those who betray him. You must go now, Jason. We are done now, yes?"

Andre leaned back into his chair and directing his gaze to the wall, sat quietly disregarding them as though he was the only one in the room, punctuating his meaning.

Jason stood, not moving for a moment. He was not sure if something else was to happen, but there was nothing. Finally, Krystal grabbed his arm to signal her desire to go. Jason looked over at her and started the turn to the door. A moment's hesitation, and Jason spun around and addressed Andre again,

"Who are you talking about? Xavier?" Jason asked.

There was no answer and Jason repeated his question more loudly, even though he knew Andre had heard him the first time,

"Andre, who are you talking about?"

The room remained silent and Jason felt his frustration grow. He wanted to grab Andre by the collar and demand an answer. He almost lunged at the old man sitting at the table, stopped only by Krystal's strong grasp on his arm.

Krystal screamed,

"No!" Attempting to hold him back,

"No Jason, let's just go!" she pleaded with him, "What's wrong with you?"

"This is not over, Andre, I'll be back," Jason stated firmly.

Andre sat stoically and without turning, continuing to stare at the wall, he said one more thing,

"You have the fifth code; you should know everything that happens on the island now. If you do not, then you are making a mistake. It seems I did also, yes?"

22

THE FAILED DIPLOMACY

The sound of a phone receiver slamming onto the cradle made Nancy Otis wince while sitting in Jacob Vanderberg's office across from his desk.

"Well, I suppose that confirms it!" Jake shouted at her from across his desk, "Our little breach of security a few weeks ago seems to have been the hard recall of our emissary from the Kringle Works! Andre Leopold was your responsibility!"

"I ... I ... Everything was arranged! I don't know what happened. How could we have known?" she weakly defended herself.

"Uh huh, I just received notification that we have a new envoy from the Kringle Works and I'm pretty darn sure that he will not be extending the same offer! What the fuck went wrong?!" Jake sprung from his chair and leaned against his desk, pounding his finger.

I want my ... what'd he call it? ICU! The president wants it! Goddamit! If I loose access to this deal, so help me, sweetheart, you will disappear from the face of this earth!"

Nancy cowered quietly; with nothing to add, she simply sat there letting Jake take his punitive tone, suffered it and counted down the moments until it would end. She felt like the victim of circumstance but knew that this would be of little help. Wallowing in her own thoughts and frustrations she heard nothing until the fateful moment when Jake coughed and took a belabored breath and then screamed,

"Now get out! You useless ..."

She did not wait for him to finish before leaving and closing the door behind her. Tears filled her eyes as she hurried down the hall, trying not to allow anyone to see her face. Jake was highly respected by their younger president and although she had a good relationship with the president, she knew that without Jake's support or, at minimum, disregard for her, it would be only a matter of time before her career at the White House was over.

Jason Pelham suspected that meeting the United States government representative might be dangerous as they might arrest him in order to use him as a bargaining chip if they felt that his offer was not what they wanted. He also felt that it was not in the Kringle Works's best interest to have anyone come to the distribution center. Based on the little information he had, he thought it prudent to allow this NTA facility to remain hidden in plain sight. Besides, he also felt a discomfort in letting the US government get any closer to Andre Leopold again. It seemed dangerous just to have them on the same grounds, even if neither knew they were there.

"A neutral meeting point, then," he thought, "Specify a minimum of security and people."

This would make the most sense and he sought to have the preparations made. Vic Clifford saw to the arrangements for Jason. He suggested they meet at an obscure little hotel outside the city limits of Fairfax. It was a simple, unassuming place, but allowed them to book a conference room where they could meet privately and securely.

Jason had gotten to the facility early. He and Vic arrived in a black NTA van and were followed by a black NTA cargo van, both of which were staffed with a driver and another NTA team member in the event that they might be needed. The plan was for them to wait with the engines running while Jason met with the appointed United States representative. Vic would stand in the hotel lobby to attend to them when they arrived as well as to watch for any situations that would require action.

An hour later a long, black limousine arrived with two SUVs following behind. Pulling up at the front entrance; two dark-suited security personnel jumped out of the SUVs and ran to the back door of the limousine. The driver walked around and opened the door. The two security personnel watched for the rotund and slightly disheveled figure of Jacob Vanderberg to emerge. He did so with what appeared to be more effort that it should have required, but upon standing Jake brushed himself off and straightened his jacket and tie. He gave a contemptuous look to the security team and started to walk toward the front door and into the hotel.

Once he entered the lobby of the hotel he was immediately greeted by Vic Clifford, who introduced himself and then led Jake to the conference room they had rented.

In the room sitting alone was Jason.

Introductions were made. Jason asked Vic to leave them alone and then addressed Jake again and asked him to sit. As they did so, Jason immediately started to lay out his agenda.

"Mister Vanderberg, the Kringle Works is prepared to offer you a full resolution to the issue that spurred your original investigation of our techniques," Jason stated firmly.

Jake grunted in response.

"You have been made aware of our ICU technology, which although completely within the parameters of the SANTA Clause, has given you cause for concern."

Jake eyed Jason suspiciously.

"Go on, Mister Pelham," he encouraged Jason with a wave of his hand.

"Mister Vanderberg, the Kringle Works is willing to cease all activities associated directly with the ICU technology, which includes disabling all ICU workstations and will effectively render all Kringle Works Integrated Communications Units, also known as ICU, useless. This will effectively make any ICU surveillance chips resident in any electronics and electronic infrastructure mute, allowing the original machines to function without ICU monitoring. We are prepared to shut down the entire ICU network over the course of three years starting with the monitoring of all governmental agencies first and following with general civilian activities until the network has been migrated back to the pre-ICU systems and technology. Note also that the Kringle Works will ask for nothing in return for this effort."

Jake sat back for a moment and as if to show off his rounded figure placed his hands on his belly. With a cough, he cleared his throat and seemed to drift into a laugh.

"Mister Pelham, you are working with a rather grave misconception," Jake noted and continued, "We do not want you to disable anything. No, on the contrary we are very encouraged by your technology. We would simply like access to the information as you gather it," Jake sounded a little amused.

Jason shook his head.

"I assumed that this might be the case, but I'm afraid that this option is not available to you. In fact, we are going to disable it in order to keep it out of the hands of any powers outside the Kringle Works," Jason said forcefully.

"Oh yes, Mister Pelham, I understand how dangerous this technology would be in the wrong hands. Don't you see? That's why the United States must have access to it. To keep it safe." Jake responded with a level of lighthearted condescension in his voice.

"No. I'm afraid that our position is nonnegotiable, we do not believe the technology is safe in anyone's hands, even the United States," Jason stated.

Jake now leaned closer to the table and with a deep breath and cough, he responded,

"Then I'm afraid that we find ourselves at a crossroads, Mister Pelham," in a tone sounding like an odd combination of amusement and menace.

"You see? I'm prepared to pay the Kringle Works some significant dollars and whatever resources you need to become a party to your technology," Jake said, trying to add some charm back into his demeanor, "Monies to improve the technology and resources to help you secure it. Add fail-safes, checks and balances that will keep others from accessing it and abusing it. In turn the US would use it only to assist in your efforts to review the data in the interest of your and our national security. This technology is far too valuable to 'disable' it! You understand," Jake followed up, now sounding strangely and unnaturally cheery.

Jason was starting to get irritated and held back the next comment, allowing Jake to fill the gap in the conversation,

"We have already offered one trillion dollars for access to the technology. I'm authorized to double that!" Jake said, "What's that? Four times your GDP? A one-time payment of two trillion dollars and the cost of maintenance, how 'bout that, Mister Pelham?"

"No! Your willingness to dig so deep into your pockets is a perfect indication why we must disable the technology," Jason spouted, sounding vexed.

Jake snorted, looking irritated and pleased at the same time. He leaned back lightly, scratching his waistline.

"Everyone has their price, Mister Pelham, what's yours? If it's not money, what is it? Control of the Kringle Works, perhaps?" Jake seemed to follow a deliberate line of thought, though it seemed to be made up of random examples, "Not money, power? I can tell you're ambitious. How do you measure happiness, I wonder? A warmer climate? Your own private island? Self-worth and honor, perhaps? No, outdated and naïve, that can't be it! Can it, Mister Pelham? Are you just playing cat and mouse with the United States of America? Is *that* giving you your high?"

"Mister Vanderberg, I believe I have made our offer. Take it or leave it. It's all the same," Jason snarled back.

"Our offer," Jake said softly, "You see, you haven't given me 'your' offer, yet. Are you just a simple mouthpiece for Santa Claus? Oh! We wouldn't want to step on those toes, would we? That is unless you can have what he has without fear of retribution."

Jake now spoke at barely a whisper,

"I can help you get it all. Isn't that what you want? How far will your loyalty take you? The Kringle Works will be forever in the hands of that family. You're still young; you've probably already hit the ceiling, since you are important enough to come here on their behalf."

Jason looked back at Jake in disgust and growled slowly,

"You're desperate! You couldn't possibly handle this technology!" Jason snarled, "We will disable it."

"You will not," Jake insisted.

Jason dismissed this comment and responded curtly,

"I think we're done here."

Jake watched him for a moment.

"Mister Pelham, to come to me with a predetermined resolution and suggest we were here to negotiate ... well ... it's simply disingenuous. We're not negotiating, you're dictating," Jake growled.

Jason narrowed his gaze.

"Good day, Mister Vanderberg," he said with a tone of finality.

Jason got up from the table, collected his belongings and started to walk out.

Jake did not seem to feel this action warranted a response and watched Jason leave the room.

Upon Jason's exit, Jake sat back with an irritated grin, pulled out a cell phone and spoke into it,

"Make sure that little shit doesn't get away!"

Jason met Vic out in the lobby and casually walked up to him. He leaned over, eyeing the security personnel there on Jake's behalf.

"Let's get out of here quickly," Jason said quietly, "I think it's about to get very ugly. Act naturally but be quick."

Vic nodded.

"The vans are running; just jump into the back of the cargo van," he said and the two started to walk out.

They noticed the two men in dark suits start to close ranks in front of the door as they approached. They quickened their pace.

Just as it seemed the two men were going to block their path out the door, they heard the voice of another man in hotel staff uniform.

"Yoooo whoooo!" he shouted at one of the security agents with a mockingly feminine voice, causing him to momentarily turn his attention.

In an instant, a fist careened into the agent's face. The other tried to lunge forward at them, but suddenly felt a paralyzing pain course through his body. He felt the pinch of needles in his back and a painful jolt that caused his body to shake and tremble uncontrollably and he fell to the ground in a quivering mass.

In their haste, Jason only noted the wires coming from the other security agent's back, attached to a device held by another person in hotel staff attire. Jason was not sure, but he thought he caught a look of extreme satisfaction on Vic's face from the corner of his eye.

They ran out the door. Jason noticed the black cargo van ahead of them with the back doors wide open. A figure at the doors was waving them in. They ran. Jason became acutely aware of the fact that he was no longer noticing much of their environment, just the elements that his adrenaline rush would allow him to focus on. He felt the cool air as they exited the building. He thought he heard Vic screaming,

"Go! Go! Go!"

Jason was not sure, but he thought he saw a black van take off and slam into one of the SUVs.

And now all he saw was the black cargo van and the open back doors ahead of him. He turned the corner and tried to jump in. However, his foot did not seem to hit the mark and he could feel himself fall. He felt the grip of someone's hand on his collar and he started to loose all of his ability to balance as the van started to move. Jason hit the floor of the van hard, his legs still hanging out of the back. He could feel one of his shoes dragging the ground, bouncing up and down, as he tried to pull his other leg in. Then there was a heavy jolt and he felt a nondescript weight on top of him. He grunted loudly as the air was pushed from his lungs and he could not seem to inhale again. The weight shifted and he caught his breath. He could feel himself get dragged into the van and the door close.

"Sorry 'bout that," he heard a voice say, "If ya weren't layin' on the floor I wouldn't have fallen on top of you."

Jason now recognized the voice of Vic Clifford,

"You okay?"

Jason nodded, sitting on the floor of the van.

"Yeah, I think so," Jason said.

He felt two sets of hands pull him to his feet.

"Well, there'll be hell to pay later," Vic said as they sat down.

"Thanks, guys!" he followed up addressing the man who pulled them in and the driver, "Good job! Fuckin' amazin'!"

"Thanks, Vic!" the driver responded, "But I think there'll be hell to pay, NOW! I guess Bobby didn't manage to block 'em all! Hang on! Looks like we have company!"

Jason looked at Vic inquisitively.

"I guess we're being chased," Vic responded. Then addressing the driver, he shouted, "Can't you lose 'em?"

The driver made a quick move and shouted,

"Workin' on it!"

They could feel the vehicle moving faster and more erratically as the driver took more evasive actions. The sound of the wheels squealing became more obvious as the seconds passed and the smell of burning rubber now permeated the rear of the van. Jason was frustrated by his inability to see what was going on behind them. He grasped the small seat in the van, holding on to it as the van shifted from side to side, and rolled with the turns.

"I'm afraid Fairfax isn't designed for this," the driver shouted, "Someone's gonna get hurt; I got one very unfriendly SUV on my tail!"

Then came a loud crash and a jolt that knocked the three men in the back out of their seats; Jason surmised it was the SUV purposely ramming into the rear of the van. Still, the fact that this was a cargo van allowed them no visibility other than the view out of the windshield.

They felt the vehicle lurch again and a small crack of light appeared at the base of the rear doors as the damage distorted their fit. They could smell antifreeze now. The smell was punctuated by another jerk of the van's position. A loud crash and the chirp of a pair of tires being pushed along the road beyond their current speed seemed to signal a hit so hard that they could feel the rear axle lift slightly. The engine of the van labored. The smell of gasoline and exhaust was accompanied by the sound of metal dragging on the ground and seemed to signal something else had just happened.

With one more jolt, the van seemed to drive more deliberately. Fast and straight, he could now hear the driver laughing over the sound of the scraping metal.

"Well, Vic, I lost 'em! Told you I would," the driver exclaimed, "What a dumbass!"

"Why? What happened?" Vic shouted.

"Well, I think he pushed his own radiator into his own motor," the driver jeered, "Brilliant! What a rocket scientist! Hey, I'm gonna put some more distance between us and then we need to pull over so we can see what we have to do to fix up this van. I'm not even sure where we are."

"Nice work, man!" Vic responded, "You do that! And roll down the windows. We need a little air back here."

He looked over to Jason with a self-satisfied expression.

"Vic? Those men in the hotel, who were they?" Jason asked, "They looked like hotel staff."

Vic leaned back, sliding lower in his seat, trying to look more casual, confident, and relaxed.

"Well, why do you think I recommended that hotel?" Vic suggested, "I had it all in hand. We're the NTA, Mister Pelham. We always have a contingency plan."

An ear to ear grin crossed his face, as he felt confident that he had just impressed a senior level manager in the company.

At that moment Jason understood why Vic was a successful supervisor. More so when he followed up with an insightful comment,

"Mister Pelham, we have to get you and Mister Leopold back to the island. You can't stay in the US any longer. I think it would be best if you hitched a ride on one of our regular cargo flights. You'll have to make like a package. You need to just disappear. We'll sort things out here once you're out of the country."

The guard who watched the entrance of the NTA's southeastern distribution center looked a little perplexed when noting the condition of their cargo van as he recorded their entry through the chain-link gate. More so, when he heard the driver say,

"Don't sweat it, man, just a little fender bender."

In fact, he was particularly alarmed when he thought he heard something fall off the vehicle as they drove past the threshold, through the intercom.

Driving toward the main building's parking lot, they noticed a crowd of people. Jason and Vic were staring through the windshield to try to discern what was going on. They pulled forward and the crowd seemed to follow them into their space.

As they opened the doors and stepped out, cheers erupted spontaneously. Each was swarmed and greeted by the crowd. Vic stepped forward and got a slap on the back and a handshake from his colleagues, followed by an update.

"Bobby showed up about an hour ago. His van was totaled. He suggested that he slipped off of his brake pedal and accidentally ran into two parked SUVs. They didn't believe him, but they apparently wanted to go after you," one employee told him, "He wrote them a check for all damages and took off. I think they were too confused to figure out what had happened. The government was not about to admit they wanted to kidnap someone, but they were pissed! We were a little worried that we hadn't heard from you."

"We had to shake one of them off but all went well," Vic said, "by the way, the beers are on me tonight! Company tab! Eh, assuming it's okay with the boss man over there."

He pointed toward Jason, who seemed to have found himself in a rather tight embrace, as he and Krystal were tightly interlocked. A tender moment, were it not for the momentary scolding he received from her about unnecessarily taking a risk with his life. Still, it seemed he heard Vic, and releasing one hand from the wrap around Krystal's body, he gave him a thumbs-up.

"There, you see?" Vic then continued, "Anyway, before we do anything else, get me one of those big cargo helicopters. I need to get our guests to a D.C. with a runway. I want them on an NTA plane back to the island, but schedule it as part of a regular route, a common flight that won't get too much scrutiny. I think we need to keep them out of the regular airports."

The man nodded.

"No problem, Vic, but keep in mind it's not the time of year for frequent flights. It may take a week," he noted.

"Yeah, I figured," Vic responded, "Just make it happen. Tell 'em no delays. It's important, but don't mention our cargo. Oh, and decommission this van. It's kinda shot."

The man nodded in acknowledgement.

The next morning the sun rose with an orange glow over the distribution center's grounds. The light streamed in through the window of Jason's condo. Signaling the impending spring, the warmth of the tone had Jason mesmerized. The sunlight seemed to make the white bedsheets glow gold as if they were their own light source.

He had been sitting up at a small desk set near the door of the condo's rather unassuming bedroom since five a.m., trying to collect his thoughts. Now as the sun came up he became fixated on the golden shapes that defined the window and were projected and distorted as they caressed the uneven shapes of the rumpled bed linens.

The room further illuminated, and he watched as the glow moved from the edge of the bed up toward the pillows. It was now illuminating Krystal's face and he watched as the sun highlighted it. Fixated on her, he could now see eyelashes moving and her closed eyes twitching under the lids with the subconscious knowledge that the morning had come. He wondered now how long it would be before she woke. He also wondered how it came to pass that these few hours born of his inability to sleep, stolen for himself to think alone, would have concluded in quiet reflection of her sleeping figure. Her nose and eyelids wrinkled as she clenched them shut tighter, becoming aware of the light as she quietly drifted into consciousness. She shifted her head away from the light and her eyes opened slowly. With a twist of her body under the covers she became aware of Jason's figure sitting at the desk. A smile crossed her face as she quietly addressed him,

"Good morning! How long have you been up?"

"A few hours. I couldn't sleep anymore," he responded.

"I could guess, but what's keeping you awake?" she asked.

"I have to talk to Andre. I should do it this morning," Jason suggested, "I have to get more answers."

"Yes, I know. Do you want me there?" she asked.

Jason nodded.

"I think you'd be helpful," he said, "I'd like you to try to remember some of the conversations you had with your kidnappers and ask him about them. Andre seems to be confused, even nervous, about some things and not just because he is in trouble, but something else--and it scares me. I need to find out what his agenda was, where his ends and someone else's agenda starts. That's what's bothering me. It seems that even if I knew everything he knows we may not know what's really going on. Remember what he said? *If we do not know what's going on, then we're making a mistake. It seems he did also.*" Jason recalled and continued, "The problem is; I don't know what that means, at least not what he meant by it."

Krystal drew her knees up toward her chest as she sat up in the bed. She watched him for a moment, studying his frustration with sympathetic eyes.

"I know, I don't either," she noted, "I'll try to remember what I can. Together, we'll figure this out. I promise!"

He agreed, and later that morning Jason made arrangements with Vic to set up another secure meeting with Andre Leopold, and within the hour the meeting was prepared.

Jason and Krystal took their time entering the same conference room where they met Andre the last time, resolute but apprehensive.

It was odd, he thought, as Jason had the sense that Andre had not moved in several days. Indeed Andre sat stoically, not moving, looking at the same wall same as he was when they last spoke. More so as his first comment was not dissimilar to the last he had made,

"I have already told you, I will say nothing more. You have no need of me, yes?"

With little effort to hide his contempt, Jason responded rhetorically,

"One trillion dollars? Andre! One trillion dollars?"

With this the businessman surfaced in the beaten old man and Andre turned to face them. A smile born of cunning and arrogance seemed to color his face,

"Yes, Jason! Yes! One trillion dollars and hundreds of billions for every year thereafter, that was the price of my loyalty."

"Loyalty! You have none!" Jason insisted, "You've betrayed your team, your friends, and your company!"

"No, Jason," Andre answered regretfully, "I have betrayed only one and I am sorry I have had to do so. You have the fifth code. You must see for yourself. I will say no more."

Jason watched him with frustration.

"We've used the fifth code and it exposed you! What else should I see?" he snapped back.

"If that is all you have found, then you have made the same mistake that I have," Andre answered.

"What should I see?" Jason asked.

Andre shook his head,

"You have the fifth code. I will say no more."

"Simple greed!" Jason shouted, "You've sold us out for money!"

Andre shook his head. He seemed to want to defend his position but then in a moment thought better of it and simply repeated,

"You have the fifth code. I will say no more."

"A trillion dollars!" Jason countered, "How much do you need? You're one of the richest men I know! What depth of depravity would drive you to want so much more? Simple, unadulterated greed!"

"Do not judge me!" Andre defiantly snarled, "You do not understand! Now it is too late. You have the fifth code. You should have used it! I will say no more."

"I do not need to use the fifth code to see what you have done!" Jason growled, "You were a great man, Andre. You've squandered it for a love of money! Simple greed!"

"No!" Andre's anger welled up, "The money was great, yes! But it was for the sustainability of the Kringle Works that I did what I have!"

"How?" Jason fired back, "How can you presume to say that?"

Andre shook his head again.

"Look at what we have built! A global logistics infrastructure that is second only to our own electronic infrastructure. It is a genius that we have let go to waste for the love of the status quo." He became more animated as his

322

passions grew, "Billions in research, years of development, the greatest minds in the world, for what? So that we could do the same job we have done for centuries!"

"And we have built one of the greatest businesses in the world!" Jason interrupted in justification.

Andre shook his head and continued,

"Bah! We are big, yes, but great, no! To be truly great, we must seize our potential, yes? We have not done so."

Andre leaned forward.

"It is like chess, we are merely a pawn in the game played by the nations of the world. Should we not be a bigger, more important piece in the game? Are we not capable of playing the part of the king or queen?" he submitted.

"So you *do* want to take over the world!" Krystal jumped in.

"Take *over* the world?" Andre shot her an indignant look, "No, to be a *great* part in the world, eh! That is what we must be, yes?"

Andre turned back to face Jason and continued,

"Look at what America is willing to pay. All of us on the island, all could be rich beyond our wildest dreams, yes, but you see that all we do is to deliver a service once a year. We are letting the world do as they please and we play a small part in it, but we are vulnerable. Someday they will grow tired of us and then it will be over. However, if they *need* us, then they cannot tire. It is not Christmas we should provide. A service that becomes the life blood of those we will keep in power is what we should provide. Only that will seal our future. You understand this, yes?"

"You're mad!" Jason snarled, "The Kringle Works has been operating for centuries because we have become an integral part of the world economy! Their own people hold those you suggest would grow tired of us at bay. The people demand the service. Their governments pay us because they are powerless against us. They do need us. They can't stay in power without us. They will not grow tired!"

"Jason, you are a brilliant businessman but you are young and a naïve idealist! We make gifts, deliver and sell them to appease the peoples. But the peoples do not pay us; it is their governments that do. These are our customers and it is those customers that seek only to keep the people sedate and happy so that they could be distracted long enough to keep themselves in power. Well, if it is power they want, it is power we should sell. This is simply good business, yes? We can do this? And we can charge much, much more for this service. Do you not see? It is not the gifts we should deliver, it is the information we gather that our customers want. If we sell this to them they will always be beholden to us; if we do not, someday, they will take it by force. They will abuse it and destroy it, and then no one wins, yes? The Kringles are rich; they wish for nothing more. Nothing more than to remain so, and their complacency has clouded their judgment."

"They will dismantle the Kringle Works and resurrect it as a global government sitting in the shadows just under the surface of those governments everyone else sees," Krystal interrupted him, "What does that mean? Whose agenda does that sound like?"

Andre swung his head in her direction. He had a look of extreme distress and melancholy and with no acknowledgement of her question continued talking,

"No one will shed a tear for me. No one will understand what I wanted to do. For the love of the Kringle Works, I have destroyed her. I have handed her to those with the ability to wield her power and do so with a sense of the righteousness of a false interpretation of her history. They have used me to drive their agenda and now useless, have sacrificed me at the foot of their altar. No, no one will cry for the betrayed betrayer."

He turned to Jason with a forlorn look.

"I do not want to go back to the island, Jason, leave me here in exile," Andre pleaded.

Jason shook his head.

"I can't do that! Xavier would think you are far too dangerous to the Kringle Works to remain in the United States. You know that," Jason suggested.

Andre laughed nervously and responded,

"I am afraid that in time you will find that I am not the one that is so dangerous to the Kringle Works. For its sake, you should deal with the United States. They will come if you do not. Save the Kringle Works, Jason! I love it and I always will." He paused, "I am just an old man. I must rest now. We are done now, yes?"

"Okay, Andre, we are done, for now. I have just one more question. Who betrayed you?" Jason asked.

Andre nodded and responded his voice broken and low,

"I do not know. I'm sorry. I am blind now. They have taken my mobile device to keep me from trying to escape and there are those on the island who have probably locked it out by now. No, I am powerless and blind. I am nothing more than an old man now. I have nothing. I am nothing." He took a deep breath and followed up, "We are done now."

Jason had intended to question Andre further in the following days, but the opportunity never seemed to present itself. Then, as Vic had promised, they were given the notice that they would be leaving in twenty-four hours.

Each of the island's natives was given a chance to pack and prepare for the flight. Jason and Krystal were met out in front of the condos, where NTA staff shuttled them to the distribution center's helicopter landing pad. Upon arrival they noticed Andre Leopold also standing at the landing pad under guard and bound by a plastic tie at the wrists. He seemed resigned and cooperative, but the whole scene made Jason uncomfortable.

Upon the helicopter's arrival the team was escorted on to the aircraft, their luggage brought abroad with several gaylords and palettes of returning and rerouted inventory.

As Vic suggested, in an effort to draw no attention, they had arranged for them to return as part of regularly scheduled flight to the island. They were to be taken to one of the largest hubs which served as one of the primary distribution points for the northern Midwest just outside Cleveland, Ohio, in neighboring Solon. This distribution center was not only one of the largest but served as one of the key staging points for inventory coming directly from the Kringle Works island via NTA aircraft and, as such, had its own private airfield on the grounds of the compound.

Their stay in Ohio was unceremonious and brief. In a matter of just a couple hours they were boarding an NTA cargo jet along with two large shipping containers.

With the number of routine flights back and forth to the island, the local border patrol agent, employed by the United States government and whose job it was to work on the distribution center grounds, barely glanced at the paperwork that might have included Jason Pelham's passport. The agent had grown so accustomed and complacent he hardly counted to see if the number of persons boarding alongside of the cargo matched the paperwork he received. Having gotten used to the numerous aircraft crews' Canadian- and Danish-issued passports on the behalf of the Kringle Works, he tended to wave them through with little process or thought.

The NTA's 747 Dreamlifter could make the trip in just under five hours and was starting to roll. Jason felt a strong sense of relief at the thought that he was now on the returning leg of their trip. It filled him with a level of comfort to know that his next stop would be the NTA Main Airport.

Whether born of this sense of comfort or pity, Jason agreed one hour into the flight that the plastic tie be removed from the wrists of Andre Leopold upon noting the trickle of blood discoloring the ties as they cut into Andre's flesh.

"The next stop will be the Kringle Works. We will be met by security on the tarmac. What can the old man do? We'll let him have his dignity and comfort for the flight. Cut the ties!" Jason commanded upon Andre's whimpering pleas.

Grateful, Andre conducted himself with dignity and respect. Though Jason thought he could feel Andre's nerves churning within him as the hours before facing his judgment ticked away, Andre remained quiet, sitting and reading for a time, then pacing the aircraft and stopping occasionally at the aircraft's side door to look at the passing landscape 30,000 feet below.

The glow of a distant setting sun illuminated the aircraft through the windows and slowly the light in the cabin slipped away.

The sound of four large jet engines droned on to the point where Jason did not hear them anymore. He focused his attention instead on Krystal, whose head nodded forward, then dropped against his shoulder as the weight of her fatigue forced her eyes to shut and she drifted to sleep.

Jason's own eyes grew heavier as he only managed to hear a portion of the pilot's announcement that they would be turning to make their final approach in twenty minutes. He looked over to check Krystal's seat belt as she slept and then checked his own. His eyes burned and he felt some genuine relief when he closed them again.

With a jolt, Jason woke up. It was suddenly bitterly cold and he could feel the air getting sucked from his lungs. It was chaotic as small objects were flying through the cabin. His hair whipped around to the point that it disoriented him. He heard alarms blaring and Krystal screaming in confused terror. Trying to get his bearings, he looked around in the darkened cabin. The alarms continued to whine at an ear-piercing volume. The wind was whistling inside the cabin and the sound of the aircraft's engines seemed louder than ever. Then with a crash, the ceiling above the seats opened up and oxygen masks dropped down. Before anyone was completely aware of what was going on, Andre released his failing grip on the locking lever of the aircraft's door, allowing himself to fall backward and letting the change in pressure pull him out and free of the aircraft into the cold, vast blackness of the night.

23

THE OPERATION

"Jacob Vanderberg, what in the hell will you do now?" Jake asked himself rhetorically.

He coughed and cleared his throat while sitting at the desk of his White House office. He spun his chair back and forth in an effort to burn an excess of energy born of nerves and frustration. Suddenly he stopped. He thought for a while, then wheeled his chair closer to his desk and reached for a lower drawer. He pulled a small bottle and a brandy snifter from the desk and placed it down on the wooden surface. He looked up to confirm his office door was closed and poured himself half a glass.

Raising it to the light of the window, he eyed the snifter for a moment, swirling the dark amber liquid in the glass as if to inspect its movement along the edges. He lowered the glass and downed the contents in one gulp. He set the glass back down and poured himself another.

Reaching into his jacket pocket he pulled out two cigars, placed one in his desk drawer, and unwrapped the other. He ran the full length of the cigar under his nose. He placed it between his lips, rotating it as if to help it conform to his mouth, and moistened the end lightly. He then unceremoniously bit the end off and spat it onto the floor of his office. Sticking the cigar back in his mouth, he pulled a lighter from his jacket pocket and prepared to light it. Though this type of behavior was highly frowned upon in the office, Jake cared little for the rules but gave another cursory glance at the door to at least make an effort to keep his disregard for them to a level of discreteness.

He took a few puffs as he lit the cigar, creating a cloud of smoke disrupted by a cough that followed. He sat back, leaning far enough to turn his gaze to the ceiling. He rolled the cigar between his fingers as he puffed away.

Then with a level of energy uncommon to Jake's normal demeanor, he jumped to his feet and wandered over to a bookcase and pulled out a binder with a combination lock. He looked at it carefully and then burst out laughing.

"Andy, old boy, perhaps you have given me the answer I needed right here," Jake said to himself.

He brought the binder to his desk, sat down and pushed a button on his phone,

"Gretchen, tell the president I'm ready to give him his briefing and recommendations."

Jake made the decision to present the president with the binder and suggest they use the plans drafted by Andre Leopold for their own purposes. If the Kringle Works would not give them what they wanted, they would take it by force. Jake thought this plan would appeal to his president and it would allow him to save face after allowing the original agreement to slip away.

The binder contained a detailed outline of Andre's plan to undermine and overthrow the leadership at the Kringle Works. It contained maps and notes as to the command and control systems, location of security personnel, and other information needed to topple the island's command infrastructure. Therefore, it would not take long for the Pentagon to get involved. Soon a plan was hatched to take the Kringle Works technology by way of military might and starting with Andre's detailed operation, a new one was drafted using his information to seize control and confiscate what they wanted.

They planned to nullify the leadership, assume control of the ICU technology and reverse engineer it.

Within a few weeks the aptly named, 'Operation: How the Grinch Stole Christmas,' was born silently of their collective lust for the technology. Operation Grinch was prepared to raze to the ground all that which would lie in their path in the effort to seize all equipment associated with the monitoring of the ICU network. Grinch's secrecy was absolute because the expected operation's lack of popularity would irreparably damage the reputation of the administration which commanded it. Indeed, it was suggested that the public outrage would be so extreme, were the target and the objective to become common knowledge, that impeachment, recalls, special elections, and even violent revolt seemed a plausible result. Still, they felt that the rewards of success would outweigh the risks, noting that if successful the technology itself could help them to limit the damage if information leaked out, as the administration would then have unlimited access to the public and the specifics of their dissent could be monitored. To that end, the administration also decided to move forward without any involvement from Congress or any other branch of the government in hopes of limiting knowledge or debate of the matter by invoking a series of arcane laws with questionable interpretations of intent, which allowed the executive branch to act on its own accord with speed and impunity.

"We're doing everyone a favor!" Jake insisted, "We're offering them plausible deniability, political cover, if all goes badly."

It was also suggested that, as this was an issue of extreme national security, the absolute secrecy surrounding this operation was completely appropriate and necessary. The public was not to be informed.

"What they don't know won't hurt them. Besides, the Kringle Works doesn't have any real defenses. We can't fail!" Jake suggested to the bobbing heads of several heads of state including the currently nearly salivating secretary of defense.

While the administration relished the technology to gain access to their own population, which they felt would help them to revive a failing presidency and ensure their party's re-election time and time again, the department of defense was excited by the ability to see the goings-on within the halls of governments around the globe.

The nearly desperate want for these abilities seemed to fuel an arrogant self-appointed right to the technology that became easier and easier to justify as the discussions regarding the implementation of Operation Grinch went on.

"We owe it to the country and the public to implement Operation Grinch," the secretary of defense insisted, "In the name of national security, we must have this technology! It should have been the duty of the Kringle Works to turn this technology over to the United States in the interest of democracy throughout the world. They have given us no choice."

Again, a collective cabinet bobbed their heads in blind agreement.

Then on April first, in a backroom of the White House, in the absence of a broader debate, with no congressional approvals, with a disregard for constitutional protocol, and with no discussion with the American people, the equivalent of a declaration of war was drafted and before the beaming and self-righteous faces of the executive branch of the United States government stood Operation Grinch ready for implementation.

"They will be coming to get what they want," Jason Pelham suggested to Xavier in his debrief back on the island, "They will try to take the technology by force."

Xavier sat back into his ornately decorated chair and pondered the situation.

"If they come, we will be powerless to stop them," Jason followed up, "I don't believe we have the luxury of time. We've got to draft a plan to counter their intentions."

Xavier sat silently for another moment.

"And what do you suggest?" Xavier inquired.

"Accelerate our plan to phase out the ICU technology before they come," Jason answered without hesitation, "Give them nothing to come for. Destroy it and present them with proof we have done so."

Xavier shook his head in resigned frustration.

"Your team will resist this option. How long do you believe we have to dismantle the ICU network?" Xavier asked.

"Thirty days," Jason responded, "Sixty, tops."

"Preposterous!" Xavier cried, "You know that's impossible! We are completely reliant on these systems. We can't just shut them down! Surely it would take the United States longer than that to launch an operation against us? They have to study our island, work out the details of our infrastructures, locate their prize and determine entry points, study the weather, review our command and control, establish our ability to respond; we have been hiding in the cold for a reason-- they know nothing about us! Jason, we need at least a year!"

Jason shook his head.

"I'm afraid not. In his final act of betrayal, I believe that Andre may have outlined a plan for them to work from. I think they have what they need. I have no proof, but I'm certain of it."

Xavier grew quiet and thoughtful. His eyes glistened. Whether it was the depth of his old friend's betrayal or the unfortunate way he chose to end his life, Xavier was having trouble reconciling the events of the last few months. Then with a deep breath, his voice low, broken, and quivering, Xavier spoke,

"Do what you have to do."

Jason's plan would be one of extreme complexity and challenge. He needed to rebuild the old, pre-ICU surveillance infrastructure and be able to covertly run it in tandem while making the provisions to dismantle the ICU network. His plan was to drive production ahead in an effort to allow for the inevitable 'black out' period that would result from the forced transition. He would have to document every step to be able to provide credible proof to the United States and others who would need to understand that the network had been effectively disabled. And though he did not know whom he could trust without alerting those who would fight his effort, or who might have been associated with the emerging conspiracy which motivated Andre, he felt he had at least Henry and Krystal whom he could rely on. Indeed, in Henry, Jason had a powerful ally. He could help him to execute the plan and was in the unique position to direct his team without raising suspicions.

Jason confidentially shared that he was drafting a plan with him; a plan to thwart an attack by the United States, which he felt was imminent. He was pleased to hear that Henry seemed enthusiastic about the concept and that he was willing to assist him in any way he could. Knowing he could count on him was a major step. He trusted his entire staff and though he felt that he could count on Raymond Dunbar, he also knew that he would get a great deal of resistance from Edward Grubb and Lorraine Barlow due to their dependence on the technology. So having Henry Foster's support was key, especially since it would be imperative that most of their activities be kept covert so as not to alert anyone who might have been sympathetic to Andre's cause.

For the next two days he worked tirelessly on the outline for this effort. Once it was in a state that made sense, he sent it to Henry in hopes of getting the granularity it needed to make it possible for implementation. To this end, he worked nearly the full forty-eight hours before getting it done. That morning he called Krystal. Determined not to allow himself to let work come between them again, he had set the goal that the day that he sent the plan to Henry would be the day he would join Krystal for lunch.

"So, finally a free moment, mister senior VP workaholic?" she derided him with a mocking tone but friendly smile, "Rumors have it that you didn't even go home last night!"

He smirked, watching her as she entered his office and sat down in the chair across from his desk.

"It's been a tough couple days," he responded apologetically.

"Well then? Should I be sympathetic or are you doing this to yourself?" she asked, folding her arms. Her tone was friendly and playful but her expression and body language became judgmental. She narrowed her eyes into a disapproving stare. She held this expression, waiting for his response, but found it hard to conceal the laugh that was building as she watched him fish for words in his mind.

Finally, knowing there was no right answer, he told the truth,

"Both!" he said plainly.

"Well, at least you're being honest," she noted with a chuckle, "In the past you would have made up some excuse, like you had no choice or it couldn't be helped."

She leaned forward, touching her cheek pensively,

"So, mister senior VP, where do you want to take me; you still owe me, you know?"

He nodded.

"Yes I do," he admitted, "I was thinking about a small place just outside the compound. Do you think you'll have time if--?"

The door to his office, which was slightly ajar now, flew open with a crash. Henry Foster flew in, obviously panic-stricken.

"Jason!" he exclaimed dramatically as he swung the door deliberately shut, "Have you lost all of your senses?"

Jason looked back at a wild-eyed Henry Foster, somewhat confused.

"What in the name of Christmas?" he questioned, "What is it? Henry, what's wrong?"

"Dismantle the ICU network? Are you out of your mind?" Henry responded, "Do you have any idea how ridiculous that plan is? No, no, no, we will not be dismantling it! It's too important!"

Jason tried to tone down the volume and addressed this emotionally driven outburst. He spoke very measured and quietly,

"Henry, you of all people? I thought this was what you might have wanted also. I thought you understood what I was going to try to do."

"No, no, no! Hide it! Protect it from attack! Defend us from a US invasion, trick them, or beat them! But dismantle the network? No way! There's got to be a better option!" he fired back intensely.

"Henry, this technology is bad," Jason responded, "If not now, someday soon, someone will take it from us. We have to get rid of it. There is no other way. Xavier has already agreed to it. He sees how vulnerable it is. He learned that when he realized that Andre was willing to betray him and the Kringle Works just for its value."

Henry shook his head.

"No! Jason, don't you understand how important the ICU technology is?" he defended his position, "The technology itself will keep us from losing it."

"I know, Henry!" Jason noted, "But even with its awesome capabilities it can't defend us."

"Yes it can!" Henry shouted, "Look; with the codes we can extend its capabilities!"

Jason thought he knew what Henry was trying to imply and reached into his desk drawer and pulled out the envelope which had both the card with the four published codes inside and the five codes written on the back. He held it up.

"Even with all five codes," Jason started to explain his position, "We can see the enemy coming. Once they are at the front door, the fifth code allows us to see them right here on the island, but that would be a great advantage only if we had an army. If we had a significant defense force, only then, Henry, only then would the ICU really help us. No, Henry. We must give them no reason to come. It's the only way. The technology has become a liability. They won't stop as long as it exists."

"We can stop them!" Henry insisted, "There is a better way than to destroy it."

Jason continued to preach his plan,

"Henry, I know it's a huge step, but even if we could stop them they would come again, and again. Soon others would try to take it as well. I know how important the technology is. I get it! That's why it has to be dismantled. There's no better way! You know it and I know it. You've worked for years on the technology, it's your baby, but you've been just as successful with the old system, a system of brilliant process and execution, one that allowed us to do the job better than anyone in the world without offering a technology that they can exploit. For years they have tried to get access to our capabilities but it has never been so simple to take it from us. No, Henry this is for the best. It's a morally challenged technology, anyway."

Jason placed the envelope on his desk and pointed at it.

"There is no other way! This has made it too easy." He extended his pointing at the envelope by tapping it with his forefinger, "This technology has made it too easy for them to steal it. In the past they would have needed us to help them use our surveillance network, but with the ICU, they just need these codes and the equipment."

Henry shook his head.

"You're wrong. There is a better way," Henry demanded.

"No, Henry, there's no better way. Look, we have all five codes. When they come we will know it, but what good will that do? We are powerless to stop them," Jason suggested, picking up the envelope and waving it in the air.

"We do have the power," Henry said smugly, "ICU2!"

Jason's heart pounded. Something was suddenly going very wrong. What was happening? Where was this leading them? Unsure, he became terrified. He started to think about a number of unanswered questions. What was ICU2? He had asked the question before but no one seemed to know. He had since disregarded it, but now the question was filling him with dread. Why had he never gotten a real answer before? His jaw dropped and his mouth hung open. He was incapable of uttering another word.

Henry frantically motioned for the envelope; Jason, unsure, reached forward to hand it to him. He regretted it the moment Henry grabbed it.

Pulling a pen from his shirt pocket, Henry started writing on the envelope. As he did, he started to explain,

"Jason, a few years back we started to amend the ICU technology. Look at the world around you. It's a mess. Corruption is everywhere. Morality has fallen from grace. The people are corrupt. Their communities are corrupt. Their leaders are corrupt, and their governments are corrupt. Someone has to take control before the whole planet implodes. With ICU2, we can do just that."

Henry continued to write some numbers on the envelope. It seemed to Jason he was calculating them.

"What are you talking about?" Jason asked watching him intently writing on the envelope.

"The ICU2 technology is code-based and can be activated by use of an additional code," Henry suggested, "But because of the nature of what it can do, we kept this code from being published … anywhere."

Henry finished writing and handed the envelope back to Jason. As he did he continued his explanation,

"This code is so important but so dangerous in the wrong hands, we had to keep it a complete secret. First, you have to know all of the first five codes. Then add them together digit by digit, disregarding any numbers you would carry over and you have the sixth and final code."

Jason looked wide-eyed. He took a deep breath and worked up the courage to ask,

"Henry, what does this sixth code do?"

Henry smiled broadly.

"It transmits!" he said proudly, "It transmits information back to the original data source!"

The office fell silent for a moment. Waiting for a reaction that did not come, Henry spoke again,

"Don't you understand? It sends information back to the originating device. We use the ICU chip to gather data, with ICU2 we can send it back! It's brilliant! We can choose what information goes back. With the ICU2 technology, we can manipulate information that people see and consequently we use that to make them act in the way we would want … eh … need them to."

"What have you done?" Jason questioned harshly.

Henry, looking shocked, answered curtly,

"I've given the world a fighting chance!" he shook his head in bewilderment, "Don't you see? With ICU2 we can control anyone's actions! Unbeknownst to them they will do what we want because they will react to the information we feed them. They will act on the environment they perceive, not the one that is their reality. In some cases we are even able to control the device ourselves."

Henry started to become more excited,

"You've heard of the Israeli technology that nearly thwarted the Iranian ambitions to nuclear weapons, or the Aurora project, which would allow hackers to destroy the diesel generators in power plants right under the noses of their caretakers? Computer viruses that allowed for control of armed, unmanned drones to fall into the hands of those they were attacking. The ICU2 does this on a far more sophisticated level. The world would be the unwitting slaves of our technology. Even those here on the island who might watch from afar can be controlled, because they too are slaves to the information they receive through their dependence on technology. As long as some of the ICU2 technology is present, we can control everything whether directly or indirectly. Without the cumbersome task of slowly reversing all of the evil in the world we can instead shift and nudge it in the right direction and save it in spite of itself. But for now, we do have a more practical application. We can stop any attack on our soil. We will win this! My team can make it so they never even reach us!"

He stopped talking. The pause he thought might contain Jason's and Krystal's impressed voices asking him to save their island from doom was instead a moment of uncomfortable silence. Bemused, Henry continued his argument,

"Look, for a while it will not be pretty. I know that. Still, consider how many people are hurt, taken captive, killed every day to appease the whims of a few morally bankrupt governments. Any collateral damage we would cause would be no worse! But in the long run," Henry smiled broadly eyes wide, "In the long run, we have the opportunity to correct the ills that have festered across the globe for decades. For now we must simply defeat a single point of resistance. We can seize control of their aircraft, weapons, or at minimum guide them away from their targets. If it is done with the right level of finesse it will look like a miscalculation, an accident, or incompetence. The United States would never even admit they tried, out of embarrassment. We will win this! It's no problem! Our plans are too valuable to the world to allow this little issue to have us run for cover."

Henry shook his head again in frustration when he saw their judgmental looks and whined,

"Don't you get it? We can control them if we need to. We can take down their infrastructure, shut down buildings, power plants, and yes, even crash planes…"

"Crash planes?!" Jason shouted in horror, "You said you had a plane to catch when the Americans left last year. You said you had a plane to catch, and then I never saw the trip you implied. I didn't think anything of it at the time, but you said it, cynically, and then you had the plane crashed with them on it! Didn't you? That's why you weren't worried about Andre's offer! You planned to keep the plane from making it back to the mainland all along! See? Your plans are not infallible! You miscalculated. Andre still made his offer."

"Andre was a fool!" Henry snapped back, "We just latched on to his twenty-year effort to overthrow the Kringles to get his followers and resources. If he had any idea how far we were able to take the technology…" he paused, "Look, Andre sought to sell the technology to gain power, but failed to realize the true power to be gained with the application of the technology. He didn't understand the full potential. The latest application and the opportunities created by the use of the ICU2."

Jason took a stern tone and started lecturing,

"Henry, how could you do this? What gives you the right? Think of how many lives you have disrupted, ruined, or even ended. How many more will you take in this errand? Do you realize the peril you've put us all in? It's because of you and those that follow you that the United States might be coming! And if? And if, by some measure they succeed, then you have given them the power you sought to control them with! Do you have any concept of the potential cost and the suffering you've placed on our island? On the world?"

Krystal could not believe what she was hearing, and in an effort to support Jason's point she chimed in,

"My God, Henry! You killed those people!" she forcefully stated, "In turn you might be killing many more!"

Henry gave her a blank stare and noted with a strangely passive voice,

340

"Well, it's just as Christopher Kringle originally said, *'Do not lament the suffering we have to endure to fulfill the dream but rejoice in the courage with which we will face it.'*"

"Oh my God, spare me the history … lesson …" Krystal slowed her speech to a stop and paused to think.

"It was you!" she suddenly exclaimed, "You! You kept me a prisoner!"

"We kept you contained. You interfered," Henry responded, "We treated you well. You were made comfortable and provided for," he followed up.

"But I was a prisoner!" she shouted.

"You were a liability," he said coldly.

"Don't you realize that Marcus was going to…" she stopped to process the information before continuing, "You might have had me killed!" she shouted in disgust.

"I had you rescued," he responded confidently, "You were in no danger. I had Marcus fully controlled."

"You killed him!" Krystal shouted.

"He was a liability," he responded.

"Like me?" she questioned sternly.

"No, that was different," he suggested coldly.

"How? Why?" she fired back, "So if I had been someone else you would have let me be killed? How dare you claim the mantle of morality?"

Henry shook his head.

"You just aren't understanding. All great ideas, all great leaps of progress, all have a wake of sacrificial bodies. It can't be helped. We try to minimize it. But it can't be helped. All we can do is to try to protect the innocents as much as possible. But it can't be completely avoided," he suggested.

He reached inside his sport coat and pulled out a .38-caliber revolver and pointed it at them.

"Look, I didn't want it to come to this but you're leaving me no choice," he said, cocking his head with an apologetic look.

Jason looked at the firearm in horror as he heard the sound of the hammer being cocked.

"Henry, what is that?" Jason asked, "Why do you have a gun? We don't have guns here! There are no guns on the Kringle Works Island!"

"Is that right? Huh? Well then, that would be why this particular gun is so very, very effective, here on the island. Isn't it?" Henry commented mockingly.

Krystal watched Henry. She slowly got out of her chair with her hands raised and away from her body. She stood up facing him. A combination of fear and anger was bubbling inside her. Her eyes moistened, but her expression and demeanor remained defiant and resolute. She started moving around the desk slowly; she felt the need to be closer to Jason.

"Stop!" Henry's voice cracked as he turned the gun on Krystal, "Don't move!"

She shook her head in disbelief, but stopped just as he commanded. She froze. Her chest tightened. She could hardly breathe.

"Henry, you don't want to do this!" she said, her voice shaking.

"You're right," he answered, "But it seems I don't have a choice. Do I?"

Henry pointed the gun back at Jason, who stood paralyzed.

"Henry," she addressed him, "All your talk of making the world better. I see your conviction, your passion for it. You don't want to hurt us. Let's talk about this. Okay?"

She stretched out her hand. Whether in a gesture of goodwill or to ask for the gun, Henry was not sure. He kept the gun pointed at Jason but watched Krystal's movements.

342

"Henry, we may not agree, but this is not the way you want this to play out. Is it?" she suggested.

"No, it's not," he answered, watching her.

Jason started lowering his hands. As he did, Henry caught the movements peripherally. His hand twitched. The gun still firmly pointed at Jason, the signal was silent but clear, *'stop moving, keep you're hands where I can see them.'* Jason froze. Henry's gaze turned back toward him.

Krystal saw what she thought was deep regret in Henry's eyes. This was not how he wanted this to go. This was a desperate move. Just moments ago, she thought to herself, Henry was trying to convince them that he had a better way. An alternative they could all embrace. He was making an appeal for his solution, but was backed against the wall by their distaste for his plan. She took a slow, unthreatening step toward him. Her eyes were understanding, her voice diminutive, as she spoke,

"Henry?"

She miscalculated. He saw the movement toward him and reacted. The gun swung in her direction and he pulled the trigger.

In a place where guns were never heard the sound of one firing seemed to echo much more loudly. The sound of the gunshot was punctuated by the almost instantaneous scream which burst from Jason's throat in an explosion of overwhelming terror. Low and guttural, it shocked Krystal for a moment. Did Henry just shoot Jason? She could not bear the thought.

She felt a jolt at the top of her body, which made her pivot at the waist by a force she did not see. She felt a wet spray on the side of her face; it stung in her eyes, and horrified, she thought that it looked like blood.

"Oh no! Jason was hit!" she thought.

The unseen force threw her off balance and she stumbled back against Jason's desk. It was just two steps but they seemed to drain her of all her energy. Her rear was leaning on the edge of the desk, which stopped her from falling for a fraction of a second, but then her knees buckled and she dropped to the floor. She thought she could feel her head impact the desk as she fell, but was powerless to stop it. There was a sharp pain in her chest and shoulder. It was hard to breathe. She looked up when she heard a commotion of movement. Suddenly office supplies rained down on her from the desk above, followed the figure of Jason Pelham coming to her aid. Dizzy and disoriented, it was as though he flew in from above the desk. She could feel his hands wrap around her in an embrace. Was he screaming? Her ears were ringing from the sound of the gunshot, so she heard him but could not make out his muffled cries. Still, he seemed okay.

"That's good! He's not hurt," she thought.

She could feel his breath on her face. She tried to caress his cheek, but could not seem to move her arm enough to reach it. Why was she so tired? She wanted to quiet his terrified cries so she looked into his eyes, smiled and whispered to him,

"Don't cry, Jason. You're okay. I don't think he hit you. You're just scared, that's all. He missed."

24

THE GRINCH THAT STOLE CHRISTMAS

"This is wrong on so many levels," John suggested, "When are they supposed to launch?"

"Zero six hundred, Agent Evans," a uniformed officer responded, "No need to go in under cover of darkness, we are expecting them to know exactly when we are coming, so we go in with overwhelming force."

John nodded and continued walking along the tarmac.

"Yes, they will know we are coming," he repeated quietly.

John stopped and the officer stopped obediently with a snap. John turned, not to face him but to look past him and take in the sight of what he was told would be nearly fifty aircraft. On either side of the lineup were smaller, heavily armed F-16 Fighting Falcon jet aircraft and in the center were larger personnel- and equipment-carrying C-17 Globemaster III military transport aircraft, which would be the 'business end' of the operation.

The tarmac was wet and reflected the pale gray images of the aircraft. One by one each stuck its nose out in a row, lined up at attention, standing quietly in line like the military men and women who would board them in the morning. There was a strange calm about the sight; all had been readied for the mission and now the aircraft stood, obediently waiting for dawn.

The day was ending and John stood and stared as he contemplated the sight. The orange glow of lowering sun defined the edges of each aircraft. It was incredible. It was awe-inspiring. It was intimidating. Yet it would be the first time in John's life that he was not filled with pride at a sight such as this, for in his mind, it was the physical manifestation of the most powerful country in the world acting on the behest of the bruised egos of its leadership. This was going to be an overwhelming act of aggression against a largely unarmed people whose primary purpose was to deliver joy across the globe, and John had some significant reservations about the whole concept.

"We're launching a military action against Santa Claus," John noted quietly, shaking his head.

"The Kringle Works, sir, in the interest of national security," the voice of the officer offered in answer.

"They will do a good job," John said to himself.

Indeed, he was certain of it. The men and women sworn to do their duty would do exactly as they were told. They would execute with an uncompromised precision the tasks presented to them in the line of duty. Their perfect and professional work, worthy of praise, would likely be recorded by history as an ill-tempered, even childish overreaction, and their efforts besmirched by the flawed policy and leadership that would command them to do so.

For now, it was quiet. The men and women who would take part in the operation had retired at the command of their superiors. They would be fresh in the morning. The shift would start early and this evening was their last opportunity to get the rest they needed. They had spent the last few weeks in briefings and training sessions in which they would prepare for every move and every conceivable countermove of the pending operation. In the morning they would execute.

John did not sleep well that night.

As the only survivor of the team that flew to the island eight months earlier and as an agent of the FBI, he was asked to spend this time on base with the troops participating in the briefings, and then to offer his perspective to command on the operation. Though he voiced his apprehension regarding the need to execute the operation at all, it was made clear this was not in question.

Similarly, Tom Bradley had also been tapped for his insight into the technology. Reams of data which Tom had compiled were sent from

Washington, DC to the base. However, like John, Tom's purpose was not to evaluate but to aid and confirm. Any misgivings on either of their parts were disregarded.

"The operation will take place," Director Patterson told both men in a conference call, "What we want from you are the details regarding your research, your experience with the island, the people, and the technology. Nothing more."

For their part, they were promised great rewards by the administration for their efforts. It was vague, but it still seemed odd to John that so much of the executive branch started to talk as though they would be in a position to grant long-term favors even though the recent polling data with the public was starting to suggest they would not survive the next election.

How was it that this, a secret operation of potentially unprecedented unpopularity if it were publicized, was making the administration so confident? He dreaded to think of what they may have considered would be their ultimate prize if all went as planned.

"We cannot allow an outside power such as the Kringle Works to spy on our activities, in the name of national security," a senior officer suggested in one of the briefings when asked, "There is even evidence that they may have had a part in sabotaging the aircraft that was sent to the Kringle Works on a diplomatic mission. We are acting in the interest of the United States to eliminate and seize any and all of the technology associated with this illegal act of continued espionage."

"But why seize it? Why not just disable it by taking out the control centers of the technology with air strikes? Wouldn't that dramatically reduce the risk and the number of troops needed on the ground?" one of the airmen asked. The follow-up questions hung in the air like some foul smell on a hot and humid day, waiting for a decisive response, which instead was shut down with, "Those are our orders!"

This left John scratching his head; for one, the surveillance may have been intrusive and questionably inappropriate, but based on the long-standing treaties with the United States they were not illegal. Secondly, though he knew that Tom felt strongly that the plane crash that almost killed him was an act of sabotage, there was no conclusive evidence in any of the official reporting and the administration's citing of this as justification for their invasion was dubious at best.

Neither John nor Tom had any love for the ICU technology, but both felt that there was a disquieting and untold agenda specific to the current administration. It seemed dark and sinister and, as such, it was no longer the Kringle Works that concerned them. During the weeks John spent on base working with the military he tried to uncover what he could. Knowing he felt similarly, he broached the subject several times with Tom Bradley, who also voiced his misgivings. Still, they were stationed a thousand miles apart during the lead up to the mission, so they could only communicate by phone and that was something that Tom was absolutely unwilling to do. He talked instead in riddles and metaphors, which kept John thoroughly frustrated. Every conversation would be short, unproductive, and ended the same way,

"Look, we'll talk about it face-to-face, okay?" Tom suggested, closing the conversation, "We can't discuss it now! Not on the phone, not like this! Just be careful."

"Even on a secure line?" John tried asking.

"Just be careful," Tom responded predictably time and time again.

The technology had Tom so spooked that he could no longer be relied on to correspond with anyone in any form other than face-to-face, though even then Tom had taken on an air of paranoia that had him always looking over his shoulder and whispering.

"You're becoming a tormented, sociopathic, and introverted nerd," John told him on one of his calls to Washington, DC.

Tom simply responded,

"Just tell them not to trust their instruments."

Tom's unease made John very anxious and now the night before the launch of Operation Grinch, John was restless to the point of waking every hour. By three a.m., it no longer made sense to stay in bed and he got up, splashed water in his face and turned on the television. Watching a few moments of the twenty-four hour cable news cycle did not help, and he decided to take his shower and get dressed.

By zero four hundred, the tarmac was a flurry of activity. Aircraft and personnel were being outfitted and loaded. This was their Danse Macabre for the Kringle Works and with the precision of the finest Swiss watch, the first of the aircraft would be airborne exactly two hours later. At zero six hundred hours Operation: How the Grinch Stole Christmas was underway.

Krystal Gardener awoke from her coma three weeks after being shot in the chest. She'd had a collapsed lung and a 38-caliber bullet lodged on the inside of her shoulder blade. She was considered lucky. Her survival had been far from certain, but it seemed that she was now on the path to recovery. During this time Jason spent every moment at her side, which forced Xavier's hand with regards to the execution of Jason's plan to dismantle the ICU network. In the absence of a better alternative the plan now degenerated to a security operation versus the elegant weaning that Jason had originally sought. At Xavier's command, Peter Sharp would work with Randall Blake to identify all active ICU workstations and remove them. Document their removal and bring them to a single warehouse, which Xavier had ordered be set aside. The consequences of the complete disconnection of each of the machines was not considered, and the obvious negative impact of this move prompted some members of the NTA teams to stand in protest, forcing Peter's security force to arrest members of both Lorraine's and Henry's teams. Systematically, Peter went down the list of currently active and commissioned ICU workstations, and workstation-by-workstation his team took them away.

The greatest amount of resistance met was from the department of data acquisition, and in the data hall. Edward Grubb's team, on the other hand, seemed to be resigned to the operation. They would be able to build their behavioral algorithms with the data from any number of sources, and where that data came from would be Lorraine's problem anyway. However, it was Henry's team in the user interface and technology departments that proved to be the most unpredictable; while half of the team was now missing and had been so for a couple weeks, the other members who remained ranged in reaction from a willingness to throw themselves before the machines in an effort to protect them from being seized, to those who stepped back and applauded as the machines were being wheeled out.

"And thus the pendulum must swing right to correct what is wrong so that it can in turn swing back when all that is wrong will be blamed on those who are right," Xavier noted while reading the report from Peter Sharp upon the completion of the task.

"Have the warehouse shut, guarded, and locked until I tell you to do otherwise," he followed up.

Peter acknowledged and turned to leave.

"Thank you, Peter," Xavier said as Peter started to walk out, "You know what we will have to do next? I will send a letter to the United States telling them the workstations will be destroyed."

Peter turned around in the doorway and nodded,

"Just let me know when."

"Even if I convince the United States to abandon their quest for this technology, Henry might still try to get at it. Have you found him or those who are hiding him?" Xavier asked.

Peter nodded in acknowledgement again and then shook his head.

"No, he is nowhere to be found but we will keep a look out for him," he answered.

Henry Foster had not been seen for a number of weeks. Peter's forces had made a comprehensive effort to sweep the island but had turned up nothing.

When the shot from Henry's gun rang out, it was not Peter's security team that arrived first. Indeed, with the precision of the NTA, a number of Henry's own team came in and whisked him away. Shortly thereafter nearly half of his team disappeared. In the following weeks, as Peter attempted to gather the workstations, more employees vanished; no longer specific to Henry's team, these now were individuals from all departments and even from the factory floors of ELF.

"The news was out," Peter suggested during his search for Henry, "It is unfortunate that we are not in a position to seek out all his supporters. They are on the run but always seem to be a step ahead. The good news is that we were able to gather all the commissioned workstations before they could hide any of them. So hopefully we will get ahead of them now."

It seemed that the conspiracy that Jason Pelham was trying to expose was now coming apart. He allowed himself to feel a moment of relief at the thought that Peter had confiscated all of the workstations. This would be a challenging time for the company, but with the circumstances being what they were he did not seem to care too much about that.

He was focused on Krystal. Indeed, for Jason things changed a great deal the day that Henry walked into his office for that last time. Jason put up no resistance when he saw her collapse after Henry's gun fired. He made no effort to stop him. Jason was focused on just one thing and with no concern for his own safety he instead rushed to be at her side. He had not left it since. From the moment she hit the ground, was shuttled to the hospital, went into surgery, and through her weeks of unconscious recovery, he was there. And he was at her side when they heard the explosions in the distance.

The date was chosen to exploit the warmer weather and the almost constant daylight. Still, it seemed almost as though the civilian leadership was being a little tongue-in-cheek when they selected June sixth, the anniversary of D-Day at Normandy, for the invasion.

Their operation had anticipated some resistance but found the Kringle Works Island largely undefended. The plan was to disable any potential for retaliation in the air and to first take control of the NTA Main Airport. F-16s would circle the island and take control of and defend the airspace. For its lack of strategic importance the island's only other airport, located twenty miles from the Kringle Works compound, would suffer complete obliteration so as to remove it as a variable to be monitored.

Several aircraft now approached NTA Main Airport and with a number of strategically placed bombs disabled several aircraft and taxi ways to the main runways, eliminating the ability for NTA planes to taxi for take off. The next wave of the invasion was to place troops and equipment on the ground. In tight formation and well-escorted, two of the larger C-17 transport aircraft landed. The escorting F-16s broke formation and flew overhead as the C-17s touched down. Barely stopped at the end of the runway, heavily armed troops sprung from the rear of the bloated aircraft. Like a bug-infested box of sugar that had just been pushed over they spread, fanning out in perfect formation. Immediately they formed a defensive perimeter around their aircraft and as the number of troops increased, the perimeter grew. More aircraft landed and like those a moment before, they took control quickly. The runways were theirs.

Running down the heated tarmac a platoon followed two large, armored vehicles which were led by a young lieutenant. They proceeded to the tower. The activity was chaotic as more C-17s landed and as the number of troops grew, so did the number of Kringle Works security personnel. Preparing for a confrontation, the marines had their weapons at the ready when they realized the majority of the security force had their guns slung and attempted to do no more than aid those who had been injured in the blasts that preceded the marines' arrival.

"Quickly!" the young lieutenant shouted, "You take your men and help them, but take their weapons!"

A couple hand gestures, and the rest were back on the move to the base of the tower. A small contingent of security outside of the control tower building seemed ready to stand their ground, but in the face of the oncoming marines dropped to their knees with their hands behind their heads. As the marines descended upon them, the young lieutenant heard one of the security team's members comment,

"We know why you are here and you won't get them."

The young lieutenant looked confused, but with a job to do, signaled for his team to seize their adversary's weapons and proceeded to the tower entrance. For security purposes it was always locked, requiring an access key.

"Marine!" he addressed one of his men and commanded, "Get that door!"

Dressed in winter fatigues, one marine hustled to the door, checked it for just a moment and with a small and precise explosion, the door sprung open. They entered, guns at the ready, and in a choreographed dance of twists and turns confirmed the area was clear. Airport personnel shrieked at the sight of the heavily armed force and pinned themselves to walls or dropped to the ground whimpering. Some of he troops remained and secured the area while the rest proceeded up a flight of stairs.

The door to the control room burst open and an already confused and panicked team of air traffic controllers were busily trying to gain an understanding of what was happening and get control of the situation. The marines quickly spread into the room and pulled the air traffic team from their seats and took their communications equipment. The young lieutenant pointed at several members of his team and with a nod they jumped into action, taking the controllers' communications headsets; they removed their helmets and sat down. With a quick scan of the equipment the marines gave an affirmative nod to their commander and proceeded to change the tower communications frequency and addressed the inbound military aircraft,

"Foxtrot echo five, we are live! Come on in and sit on Papa Christmas's lap, we've rolled out the red carpet for yah!"

Just minutes beyond their arrival the incoming marines had secured the NTA Main Airport.

The intention was not to take control of the island but rather to cut off and secure just the Kringle Works compound. As the aircraft landed, more troops and equipment emerged from the airport grounds. Troops marched down the roads with large armored vehicles outfitted with treads or studded tires to deal with the island's terrain that tore into the ice covered roads of the compound.

With a combination of diplomacy and persuasive force the troops cleared the traffic of people, snowmobiles, sleighs, and commercial vehicles that normally moved unencumbered throughout the compound in order to open the roads ahead of them. A testament to training and practiced simulations, they navigated the compound as though they had done so a hundred times. With the roads cleared by the armored vehicles, personnel carriers followed behind. Several were deployed at each of the entrances of the compound in an attempt to secure it from the rest of the island. Gates were shut and chained.

Within only a few hours and with little resistance, the United States Marines Aviation Combat Element took control of the skies and the Ground Combat Element had secured and isolated the perimeter of the Kringle Works compound. The next phase was to secure and occupy various buildings of particular interest. Andre would have seen this phase as his opportunity to take control of the Kringle Works; and with the United States Marines at his command as the new security force no one would have been in a position to question his authority.

However, with Andre Leopold no longer part of their equation, the United States executive branch was now executing a different agenda.

25

The Occupation

Jason had his hands firmly wrapped around Krystal's when he told her he had to go. He had just heard one of the hospital staff say,

"The Compound is under attack!"

A sense of panic permeated the very air around them. There was a buzz of activity and chatter. Outside their room the drone of ongoing discussions was punctuated by gasps and even screams of horror as news started to filter in.

Jason leaned closer to her at the bedside.

"Krystal, I have to go. I have to find out what's going on," he whispered into her ear.

She closed her eyes and nodded; her voice was low, grumbling, and squeaked as she drew labored breaths between her words as she said,

"I know you do. Go. Just be careful."

Reluctantly he left her to go to the Kringle Works compound. His heart pounded as he pondered what he would find. The streets and people seemed normal but there was a strangeness in the air that he could not identify. As he saw the walls of the compound getting closer he was surprised to see all seemed unchanged and undisturbed from the outside.

The gate was now coming into view.

It was unusual to see the gate closed, he thought as he approached. Indeed it had been decades since the last time the compound had been closed up. As the demand for the Christmas service grew around the world, the Kringle works implemented longer shifts and eventually twenty-four hour manufacturing at ELF. By now it might have been thirty to forty years since the last time the tall iron gates to the compound had been shut.

To see security guards at the gate was, however, not unusual; but these were not men dressed in the fanciful, old-world, dark green uniforms of Peter Sharp's security force. No, by contrast these were marines, heavily armed and dressed in highly sophisticated, winter battle fatigues. Armored vehicles stood behind them and blocked much of his view of the compound beyond.

Jason approached the gate cautiously.

"What is your name, sir?" one of the marines addressed him from behind the gate.

"Jason..." he started and hesitated as he noted the sudden look of interest on the guard's face.

"Jason? Jason who?" the marine asked.

"Jason ... Lies," Jason answered with the first thing he could think of.

The marine guard gave him a rather suspicious look and responded slowly,

"Well, Mister," he paused, "Lies. I will need to see some identification."

The marine looked down for a moment, scanning a clipboard that looked like a list of coveted invitees to an exclusive party.

Jason took this moment and quickly backed away. The guard looked up, seeing Jason retreating.

"Hey!" the guard yelled after him.

Another marine put his hand on his arm and quietly suggested,

"Let him go. We have everything we need in here. If we need him we will track him down later."

Jason ran back to his vehicle and decided to make his way to another of the compound's gates. With the size of the compound it would take him nearly and hour to get there.

At the next gate the situation inside the compound was similar, but by now a crowd of people stood at a distance hoping to catch glimpses of what was happening inside.

The marine guards stood ready behind the gate watching the crowd carefully. Jason exited his vehicle and meandered into the crowd as it grew. He started to make his way to the front.

Being modestly famous on the island, a man now turned to Jason and, recognizing him, said,

"Mister Pelham! What do …?"

Jason shook his head and put his forefinger to his mouth to signal the man to remain silent. The man acknowledged with a nod. Jason now stood shoulder to shoulder with other island residents and tried to get a sense of what was going on inside.

Then the crowd started to stir. A buzz of chatter swept over them and at the point at which it originated, the mass of people parted as a dozen Kringle Works security personnel now approached the marines. They had their weapons drawn and at least two of them seemed equipped to cut the chains and break open the gate.

The marines raised their weapons.

"Stand back," one marine commanded from behind the gate, "We will not let you enter."

Undaunted, the security team quickened their pace. The marines maintained their position, their guns pointed at the approaching security team. Then with a nod from the commanding officer one marine fired his weapon over the heads of the team. The crowd seemed to recoil in unison. Gasps and screams punctuated the movement as about sixty people all stepped back as a group. The security team, however, continued forward.

The senior marine shook his head in a combination of disappointment, disbelief, and admiration. He gave another signal and the marine who just fired aimed again and took a single shot at the approaching team. One of the security team dropped to the ground. They continued their advance. The marine took another shot and a second security team member dropped. The team stopped their advance.

The senior marine addressed the security team and the crowd beyond,

"Stop your advance and lower your weapons. We will not yield our position. Tend to your wounded. We will not hamper your efforts. If you make no attempts to enter this compound, we will not cause you any harm. However, if you choose to approach or attempt to breach these gates, we will use deadly force to defend our position. We have no business outside of this compound and you may go about your business unencumbered."

It was a sad fact that Andre Leopold had accomplished a great many things in his long life, but that his legacy would now be a plan which would never be executed on his behalf. It was the details of his plan that gave the United States the foundation that would become the current operation, 'How the Grinch Stole Christmas' and told the invaders exactly what they needed to know. How the compound was laid out, what buildings housed security, how well-armed was that security, command and control systems, what buildings housed key interests and personnel, who were the key personnel and most importantly, where the ICU technology was housed, how many machines were in operation, who might be sympathetic and who would be likely to oppose them. Indeed, the marines and their commanders now knew more about the Kringle Works compound on a theoretical level than ninety-nine percent of the population of the Kringle Works Island.

As Jason watched two security personnel lying on the ice in a puddle of their own blood with members of their team attempting to aid them and a crowd of confused, terrified and angry people slowly starting to disperse, he felt an overwhelming sense of helplessness. It seemed that any efforts to gain access to the compound directly were likely to be fruitless. He chose to go back to his vehicle and return to the hospital. He would have to think on this situation.

The compound was designed to be defendable with a small force but that design was conceived at a time when flight was still a dream and the very location of the island was defense enough. In the not-too-distant past people routinely died just trying to get to the island and adjustments to national security seemed to fall low on any priority list since the Kringle Works never sought to be an active threat and exerted its power through the very governments that might seek to engage them in a reciprocal partnership. The thought that the compound would fall from within and then use its antiquated defense posture to lock out any chance for reinforcements to aid them was never considered.

Jason decided to see if there had been any other developments at the other entrances by going back to the original gate.

He drove along the wall of the compound and turned the corner, bringing the gate area into view. What he saw now was the result of a rebuffed attack. There was evidence of an artillery round having been exploded in the street in front of the gate. Jason counted about twenty bodies which lay in the slushy, blood-stained ice. The exact number was difficult to determine, as the blast appeared to have disarticulated the bodies of those who were closest to it. Gunshots from outside were evident but the gate remained intact and guards behind were going about their tasks with several watching as civilian medical personnel tended the fallen Kringle Works security team. To his horror, it seemed that the attack at the gate that he witnessed was part of a more overall coordinated effort, the consequences more dire depending on the resolve of the security team or the reaction of the marines.

With Peter Sharp and his senior leadership of their security force inside the compound along with most of its resources, it seemed that any attack from the outside was likely more reactionary and desperate than well-thought through. With the destruction of the island's lower airport and the NTA Main Airport part of the seizure in the compound, any attack would have to be at ground level. The most significant ground forces were already in the compound. By now communication was compromised and the apparent fact that the resistance inside showed no visible signs to the outside did not bode well for its success.

The attack and aftermath that Jason witnessed at the gates was a last effort to try to maintain access to the compound before it was completely cut off and had to be left to the marines. They were two of many staged at each of the five gates. Unfortunately, all met with the same level of failure. The number of dead and wounded varied, dependent on the speed of assembly, the available size and resolve of the security team at each location. Hopelessly out gunned, the series of attacks from the outside were rebuffed and the security teams retreated, licking their wounds. The United States Marines Corps would be left to continue with their agenda inside.

The chatter of treads running along the side of the building which housed the senior executive staff had Peter Sharp feeling the confrontation was imminent. These were the executive offices of the Kringle Works; they must be defended after all. It was also the main office of Peter's security force from which he commanded most of the actions of his team within the compound and to some degree the rest of the island.

Xavier and Peter had discussed the likelihood of an invasion by the United States and the options they would have if it should come to pass that Xavier's efforts to defuse it failed, but neither had been able to prepare for its coming so quickly. Their efforts were to create the environment so as to avoid the attack in the first place by eliminating the incentive to come. By destroying the ICU technology, as Jason had suggested, Xavier had hoped to present the United States with a case for disengagement. However, it was the United States' desperate desire for the ICU technology and the depth of the information that Andre Leopold had presented them that made their preparations so efficient and quick. Xavier had neither the time to eliminate the incentive for them to come to the island for the technology, nor to sell the case that the technology would not be here when they did. It was Peter's assistance in this effort that kept him from planning for the invasion, more so since the disconnection of the ICU technology left them even more vulnerable. It was a time in which the all-seeing and all-knowing Kringle Works would be blind and ignorant for a second, and in a lamentable moment of bad timing, it left them hopelessly unprepared.

The muffled sounds of commands and feet on the ground could be heard from behind the locked door in the deathly quiet of the building's foyer. Peter raised his firearm and with a nod to his left and to his right he signaled his team to do the same.

Who of the executive staff was still here? For all he knew the building was empty. With the news of the taking of the NTA Main Airport, his team jumped into action and hurried out all staff and support personnel they could, knowing this building would be a target. Time was short and they left their posts to arm themselves, leaving the regimented protocol of monitoring who entered and exited unattended for just a moment. It did not matter; they would defend this position no matter who remained.

There were sounds at the entry outside; Peter's heart pounded and they aimed their weapons. The door burst open. Peter saw the first of many marines enter, and started to fire. He thought he saw a soldier fall when he heard the clanking sound of metal hitting the tile floor of the foyer. He looked over to see a metal canister; smoke was billowing from the side. Then with a flash it seemed to explode in a cloud of white smoke. Peter's eyes watered; he could no longer see. The smoke now filled the foyer. He heard gunfire and commotion. He shifted position trying to see through the smoke. He turned to the left and then to the right, his handgun out in front. It was useless; he was unable to fix on anything, just shadowy figures, and was too afraid that he might hit one of his own men. It was hard to breathe. The sound of gunshots seemed random and desperate. Unrecognizable figures moved in and out of the smoke. Then Peter noticed a figure approach him intently through the smoke. He raised his firearm again and before he could make the decision to fire, he saw a flash. A sudden pain in his arm, and he dropped his gun. His right arm fell to his side and he could not seem to move it. The pain was starting to heighten and he fell to his knees.

"Area secured!" an unfamiliar voice shouted.

The smoke was starting to clear.

A marine approached Peter. He eyed him carefully, his M16 rifle pointed at him. Peter, still kneeling on the ground helplessly, looked up at him. He felt a tingle in his forearm and a searing pain in his upper arm and shoulder. He could feel the warm blood running down his arm and along his torso underneath his uniform.

"Medic!" the marine yelled out, looking at Peter sympathetically.

As the United States Marines' combat physician tended to Peter's wound, another marine tied his left arm behind him and to his belt with a plastic zip tie. Peter looked over, noting that most of his team had had a similar fate befall them. The marines had placed them to one side of the foyer kneeling on the floor, bound and guarded. Peter watched as a marine commander talked to one of his security team and noted that he had pointed him out. The commander looked at Peter and nodded in response and understanding. He started across the foyer and as he walked pulled out a small clipboard.

"Peter Sharp, head of Kringle Works's security, I presume?" the marine commander addressed Peter upon his arrival in front of him.

Peter winced as the medic continued to dress his wound, but acknowledged the commander's assessment.

"Very good, Mister Sharp. I am looking for some specific people and their offices, which should be in this building. Xavier Kringle, Malcolm Kringle, Andre Leopold, François Tribert, Nicholas Kasner, Vladimir Khovsky and Isabella Roman," the marine commander inquired with the list of top Kringle Works's executives and continued, "Two of these offices, Xavier Kringle's and Andre Leopold's, contain something we are instructed to take. Please show me to them. Note that these will be our honored guests. No one will be hurt."

Peter shook his head.

"We know why you're here and you won't find what you're looking for in these offices," Peter suggested, "As far as the executive staff, emergency procedures; I believe they're all gone."

The physician had completed dressing Peter's wound and put his right arm into a sling. With the left arm still bound to his back, the commander helped him to his feet and said,

"Show me!"

Peter nodded and with the commander and two armed marines escorting them they started up the stairs to the executive offices. One by one they entered each office. They found each empty. Computers, papers, and coffee cups left as though any might return at any moment. The marines were dumbfounded by the size, old-world design, and opulence of these spaces. Still, it was not until they entered Xavier Kringle's office that Peter heard one of them gasp in amazement as they scanned the walls, portraits, and furniture.

"So, this is Santa Claus's personal office ... and the ICU workstation, Mister Sharp?" the commander requested.

"That space. That's where it was. I told you, you won't find them. They're not here. Look for yourself, but please be respectful of these offices," Peter answered. He was quietly relieved that it appeared that none of the staff remained here.

"And Andre Leopold's station, too?" the marine commander asked rhetorically, now visibly frustrated and shaking his head, "Mister Sharp, I have been instructed to seek out Mister Leopold; I insist you allow me to talk to him."

"No, I'm afraid that won't be possible," Peter responded.

The two support marines immediately raised their weapons, pointing them casually at Peter. Their commander now followed up, smiling,

"I don't think you understand. It's not a luxury you have to deny me," he leaned closer to Peter, sounding mildly condescending and continued, "I insist you take me to him. As I understand it he is likely incarcerated and being held here on the Kringle Works compound."

"No, I'm afraid that won't be possible," Peter responded again, "You see it's not a luxury I have to present him to you," Peter suggested, mockingly paraphrasing his captor, "Andre Leopold committed suicide a couple months ago. According to those who witnessed it, he jumped from a plane."

The marine commander leaned back, trying to hide his shock and frustration. He turned to one of his men and commanded,

"Take him back down with the others. Hold him until you get further instructions."

He then turned to the other marine,

"You come with me. We are setting our command center in the vacant office of Andre Leopold. Leave the others undisturbed," he then turned to Peter, "Within a few days we hope to allow you to resume your operations. We want to minimize the impact of our presence here, but understand this; we will get what we came for." And with a hand gesture, Peter was escorted back down to the lobby.

The tears were starting to moisten Krystal's eyes as she listened to Jason's emotional account of the day's events. He paced nervously in her hospital room as he recited the actions that led to the futile attempts at attacking the gates of the compound. His voice shook with a combination of extreme pain and anger. Somehow, recounting what he witnessed now genuinely penetrated him as the gravity of the moment gave way to the pensiveness of a recent memory. His lip quivered as he spoke. He had to pause frequently as he speculated as to what might be happening inside the compound.

Jason stopped at her bedside and dropped into the familiar chair he had been occupying almost exclusively since the day that she was shot. He felt helpless then, and he felt helpless now. It was a similar moment. It was when she was shot that his true love for her bubbled to the surface, no longer shrouded in a façade of professionalism that had otherwise ruled his life to that point, and for the first time he had been able to let go of all else. However, as he witnessed the attack on the compound, he was reminded of his passion for the Kringle Works, his love for her and the island-nation that existed to serve her. He buried his face in his hands and in a moment of weakness wept in frustration.

Krystal rolled onto her side and reached out toward him. Dragging with her hand the monitoring wires and intravenous lines, she clasped his shoulder.

"You knew this would happen," she said to him softly, "You warned them. You gave them a plan to avoid it. There's nothing else you could've done."

He reached up and took her hand and leaning closer to her, he was able to allow her to roll back. He could see that she was still in pain if she put weight on her side. She fell back into position with a wince and a gasp. Then she held his hand tighter and clenching the other into a fist, she growled in frustration,

"This is all his fault!" she snarled through her teeth, "Henry brought this on us!"

Jason nodded.

"And Andre. And a whole lot of others whom we don't yet know," he added.

"There's nothing you can do now," she said trying to comfort him.

He shook his head,

"I've got to do something! I can't just sit here! I can't imagine what's going on inside! I can't get through to anyone, we're helpless!"

Krystal watched him sympathetically as he got up again to resume his pacing as he attempted to think things through.

"Mister Pelham, I'm sorry to interrupt, but there's someone here to see you!" a nurse said frantically, entering Krystal's room abruptly, "Please, Mister Pelham, come with me!"

Jason's heart jumped. He looked back at Krystal and saw the concern on her face. He smiled at her.

"Don't worry, I'll be right back!" he said to her cavalierly.

Jason escorted the nurse down the hospital corridor. His heart pounded as they silently walked past rooms and equipment. There seemed to be a lot more activity in the hospital. The nurse then directed him to a waiting room. As he entered, he saw the disheveled figure of a younger man sitting alone, harried and unkempt but apparently unhurt.

"Raymond!" Jason exclaimed, "How did you get here? What's going on?"

Raymond Dunbar looked up at him and took a sip of water from a cup as he gathered his thoughts.

"They came in from the NTA Main Airport," Raymond took another sip of water and drew a deep breath, "They made their way to the gates and were swarming all over the NTA and executive offices. They rolled over Peter's security teams like a stampede of caribou."

"How did you get out?" Jason asked frantically.

Raymond shook his head,

"Much of the compound is undefended and the only way out is on a gurney or in a body bag. They're locking it all down! I was at ELF when the attacks started. I was able to get out before they had secured all the gates. I have a feeling I was only seconds ahead of them."

He whimpered for a moment and took another sip of water. Jason sat down next to him and put his hands on his shoulders.

"They have no business outside the compound," Jason said calmly, "We're safe here. Tell me what else you know."

Raymond nodded and continued,

"Here is what I have seen and heard; Xavier and the executive staff disappeared. They're still in the compound but hiding; Peter was defending the executive offices and they were heading for the NTA and the data hall; all communications have been cut or jammed; they are guarding everyone and rounding up those who are important to them. They've come for the technology, Jason, but Xavier has already taken it away; they won't find it where they think it will be!"

Raymond's face contorted in fear and looked Jason in the eye,

"I don't know what they will do when they can't find it! They'll tear the place apart! They'll destroy the whole compound, and worse, they'll eventually find the workstations. They won't stop until they do!"

Jason nodded in understanding and agreement.

"Raymond, do you know where Xavier is?" he asked.

"I think so, but we can't reach him," Raymond suggested, shaking his head.

"We have to," Jason followed up sternly, "We have to make sure Xavier can finish what he started…" he fell silent rather suddenly for a moment.

Then a smile crossed his face and he said, "… And I think I know how. I think I remember a way in."

The doors burst open violently at the NTA offices and a large number of marines marched in, guns up. Papers, files, and even laptops flew through the air as employees of the Kringle Works NTA dove to the ground or threw their hands up in terror. Startled screams added to the chaos as the troops came through. A couple of marines approached an apparently abandoned security station. One leaned over the counter to find a single security guard hiding behind the desk. He reached down and pulled him to his feet by his jacket, the other marine keeping his gun aimed at him.

"Over here!" the first marine yelled out. He then stepped back and raised his weapon as well. Then addressing the lone security guard, who now stood hands up, lip quivering and trembling,

"It's just you here?"

The security guard nodded frantically. The marine smiled.

"Where are the others?" he asked the security guard.

Trying to answer, the only sound was a broken squeak. The security guard cleared his throat and tried again,

"They … they all ran down to the airport!" stuttering and wincing, "They're … they're all gone … not here. I'm alone … I think."

The marine nodded and keeping his gun aimed, turned his head back.

"Is the area secured?" he shouted back.

A voice from a distance responded,

"Area secured!"

A marine lieutenant now approached the two marines holding the lone security guard.

"And what do we have here?" the lieutenant asked.

"Security, says he's the only one, almost wet himself," the first marine noted.

The lieutenant turned to the security guard, which seemed to make him try to raise his already erect arms even higher.

"What is your name?" the lieutenant asked him.

"Frederick Hollander," he answered with another squeak.

"Well Mister Hollander, where are all your friends?" the lieutenant asked.

"All ran out to the airport. When you arrived. I haven't seen them since," the guard responded.

The lieutenant looked around. A large number of office workers were seated in the area near the front door, guarded by a few marines. The area beyond had offices, open desks, and conference rooms, which were now being systematically searched, personnel being rounded up, brought to either the area near the door or one of the conference rooms to be watched and guarded. He turned back to the security guard.

"Mister Hollander, as the representative of the United States Marine Corps and in the interest of the office of Homeland Security, I am instructed to meet with the following persons: Jason Pelham, Henry Foster, Lorraine Barlow, Edward Grubb and Raymond Dunbar," the lieutenant started reading from a small note pad which contained these specific references, "I am also to be given access to the following offices in order to commandeer the following equipment: one ICU workstation in the office of Lorraine Barlow, eight ICU workstations in the offices of Henry Foster and his staff, and four ICU workstations and two data servers in the offices of Edward Grubb's department of data analysis and implementation."

The security guard nodded frantically.

"Yes, they're upstairs," he responded obediently.

"You will take me there," the lieutenant commanded.

The lieutenant turned to one of his men.

"Bind his hands. He's liable to give himself an aneurysm or something if he keeps his hands raised any longer."

One marine took out a plastic tie and bound the security guard's hands behind his back and then motioned for him to lead the way. The group then followed him to the offices upstairs.

The first office they entered was that of Lorraine Barlow. She was sitting at her desk as they approached. The lieutenant and his two men, led by the security guard, should have been a startling sight. Still, she barely acknowledged them, looking up over her reading glasses without moving her head. Then addressing the security guard, said,

"Well, Frederick, would you kindly explain what we have here?"

He tried, but before the overly nervous security guard could answer, trying to work past a stutter, the lieutenant jumped in.

"Our humble apologies, Ms. Barlow," he said politely, "We regret the interruption--"

"Interruption?" she cut him off, "No, 'interruption' implies that I'm doing something of value. Unfortunately, I am not. Not since they took away our equipment. No, all I do now is follow-up on decade-old contracts and contacts that I hope are still workable for our data gathering operations."

She leaned back and folding her hands in front of her continued,

"So I'm not doing anything of value and you are not interrupting. What can I do for you fine gentlemen?"

"Thank you, Ms. Barlow," the lieutenant responded, "Actually we were going to request that you, Mister Pelham, Mister Foster and Mister Grubb assist us in our efforts to assume the technology called ICU, by our right under US law and as mandated by the Department of Homeland Security."

She sat back and pondered this thought for a moment and then responded.

"Uh huh, really? Well, you're going to be disappointed," she suggested.

The lieutenant frowned as Lorraine continued,

"First, we are not breaking any laws, US or otherwise! Second, I'm afraid that neither Jason Pelham nor Henry Foster is here nor has either been for about a month or so," she leaned forward and continued, "And as far as the ICU technology is concerned, they took it away. Why do you think I am wasting my time trying to reconnect with these ancient surveillance networks! Or haven't you been listening?"

The lieutenant, frustrated, pointed at the computer on her desk and asked intently,

"And that? What is that?"

She looked at him, cocked her head and in a slow, condescending voice suggested,

"That? That is a laptop computer, but I would have thought you might know that. I suspect you've seen one before."

"Where is the ICU workstation?" the lieutenant now asked, clenching his teeth.

"Not here," she reiterated, "They took them away. You won't find them."

The marine lieutenant looked agitated and turned to one of his men.

"Find Grubb!" he commanded, "Bring him back here!"

He turned to the other and said,

"Get some help! You know which offices to search."

Then turning back to Lorraine he followed up, trying to remain composed and courteous,

"Ms. Barlow, please come with me!" still clenching his teeth, "I insist!"

26

FIRE AND ICE

The electrical service tunnels were not considered of particular significance due to their age and limited size. Consequently they were not part of Andre's plan, which resulted in it never making it to the American operation. Indeed, the electrical service tunnels that ran underground from the junction stations outside the compound to the data hall were not viewed as a security risk or of notable value. Built in the 1930s, the small thirty–inch-tall by forty-inch-wide tunnel was designed to run several bundles of wiring and be barely large enough for a single man to slide in and service it. Largely ignored now, the tunnels were monitored by robots which tested the wiring harnesses by continuously running along them checking for fluctuations in the electrical current.

That afternoon, Jason remembered the tunnel and decided this was where he and Raymond could make their way inside the compound undetected. He wanted to start this rather arduous journey immediately and they left the hospital together. He recalled some historical text, which indicated the routes for each junction station, and attempted to select the one that would offer them the most direct route. They drove there as quickly as they could. They arrived at the station and stepped down inside. It was nearing five o'clock and the trip in the tunnel would be grueling and likely take several hours. Jason removed the metal cover to the service tunnel and after a careful inspection of the area inside with a flashlight, Jason confidently slipped inside first.

The walls of the tunnel were smooth and it seemed that the fastest way to travel it was to lie on their backs and push along with their feet. The distance was significant. The old lights in the tunnel, some long burnt out and never replaced, modestly illuminated the way. With the robotic maintenance there was no need to replace the bulbs in the recessed cages of

371

the tunnel's ceiling. Overall it was too dark without the flashlights so they kept them close, using them if needed. Jason lay on his back holding the flashlight on his chest and looked up at the old wiring harness. Raymond followed. The tunnel was covered in a fine red-orange dust, which was accented by an old, rusty, wet, metallic smell that seemed to punctuate its age.

The cluster of wires above seemed, like the rest of the island, to suffer from a state of duality of high technology and antiquity. He noted the modern cables bound to the old rusty metal conduit that protected the fabric-lined wires of a bygone age, which was offset yet again by the modern repairs of a now robotic maintenance crew. They pushed on.

It was a comfort that insects and rodents were of little concern here as the cold climate on the island kept the unwanted animal life to a minimum. However, with their clothing tightly pressed against their skin while lying in the confines of the service tunnel, the cold penetrated, chilling their backs and shoulders. Somehow, this seemed to heighten a feeling of being trapped and isolated. Raymond found this a little overwhelming and felt compelled to engage in conversation to help comfort himself. His words sounded muffled and hollow in the metal tunnel as they continued forward, sliding on their backs. Jason, found it hard to understand Raymond's words as he was focused on the effort to reach the NTA's data hall. Reaching it, he thought, was the only way for them to leave this unpleasant space.

The journey was underway for about forty-five minutes. The quiet of the tunnel seemed violated by their intrusion in this forgotten space. Jason could hear every fiber of his clothing as it rubbed along the metal floor and walls of the tunnel. Every word that Raymond spoke in his effort to comfort himself seemed to vibrate along the walls, and now Jason could hear the panic in his voice starting to build. Raymond's voice squeaked and then he started to hyperventilate.

"Raymond! Stay calm! You can't turn around. Just a couple hours and we're there! It's much harder now to go back! The space is too small, you can't turn around!" Jason demanded.

"I can't do it!" Raymond insisted, the pitch of his voice elevated to a whimper, "We'll die in here! We have to go back!"

Jason could hear Raymond stop moving.

"Raymond! It's a straight line! It's just a couple hours in the dark! It's much harder to go back now!"

There was silence. Both had stopped moving.

"Jason," Raymond called out, in a voice unconvincingly trying to sound calm, rational, and thoughtful, "You'll need me to make preparations … outside. I'll be working toward the next steps. I'll follow up with you outside! I know it's just a couple hours, but you'll need someone to make preparations. I'll go back and follow up with you, outside."

Jason could not think of any significant preparations Raymond could do for them. Their current plan was, after all, an almost impromptu effort born of complete desperation. Jason actually had little idea what they were going to do once they got inside the compound. Perhaps, he thought, it was a fool's errand, but Jason felt he had to try. He had to do something. Still, perhaps he had asked too much of his employee. Jason sought to release him and allowing him his dignity, said,

"Good idea, Raymond! I could use your help outside. I'll follow up with you!"

Dragging himself backwards back down the tunnel to the junction station for nearly an hour was not going to be easy, but the thought of going back calmed Raymond. The dark unknown ahead intimidated him and the idea that he was going back into the compound after his narrow escape that morning, crushed his courage. But with Jason's release, he was able to breathe easier.

"Of course, Jason," Raymond said obediently, "I'll catch up with you outside. Okay?"

Then after a moment Jason could hear the sound of Raymond starting back down the tunnel toward the junction station. Jason closed his eyes as the sound faded into the distance and started to move forward again.

Another hour passed as Jason tried to keep up a fevered pace. He was not sure what time it was and he did not bother to check. He simply assumed he would deal with whatever situation faced him at the other end of the tunnel and that would define his next steps. Still, if he kept up this pace then perhaps he could still find Xavier and help him destroy the ICU technology before the United States got their hands on it. He had estimated that he would reach the data hall by nine o'clock that evening and he kept moving as fast as he could.

The architecture of the island was built in stone and set deep into the permafrost; as such, features like this tunnel were like spending time in a refrigerator and though his clothing was designed to shield him from the cold, he was starting to feel the effects. He was starting to shiver.

Alone with his thoughts, he continued to focus on the end of this journey to give him the strength to finish. He pressed on.

The soft whirring sound of fans that moved the air in the tunnel was apparent as he neared them and then faded as he passed them. Indeed, all of the sounds in the tunnel were becoming familiar; the brush of his clothing against the metal surfaces, his own breathing, the ventilation fans, and the silence. Then, after another hour, he heard something new. Something was approaching. He twisted his body and turned his head to try to see what was up ahead. He saw nothing, but realized that the sound was coming closer. It was a mechanical clattering, a clicking of some sort. Still committed to his task, he felt he had no choice and continued forward anyway. Whatever it was, he would have to confront it at some point. Then the sound stopped. Again, Jason tried to look ahead. He watched for a moment silently. Then came a popping sound, accented by a flash, which broke both the silence and the dark. Momentarily the tunnel was brightly illuminated as a shower of sparks covered the diameter of the tunnel ahead. A beep sounded. A red light flashed. Then the tunnel went dark and silent again. The smell of burned plastic permeated his next breath. Another second passed and the new sound started up again. The mechanical clicking and the sound of small motors were now approaching again. Jason thought he knew what it was.

"Just a robot," he said to himself.

Then as the sound came closer he felt a hard metal object strike his head. The sharp pain startled him. He reached up and tried to push it away. However, the object insisted on its path and struck him again, and again he reached forward above his head and tried to move it out of the way. He felt the object shift and maneuver; various articulated appendages protruded from its side, flailing about in a seemingly random manner. Jason attempted to lift it off the floor and toss it out of his way. The sound of metal parts clattering in the tunnel made him flinch. Then he heard it presumably right itself and stubbornly approach again. This time he shielded his head with his outstretched hand. The metal menace tried again and hit him in the head in an effort to pass, disregarding his being in its way.

Fumbling in the dark over his head, he lifted the device again and hoped to throw it past his body and feet, but found that it was too large and too animated to do so safely. In desperation, Jason grabbed his flashlight and rolling on his side for leverage, struck the metal robot several times. The flashlight flickered and went dark just as the mechanical beast stopped moving.

He lay there a few seconds while his eyes adjusted. Without his flashlight, he could see only the yellow glow of antique lights faintly illuminating the tunnel. With many of them burnt out and there being no incentive to repair them, they created an uneven pattern of yellow dots which ran in a straight line into the distance.

Jason reached up and started to pull the articulated limbs of the now lifeless robot. Twisting and pulling parts off of it, he tossed them into the tunnel beyond his feet. With it disarticulated, he now had the room to get the thing out of his path and out of his way. He pressed on, hoping to get to the data hall before it was too late, for what he was not sure.

It would be another hour before Jason reached the data hall junction area. It was dark but not as cold; the area was barely visible in the low light. Jason slipped out of the tunnel and crouched in the four-foot by four-foot space and looked up at the small shaft that led upward by way of a steel ladder, which ran alongside of the thick cluster of wires and cables. Quietly he started to climb. At the top, he stopped and listened. He heard nothing. He waited for a while longer, listening intently; still he heard nothing and then very carefully he started to push up on the metal plate that covered the shaft at the top.

The scraping of the metal plate against the metal frame seemed deafeningly loud as it released. So too, the sound of the plate scraping the floor of the electrical equipment closet, but after a moment Jason thought it was safe to pull himself out and up into the room. He stretched his legs and back, which had stiffened from the long journey lying on his back. He fumbled in the dark for a moment looking for a wall. Following along it, he ran his hands up and down the wall looking for a light-switch.

Shielding his eyes, he turned on the light and allowed them to adjust. He looked around. Jason had not spent much time in the electrical equipment closet, but he was familiar with it--and it had changed. The once fully loaded racks were only partly occupied by the data servers, networking hubs, and ERP management systems that ran the basic company infrastructure. Shelves full of equipment with wires and flashing lights stood next to empty spaces where various ICU servers and equipment had once resided.

"Wow, he really did it," Jason whispered to himself, "He had all the ICU technology taken out."

He looked around once more and then proceeded to the door. Quietly he started to open it. Looking out into the main room of the data hall, he noted just a handful of the three hundred or so employees who normally would occupy all the desks in the large room. It seemed unusually empty and similar to the closet he was standing in; all of the ICU workstations that normally graced each desk were conspicuously missing. The screens of a handful of laptops flickered in front of each of the members of the skeleton crew that was here working. Normally each of the staff here would have a laptop, which they used for their day-to-day activities such as e-mail, documentation, and spreadsheets, and an ICU workstation, which remained permanently in the hall for their function as data miners. Part of data acquisition, this team's primary activity focused on the gathering and sorting of data via the ICU workstation, roughly monitoring the world's population of Christmas Service subscribers whose data would be consolidated, filtered, and passed on to Edward Grubb's team at data analysis and implementation to discern and reward based on their behaviors.

Seeing no sign of any potentially unfriendly personnel, Jason quietly stepped into the large, dimly lit room. Whether it was because of the fact that no one would have expected someone to emerge from the equipment closet without seeing them first entering it or because of his disheveled appearance or because of who he was, the entire room turned and stared in disbelief at Jason as he started walking up the hall.

As Jason approached the front of the hall, he noticed the sudden, animated reaction from the figure nearest the main door.

"Bloody hell! Mister Pelham?" the now-approaching figure of Randall Blake exclaimed, "How on earth did you get in here?"

He scanned Jason for a moment.

"You look like hell!" Randall noted, dropping his usually polite demeanor, "What did you do, crawl in on your belly?"

"On my back, actually," Jason quipped, smiling broadly.

Randall looked confused, but quickly his mood became quite serious.

"You shouldn't be here," Randall suggested, "They'll be coming soon, no doubt. The building, and its equipment, is a target for sure. They're coming for the technology. It's dangerous here, especially for you. No doubt they are looking for you."

Jason nodded.

"I know," he said resolutely, "I have to find Xavier. Do you know where the ICU technology is hidden?"

"I do," Randall explained, "It's not hidden at all. Xavier placed it all in the old warehouse on Julenissen's Path. He planned to have it dismantled, parts of each ICU station, like a cut-up motherboard or something, kept as proof of its destruction with documentation about every machine assembled for audits by the United States. He expected to present this as proof of the complete destruction of the technology that monitored the chips. You know, to make the chips useless and to keep them from coming."

Jason nodded,

"Well, it's too late for that now, but we have to keep it out of their hands. Somehow we have to convince them it's gone. We still have to destroy it so it can't be recreated, and then you and I are going to have to figure out how to spy on the world like we used to a decade ago."

Jason reached out and tapped Randall on the shoulder.

"So, where's the rest of your team?" he asked lightheartedly, looking around.

"It's late," Randall suggested, "They can't go home. The compound is locked. Their families must be beside themselves!!" he paused with a sigh,

"So, anyway, I suggested they find some rooms at the Inn or the hotels near the training center or by the auditorium. I didn't want them to stay here. It's too dangerous. They'll be coming for the technology. It's only a matter of time … Look, Mister Pelham, as I said, you have to go! You shouldn't be here. They'll be looking for you."

Jason nodded in acknowledgement and asked,

"Do you know where Xavier is?"

"Go to the warehouse. Take my vehicle. I'll be here," Randall said, tossing him the keys.

Randall turned to face the staff in the hall and loudly announced,

"This man!" he pointed at Jason, "Was never here! Got that? I don't care who asks you, answer any other questions truthfully, but this man, was never here!"

He turned back toward Jason.

"When they come, what should I do? They will want the technology," he followed up.

Jason thought for a moment. Then answered simply,

"Tell them where it is. Don't let them hurt anyone. But buy me as much time as you can."

The compound now bore the scars of the American occupation as heavy vehicles chewed the snow and ice while moving troops and equipment. Broken doors and makeshift signs marked seized and occupied buildings and defended positions were awash in bullet holes and blood. Like an old tree overrun by ants, the United States troops walked the streets with authority, while the indigenous population cowered and hid or was rounded up and guarded.

The United States forces continued their operations, taking advantage of the nearly constant daylight, and later that evening one marine Captain and his men were tasked with the securing of the NTA's data hall and seizure of the ICU technology. This was a mission focused only on the recovery of the equipment and all personnel encountered were to be categorized for the operation as cooperative, passive, or neutralized. He and his troops made their way to the building and stopped at the base of the steps leading to the entrance. Weapons at the ready, they approached the security team that stood at the doorway.

"This is the United States Marine Corps. Our mission is to take this facility!" the officer addressed the Kringle Works's security team. "If you resist, we will do so by force, if you comply and allow us access, there will be no violence. The choice is yours."

The security team remained in position.

"If you stand your ground, we will shoot!" the officer clarified and signaled his men to raise their weapons and step forward. "Drop your weapons, get on your knees, and put your hands behind your head, and no one will be hurt."

They stepped forward, guns up.

Hopelessly outgunned, the security team looked to their leader. He gave them a nod and placed his weapon down, then got on his knees and put his hands behind his head. His team watched him for a moment and slowly started to do the same. The marines kept their guns up. Once all of the security team had complied, the Captain commanded some members of his team to secure the enemy-combatants. Approaching the security team were as many marines. Guns still up, they moved in around them and once behind them, they lowered their weapons in the knowledge that the rest of their team remained ready. Each grabbed the hands of the kneeling men and bound their wrists with plastic ties and helped them to their feet. The remaining team now moved forward and collected the weapons on the ground. The security team was escorted into the building in front of their captors.

Two security guards sat at the security desk in the lobby. With no significant level of surprise they each stood up slowly with their hands raised. A young marine bade them to come forward and join their comrades. A marine bound their hands and had them sit on the lobby floor in a group with the others. Several marines moved into position to guard them. The remaining marines and their commanding officer now entered and addressed the captured security team,

"We are looking for Randall Blake."

"Right here!" a voice came from the main entrance behind the security desk. The figure of Randall Blake walked toward them.

Several marines turned and aimed their weapons with a snap.

"Bloody hell!" Randall exclaimed as he froze in place. With a nervous shake in his voice, he continued, "Randall Blake at your service." His voice cracked, "Please lower your weapons. We knew you'd be coming."

"I suppose you did," the senior officer acknowledged.

He gave his troops a nod and they lowered their guns to a visibly relieved Randall Blake.

"Mister Blake, in the name of the department of Homeland Security of the United States of America, we demand you allow us access to all of the technology housed here in your data hall, which you refer to as ICU," the Captain commanded in a well-rehearsed statement.

"They're not here," Randall informed them.

Somehow this simple statement acted like a command for several of the lead marines to, once again, fix their weapons on him. Randall's eyes widened. With an audible squeak, he raised his hands as if to shield himself.

The Captain smiled, apparently amused by his reaction.

"What do you mean they're not here?" the officer asked, now looking more serious.

Randall remained fixated on the guns as he answered,

"Eh … they're not here. They took them away. They're not here."

"I'm afraid, Mister Blake, we'll have to confirm that for ourselves," the officer suggested and continued, "So, show us the hall and then tell us where the ICU technology is."

The Captain assigned a guard for Randall and assembled a team to follow him to the primary area of the data hall. In recent days it would have been dimly lit to allow for the best viewing of the ICU workstations' screens, but what Randall was now able to show the marine officer was a brightly lit space. Most of Randall's remaining staff was working on the phones, seated at desks that stretched as far as they could see. Notably absent from these were the workstations. Each desk looked lonely and forlorn, with a series of cables and ports leading to a device that was no longer there.

The Captain commanded four of his men, "Walk the hall. Stop at every desk and confirm there are no devices connected. Ask the staff what they know."

The marines jumped into action and walked down the rows of desks.

"Mister Blake, where are they?" the Captain asked.

Randall shrugged.

"They're not here, but I think you should see for yourself. Please take you time, check every corner."

The Captain eyed Randall suspiciously.

"Right, you should look in each of the offices and conference rooms, too," Randall noted.

The Marine Captain scowled at him, then turned to another of his men and suggested he search the adjacent offices.

"Interrogate all of the personnel you see, find out what their story is," the Captain commanded of his man.

"It's getting late, Mister Blake, I'm not playing games," he said.

Randall answered quickly,

"No! No, I know you're not! I just want to be sure you know, for a fact, that they are not here."

"Where are they?" the Captain asked again.

"You won't find them here," Randall reiterated, "See for yourself."

"Yes, we are going to be sure of that, but you will tell me where they are!"

With a nod from their commanding officer, two guns went up and were aimed at Randall.

He recoiled, putting his hands up.

"It's getting very late, Mister Blake! Where are they?"

"Right, well, they're in a warehouse, aren't they? Locked up. All the stations were brought there as ordered by our top management," Randall noted with a hint of disapproval.

"Address, Mister Blake!" the officer insisted.

The four marines returned as Randall gave him the address. They confirmed that it appeared that there was no ICU equipment at any of the desks. The Captain tapped a button on a communications device hanging from his uniform on his chest and using the headset which was integrated into his helmet, he confirmed the story was the same at all of the facilities they had targeted, executive management, NTA headquarters, NTA technology, data analysis, and several other NTA functions which were connected to the technology.

"If you are lying, Mister Blake, I will be back," the officer threatened.

Visibly frustrated, he commanded a few of his men to remain behind and keep the building secured. He then commanded the remainder to join him outside and he and his team exited. If this was the address in which all of this technology was stored, then it must be well-defended. He planned to consult with the other commanders and coordinate an offensive operation.

Jason drove as fast as he could, but when he arrived at the warehouse he found it completely locked up. Attractive for a building with such a utility purpose, it was made of stone and timber much as the rest of the island's architecture. It stood just two stories tall but had huge, arched windows that ran base to roof. The doorway was equally impressive with a large glass arch above ornately decorated metal doors. A little out of place was the modern scanning pad that beckoned him for his security badge, which he unfortunately did not have with him. And there were no security personnel to allow him access by virtue of his title. He cupped his hands around his eyes and against the window in order to see inside. In the dark of the interior he was able to make out what seemed to be a huge store of computer equipment. He studied it for a moment longer and was able to make out the familiar shape of the ICU workstations. There appeared to be hundreds, perhaps even as many as a thousand workstations and servers.

Jason started to walk around the building to see if he could find a way in, but all the doors, loading and receiving docks, and windows were locked. Finally, in desperation, his attention focused on a door next to the receiving docks. It was a small side entrance. The steel door was locked but it had a glass paned window reinforced with wire at the top. It did not have a security scanner and was presumably used only by the team at the receiving dock during the hours of operation, never to act as a general entrance.

He looked around and noticed several heavy hoses which hung between the receiving dock doors. These were attached to large, underground fuel tanks which were used to fuel the larger transport vehicles after loading or unloading. At the end of these hoses were heavy metal nozzles. He grabbed one of the hoses and started to remove the nozzle at the end. Uncoiling the hose, he used the heavy metal nozzle and proceeded to strike the window with it. After several hard blows, the window cracked. It would not give. The wire kept it stable. He struck it again and again, harder and more frequently. Finally, after multiple well-placed swings, he was able to punch a small hole into the now nearly completely shattered but unyielding glass pane.

Jason jammed the nozzle through the hole. He twisted and wrenched it until the hole was large enough for him to reach in with his arm and unlock the door from the inside.

With a click the door was open. Jason stepped inside, but before he realized what was happening, a flashing red light on the wall next to the door gave way to the piercing screams of an alarm. Jason panicked. He was not concerned about explaining himself to the Kringle Works's security team, but an alarm at a remote warehouse during the United States' occupation might attract attention from a different source and right now he wanted to attract as little attention as possible.

The alarm squealed. Jason looked around for a clue as to how to stop it. The area inside the door was open but dark and he had trouble making out his surroundings. Then suddenly, the sound stopped.

"Who is it?" a forceful voice demanded.

Jason squinted, trying to make out the broad, imposing silhouette up ahead.

"A friend," Jason answered, thinking this would be the best response in all circumstances.

"Jason, is that you?" the now familiar voice of Xavier Kringle questioned.

"It is," he responded enthusiastically, "But if you didn't know it was me, why did you turn off the alarm?"

Xavier chuckled as he walked closer.

"Well, if it was anyone unfriendly, I was not about to die with the last sound I heard being that infernal alarm blaring at top volume. Besides, the armed forces taking control of our compound would not have tried to break in one at a time. They would likely have taken a complete wall out and stormed in guns blazing. Don't you think?" Xavier said with amusement.

Jason acknowledged the comment. He and Xavier then walked into the warehouse. Xavier explained how he had gathered all commissioned ICU workstations and servers here for the purpose of dismantling them, but the attack on the island happened too soon and too fast. He also noted that with the sudden intelligence blackout period that resulted from the machines being disconnected, they had no way of anticipating the exact time and manner of the United States' arrival.

So now Xavier suggested he would come here alone to destroy as many machines as he could, fight the invaders when they came and die doing what he could to keep as much of the technology out of anyone else's hands, even if the effort was going to be futile.

Jason noticed a significant pile of broken machines near the back of the great warehouse's main area, smashed with varying blows to the screens and the main bodies with whatever hardware Xavier could find. Now as he got his bearings he could see that the old man was exhausted. Xavier collapsed in fatigue, sitting down on one of the lower conveyers designed to move goods throughout the building.

"Xavier," Jason addressed him sitting down at his side, "We don't have enough time. They'll be coming soon, but we have to make sure they see the machines being destroyed and we can't leave them intact enough for them to backwards engineer them. They have to be utterly destroyed. Otherwise this was all for naught."

Xavier nodded, but said nothing. His head slumped forward. He looked old and beaten, which was something that Jason did not see very often but it was becoming more frequent. The two sat quietly for a moment.

Jason jumped up.

"Xavier!" he exclaimed, "This warehouse was still in full operation before you had the ICU technology brought here, right?"

Xavier nodded.

Jason smiled broadly as an epiphany took shape in his mind.

"Get up, Santa Claus! We have a demonstration to set up for!" he shouted excitedly, "Quickly, we don't have much time! You have a show to put on!"

Xavier got to his feet.

"Okay, my boy, what are we going to do?" he asked.

"We have to pull the PA system from the supervisor's mezzanine office. Then help me drag the fuel hoses inside through the loading and receiving dock doors."

It was about five in the morning when the Marine Captain reassembled his platoon and waited for his counterparts to rendezvous with them. The sun hung low in the sky, having never dipped below the horizon; this seemed less like a sunrise than a stalled sunset reversing direction.

The Captain and his lieutenants then commanded their men and accompanying support vehicles to march together to this warehouse. As they approached, they made out the features of the warehouse. The two-story-tall arched windows did little to illuminate the contents with the interior lights off and with the remaining sides of the building sealed. On the right, one could see the closed bays which allowed for thirty or so transport vehicles to access the inventory and at the left, some receiving bays. Still, the area around the building seemed to have been completely cleared of vehicles and personnel. It was eerily still.

Then a movement! They stopped and raised their weapons. Was that a figure on the roof? A single person, it was too ludicrous to think that this one man might be part of a trap. They kept him in sight and continued their approach.

"Stop! Come no closer! It will be at your peril if you do," the commanding voice of Xavier Kringle echoed across the landscape with the aid of an audio system.

Even in the distance the charismatic and imposing figure seemed to stop the marching troops in their tracks. They kept their weapons fixed, but now stood still.

"Is that who I think it is?" a young marine inquired.

"It is," the Captain confirmed quietly with a sharp nod. He followed up with an order,

"Hold your fire!"

He tapped a button on the communications device on his chest, and reiterated,

"Do you copy, hold your fire! I will not have Santa Claus himself shot by anyone under my command! Do I make myself clear?" the Captain barked into his headset.

Disciplined and quick, they held their weapons and watched as the figure they all now recognized continued to address them,

"We do not have the might or the resources to fight you! We have never expected to have to.

"Our island has never needed to defend itself from an enemy. We do not have a military. All we have is a security force to maintain a level of judicial order, which allowed us to live as free, but as orderly, as we could.

"And we do live free. But with this high level of freedom comes individual responsibility.

"No, the world is not perfect, because the individual is not. And this has been our failing.

"Indeed, we have allowed for some amongst us to exploit their freedom in a quest for a perfect world, but they did so without responsibility. A failing that resulted from a quest for perfection that would turn into a quest for power. A quest for the power needed to execute a misguided attempt to build a world, but one that might be perfect by removing the freedom from the individual.

"An ultimately imperfect individual."

Xavier fell silent for a second. He thought for a moment, shook his head and continued,

"Still, it is the individual who guides the winds of progress in the world. A free individual can make changes. To better themselves, to improve the world and those around them, but this must be done by the totality of all the individuals in a society and of their own free will. Not by the dictates of a few. Without that, you will only be as good, as changing, as imaginative as those who control you and who would presume to be so perfect that society will benefit from these few individuals at the expense of the freedoms of all the others.

"You cannot achieve a perfect world, because there is no perfect individual.

"The best we can do is to allow the individual to prosper and thrive. Embrace the positive contributions and understand the imperfections. There is none perfect enough to allow us the luxury of relinquishing our freedom to them and, as such, of each individual we must limit the power that any might have.

"For it is the imperfect nature of the individual that is as constant as the inability for the imperfect to wield the sword of ultimate power. Ultimate power, whether by force, as you who would march onto foreign soil to impose your will, or by persuasion, as those who would seek to exploit the Kringle Works technology, is too perfect a medium for such flawed individuals.

"I must stand in the way of any pursuit of such a quest for power!

"For power is an ill-tempered and treacherous mistress. She corrupts even the incorruptible. If you value your freedoms you will have to bind her and keep her from your lands and leaders, because she will seize their minds and seduce their consciences until they give in to her insatiable appetite.

"Access to such power must be denied. You may not seek her, but she will find you. You may not be vulnerable, but she will eat at your convictions until you yield. You cannot resist her and if you lust for her she will swallow you in an instant and make you her servant.

"Even for those who would have power at their call, freedom will be fleeting.

"As the flag of power ascends, she will oppress the masses and she will enslave the masters. Freedom will fail and the world will be razed to ruin, no matter how honorable the intentions might have been. It is the inevitable outcome, because the individual is not perfect and, as such, the world will never be.

"To aspire to utopia at all cost, especially at the cost of freedom, is to seal your fate either to live bitter and frustrated with the impossible quest, or to wallow in a dystopian slum with power as your landlord.

"Below me, within the walls of this warehouse, there lie the objects of your misguided desires. We have rounded up all the machines. We have rounded up all of the workstations, all the processing machines, all the translators and ICU servers that reside on the island and placed them here."

The large, arched windows on the façade of the building suddenly lit up as the flicker of the building's interior overhead lighting illuminated. Through the windows, the troops could see the rows of computer stations. Too numerous to count, the view seemed to highlight hundreds of them. Xavier gave them a moment to take in the sight and continued,

"See for yourselves, the members of my security team have used our technology deployment data and inventory records to confirm that all of the machines are here.

"You come here under the guise of national security, but I know what your leaders really want. You would seize all this technology to keep it safe? No, I cannot let you have it. Not a single machine must land in your hands, as it should never have been in ours. No, every last machine must be destroyed. To protect the freethinking people of the world, to protect the individual no matter how imperfect, we must destroy this technology utterly … and you will be a witness to it.

"Now, I implore you, do not come closer!"

Xavier nodded and cupping the microphone before him he said quietly,

"Now, Jason."

He turned and disappeared from sight as he walked toward the back of the building's flat roof.

The marines watched, bewildered.

"Captain, do we go in?" the young marine asked.

"No, hold! I want to see his next move," the senior officer commanded.

"You don't think he will really destroy it?" the marine inquired.

"I'm not sure, but I think he will," his superior suggested.

"Sir?" the marine cried in confusion. "What about our mission?" the marine then followed up.

Almost cutting him off, the officer corrected him casually,

"Our mission," he paused and started his sentence again. "Our mission is to seize all the technology in the name of national security so that it can be destroyed by our government. Well, if Santa Claus himself wants to destroy it for us? Let him," the Captain answered.

He shrugged and glanced back at his subordinate.

"Now hold your position, marine," he followed up.

For a few minutes that seemed like an eternity, the troops stood quietly. Then as if to signal that they had worn out their patience, a loud warning siren squealed for about five minutes. Once silent again, they noticed sparks on either side inside the warehouse. Punctuated with a roar, the lights went out and a violent swirl of yellow and orange flames suddenly filled the view through the tall windows.

Contained by the building's large stone walls, they could see the interior burning angrily. Some of the windows cracked as the heat from the flames increased and even at their distance the troops could now feel the warmth that seemed so out of place in this environment.

Helpless and confused, they watched. As the building continued to burn, smoke and flame slowly started to break free of the interior of the building and found its way out through the doors and windows. The smell of burning wood, rubber, and plastic filled the air. A large column of dark smoke was now starting to work its way skyward as the open points of the building at the doors and windows now allowed the smoke to billow unencumbered from the interior.

The flames continued to lick the interior walls until they too broke free and the golden-colored flames now followed the smoke out of the windows. The flames reached up and out, hugging the top of the building and curling around the roofline.

With the sound of a crack and the tinkling of glass, the framework of the tall windows collapsed. The flames, released from bondage, now burst out, protruding from the building's walls, blackening the stone from top to bottom. The roof, superheated by the fire below, started to smoke and as the white smoke billowed from it, it mixed with the column of black smoke from the interior. Breaches in the roof started to form, which allowed the fire to reach out from the top of the building. Then with a sound akin to an explosion, the roof collapsed and the four walls stood open.

The fire remained contained on the grounds of the warehouse and was allowed to rage on for nearly three hours unchallenged. It grew so intense that it forced some of the patrolling aircraft to land before the sound of sirens filled the air again. A significant number of yellow vehicles now approached. Their purpose was obvious and no one made an effort to stop them. On treads designed to allow for fast movement on the snow, they had guns mounted on turrets which would start to shoot flame-suppressing foam into the building's now hollow shell. The Kringle Works's fire departments never used water to combat fires on the island as it froze too readily.

After the fire, Xavier Kringle officially gave himself up to the senior command of the United States Marines and presented a list of ICU workstations, their commission dates, and serial numbers. The marines were also given the opportunity to review all formal records and granted access to the now-destroyed warehouse. This gave the United States complete access to the remains of the destroyed ICU workstations and servers. In this the Kringle Works attempted to offer enough evidence that any particular machine could be identified and its destruction verified without the technology being in a state to be reverse engineered by either the Kringle Works or anyone else.

With the technology now destroyed, it seemed the United States' executive branch had miscalculated. Their efforts were to acquire the technology without being judged by their constituency. This mission was so sensitive, so controversial, that only the very highest positions in the government were informed of it. Consequently, the Administration assigned the mission to seize the technology in the interest of national security with the intent to destroy it personally, diverting from the covert intent of seizing and implementing it for their own use. Still, the rumors of the mission's true intent were widespread within the senior ranks of the armed forces and some were unofficially accused of actions that would lead to the failure of the technology making it to US shores.

In light of the mission's conclusion, terms and conditions for the release of all Kringle Works personnel, property, and the resumption of all non-ICU-based activity were implemented. As part of these negotiations the Kringle Works agreed to have a small military contingent remain on the island to monitor its data gathering operation, managed under Lorraine Barlow, confirming that the ICU technology was no longer in practice.

27

THE UNINTENDED CONSEQUENCES

If one were to review the history of the Kringle Works, there would only be a small number of times in which the delivery of the Christmas holiday was in question. The last was subverted by the efforts of Jason Pelham, now nearly sixteen years past. Indeed, through geographic transitions, updates in technologies, changes in logistics, business model shifts, political and social unrest, weather and two world wars, the service had been delivered year over year with only minor discernable disruptions since Christopher Kringle founded the company in 1828.

This year, however, the company's vulnerability due to its modern operating systems and inflexibility of process since its integration and reliance on the ICU technology, would not allow them to recover from the forced removal of the system. It became inevitable that even with the inventory available, the NTA logistics had been so crippled that execution was now going to be impossible. Indeed, other than some minor regional deliveries, the global nature of their business model and the removal of the ICU portion of their electronic infrastructure would result in a complete collapse of deliveries as product sat both in global warehouses and in the island's own ELF facilities, with no ability to move.

"We have the product and the delivery systems, but we don't know what goes to whom and when!" noted Raymond Dunbar, the vice president of gift delivery in a statement to the media.

The resulting cost to the Kringle Works was in excess of four hundred billion US dollars in top line revenues. The cost to its customers was estimated at nearly three trillion dollars in tangibles, like delivered gifts, and intangibles such as political capitol. A global impact of such proportions had the rather unfortunate effect of making the United States' recent military operation a very public discussion. Furthermore, with the administration's failure to capture the ICU technology, they had no ability to monitor or control the narrative, which was now spreading across the globe. Calls for investigations and restitution were taking on a fevered pitch in the world community. Subsequently nearly forty percent of the White House staff was either fired or resigned in the first week after the operation's conclusion.

In a twist that seemed to confuse most of the American people, Jacob Vanderberg broke with the rest of the administration and took a lead role in the charge to have the president himself recalled, siding instead with many of his own party in the legislative branch who now distanced themselves from the "rogue efforts of an out-of-control presidency."

The United States was facing a catastrophic plummet in credibility in its domestic agenda, and a diplomatic nightmare which now plagued their foreign policy to the degree that it threatened to throw the entire global community out of balance. So much so, that cries for Xavier Kringle himself to join the discussions became too loud to ignore and he left the island for meetings throughout Europe to mediate in the discussions with the United States.

With Xavier away and the company's desperation growing, demands that Jason return to work grew equally loud and in mid-July, after Krystal was released from the hospital, he did so.

Recovery and restoration of functional operations at the Kringle Works preoccupied him and he worked with Raymond Dunbar to scratch out process maps and write up plans to rebuild the company's infrastructure with a less intrusive data management and customer-monitoring system. This was to be similar to what he anticipated using with his own plan, which was to wean the business off of the ICU more strategically.

Though Jason had been getting general updates and working remotely for the last month, it still seemed to be hard for him to get back into the swing of his routine. He had not been back to the compound since the occupation by the United States and though anxious to get back to work and solve the issues with his team, he found the idea of returning strangely disquieting. The morning of July fifteenth he chose to return. Feeling the need to think or to slow his arrival time, he did not know which, he chose to walk to work. The everlasting sun shone and it was a balmy forty degrees Fahrenheit. He felt he deserved the time outside. The walk to the compound from his house would only last forty-five minutes, the trip inside the compound would be much longer but he could take a snowmobile at the gate.

The United States invasion a month and a half earlier had done a significant amount of damage to the compound, though it was only visible to a discerning eye. The damage at the gate where it was chained and welded, the roads which had showed a splotchy patchwork of grays and blues where they had been repaired and ice from different water sources and aging used to fill the holes, seemed to fade with every passing day. For the most part the damage was in the functionality of the Kringle Works. Though the physical damage was mostly relegated to the airfields, the deployment and defense of the men and equipment that spent a week holding the compound under the occupation seemed to have taken a toll on the overall demeanor of the place. Jason knew that the United States Marine Corps still had five officers set up in Andre Leopold's old office. No doubt he would have to run his new processes by them for approval, but for now he was happy that he could avoid them by staying away from the executive offices and hiding out at the NTA.

Entering the compound, he made his way to the half-timbered barn. As he approached the front office, his heart started to pound. He knew she would not be there, but somehow his heart felt as though he would find Krystal at the desk or in the back with the animals.

"So what will it be, gasoline or grain?" a young man asked without looking up.

Jason pondered for a moment before answering. He had heard that question asked that way before. Hearing it adopted by others this way made him smile.

"Good morning, Eric! I think gasoline for today," Jason answered.

"Morning? Nah, it's just about afternoon …" the young man looked up as he made the comment.

"Mister Pelham!" he suddenly exclaimed, "Holy Christmas, it's good to see yah! Eh, yeah, gasoline, yeah! Right away!"

The young man grabbed a key and handed it to Jason.

"In the back, number twenty-two," he said enthusiastically, "Now that you're back, things can start getting back to normal!"

Jason shook his head and with a hint of melancholy answered the rhetorical question,

"Things have changed, Eric; they'll never be the same."

The young man nodded.

"We miss her, Mister Pelham, how's she doing?"

Jason smiled.

"Krystal is doing well. I think she will be fine, Eric, but she has a long way to go yet."

Jason started toward the snowmobiles, when he heard the young man's voice behind him,

"I don't miss him! I hate to say it, Mister Pelham, but I don't miss Marcus Mill--"

"Then don't say it, Eric!" Jason cut him off, "Just don't say it! We have a lot of healing to do and it will have to start with each one of us!"

The young man nodded, looking contrite, and turned back to the desk silently.

Jason arrived at his office at the NTA. The familiar cross of an airport control tower and Victorian manner, his office seemed unchanged, were it not for the disarray on his desk with hastily picked up materials that had fallen to the floor, the chairs shifted to the side so that a gurney could be brought in, and the discoloration on the floor where Krystal's blood had pooled and been cleaned up after the investigation was completed. His chest tightened. He decided to move the chairs back into place, thinking it would make him feel better, but he stopped at just one.

He sat down at his desk and set down a stack of papers. They were his drafts, thoughts, calculations, and process maps. There was work to be done, but he needed to allow his head to clear.

He turned around to look outside and through the huge windows that lined the walls of his office, were reminders of coming changes. The NTA airport had United States aircraft and men stationed on the tarmac. Around the runways was construction to repair the damage from the attacks a month ago. Unnerved, he tried to look past it to railways, distribution centers, trucking lanes, and at the harbor in the distance, but it all looked as though it had been somehow soiled.

He swiveled in his chair, scanning the office, when he noticed something that made his heart stop. He stood up and recoiled. He slowly backed up and stepped around his desk. His eyes were fixated on the credenza behind his desk. Loosely covered, was a familiar shape of something he had not expected to see. He continued to back up, and once around his desk, he hastened to the door of his office. He continued to look at the covered object, and with a quick glance out of his office to look for activity, he slowly and quietly shut the door. With the sound of the latch he proceeded to turn the lever that would lock it, something that Jason had rarely done. It was not uncommon for him to close the door, but he never felt compelled to lock himself in.

Even though he knew he was alone in the office he looked around with a sense of paranoia. He rushed back to his desk. His eyes never strayed from the covered object. He reached for the cover and hesitated. He then reached behind it and let down the blind of the window just beyond. He stepped back. He put his hands gingerly on the cover again and with the apprehension of a person about to roll back the sheet on a cadaver in a morgue asking for a positive identification, Jason lifted back the cover.

Like a relic of a golden age that was now coming to a close, before him stood a ghost of all the evil that had precipitated its passing. Jason allowed himself to fall into his chair, his eyes never leaving the lone ICU workstation that sat dormant before him. Silent and quiet, it was the sole remaining commander of a sleeping army of chips that had, by one way or another, infiltrated the majority of the world's electronic infrastructure. The workstation need only be turned on and it would awaken the network that was connected to it, either directly or indirectly; it would be allowed to talk to a world that sat at the fingertips of mankind whose reliance on its own technology would unwittingly offer up its activities for unencumbered review.

Jason sat silently in his chair, eyeing the machine contemptuously. What was worse, he thought, was that this particular machine had the codes that would activate it hard-coded in and with the information contained on an envelope just behind him in a desk drawer was a fifth and sixth code that could unwittingly allow the user to manipulate the data that was seen by someone at the other end.

A simple oversight that now threatened the world. How did this happen? How did this machine escape Xavier's clutches? All of the machines were well documented; where they were, who they were assigned to, what point in their life cycle they were, like an arsenal of nuclear weapons, everything was tracked. The machines were always considered too dangerous in the wrong hands. So by a twist of fate Jason inherited one machine, on the books to be dismantled and destroyed. Unassigned, Andre's old machine was a ghost born of paperwork to decommission it, and yet saved from destruction by Randall, to land in Jason's hands. He pondered this question afraid of the potential consequences if anyone knew it was here.

He thought about turning it on, but he could not muster the courage to do so. The machine would operate silently, unknown to those whom he might be watching or manipulating, but somehow he felt as though turning it on would alert the world to its existence. Jason got up and covered it again. It had to remain a secret, but there were those who did know the machine existed. Jason never hid his having it from anyone who knew the technology existed at all; Randall, Xavier, Krystal, and Henry, they all knew he had it. Still, off the books, it was overlooked, hidden in plain sight. Indeed, Peter Sharp, who had taken Xavier's lead to round up all the machines, worked from the very documentation that neglected to follow this workstation to Jason's office. Andre never knew Jason had a machine, at least not until after he developed his plan, which he presented to the United States, and as such, it was never outlined in the material the United States used for their operation. Their information was so complete they never sought it out. It simply ceased to exist once it was decommissioned on paper, and a momentary lapse of procedure, a modest amount of well-intentioned deviation, and a device of great power slipped through the fingers of control.

This was a machine that could change the world of politics, expose agendas, shackle communities, even crash planes ... Jason's mind reeled when it occurred to him the depth of what Henry had told him on that fateful day in this very office. This machine could manipulate people to unwittingly self-destruct. This machine could command an innocent party to execute acts of great destruction. This machine was designed to identify and understand anyone's intentions by monitoring what they did and with its unlocked capability to feed information back, then manipulate them into doing ... anything within their power to do. You need only to find the right person on the right device.

Henry sought to use this capability in a misguided effort to better mankind by taking control of an out-of-control world, but what could a device like this do in the hands of one who might use it to destroy or disable their dissenters? Worse, used cunningly, there would never be dissent.

"And no one knows to look for it," Jason whispered to himself.

Jason felt he had only one choice. He had to destroy it. Smash it. Break it into pieces so no one could get their hands on it, but herein lay a problem. The control of the technology was due to its anonymity; its secrecy now exposed, all would want to have it. The contingent of United States troops were not here just for mop-up efforts, they were actively looking for remnants of the technology. They were sifting through the charred remains of hundreds of ICU workstations. Engineers and scientists were still trying to decipher and reverse engineer blackened metal parts, twisted lumps of glass, hardened puddles of plastic and electronics that were little more than a handful of dust and ash. If he tried to destroy it he would have to do so utterly, so completely that once aware, no one, not even the greatest minds of technology, could reassemble it. He and Xavier had done a good job with the other machines and the United States' window of opportunity to capture the technology was coming to an end as the world community debated the validity of their operation. Could he burn it? Like the other machines, to get the fire so hot so long as to keep the technology hidden, he might have to burn down his entire office and perhaps even the building around it. No, even if this were an option, as one of the key leaders in the company he had little ability to make any significant moves; he would draw attention to himself far too quickly to try to complete the task. He could neither destroy it here nor remove it. For now, the only reason the machine was not in the hands of the enemy was because no one knew it existed. Hoping it would remain hidden was too risky. So for now he sat in a locked office, a virtual prisoner of the machine covered before him on his credenza.

Silently, an hour passed. Why did Xavier not take this machine? Why must he now be burdened with this calamitous circumstance? Trying to think it through, Jason resolved to call Xavier who, steeped in the morass of global politics connected to this situation, might have some insight, some knowledge that could resolve this issue without compromising their position. Perhaps he could help.

Jason dialed from his mobile device,

"Xavier, it's Jason!" Jason whispered, "I'm sorry to call you, I assume it's late. Where are you now?"

"Geneva, no problem," Xavier's voice responded reassuringly, "What can I do for you, my boy?"

"I have one. One survived!" Jason said quietly with intensity, "You know what I mean?"

The phone was silent.

"Xavier!" Jason asked hastily, "Do you understand me?"

Another moment of silence passed before Xavier acknowledged,

"This is a devastatingly bad problem, yes, I do," Xavier said calmly. He paused and then asked, "Jason, what are you working on? How far are you on your plans for the new systems?"

"Raymond and I have the basic outline and process maps for resurrecting the old surveillance networks. We expect to reengage with local law enforcement and non-direct monitoring of systems more like the old days of SANTA. We were good at it," Jason answered. Proud of the work he had done so far, but confused as to why this was of interest at this moment,

"But why do--?" he started to ask, before Xavier interrupted him.

"Take your plans," Xavier suggested, "Take your plans to Andre's old office. Engage the senior command of the United States' team. Tell them about your plans. Keep them occupied for a minimum of two hours. Their subordinates won't move without them, so engage them. I'll take care of it from here. I know who we can trust. You can't do anything, they are too aware of you. Go, talk to them. Leave your office. Lock it. Then go to ELF. Talk to someone, anyone, then visit with Krystal; she'd love to see you.

When you return later today, it will be taken care of. The workstation will be gone. I promise."

Jason was skeptical, but his old mentor's confidence reassured him and he did as Xavier asked.

28

THE ENVELOPE, PLEASE

Xavier Kringle, as the personified representative of the Christmas holiday in the eyes of the world communities, was now taking a center stage position in what would become the efforts to restore the world back to order. He remained a popular figure. He had an uncanny ability to use deep insight and broad awareness of global activities in the effort to bring to a close most of the discussions that were engaging many of the world's leaders in the wake of the military action against the Kringle Works.

In the months that followed, Xavier was able to calm the global rhetoric and was a formidable foil for the current United States leadership's defense of their actions. This became, however, a multifaceted discussion as Xavier exposed some of the unpleasantries of many of the rest of the world's governments as they hypocritically chided the American president.

"It is hard to argue with someone who knows if you have been naughty or nice," one newspaper suggested in an article titled, '*Lumps of Coal for All.*'

The public's frustrations grew with many of the western world leaders, and movements to recall the heads of a number of governments started to take on an ugly tone. It was at this moment that Xavier started to seize the platform and assert his vision.

Jason Pelham was not in a position to keep track of his absentee boss, but his curiosity was piqued when he heard that Xavier was being asked to run for office and surprisingly, after several months, he had considered doing so.

"What is the old man going to get into next?" Jason asked himself, shaking his head as he read some of the account in The Work's Weekly.

The article noted that Xavier was planning on using his old family's estate in upstate New York and the citizenship he bore all his life to allow him to qualify, suggesting he would consider a candidacy for elected office once he felt the work of routing out the corruption in the government was complete.

As November of that year approached, it appeared that the US public was primed for an off-cycle presidential election driven by the opposition party, who now aligned themselves with Xavier in an effort to drive awareness and stoke the flames of discontent. They had adopted Xavier's anticorruption stance.

The American president reportedly spent no time in the Oval Office anymore. He instead moved from one speaking engagement to the next to defend his position and rally the small percentage of his remaining supporters. Even with a number of blind followers, this proved to be no easy task as the news cycle was awash, between campaign ads, with coverage of members of his administration being interrogated by Congress.

Still, Jason was acutely aware of the fact that even Xavier Kringle would have a tough time in this politically charged environment. Jason was forced to cancel all of the Christmas service shipments for the first time in the history of the company, and with the American president desperate to defend himself, a great deal of attention was drawn to the Kringle Works's practices and it seemed there was a groundswell of discomfort building. So much so, that when Xavier held a press conference suggesting that he would permanently remain in the United States in his family's estate and announced his intention to run for the State of New York's senatorial office in the coming year, there was a small number of demonstrators holding signs.

"How can they protest Father Christmas?" Jason asked in a phone conversation with Xavier, "I wish I could help you, Xavier, but nothing is up and running yet."

"Jason! You know better than that! That is the kind of thinking that got us in trouble in the first place," Xavier scolded him, "No, Jason, don't worry about me. I think I can handle it. I still have my ways of finding out how and what people are thinking."

And indeed, it seemed that Xavier did, being able to deflect any questions as though he knew they would be asked. He always seemed to say the right things. He was always a step ahead and he managed to remain quite popular even though it was becoming apparent that the general public had little interest in Santa Claus when there was no Christmas Service to be delivered. Filling entire stadiums with jubilant crowds of excited supporters, there was always an element of the media and the public that dogged him, and at one such event, Xavier managed to give a performance that would win accolades and cheers from tens of thousands, only to be disrupted by a modest few holding signs and chanting,

"No Gifts, no votes! We've been nice, you're being Naughty! No Gifts, no votes! You've got yours, where's ours!"

The public now knew that Christmas would not come this year and with significant segments of the media who remained suspicious of Xavier and strangely vested and sympathetic to the former American administration, his frustrations grew. It seemed that no matter how he tried he could not control the narrative.

That November during the special election for the president of the United States, he spent his time campaigning against the incumbent administration and while laying the groundwork for his own senatorial campaign for the following year, Xavier found himself perpetually on the defensive. He was continually deflecting questions about his birthplace and legitimacy of citizenship, answering to the Christmas Holiday that was not to come this year, defending his company's intrusive practices and losing his message of anticorruption, personal freedom, and individual responsibility. Then, in a moment of extreme frustration, Xavier reached out to his old friend and employee.

"In some ways Henry was right," Xavier suggested in a phone conversation with Jason, "It seems that much of the public doesn't really know what's good for them. Why would they be so blindly self-destructive? So willing to enslave themselves for a free trinket or empty promise? It's so frustrating! I can see why he wanted to be able to control them."

"Why he wanted to? Yes, I understand why he wanted to," Jason acknowledged, "But to justify it in his own mind Henry became twisted and diabolical, he had to convince himself that the people were no longer important and that his methods would be justified."

"Methods! Yes, he certainly had his methods," Xavier noted, "How did he do it? Jason, how did he use the same ICU workstation we all had, so that he alone could control the public?"

"It was all about the ICU2 chips," Jason answered, "The workstation was just a conduit, the ICU2 chips were able to communicate back to any device they were installed in or connected to, not just monitor it. He kept this functionality from anyone who wasn't part of his agenda, from their accidentally stumbling onto the capability by protecting it with more codes. Just like the ones used to activate the old chips. I suspect that he knew that if he had tried to build entirely new workstations, more questions would have arisen. So he and his team just changed the chips."

Xavier was silent for a moment before he pensively said,

"Brilliant. He was quite the genius, he and his team. So, you know the codes? That makes you dangerous, that is, if we hadn't destroyed all of the workstations," he chuckled a little, taunting Jason.

"I suppose," Jason acknowledged, "I think I still have an envelope with the codes on it. For some reason I kept it, sort of a reminder of how far we can stray from a virtuous path. How misguided we can become. Henry became so blinded by his agenda he was even driven to kill, " Jason's voice started to become very agitated, "Once down that path, he would never be able to return. He kidnapped and shot Krystal! What could drive anyone to that?"

"How is she?" Xavier asked, interrupting him, defusing the impending emotional rant.

There was a pause before the conversation restarted.

"She's ... recovering," Jason recounted as he regained his composure.

"I'm sorry, Jason," Xavier responded pensively, "I shouldn't have brought Henry up. He's hurt you, and a great many people, a great deal."

"Thanks, Xavier," Jason responded with a whisper.

"Jason," Xavier then started with a notable infusion of positive energy, "I will have a lot to do. I'm not coming back to the island, not for a long time, anyway. I've made some decisions that I want you to advise me on, and then execute for me. Can you come to America? For a week or so? Please, bring Krystal if she is well enough to travel. I would love to see her."

"Sure, Xavier, immediately. I'll have Justin contact you for some details," Jason responded.

"Great!" Xavier exclaimed, "My friend, I look forward to seeing you again! We have much to discuss."

He paused.

"Jason?" Xavier asked, following up, "Bring that envelope. It's an important part of the Kringle Works history now. I'd like to see it! You don't mind, do you?"

"Of course, Xavier," Jason responded, "I'll see you in a few days!"

Unlike any of the other guests, Jason and Krystal left the window wide open in their luxury Essex County hotel near the Kringle estate in Lake Placid, New York. The late November air felt like a summer breeze on their island to them. They had arrived the evening before and once settled in the room they went straight to bed, weary from the travel; still, Jason woke up frequently that night and as the sun started to rise, he lay quietly, watching Krystal sleep.

Gingerly, he brushed a few strands of hair from her face. She twitched as the ends passed over her nose. He ran the back of his hand along her cheek and down her neck and shoulder. Tracing the curve of her arm, he watched as the sun started to illuminate her from behind. His eyes traced her shape under the sheets as she lay on her side facing him. Her arm exposed, he fixated for a moment on the curve of her uncovered left breast. The youthful perfection of her fair skin was interrupted by a red dimple two inches north of the nipple; it was the scar of the bullet that might have killed her.

Whether it was due to the discomfort in his eyes from a lack of sleep or the quiet reflection as he watched Krystal, his eyes moistened. He could feel a single tear build. He could close his eyes but instead he remained fixated, his eyes open, allowing the salty water accumulate and blur his vision. He blinked, feeling the teardrop breach the corner of his eye and run down his cheek and drop on to the pillow. He turned his head to wipe himself dry on it. Then he pulled the sheets tighter over his shoulders.

"So this is what happens when I take some time off. I become emotional and introspective," Jason thought to himself.

He continued to watch Krystal sleep. The hair he had brushed aside had now fallen back into her face. Though he felt he would never be rash, there was a level of discomfort knowing that the events of the last year had made him much less measured and calculating. He relied more on feeling and intuition; he was starting to rely on other people, and he relied on her more than ever before. It made him feel less in control, more vulnerable, but strangely more secure. Like allowing yourself to fall, giving up the effort to learn how to fly, knowing someone will be there to catch you. Was this growing up or growing old, maturity or dependency? He shuddered to think that he could no longer live without her. Whatever lay ahead they would now face it together.

He turned around to face the alarm clock and watched the red LED display flip to 7:10 a.m. He lay there for another twenty minutes before he decided to get up and take a shower. As the warm water hit his face, he pondered his meeting that morning. Certainly there was much to discuss with the boss he had hardly seen in the last six months.

When Jason and Krystal arrived at the coffee shop that morning, they were struck by the number of security personnel clad in dark suits, sunglasses, and communications devices standing just outside the quaint and unassuming shop front. They approached with some apprehension when one of them addressed Jason,

"Mister Pelham?" the sturdy younger man asked rhetorically.

"Yes," Jason responded.

The man nodded and bade them to enter. As they did, the warm and animated greeting by Xavier Kringle seemed to draw a particularly stark contrast to the cold formality of the greeting outside.

"Jason! Krystal! What a great pleasure it is to see you!!" Xavier exclaimed, jumping to his feet.

He looked sharp, well-groomed but strangely acclimated to the local fashion. Gone were the long robes and heavy trim common to the aesthetic of the Kringle Works Island. Instead, he'd donned a gray pinstripe suit and a dark red tie. His white beard, flowing white hair, and gold-rimmed spectacles, however, were unmistakably those of Xavier Kringle.

"Come, come, come!" he said anxiously, "Sit down, sit down!"

Krystal looked over at Jason smiling, amused by Xavier's overly exuberant enthusiasm as they made their way to the table.

As they sat, Xavier leaned over to Krystal and with a twinkle in his eye said,

"I love the hazelnut coffee here, but I think you would enjoy their uncommonly good chai tea. I highly recommend it!" He nodded at a shop employee who came by to give Xavier a refill and take their additional orders as he spoke.

He turned to Jason,

"You look good, my friend! How are things coming along at home?"

Jason looked around, suddenly realizing there were no other patrons in the shop. Inquisitively he looked back at Xavier, but before he could ask, Xavier offhandedly addressed his confusion.

"No need to be concerned, my friend. You may speak freely here. I often stop in this shop to talk to the people. It's a great place for some one-on-ones and a terrific photo opportunity for my campaign. Local people and a local business--it has served me well and I have brought a great deal of interest and awareness to the shop so the owner is happy, also. With that, I asked to have some private time with you and Krystal; he was more than happy to oblige, and no one likes to say no to Santa Claus!" Xavier finished with a chuckle and winking at Jason as he looked over his glasses.

Jason nodded understandingly and proceeded to describe some of the elaborate actions he was directing his team and the business to take in Xavier's absence and to accommodate the company's new reality.

"Lorraine has been rebuilding the data gathering network using the old model," Jason noted as he accepted his cup of coffee.

"She has been working with Raymond to activate local surveillance hubs and linking to law enforcement, local community leaders, and the press at each of the logistics sites. You know, much like we did about ten years ago. Grubb thinks he can work with his team to build his delivery lists with the data in this raw form, so we should be all set for next year's Christmas delivery," he continued down the list of significant activities, "I will have to renegotiate with the United States in light of the development this year. We need to have a revised contract that protects us from any action like this past summer in the future. They'll want to get some surveillance exemptions for their government for purposes of national security in return. We have been working with Peter's team to find any remaining decent within our ranks and I am considering replacing Henry from within. Finally, I have been managing ELF with Marcus ... well ... dead. All is on track from a manufacturing perspective."

Xavier nodded.

"And Henry, did you ever get any leads as to his whereabouts?" Xavier asked.

"No, but there is little he can do now; he's on the run somewhere. Peter will find him!" Jason suggested.

"I'm confident he will. I figured you would have it all in hand, even in my absence," he confessed to Jason, "That is why I have taken steps to make some changes in our organization."

Xavier pulled out a large envelope from a briefcase next to his chair. He opened it, unraveling a string that sealed it closed at the top and fanned out some paperwork. He pulled a pen from his jacket pocket and proceeded to sign each of the pages.

"Jason, these documents are going to set a number of things in motion," Xavier suggested as he went from document to document, "One is a letter of my resignation."

Krystal gasped.

"No, Xavier!" Jason exclaimed, "Not now, I will run things for you until you can return."

"I know you will," Xavier answered, "That's why I am naming you the new CEO of the Kringle Works."

Jason fell back into his chair, stunned.

"It has all been arranged, Jason," Xavier said as he signed the last document and slid it over to Jason, "The executive committee is in agreement and the terms with my family and my brother Malcolm's children have been negotiated. My family will have their financial stake in the business but they will no longer have the exclusive right to run it. I will remain as chairman of the committee, but you will run all the operations and the business as a whole. All you have to do is sign here."

Xavier pointed at the base of the last document under his own signature and placed the pen on the paper.

Jason remained speechless.

"It's the right thing to do, Jason," Xavier followed up, "We will ease you into the position. You'll have help, guidance. You're already running the business. You'll do fine. My family has been running it for long enough. It's your turn now."

Krystal turned to Jason, trying to read his thoughts, proud, smiling but sympathetically apprehensive. She gave him a nod as if to say it was going to be okay, that she would be there with him.

"You're not in this alone," she whispered.

Slowly Jason leaned over, dragging the paper toward himself, and with a moment's pause he picked up the pen and signed under Xavier's name.

"Excellent!" Xavier exclaimed, "Congratulations, my friend! By the way, the committee was unanimously in favor of your taking this job. This is one move which will help me personally overcome one of the many failings in my long career as CEO. Thank you, Jason!"

"I'm so proud of you!" Krystal insisted, "You will do great things!"

Jason nodded but remained silent. He was unsure of what to say and he was sure there were no words to describe what he was feeling.

Xavier gathered the documents and placed them back into the large envelope, sealing it with the string tie. Then he tucked it back into the briefcase.

"Okay," he said with a sense of accomplishment, "That's that, one envelope down and one to go. So, Jason, do you have that envelope we discussed? The one with the codes on it."

Jason reacted as if shocked out of a trance.

"Yes," he answered, "yes, of course."

He pulled the small, white envelope from his jacket pocket and handed it to Xavier. It was worn and soiled from months of handling. It bore numerous creases. As Xavier inspected it he noted the numbers written on the outside. Hastily written in pen, a partial code followed by a full one and just below, another written by a different hand. He opened it. Inside was a card. It too had codes on it; four were printed, the fifth was added in pen, and yet a third hand suggested, *'Keep this card but remember the codes are hard-coded into this machine. Let me know if you have any questions. Cheers, Randall.'*

"This envelope, it's obvious that there is a long, sordid story attached to it," Xavier noted as he continued to examine it, "Please tell me about it."

Jason proceeded to describe how he first took the envelope from Andre's office and noted the unique fifth code. How he transcribed it to the card and placed it in the envelope, and how it came to pass that Henry himself wrote the sixth and final code on the envelope just moments before he shot Krystal.

"The first four codes you're familiar with," Jason suggested, "They are the base of the technology. The fifth code was one commissioned by Andre to allow him to spy on ... well ... you, Xavier. The sixth was the key to Henry's agenda, which allowed him to manipulate the data feed and transmit the information back to the source, allowing Henry and his team to activate the ICU2 chips and change what the people at the other end saw. This would allow them to control the actions of anyone they targeted; whether it was as passive as adjusting a news report to control a message or as direct as an effort to control someone to destroy or disable a system or device."

Xavier nodded in acknowledgement and continued to study it. Finally he placed it on the table, but without letting it go. He looked Jason in the eye apologetically and asked,

"May I keep it?"

Jason watched him, mildly bemused.

"Sure, but why?" he asked in response.

"It is a relic, Jason," Xavier suggested, "A reminder of a failing that is very personal to me. It is the physical result of my inability to control the corruption within the Kringle Works. This is what proved that it was time for a new era of leadership on the island. I will keep it to keep me from straying. It will remind me how far we can fall. That's why, Jason. That's why I would like to keep it."

Xavier drew a long, pensive breath and with a sigh, continued,

"My family has owned the rule of the Kringle Works for too long. The new era begins with you. You, Jason, are uniquely qualified in this task. Christmas will be, once again, what it was. You will usher in a better and truer Christmas for the world. And I? I will learn from my failings and do what I can to keep others from the same path. That's why I have chosen to pursue politics, so that I might change the world for the better from within the belly of the beast. That's why I have chosen to resign my post as CEO. It's a good trade, Jason. I will forward the documents to the committee. When you get back to the island, it will be as CEO."

Xavier got up, looking at his watch.

"Well, I have to get to my next meeting," Xavier noted hastily, "Jason, thank you and congratulations again!"

He reached out to grab Jason's hand and placing the other on his shoulder warmly shook it. He turned to Krystal, cocked his head and, smiling brightly, stretched out his arms and embraced her. As he did he whispered in her ear,

"Take care of him for me, child, he needs you more than he will ever know."

She nodded and stepped away, still holding his hands.

"Take care of yourself, Xavier! Don't let these people make you something you're not," she said, holding his hands.

"Mister Kringle," they were interrupted by one of the security team tapping his wrist watch, "It's almost time. I'm sorry."

"It's okay, Xavier, we'll have a chance to meet again before we head back, I hope," she followed up.

"Me too," Xavier responded.

Jason took Krystal's hand and gave Xavier a last wave as they followed the security aid out.

Xavier sat and took a last sip of his coffee, tucked the envelope in his breast pocket and readied himself to leave the coffee shop. Stepping outside, the team of aids and security personnel clad in their dark suits, sunglasses and communications devices scurried their way into a large, black SUV-based limousine. Xavier tapped his chest to check for the envelope and got in. The others made their way to their respective and similarly appointed vehicles, which were parked in a row.

Inside the vehicle Xavier sat down in the back seat, addressing a figure who had been waiting for him.

"Did you get it?" the gray-haired, tall, handsome and charismatic figure asked with a quiet confidence.

"Of course, I wouldn't want to disappoint my brand new campaign manager," Xavier answered, sporting a wry smile.

The man smiled and sat back, signaling the driver to go,

"Let's go; we're already running late."

"Yes sir, Mister Foster, we'll catch up," the driver responded.

The caravan sprung to life almost in complete unison, pulled into traffic and down the city street like an oversized, black, mechanical snake. The long

414

line of vehicles drove down the road with headlights ablaze even though the late morning November sun shone brightly, illuminating the signs on the doors of each vehicle, '*Kringle for Congress.*'

EPILOGUE

THE CAMPAIGN

It was almost uncanny how dramatically the 'Kringle for Congress' campaign seemed to turn with the new year. Last December's lack of a Christmas Holiday, public discontent with the Kringle Works' practices and suspicion of Xavier's motives was becoming a distant memory as it quickly gave way to what appeared to be a runaway train to an inevitable electoral success. The campaign that had been only moderately successful by year's end suddenly seemed to be an almost foregone conclusion, as poll numbers rose almost daily. Credited largely to a small shuffle of campaign resources and personnel, the campaign's new direction seemed to defy conventional wisdom. At the advice of his new campaign staff, Xavier adopted a new strategy of avoiding public debates and print media interviews, allowing instead the world of electronic media to drive his message.

The complete avoidance of direct one-on-one engagement on the issues outraged the opposition campaign and invited a great deal of criticism. However, any negative commentary made against the Kringle campaign seemed to fall on deaf ears. The public seemed disinterested and almost unwilling to hear any dissent. Indeed, even if Xavier made a misstep in a public appearance it seemed to quickly die down. By contrast, every comment or action by his rivals seemed to get undue public scrutiny. Even the most insignificant indiscretion accelerated like a wildfire fanned by a hot summer breeze in a pine forest and became viral, only to leave behind the charred remains of the week's campaigning which would descend into a dark, smoldering pit of apologies and justifications.

Pundits and political junkies were already studying the Kringle campaign strategy trying to understand its formula for success, but found it was nearly impossible to pinpoint how it was getting so much traction.

In an interview, one such pundit made a comment,

"It's remarkable how the Kringle campaign is dominating the public's attention. Spending only about twenty-five percent of the monies devoted to this office's election, Xavier Kringle seems to be able to do more with less to an unbelievable effect."

To the nods of agreement by the talk show host, the commentator continued,

"If Kringle brings this type of expertise to the post, he may single-handedly change the dynamic of American politics."

As an almost self-fulfilling prophecy, this comment suddenly became an internet video sensation. This simple remark from a political strategist, who proclaimed himself unbiased, now inadvertently spent nearly a month indirectly supporting the Kringle campaign, as this video seemed to flood into every household in the country, breaking record after record of viewership; surprising, because the public's usual interest and consumption of such visually mundane content oft gives way to videos of drunken college high jinks, burping babies, and silly pet tricks.

However, it should not have come as a surprise that when one network news program chose to do a man-on-the-street interview, looking for the most uninformed voter possible, they still found that people had a significant level of information regarding Xavier Kringle's platform. Even if it seemed as though they did not understand his positions, they knew what they were. When asked who was running against Kringle the camera only captured a blank stare, which gave way to an embarrassed laugh, followed by a comment,

"I'll be damned! I have no idea! Some jerk!"

To further cement the depth of this person's lack of engagement with the political landscape, when the follow-up question, "Who is the current vice president?" was posed, they again could not answer. Suggesting instead,

"Geez, I thought you'd ask me about last night's game! Hey, is it okay to say 'Hi' to my girlfriend? Hey, Lorena! Check it out! I'm on TV! Woooo!" the final comment being accentuated by two outside fingers held high in a gesture of 'Rock On' and a lurch toward the camera, tongue wagging.

This infamous report aired three months before the election and had so incensed the opposition that it would precipitate their fate, as it would give rise to an even more infamous piece of video.

Dubbed 'The Prelude to a Coronation' this gem of a video was the final nail in the coffin for the campaign of Xavier's rivals. Apparently captured on a security camera in a state building, the opposition candidate was found ranting for ninety seconds, insisting that the average voter was too stupid to be allowed the privilege of casting a ballot and that this was not a campaign but rather a prelude to a coronation. How the video managed to hit the mainstream no one knew, but once it had, it too had quickly become viral.

Xavier Kringle's favorability poll number topped at seventy-eight percent at the close of October.

Afterword

Consider for a moment that the fantasy is real and that a playful ruse has been set loose upon your existence.

What if there was a Santa Claus with his power and reach complete? Who would he be? What kind of a man would have the resources and the abilities? Whom would he employ? Whom would he trust?

A real Santa Claus would have access to our children, our homes, our lives, and our dreams. Would he be beyond reproach? Would he be immune to the power that corrupts others so completely in all other walks of life? Would the media, the law, and the government tolerate him? Indeed, would the public embrace him as they do the fantasy?

What if there was a Santa Claus; should he not lead, or like all other men would he fall victim to the trappings of wealth and power that by the nature of who Santa Claus must be, might corrupt him so completely?

If there was a Santa Claus, would you then be part of a resistance or trust him implicitly and defend him to your own ruin?

Like the politician who forgets his constituency or the company that has failed its shareholders, it will be the people who, for the sins and shortcomings of those that they elevate, will be hung to suffer the cross.